ZORRO dismounted quickly and dropped the reins over the head of his heaving horse. Working swiftly, he got off the Zorro costume and tossed it on the ground with the black hood and mask. His blade was left there also. He retained only his pistol.

He could hear Burke coming on toward the rocks. Zorro got up among them in a good hiding place. He would remain there until Burke had gone on, then get back to the rancho. If Burke stopped and found the horse and Zorro's costume, he would race on after the mule, thinking Zorro had gone on a fresh horse.

But more ill luck came to Zorro then. As Burke came thundering toward the rocks, the black horse took a few steps and revealed himself in the moonlight. Burke made a quick stop.

"Come out, Zorro!" he shouted. "I see your horse and know you are there."

"Now we have you, Zorro!" Sergeant Garcia cried. "One move, and you are a dead man! Put up your arms and hold your hands high! In the Governor's name!"

Two of the troopers had dismounted. They rushed forward suddenly and seized Burke. There was a short struggle, then the Americano was on the ground, and his wrists were being lashed behind his back.

*Under one cover — **A Task for Zorro**
and fifteen Zorro short stories
by Johnston McCulley*

Zorro: The Complete Pulp Adventures
Six-volumes collecting the original adventures of Zorro!

Zorro ®

THE COMPLETE PULP ADVENTURES™ VOL. 5

Johnston McCulley

Featuring

A Task for Zorro

and short stories
from West magazine

Introduction by John E. Petty
Story Illustrations by Joseph Farren
Cover Painting by Peter Poplaski
Title Page Illustration (16-17) by V. E. Pyles

BOLD
VENTURE

Rich Harvey / Co-Editor & Designer
Audrey Parente / Co-Editor
Peter Popaski / Cover Illustration

Special Thanks to
John R. Rose, John E. Petty

Pulp Adventures TM & © 2017 Bold Venture Press, All Rights Reserved.

"A Task For Zorro" by Johnston McCulley © 1947 Johnston McCulley. Copyright © renewed 1975 and assigned to Zorro Productions, Inc. All Rights Reserved. Originally published in *West*, June 1947.

"Zorro Saves His Honor" by Johnston McCulley © 1947 Johnston McCulley. Copyright © renewed 1975 and assigned to Zorro Productions, Inc. All Rights Reserved. Originally published in *West*, February 1947.

"Zorro and the Pirate" by Johnston McCulley © 1947 Johnston McCulley. Copyright © renewed 1975 and assigned to Zorro Productions, Inc. All Rights Reserved. Originally published in *West*, March 1947.

"Zorro Beats a Drum" by Johnston McCulley © 1947 Johnston McCulley. Copyright © renewed 1975 and assigned to Zorro Productions, Inc. All Rights Reserved. Originally published in *West*, April 1947.

"Zorro's Strange Duel" by Johnston McCulley © 1947 Johnston McCulley. Copyright © renewed 1975 and assigned to Zorro Productions, Inc. All Rights Reserved. Originally published in *West*, May 1947.

"Zorro's Masked Menace" by Johnston McCulley © 1947 Johnston McCulley. Copyright © renewed 1975 and assigned to Zorro Productions, Inc. All Rights Reserved. Originally published in *West*, July 1947.

"Zorro Aides an Invalid" by Johnston McCulley © 1947 Johnston McCulley. Copyright © renewed 1975 and assigned to Zorro Productions, Inc. All Rights Reserved. Originally published in *West*, August 1947.

"Zorro Saves an American" by Johnston McCulley © 1947 Johnston McCulley. Copyright © renewed 1975 and assigned to Zorro Productions, Inc. All Rights Reserved. Originally published in *West*, September 1947.

"Zorro Meets a Rogue" by Johnston McCulley © 1947 Johnston McCulley. Copyright © renewed 1975 and assigned to Zorro Productions, Inc. All Rights Reserved. Originally published in *West*, October 1947.

"Zorro Races with Death" by Johnston McCulley © 1947 Johnston McCulley. Copyright © renewed 1975 and assigned to Zorro Productions, Inc. All Rights Reserved. Originally published in *West*, November 1947.

"Zorro Fights for Peace" by Johnston McCulley © 1947 Johnston McCulley. Copyright © renewed 1975 and assigned to Zorro Productions, Inc. All Rights Reserved. Originally published in *West*, December 1947.

"Zorro Serenades a Siren" by Johnston McCulley © 1948 Johnston McCulley. Copyright © renewed 1976 and assigned to Zorro Productions, Inc. All Rights Reserved. Originally published in *West*, February 1948.

"Zorro Meets a Wizard" by Johnston McCulley © 1948 Johnston McCulley. Copyright © renewed 1976 and assigned to Zorro Productions, Inc. All Rights Reserved. Originally published in *West*, March 1948.

"Zorro Fights with Fire" by Johnston McCulley © 1948 Johnston McCulley. Copyright © renewed 1976 and assigned to Zorro Productions, Inc. All Rights Reserved. Originally published in *West*, April 1948.

"Gold for a Tyrant" by Johnston McCulley © 1948 Johnston McCulley. Copyright © renewed 1976 and assigned to Zorro Productions, Inc. All Rights Reserved. Originally published in *West*, May 1948.

"The Hide Hunter" by Johnston McCulley © 1948 Johnston McCulley. Copyright © renewed 1976 and assigned to Zorro Productions, Inc. All Rights Reserved. Originally published in *West*, June 1948.

"Zorro: The Unique, the Unusual, and the Bizarre" © 2017 John E. Petty. All Rights Reserved.

ISBN-13: 978-1545596104
Retail cover price $19.95

Published by Bold Venture Press
www.boldventurepress.com

Contents

Zorro Against Maciste (1963), in which Don Diego meets legendary Italian strongman Maciste.

Zorro: The Unknown, the Unusual, and the Bizarre

by John E. Petty

SO YOU think you're a true Zorro aficionado, do you? You say you've seen all the movies and can discuss the differences between Fairbanks, Power, Williams, and Banderas? You've read all the books and short stories, you've dressed up as Zorro for Halloween, you've collected both the Gold Key and the *Four Color* comics, and you splurged on a mint-in-the-box example of the rare and desirable Marx Zorro playset. You even convinced your spouse to let you hang a *Zorro's Fighting Legion* movie poster above your bed. You are, in a word, the Don Diego de la Vega of the Zorro-collecting world.

Um, not so fast, amigo.

Yep, that's a pretty good start, but the world of Zorro is vast... and sometimes weird. Let's take comic books for example. We all know about the American comics featuring Zorro, with some of the best-known released during the period in which the Disney TV show, starring Guy Williams, was on the air. But Zorro's adventures have been exploited in four colors in a number of different countries, including Brazil (100 issues between 1954 and 1962, with at least one cover [#93, Nov. 1961] featuring the Lone Ranger and Tonto), Sweden, Germany, France, the Netherlands, Norway, Great Britain (40 issues between 1952 and 1954), Italy (with some beautifully painted covers that would have been right at home on the cover of a paperback book), Portugal, Belgium, Spain, Austria, Colombia, and Japan.

The Zorro comic from Great Britain is particularly interesting. It was one

From India's Bollywood comes *Madam Zorro* (1963). An evil scientist lusts after the fabled Seven Treasures. The music is catchy and upbeat, and one song seems to draw inspiration from traditional spanish music.

of a large line of comics published by the UK firm of L. Miller & Son. Founded in 1943 by Arnold Miller, the company's bread and butter was the British rights to reprint the American Fawcett Comics titles, including *Master Comics*, *Don Winslow of the Navy*, *Nyoka the Jungle Girl*, a host of Western titles, and, most importantly, several books featuring Captain Marvel and his "family" of spin-offs — including *Captain Marvel Adventures*, *Whiz Comics*, *The Marvel Family*, and *Captain Marvel, Jr.* — all in black and white. That is, until 1954, when Fawcett lost a long-running lawsuit to DC Comics, the publisher of *Superman*, for copyright infringement leading to the cancellation of all Captain Marvel titles. But that's another story.

As part of their line, they also issued a comic called *Zorro*, which featured a black-clad, black-masked, black-hatted vigilante who helped people in distress and dispensed justice. Funny thing, though: he seems to have nothing to do with

Johnston McCulley's character. Miller wasn't above knocking off popular characters for his own use (the withdrawal of Captain Marvel from his line led to the creation of Marvelman, a thinly-disguised clone), so it's possible this Zorro was simply a retread version of the original. What little information exists on this comic suggests that Miller may have been presenting reprints of a French newspaper strip by André Oulié which ran from 1947 to 1967. Oulié also supplied Zorro material for a number of French album editions, which Miller may also have drawn upon for content.

For many, that certainly represents the unknown, as few of these foreign editions are easy to find in the wild, and little is known about many of them, with only the most tantalizing bits of information to be found online.

UNDER the category of "unusual," we might put the series of video games that have entertained keyboard warriors for decades. The first such game was titled, simply, *Zorro*, and was released for the Commodore 64 and Apple II (on a tape drive, for those of us old enough to remember that giant leap forward in technology) in 1985. A fun 8-bit adventure, it involves Zorro racing to rescue a kidnapped señorita. To do so, he must not only face a legion of foes, but also solve a number of puzzles, from the straightforward to the incredibly bizarre (where else will you see The Fox climbing a ladder with a large flowerpot balanced on his head?).

Capstone released *Zorro: A Cinematic Action Adventure*, an MS-DOS-based game on CD-Rom for the PC in 1995. The graphics were ambitious for the day, attempting to look more like paintings than simple 8-bit renderings, but the technology of the time wasn't quite up to the task. The game has a very *Castlevania* feel to it, as Zorro spends much of his time running, jumping, moving from platform to platform, and using his whip to take out enemies. Nevertheless, it sticks closely to the classic story of Zorro, showing a certain reverence for the source material.

In 1999, *The Mask of Zorro* was released on the Game Boy Color. In the gameplay, Zorro must stop Don Rafael plot to take over California. Encounters with enemies and traps deplete his life, but a kiss from the beautiful Elena replenishes his health. Released to capitalize on the popularity of the first Antonio Banderas film, the game hit shelves to largely poor reviews. Critics complained about uneven and frustrating movement/action controls, annoyingly repetitive music and sound effects, and poor realization. Clearly, Zorro deserved better.

The turn of the millennium brought new gaming opportunities to our friend

Les aventures de Zorro — a French comic strip illustrated by André Oulié, published between 1947 to 1967.

Left: Zorro Gigante Anno VIII #10 — This Italian comic featured a painted Zorro that could have passed for a Lone Ranger paperback cover. Right: *Zorro the Avenger* (Copercines, Cooperativa Cinematográfica, 1962) with a story and screenplay by cult favorite Jésus Franco

in black. 2002 saw *The Shadow of Zorro* for Windows and Playstation 2. With advances in technology, this version of Zorro looks far better than his 8-bit predecessors, but the gameplay was still lacking. 2009's *Destiny of Zorro* for the Nintendo Wii used that platform's new motion-controlled technology so players, as Zorro, could "whip, slice and of course perform Zorro's signature 'Z' slash move to bring his foes to justice." The game was promoted as taking inspiration from "… Mexican, Spanish and Native Southwest American cultures prevalent in California in the early 1800s," but in the end, it left gamers cold.

The most recent platform game featuring the black-clad hero was *Zorro: Quest for Justice*, released for the Nintendo DS in 2010. The game debuted in Europe before making its way to America, and seems to have disappeared virtually without a trace.

Many games have found a new home online, and those featuring our hero are no exception. A quick Google search will find a plethora of Zorro online slots, coloring games (viewers can digitally color black and white images), and a host of adventure and RPG-style games of various complexities. Although Zorro may not be as popular a video game hero as his thematic offspring, Batman, there's still a lot of life left in the wily old Fox as he transitions into this brave new world.

Also under the category of "unknown" are a number of movies from around the world, such as the 1962 Spanish film, *Zorro the Avenger* (not to be confused with the 1959 feature film of the same name consisting of edited-together TV episodes starring Guy Williams), with a story and screenplay by cult favorite Jésus Franco, who also lent his talents to *The Blood of Fu Manchu* (1968), *Jack the Ripper* (1976), with Klaus Kinski as Saucy Jack, and *Vampire Killer Barbys* (which he also directed).

Speaking of Spain, that country frequently partnered with Italy during the 1950s, 1960s, and 1970s to make a number of memorable films. These included many of the great "spaghetti Westerns" such as *The Good, the Bad, and the Ugly* (1966), *For a Few Dollars More* (1965), and *A Fistful of Dollars* (1964), as well as classic "sword and sandal" films such as *Goliath Against the Giants* (1961) and *The Invincible Gladiator* (1961). The latter tradition also gave us *Zorro against Maciste* (1963), also known as *Samson and the Slave Queen*, in which Don Diego meets legendary Italian strongman Maciste. This Hercules-like hero of Italy debuted in the epic *Cabiria* in 1914 and went on to headline 26 silent films between 1915 and 1927, as well as 25 sound films from 1960 to 1965.

Zorro against Maciste stars Pierce Brice as Zorro (he also played "Don Diego" in 1963's *Invincible Masked Rider*) and Alan Steel, who made a living playing Italian strongmen, as Maciste. In this film, the heroes are hired by rival factions to retrieve a dead king's will. They soon discover that they're being played and eventually team up to ensure that the worthy party gains the throne. Other Spanish/Italian co-productions included *Sword of Zorro* (1963), *Zorro the Invincible* (aka *Zorro of Monterey*, 1971), *Zorro, Rider of Vengeance* (*Zorro il cavaliere della vendetta*, 1971), and *Zorro's Latest Adventure* (*La ultima aventura del Zorro*, 1969).

Mexico contributed several Zorro films, such as *The Great Adventure of Zorro* (*La gran aventura del Zorro*, 1976), and *El Zorro de Jalisco* (1941), starring the popular Mexican actor Pedro Armendariz, perhaps best known to American audiences for his role as Kerim Bey in the second James Bond film, *From Russia with Love* (1963).

From India's Bollywood comes *Madam Zorro* (1963). Produced by A.D. Productions in Bombay and directed by Akkoo (or, alternately, Akku), who was known for his skill helming such action films. The movie is about an evil scientist — Professor Shekhar — who lusts after the fabled Seven Treasures left behind by the current Maharajah's ancestors to be used for the good of the people. Professor Shekhar creates the monstrous Faulad, who kills the Maharajah and places the blame on the ruler's son, Ajit, who is then imprisoned. He is freed by his fiancée, Maya, and when she is sent to jail, Ajit frees her in return. In the meantime, Professor Shekhar begins a reign of terror, pillaging and looting the countryside with the aid of Falaud. To oppose the Professor, Maya becomes the masked Lady Zorro and, with Ajit's help, destroys the Professor and his creation, bringing peace to the kingdom. The music is catchy and upbeat, as Bollywood music tends to be, and remains popular; a Google search on "Madam Zorro" returns any number of sites offering the songs and their lyrics for download. Interestingly, at least one of the tunes, "Ham Bhi Kho Gaye Hain Dil Bhi Kho Gaya Hai," seems to have been influenced, at least in part, by traditional Spanish music.

In 1975, the simply-titled *Zorro* was released, with Navin Nischol taking the role of the hero. The complicated plot involves Gunwar (Nischol), the bastard son of the Maharajah, donning the black mask when he sees firsthand the atrocities committed by his half-brother against the local villagers. Although transplanted to India, and immersing itself in all the cultural content of that country, the story hews closely to the Zorro with which we're all familiar.

And that brings us to the bizarre, things that are just … odd.

IN the Philippines, for example, on the campus of a university in Quezon City, a man dressed as Zorro, complete with hat, mask, cape, toy guns, and binoculars(?) roams the grounds, bringing solace, encouragement, and uplifting messages to students that need them. No one knows who he is, or why he has chosen to take up the mantle of the Fox, but his presence is appreciated by those who have met him.

The Philippine movie industry has also released several Zorro films — perhaps the inspiration for the real-life masked man — including *The Magnificent Zorro* (1968), and *Tulume Alyas Zorro* (1983). The same country also produced a TV show in 2009 aptly named *Zorro*, which loosely follows the plot of McCulley's *The Curse of Capistrano*, the novella that introduced Zorro. Filmed in Bataan, it starred Richard Guttierez as the masked man.

In Japan, there's a cartoon called *Kaiketsu Zorori* (not to be confused with *Kaiketsu Zorro* (1996-97), also from Japan, which is a more straight-ahead presentation of the masked hero). The main character is a yellow fox who wears a decidedly Zorro-like outfit: black hat, black mask, black cape with a red lining, blue tights (with a "ZZ" marked on the chest), a gold belt with a buckle in the shape of a fox's head, and red boots. His goal? To fulfill his mother's dying wish, that he become a Prankster Genius, settle down and marry a pretty girl, and live in a castle. He is adept at building machines to help him achieve his goal, many of which are powered by flatulence. One can only wonder what McCulley would think.

In his book, *Crackpot*, legendary director John Waters writes about his favorite Baltimore stripper named Lady Zorro, and tells us that she gained that name because of her strikingly rugged resemblance to Victor Mature (???). According to Waters, her campy and quirky act was one of a kind, and she remained a local favorite until her death at the age of 63 in 2001. Several photos of her are online, posing in a black hat, black mask, and little else.

Playwright Bernardo Solana has written *Zorro X 2*, which, according to its official description, "…updates the classic tale of Zorro to the 21st century, complete with immigrant laborers, a sadistic chief of security, and an ineffective computer geek who's taken in by a homeless man who claims to be the original Zorro." Apparently, the play remains unproduced, but it stands as another medium — live theater — retelling the story of Don Diego.

When something becomes popular — be it a fictional character, a political figure, or anything else — you can bet your bottom dollar the porn industry will run with it. Porn flicks based on *Batman*, *Star Wars*, *Tomb Raider*, *Edward Scissorhands*, even *E.T.* (No, I don't want to know and neither do you!) and Sarah Palin exist. You won't be shocked to learn that Zorro has been recruited by the adult entertainment industry as well. No doubt others have been produced, but records can be hard to find regarding this branch of film history.

1972 was a big year for adult Zorro, seeing the release of *Red Hot Zorro*, a French film also titled *Les aventures galantes de Zorro*, a title that sounds much more respectable than the film actually is. Interestingly, this version of Zorro actually wears his hat and his mask… at all times. This softcore film used the legend of Zorro as a backdrop, but it was overshadowed by the far funnier, softcore *The Erotic Adventures of Zorro* (aka *The Sexcapades of Don Diego*). With a great script by David F. "The Mighty Monarch of Exploitation," Friedman, known to exploitation film buffs for his partnership with Herschell Gordon Lewis on such classics as *Blood Feast* (1963) and *10,000 Maniacs!* (1964), it was billed as "the first movie rated Z." Don Diego poses as a gay man by day, and lets loose as a super-Casanova by night. Though hardcore sex films were more popular — and more profitable — by 1970, Friedman refused to have anything to do with them, and continued producing softcore pictures like this for several years. High camp, high production values, and passable acting make this a cut above many other films of its type and a truly fun watch.

More recently, *Zorro XXX* has been released by Pleasure Dynasty, the same company that brought you *Thor: A XXX Parody*, *Taxi Driver: A XXX Parody*, *Mall Ratz XXX*, and *The Real Housewives of South Beach XXX*. High production values — *Zorro XXX* won Adult Video Network Awards in 2013 for Best Art Direction and Best Parody-Drama — mark these films as something more than your usual cheapo quickie, and it boasts a solid storyline and an A-list cast. So, for those of you that *really* want to be Zorro completists ...

This is just a taste of all the weird and wonderful ways the Zorro story has been told throughout the years. For the dedicated collector, it represents a challenge to gather as many different representations of Don Diego's masked alter-ego as possible. For the casual fan, it may ignite a desire to learn more about Zorro and the way he's portrayed in other media and in other countries. But for all of us that listen for the sound of thunderous hoof beats and look for that slashing "Z" that is the trademark of the Fox, it demonstrates that we are far from alone in our interest in this legendary hero.

John Petty is a Lecturer in Film at the University of Texas at Dallas. He is also the author of Capes, Crooks, and Cliffhangers: Heroic Serials Posters of the Golden Age, *available from Ivy Press at www.HA.com/serial.*

Art: V. E. Pyles

A Task For Zorro

Don Marcos Vargas — His inherited fortunes had been squandered. He was tolerated in polite society because of his lineage and social standing, but one by one his friends were dropping away.

Pedro Ramirez — Truth and honesty were difficult virtues for him. Perhaps he was leading Vargas down the wrong path in an attempt to rebuild his fortune?

Barney Burke — The Americano traveled through the pueblo, befriending Diego Vega. His goal was to build a cattle ranch of his own. But he hoped to finance his endeavor with the reward for Señor Zorro's capture!

Diego Vega — Apathetic and languid by day, he was secretly El Zorro, the masked highwayman, by night! His sword rang true, clashed against enemy steel, in defense of the poor and downtrodden!

CHAPTER I
Don Diego

WILD yells, wilder laughter, the screeching of children and the yelping of mongrel dogs, the sounds made by galloping hoofs pounding the hard earth — Don Diego Vega heard all that as he strolled from his father's house to the plaza in Reina de Los Angeles.

Reckless, half-wild *vaqueros* of the rancho district had gathered in the plaza. They were on their way to the vicinity of San Gabriel, where the annual great slaughter of cattle was to be held on the rancho of Don Alejandro Vega.

Riders from half a score of other big ranchos would help the Vega *vaqueros* with their work. And after the work was done there would be a grand *fiesta*, with an abundance of food and wine, music and dancing, a deal of furtive love-making beneath the spreading pepper trees when the grim duennas were not looking, and undoubtedly a few fights.

This was an afternoon when the usual after-siesta promenade around the plaza was not being held. Fat señoras did not bring out their marriageable daughters to show them off to eligible males. The noise and confusion upset everybody's nerves, and the dust would ruin costumes and toilettes.

As Diego Vega approached the plaza, he heard the tumult and smiled, knowing the reason for it, but he did not quicken his stride. Those who knew him best declared that Diego Vega could not be quickened by anything.

The only son and heir of aged Don Alejandro Vega, owner of the vast rancho property near San Gabriel and of a fine house in the town, did not resemble other young caballeros of the vicinity when it came to strenuous pursuits.

Unlike them, Diego did not care to ride a horse at breakneck speed for no reason at all, fight at the mere lifting of an eyebrow, play heavily at dice and cards, drink heady wine to excess, or spend considerable time making the hearts of the dainty señoritas flutter. He seemed to avoid all physical exertion, and spent much time reading the works of the poets.

Many had a feeling of pity for old Don Alejandro because his only son, as they saw it, had turned out to be a mixture of milksop and popinjay. They did not know that Diego's languor was only a pose.

Only three men knew the entire truth about him — that Diego Vega was also the mysterious masked Señor Zorro, and rode the hills and highways with pistol, blade and whip to punish those who mistreated the poor and helpless, and in many ways aided the unfortunate and downtrodden.

ONE of the three who knew was Don Alejandro himself, who rejoiced in secret over the exploits of his son.

The second was aged Fray Felipe, a Franciscan *padre* attached to the little chapel in Reina de Los Angeles, who was Diego's father confessor and hence could reveal nothing.

The third was Bernardo, a huge mute peon who acted as Diego's body servant. He was unable to speak, but had he been able would have died rather than betray his master.

Today, Diego Vega was dressed in his resplendent best. He was on his way to the chapel to receive Fray Felipe's blessing before driving out to the rancho with his father, and also to learn what Fray Felipe required of him. For the *padre* had sent a messenger with a note asking that Diego make him a visit as soon as possible.

Diego walked slowly behind a row of adobe huts and so came to a corner of the plaza, where he could see what was happening to cause the tumult.

He saw the *vaqueros* racing their half-broken horses around the plaza through clouds of fine dust. It was a sight he had seen often before when the rancho riders were gathering for the great slaughter. He held a scented handkerchief to his nostrils and half-closed his eyes as he walked to the side of the plaza where the dust would blow away from instead of upon him.

Some of the *vaqueros* were quick to recognize him, and began shouting their greetings. Diego waved a hand languidly to acknowledge their salutes. Each year he gave prizes for riding, wrestling and other sports, and the *vaqueros* did not forget that, for Diego was always generous.

Passing the sprawling tavern building, which was filled with roistering men, Diego strolled on to the chapel. Fray Felipe was waiting for him there. He received the *padre*'s blessing, and they sat down to talk.

"I received your message, *padre*, and came at once," Diego said. "You intimated it was something urgent."

"It is indeed urgent, my son. That is why I desired to see you before you left town for the rancho. It amounts to this, Diego — Zorro has work to do."

Diego sat up straight on the bench. "Zorro?" he repeated. "What now, *padre*?"

"For some time, my son, somebody has been slaughtering cattle belonging to the Mission of San Gabriel. As you possibly know, the mission cattle graze widely, even across the hills and almost to the sea."

"So I know, *padre*."

"At first, wheeling buzzards in the sky pointed the way to several carcasses from which the hides had been stripped. The depredations have increased in number and seriousness rapidly. We of the missions have been watching. The thefts have been so widespread that there must be an organized band of thieves committing them. And the band must be headed by a clever rogue of uncanny skill."

"How much have you learned, *padre*?" Diego asked.

"Very little of importance, my son. But we do know that cart caravans have traveled up the highway to Monterey, where bales of green hides have been sold to traders. The hides did not come from any of the great ranchos, or they would have been marked."

"What do the caravan men say? Have they been questioned at all?"

"The caravan men were questioned. They declare that they bought the hides a few at a time along the highway from any who wished to sell. Since the hides do not bear earmarks, as our mission cattle are marked, who can say to whom the cattle belonged?"

"But this is monstrous!" Diego declared. "To steal like that from a Franciscan mission!"

"To some men, my son, nothing is sacred. It is my thought that Zorro could look into the matter during the great slaughter at your rancho."

"I am sure Zorro will do the best he can, *padre*," Diego replied, smiling.

"As usual, there will be much activity during the slaughter and *fiesta*. Wine will loosen men's tongues. You may overhear something that will give you a clue, or observe something. But use the utmost caution, my son. You may be encountering strong enemies in this enterprise. Zorro is badly needed now, and nothing ill must befall him."

"Have the soldiers been informed of these cattle thefts?" Diego asked.

FRAY FELIPE nodded, and sighed. "They have been informed fully, my son, and given all the facts we have gathered."

"With what result?"

"The *commandante* here claims that they can learn nothing. The way circumstances are now, Diego, with the politicians coveting the wealth of the missions and seeking to undermine our influence with the native neophytes, we cannot expect much help from the Governor's soldiers."

"How many hides have been taken, *padre*?"

"More than two hundred carcasses have been found and counted in scattered localities, a few at a time, with the buzzards gorging themselves," Fray Felipe replied. "How many more have not been discovered, we do not know. And most of the carcasses have been found where only mission cattle graze."

"Is there anything at all to point the way to the guilty?" Diego questioned.

"We have been watching certain men, but we have obtained no real proof," Fray Felipe replied. "Everything points to a well-organized band of cattle thieves, and such must have a man of ability at its head. If Zorro can locate this man and pin the guilt on him, the wholesale thievery will soon be ended."

Diego got up from the bench upon which he had been sitting.

"I have some preparations to make, *padre*," he said. "I hope to have you as our guest at the rancho no later than tomorrow evening."

"I'll come out early tomorrow on my riding mule," Fray Felipe promised.

"The door is always open to you," Diego said. "Regarding the mission cattle—have you reason to suspect any one man more than others?"

"There is a stranger in town, an Americano," Fray Felipe replied. "He arrived this morning. He appears to be a man of wild, adventurous spirit. That is the report I received about him. He may be blameless, but we are having him watched."

Chapter II
Stranger In Town

BARNEY BURKE was six feet tall and as slender as a reed, except for his shoulders. In weight and breadth they gave great driving power to his arms and fists.

He walked on the balls of his feet and swayed like a tireless Indian traveling a long trail. His steel-colored eyes always seemed to be keenly alert. His mop of sandy hair fell almost to his shoulders.

Barney Burke was dressed in a stained suit of worn buckskin, and his boots were badly run down at the heels. A wide leather belt held a sheath from which the hilt of a knife protruded, and he wore a holster in which he carried a pistol.

That morning shortly after dawn, he had ridden his bay pony into Reina de Los Angeles from the south trail. Picketing his pony behind the tavern, he had gone inside to buy and devour a heavy meal, then had asked for a room off the patio. He had slept soundly until after midday.

When he awoke, his shouts for service had made a native servant hurry to him. Burke had demanded an abundance of warm water for a bath.

Having performed his ablutions, meanwhile singing at the top of his baritone voice a song which nobody who heard it could understand, he went to the main room of the tavern and ate another huge repast, paid for it, and went out to feed and water his pony.

By this time, everybody around the tavern and plaza was watching him closely and speculating as to his identity and his business in the pueblo. They watched as he saddled his pony and tied him to one of the horse blocks at the side of the tavern building, and as he chewed off the end of a cheroot, lit it, and puffed with evident content.

All the fat tavern keeper could tell others was that the stranger spoke Spanish, but with an atrocious accent, had a name that was difficult to pronounce, and offered little information concerning himself.

He had ridden from San Diego de Alcalá, he had said, where he had left a ship in which he had sailed from a small port in Mexico. But there the self-offered information had ended.

Sitting later on a bench in front of the tavern, he watched the scene in the plaza. He never had seen anything like it before, and his eyes sparkled as he watched.

The *vaqueros* had been drinking quantities of wine from the wineskins they had brought with them attached to their saddles. They had reached the stage where they were boasting and arranging horse races and wrestling matches.

Barney Burke ignited a fresh cheroot. He glanced up when he heard boots crunching the sandy earth, to see approaching him a huge man wearing the uniform of a sergeant of the Governor's troopers.

The sergeant stopped in front of Burke, to stand with his feet apart and his fists planted against his hips. He blew out the ends of his enormous mustache, glared, and spoke in a raucous voice.

"I have the honor, señor, to be Sergeant Manuel Garcia, of His Excellency's soldiery, at present in official charge here in Reina de Los Angeles during the indisposition of our *commandante*."

Burke blinked rapidly as if dazzled by the sergeant's uniform. He forced back a smile, then got up off the bench slowly, stretched his lanky form, and gave the burly sergeant an elaborate bow.

"It is always pleasant to meet an important man," Burke said, in his 'atrocious Spanish'.

"According to the official report that has been made to me, señor, you rode into the pueblo at an early hour this morning," the sergeant accused, his manner arrogant. "Is that the truth?"

"That's correct," Burke admitted.

"And you neglected to report your presence at the barracks," the sergeant continued.

"Should I have done that?"

"It is a thing required by the law in the case of an alien. Your quaint manner of speech, the color of your hair and eyes, your clothing — everything about you indicates that you are an alien. Do you happen to be an Americano?"

"That's correct."

"Such was my own belief. Be kind enough to explain yourself to me, señor. And do not allow your tongue to wander from the truth. I have heard that all Americanos are adept at deception."

"My name is Barney Burke. I'm twenty-eight years old and stand six feet in my socks. I don't know my exact weight at this moment, because the food a man gets in this country doesn't keep him built up."

THE sergeant drew himself up, and puffed out his cheeks.

"Ha! You complain of our food? You say that it doesn't keep a man built up? Observe me!"

"A mere mass of flabby fat," Burke judged. "Bulk, but no muscle, no solid meat, no stamina."

"Indeed, señor? Is it customary for you to insult the officials wherever you travel? Is that a sure manner of winning their friendship and respect? Now, señor, to business! You came from where?"

"I landed at San Diego de Alcalá from a ship upon which I took passage from Mexico. I bought a bay pony and rode north to have a look at the country. I have a bill of sale for the pony."

"Have I given you the slightest intimation, señor, that I thought you stole the pony?" Sergeant Garcia asked, with a trace of anger in his manner. "A swift glance at the animal convinces me he would not be worth stealing."

Barney Burke's eyes glittered an instant. "Never judge a horse by a swift glance," he advised. "And don't ever be foolish enough to bet against mine if you ever find him entered in a race."

Sergeant Garcia blew out the ends of his mustache again.

Ha!" he said. "As to that, señor, there probably will be horse races here in the plaza between now and sunset, if you care to race your pony against the mounts of some of our *vaqueros*."

"I'll think about that, Señor Sergeant."

"But at the moment, señor, I am less interested in your pony than I am in his owner. What is your business here in our pueblo? How long do you expect to remain, and where are you going when you depart?"

"In my own country, I was what they call a cowboy," Burke explained. "I worked for a cattle ranch. I want to see how you raise cattle in this country. I want to take a ride through the rancho district and learn things. I have money to pay my way. Anything illegal in that?"

The burly sergeant rumbled in his throat and glared again, though fully aware that his glares did not disconcert Burke in the least.

"I grant you permission to enjoy your stay among us, Señor Burke," he said flatly, as if he had made a momentous decision after long deliberation. "But do not be offended if we keep our official eyes upon you for a time."

"I'll try to keep from shivering," Burke replied.

"It is now the season of the year when they hold the usual great slaughter of cattle at the Vega rancho near San Gabriel. The Vegas are the greatest and proudest family in this part of the country. Go out to the rancho and watch the slaughter, and have fun at the *fiesta* following it, if you would learn of this country and its customs."

"Thanks!" said Burke. "And where can I get permission to visit the rancho?"

SERGEANT GARCIA laughed, with a touch of scorn in his laughter.

"It is quite apparent to me, señor, that you know little of our country," he said. "Everybody is welcome at Rancho Vega during the slaughter and *fiesta*. Don Alejandro Vega and his son, Don Diego, will drive out to the rancho during the cool of the night. There will be a full moon."

"I've heard of that big Vega rancho and would like to see it," Burke said.

"Who has not heard of the Vegas and their rancho? All these *vaqueros* in the plaza will ride out to the rancho this evening also. I'll leave with some of my troopers after sunset, to maintain order during the affair."

"Do I just ride out there and make myself welcome?" Burke asked.

"Simply jog along with the crowd, señor, and try to keep out of fights, if you do not wish to be buried in a strange land. Do not roll your eyes at the señoritas, lest some *vaquero* slip a knife between your ribs in a moment of jealousy."

Barney Burke smiled slightly. "Señor Sergeant, I've always been able to take care of myself," he replied. "Your *vaqueros* can't be any tougher than some of the hombres I've met in cowtowns and on the trails back in the States."

"Nevertheless, have a care, señor. 'Tis said that the man who treads carefully walks a long distance."

"I'll be careful," Burke promised.

Sergeant Garcia clicked his heels, bowed stiffly, and left him, to move on and shout rebukes at some roistering peons who were making more wine-induced noise than was usual.

BURKE remained sitting there and watching the *vaqueros* for a time longer, then slapped some of the dust from his clothes and entered the tavern to order a mug of wine. He sat at a table in a secluded corner of the room and sipped the wine slowly, continuing to watch the plaza scene through an open window. The din increased steadily.

Before he had been sitting there long, the fat tavern keeper approached. Behind him strutted a man whose dress and manner proclaimed him a member of the arrogant hidalgo tribe.

The man appeared to be in his middle thirties. He was tall and slender and swarthy, and wore fashionable attire. His long tapering fingers were adorned with heavy rings. At his side he wore a blade with a jeweled hilt.

The tavern keeper bowed. "Señor Burke," he said, after the manner of a man doing a great honor, "this gentleman is Don Marcos Vargas. I have told Don Marcos that you are an Americano traveling through our country, and he is doing you the honor of allowing you to meet him and converse."

The tavern keeper bowed low to Vargas and retreated.

Eyes glittering, Barney Burke looked up at the man standing so arrogantly before him, twirling one end of a tiny mustache and smiling sarcastically.

Don Marcos Vargas had inherited extensive properties some years before from his father and an uncle, and had dissipated his estates by gambling and making unsuccessful business ventures in an attempt to regain his gambling losses.

He was still tolerated in polite society because of his lineage and social standing, but one by one his friends were dropping away from him.

Marcos Vargas lived now in a bachelor establishment in town, and kept a few horses. He dressed well and made the usual annual trip to Monterey.

It was being whispered around that he had undesirable companions, and that some of his methods of keeping in funds were unscrupulous.

"Señor Burke," Vargas said now, after an uncomplimentary inspection, "I have heard much of you Americanos, and I am frank in saying that there is not much in you worthy of admiration."

"Since we're being so frank in our talk, you don't impress me much, either," Burke replied, not entirely sure he relished understanding Spanish at all.

"Señor! It will not benefit you to be insolent to a man of my standing. Attend me! I have often heard that you Americanos are always willing to risk a few coins on a wager."

"A wager on what?" Burke asked him. His tone was one of suspicion, and the manner in which he looked up at Vargas was not flattering.

"Sergeant Manuel Garcia has informed me that you are the owner of a bay pony which you fancy as an animal of fleetness. Perhaps, señor, you would care to match him in a race with a horse of mine."

"Well, I might be tempted to do something like that," Burke replied, with a smile. "Sit down and have a mug of wine with me, Don Marcos, and then we'll go out and have a look at this horse of yours."

"Your pardon, señor, but I never allow myself to drink with strangers," Vargas said softly.

Burke's face burned suddenly with mingled embarrassment and anger.

"Meaning that you're too high and mighty to clink mugs with a man like me?" he demanded.

"I meant no offense, señor. It is only a personal rule of mine."

"All right. We'll go out and take a look at your horse," Burke decided.

He gulped the remainder of the wine, tossed a small coin down upon the table in payment, and got up to follow Vargas out of the tavern.

CHAPTER III
A Wager Is Made

AT ONE side of the noisy plaza, a man was holding the reins of a large sorrel that looked like an animal of spirit and stamina. Burke walked around the horse and eyed him well, put an investigating hand upon him, and inspected his legs and feet.

"He looks like a good horse, Don Marcos," Burke praised, finally.

"Will you race?" Vargas asked.

"What kind of a race do you want?" Burke asked. "What distance, and all?"

"Look up the north trail, señor," Vargas requested, pointing in that direction. "Do you see the little adobe hut beside the trail on the left side? From there to the middle of the plaza, where we shall draw a finish line in the dirt, is exactly one mile. Let that be the course."

"Suits me," Burke agreed. "I ride my pony and you ride your sorrel. Right?"

"Pardon me again, Señor Burke, but I never ride in a race except it be against another caballero. It is a personal rule of mine."

"Too proud to ride against me, or afraid that you'll be beaten?" Burke asked him.

"Señor! A Vargas is never afraid of anything! This is my friend, Pedro Ramirez, holding the horse. He will ride the sorrel for me."

Pedro Ramirez bowed as Barney Burke gave him an appraising glance. Burke saw that Ramirez was slight in build and had beady black eyes. Burke made the instant decision that Ramirez was not a man to be trusted far.

He finally turned to face Vargas again. "I'll take you on," he decided.

"And our wager, Señor Burke?"

"I'm not a rich hidalgo," Burke informed him. "I'm a man who carries his estate in his pocket. But I can go for three or four pieces of gold."

Vargas' face revealed his disappointment.

"So small a wager, señor?" he asked. "I have heard that all Americanos are rich."

"A few of us haven't got around to making our piles yet," Burke informed him.

"Ordinarily, señor, such a small wager scarcely would interest me," Vargas replied loftily. "But my horse needs exercise and more experience in racing. Let it be for four pieces of gold, if you can go no higher. The gold is as good as in my pocket anyhow. I'll give it to Ramirez for riding."

"Who holds the stakes?"

"I believe we may trust the tavern keeper. He holds stakes for most of the races in the plaza."

"Suits me," Burke replied.

"Then we will return to the tavern and wager the money," Vargas decided. "You, Ramirez, will warn the *vaqueros* and others to clear the path for us. And have the ground swept, and scratch a finish line in the usual place in the dirt across the middle of the plaza .... "

When Diego Vega's interview with Fray Felipe was at an end, Diego left the chapel to return to his home and make some last minute preparations for his journey to the rancho.

He would have to pass the tavern, and he saw a crowd in front of the tavern door. And in the midst of the crowd was Don Marcos Vargas, a man Diego despised.

In the tavern crowd he also saw Bernardo, his huge mute peon servant, no doubt waiting there to escort him home and carry any packages Diego might have.

As Diego neared the tavern, somebody gave a shout, and he saw the *vaqueros* leaving the plaza and congregating along the sides of it. Two men waited until the dust had settled, and drew a line on the ground with a stick.

Diego knew, then, that a horse race had been arranged. He glanced up the north trail and saw two riders there, with a couple of men beside them to start the race.

Diego stepped back against the tavern building out of the press of the crowd to watch the race, and found himself standing beside the tavern keeper.

"What is this, señor?" he asked.

"Ah, Don Diego!" the tavern keeper greeted. "A cordial welcome to you! We have here a race for four pieces of gold between Don Marcos Vargas' sorrel and a little bay pony owned by a stranger who arrived this morning. He is an Americano."

"An Americano?" Diego asked, his brows lifting slightly. "I am rather eager to see him. A friend of my father's, who visited us recently, told me much concerning the Americanos. Did we have their ability and exercise ourselves performing it, we could develop our country quickly, he said."

"'Tis true that the Americanos are spreading out and encroaching everywhere," the tavern keeper declared. "It is being reported that already they have invaded the Oregon country far to the north, and they are seen frequently in San Francisco de Asis. They are brave explorers and shrewd traders."

"So I have heard."

"This man, who names himself as Barney Burke, holds himself well. He has a keen eye, and I doubt not a quick temper when aroused. Marcos Vargas coaxed him into the race, no doubt thinking to gain some gold easily."

A sudden roar came from the throats of the watching *vaqueros*, peons and natives. The race had started. In a cloud of dust, Vargas' big sorrel and the little bay owned by Barney Burke were racing toward the plaza.

Under the expert guidance of Pedro Ramirez, the rangy sorrel had managed to get away in front, but the bay was only a few strides behind him. Down the gentle slope they raced straight toward the plaza and finish line.

"Who is riding the sorrel?" Diego asked the tavern keeper.

"Pedro Ramirez."

"He is a slimy fellow," Diego declared frankly. "I would not trust him too far. How Vargas can tolerate the man and make a familiar of him is beyond my understanding."

"It has been said, Don Diego, that birds of a like feather seek to nest together. Ah, I humbly beg your pardon for that remark, Don Diego! Such as I should not speak ill of one of gentle blood."

"The pardon is granted freely, señor," Diego replied. "Gentle blood ceases to be gentle when the one in whose veins it flows befouls it himself."

The excited crowd was cheering and shouting at the two riders now. In front of the group before the tavern, Marcos Vargas was laughing loudly.

"'Tis scarcely a race!" Vargas was shouting. "An easy contest for my sorrel! I wish this race was for a hundred pieces of gold. Look at the sorrel's stride!"

Now the racers were near enough for those grouped around the plaza to hear the pounding of hoofs above all other sounds. Barney Burke was racing about a length behind Ramirez in a narrow place in the trail.

As the trail neared the plaza, it became wider. Burke bent low over his pony's neck, and those around the plaza could see that the bay was gaining gradually.

"Vargas' big sorrel is tiring, and the little bay is coming along nicely," Diego told the tavern keeper.

"But 'tis nothing more than a futile spurt, I fancy," the tavern keeper replied. "Ramirez can drive the sorrel ahead at will. He is saving the horse."

"Not so!" Diego shouted, far more excited than it was his custom to be. "Watch the little bay!"

Barney Burke had his pony neck and neck with Vargas' sorrel now, and both mounts were racing at top speed. Those around the plaza could see that Pedro Ramirez was starting to use his whip. He lashed at the sorrel's rump and flank, and the sorrel surged ahead again.

But only for an instant. Barney Burke's bay pony came on and made it a neck and neck affair once more. In the plaza, the *vaqueros* were shouting wildly. This was the sort of race they liked to see.

Marcos Vargas was yelling something nobody could understand. Ramirez was using his whip on the sorrel again. But Burke's little bay started to gain as the sorrel began tiring and falling back. Under the urge of the stinging whip, the sorrel put on a last burst of speed.

A chorus of exclamations and howls of rage came suddenly from the watchers. Facing defeat, Pedro Ramirez had lost his head. He half-turned in the saddle and began lashing Burke's pony about the head with the whip. Then, as the side of the plaza was reached and the finish line was only a short distance away, he cut at Burke.

"Foul! — foul!" somebody shouted.

Others immediately took up the cry, but ceased quickly when they realized that they were shouting against Vargas' rider, and that Vargas himself was there to hear them and might remember it afterward.

The racers came on toward the finish line with thundering hoofs. But the bay had swerved aside for an instant, bewildered by the blows he had received on his head. The sorrel went across the line a winner by two lengths.

The riders pulled up their mounts and turned and came back to the line as the crowd started to surge forward. Marcos Vargas hurried out into the plaza. The tavern keeper waddled after him, being the stakeholder. Diego Vega sauntered after the tavern man.

"An easy win!" Vargas was shouting to all about him. "It would have been a dozen lengths if Ramirez had let the sorrel out."

But Diego was not watching Vargas. He had his eyes on the Americano. He was remembering what Fray Felipe had said, and wondering whether Barney Burke had anything to do with the theft of mission cattle.

THE heaving horses were stopped at the line. Pedro Ramirez glanced strangely at Vargas and got down out of the sorrel's saddle. But Barney Burke was on the ground before Ramirez, his eyes blazing with rage. He ground-hitched his tired pony and strode forward angrily.

The bay pony had welts on his head and neck where the heavy whip had struck. Barney Burke had an ugly bruise on one cheek with a trickle of blood running from it, where the whip had cut him.

"Ramirez!" Burke shouted, his voice shaking. "One moment, you! I'll teach you not to lash my pony and strike me with a whip!"

"A poor loser," Marcos Vargas commented, loud enough for all around him to hear the words. "I have heard that all Americanos are such."

"Poor loser?" Burke raged at him. "Everybody who was watching the race saw that foul, Vargas. Can you defend your rider? So that's the way your horses win races, is it? I claim the stake because of the foul!"

"Nonsense!" Vargas declared. "There was no foul, señor. Your pony swerved and bumped the sorrel and got beneath the falling whip for an instant. Your bay was not fast enough to win, that is all."

"No foul? Look at my pony's head and neck! Look at my own face!"

Pedro Ramirez had started to make his way through the crowd, hoping to get from the neighborhood before Burke noticed his departure. But Burke darted forward and caught Ramirez in an iron grip and whirled him around.

"One minute, rat!" Burke yelled at him.

"You won't get away that easy. You'll answer to me for what you did, right here and now, if these men will stand back and give us room."

"Unhand me, señor!" Ramirez ordered.

Chapter IV
Under Protection

RAMIREZ lifted his riding whip as if to strike, and that was a bad mistake. With a cry of rage, Burke tore the whip from his hand and hurled it aside. Then he grasped Ramirez again and whirled him off balance and to a clear space near the finish line.

"Garcia!" Marcos Vargas was shouting in a frenzy at the big sergeant, who was standing not far away. "You and your troopers make a quick end of this! The Americano is a bad loser. He may try to harm Ramirez."

Sergeant Garcia, who always welcomed an opportunity to show his authority, beckoned to a couple of his men and immediately thrust his way forward.

"No brawl here, señores!" he shouted. "Keep the peace! In the Governor's name!"

But Diego Vega had a thought concerning the situation. His eyes were gleaming as he stepped forward and touched the sergeant on the shoulder.

"Sergeant Garcia, I was an unhappy witness of the entire affair," Diego said. "Without doubt, Pedro Ramirez deliberately fouled the Americano. He struck Señor Burke and the bay pony with his whip. Allow them to settle this affair themselves, Sergeant, in their own way."

Sergeant Garcia blew out the end of his mustache and squinted at Diego. He knew better than to affront one of the Vega family by refusing a just request. Between Diego Vega and Marcos Vargas, it did not take Garcia long to decide. He turned his back and strode away, motioning for his troopers to retire.

Burke had charged forward with his fists coming up. Ramirez sprang lightly to one side, and his hand flashed toward his sash. But Burke caught the gleam of the sun on the knife. He bent quickly and dodged, and the thrown weapon flew past him to clatter on the hard ground.

"You sneaking coward!" Burke shouted at him. "Try to knife me, will you? I'll make you pay double for that! Stand and take it, you scum!"

Burke charged again, and this time Ramirez could do nothing but stand and try to fight. He made a poor showing at it. Burke's fists crashed through his guard at will and thudded against his body. Beneath the barrage of blows Ramirez retreated, trying to cover up.

Ramirez' face was badly cut and bruised and one of his eyes was closed before they had been fighting more than a minute. Burke's superior strength and skill, enhanced now by his just rage, made Ramirez an easy victim.

Burke cut him up for a short time longer, by way of punishment. Then his hard right swung over and collided with Ramirez' chin, and Ramirez dropped unconscious to the ground.

Vargas was like a madman.

He sprang out into the open, but stopped quickly enough when he saw Burke striding toward him.

"Now, Señor Vargas, I'm ready to settle with you!" Burke told him.

But Sergeant Garcia barged forward again. "Stop, señor!" he ordered Burke. "One brawl is enough for today. And do not forget that you are an alien among us. A man of your kidney does not dare attack Don Marcos Vargas."

"Not dare?" Burke declared. "In a case like this, I'd take on a couple like him at the same time. It's a good thing for him that he has soldiers to protect him. Where's that tavern keeper? I want the stake money. Ramirez fouled me, and I'm entitled to the stake."

"Oh, give the fellow the few gold pieces and let us have an end of this!" Vargas said.

"So you admit that your rider fouled?" Burke asked.

"I am admitting nothing, señor. But I am sick of this cheap haggling."

Burke faced the tavern keeper again. "Then, señor, you will kindly declare this a 'no race' and call all bets off, and give me back my own stake only," he ordered. "That will be fair to us all."

The tavern keeper handed him the coins, and Burke put them into his pocket. Vargas accepted his stake also, and jingled the coins in his hand.

"If you're a fair example of a California gentleman, give me some decent waterfront scum," Burke told Vargas.

"I'll see that you pay for your insolence and insults, señor!" Vargas threatened, his eyes flashing dangerously.

"Meaning that you'll hire some fellow to knife me in the back some dark night?" Burke asked. "You'd be afraid to try it yourself."

VARGAS' face purpled with wrath. He stepped quickly to one side and tossed up his arms to attract attention.

"Vaqueros!" he shouted at the half-wild, more than half-intoxicated rancho riders. "Shall we allow this insolent Americano to insult us and this country we call home? Perhaps a little rough handling would teach him his proper place. Have your way with him."

Some held back, having a feeling toward fair play. But others yelled and started to surge forward. Burke caught up a club from the ground and prepared to defend himself against them as well as he could. He made no move to use either pistol or knife. That, he feared, might cause his arrest by the soldiers.

But Diego Vega suddenly was out in front of the *vaqueros*, between them and the man they intended to make their victim. Diego lifted his hand somewhat languidly.

"Stand back, *vaqueros*!" he said to them in a quiet voice. "This Americano has done nothing wrong. He was treated dishonestly, and resented that treatment as any proper man would. Think how you would feel in his place. Do not put your hands on him."

"What business is this of yours, Diego Vega?" Vargas asked, with heat.

"We owe it to ourselves and our country to treat an alien visitor within our gates with fairness and respect," Diego replied. "This man has done no wrong. I place him under my protection!"

Don Diego's quiet manner and fair words, and the weight his name and lineage carried, brought the angry *vaqueros* to an abrupt stop.

It was the Vega rancho to which they were going for work and fun, for both profit and pleasure. They did not want to affront Don Alejandro's son, the man who annually gave such generous prizes for horsemanship, for skill in slaying cattle, for wrestling and other sports.

Many there expected Marcos Vargas to resent Diego Vega's interference. Some also expected and hoped to witness a fight with blades, both Diego and Vargas being of gentle blood and neither able to refuse with honor a challenge by the other. In such an event, they feared for Diego, who had no reputation as a swordsman, whereas Vargas was known to have wounded three men in duels.

Sergeant Manuel Garcia was wondering what he could do about it if a quarrel and duel resulted, for the Governor had issued an edict against dueling.

But the sergeant was spared the embarrassment of making a decision.

Marcos Vargas only glared at Diego for a moment and met the latter's level gaze, then turned away to pass through the crowd, which opened to make a lane for him. But first he gave orders for a couple of men standing near to pick up Pedro Ramirez and carry him to the horse trough, and there throw water on him until he returned to consciousness.

Diego glanced through the crowd and beckoned. Bernardo, his mute servant, saw the gesture and thrust his way forward. Diego beckoned a second time, and Barney Burke stepped up to him, leading his pony.

"I am Diego Vega, señor," the scion of the Vega family introduced himself. "I am very happy to have been of some little service to you."

"I've heard of your family and your big rancho, Don Diego," Burke admitted. "And the service you just did me was something special. Thanks for keeping those wild *vaqueros* off my neck. But I sure wish I could have had a little argument with the owner of the sorrel. I do not care for him."

"Let Bernardo, my servant, handle your pony while we have a little talk, señor," Diego suggested. "He is a wonder with horses, and will take good care of your little bay. He handles the Vega racing ponies."

"That's good enough for me, Don Diego. Thanks!" Burke handed his reins to the mute.

Diego gave Bernardo his instructions and received his guttural assurance that he understood. The mute led the pony away to cool him off and rub him down and give him water after he had cooled.

The *vaqueros* had drifted away, the excitement being at an end, some to enter the tavern again and shout for wine, and others to continue their rough games.

DIEGO took Burke into the tavern. They sat on a bench beside a table in a far corner of the big room, and the tavern keeper hastened to take a skin of his best wine and his finest goblets to them. The goblets were filled; they saluted each other and drank.

"I understand that you are an Americano, Señor Burke," Diego said.

"That is correct," Burke replied, answering Diego's warming smile with one of his own.

He was estimating the great difference between the manner of this hidalgo and that of Marcos Vargas, and Vargas suffered much in the comparison.

"I have heard much of you Americanos," Diego said, "but this is the first time I have had the pleasure of meeting one."

"A happy meeting for me, Don Diego!"

"There are some of us who believe it would be beneficial for both if we Californians and the Americanos knew each other better."

"I think the same, Don Diego."

"Though we are separated by lofty mountain ranges and great stretches of semi-desert land, we of California are really as close neighbors with you as we are with Mother Mexico. Tell me something of yourself."

Barney Burke was more than willing to do that. Already he was warming toward this resplendently dressed son of the dons whose manner was so gracious. And he was enthusiastic in his ambitions.

He explained to Diego how he had been a cowboy and trail boss back home, and told about the great wide grazing areas, the long drives to markets and shipping points, and the continual warfare against Indians and rustlers, against disease and blizzard and drought.

He explained also how wanderlust and the hunger for knowledge had lured him through Texas to Mexico and then up to Alta California.

"I have heard about your big Vega rancho and the others, and of how you raise cattle and horses and sheep," he concluded. "I would like to have a good look at it all, and perhaps learn something."

"Then you have come at an opportune time, señor," Diego replied. "We are to leave this evening for the Vega rancho, where the annual great slaughter of cattle is to be held. We kill cattle mostly for hides and fat, and burn what meat we cannot use or give away."

"But that is a sinful waste, Don Diego," Burke declared, frankly. "We raise cattle for the meat, and hides and fat are secondary with us."

"Señor Burke, it would please me if you would be my guest at the rancho for as long as you may desire to remain," Diego said. "We may learn much from each other."

Diego was not forgetting that this man might have something to do with the slaughtering of the mission cattle. And Barney Burke's reply to the invitation was swift.

"I would like that, Don Diego, and thanks for asking me," he said. "But would I be free to come and go as I pleased, and watch your men work?"

"Certainly, señor," Diego assured him. "Your movements will be entirely without restraint. You will be assigned one of our guest rooms and eat at the family table. Mounts will be supplied you whenever your own pony is tired and needs a day of rest."

CHAPTER V
Unexpected Enemy

DIEGO decided he would give Burke every chance to betray himself, if he really had a hand in the mission cattle business. But wherever this Barney Burke rode, Zorro could follow.

Burke took another sip of wine, glanced around to make sure nobody was within hearing distance, and bent slightly over the table when he spoke again.

"It is like this, Don Diego," he said. "I believe you are my kind of man, a square man as we say, meaning that you are honest and fair in your dealings. So I want to be honest with you, too, and not accept your hospitality until I tell you a certain thing."

"If you insist, Señor Burke."

"It is true that I want to study your methods of stock raising. But I am here on another mission, too. It will probably meet with your approval, but I want to be sure. I have heard of this mysterious Señor Zorro, the masked man who rides the hills and highways."

"Ah, yes!" Diego replied, hiding his swift smile by brushing his handkerchief quickly across his face. "I understand he is a rather turbulent fellow."

"I have learned that your Governor has proclaimed him to be a highwayman and outlaw, and has offered a large reward for his capture. I could use that money to start a little ranch of my own."

"And do you really think that you could catch this mysterious Señor Zorro when the soldiers have failed to do it?" Diego asked.

"Well, I know a lot of tricks in man-tracking that your soldiers may not know, Don Diego. Back home, I have dealt with Indian cattle thieves and white renegade rustlers. I know how to find a trail and how to track a man."

"That should be a great advantage," Diego said. He was thinking that experience like that would be of great assistance to the head of a cattle-stealing gang, too.

"I think I can learn where this Señor Zorro lives, and who his friends are, and finally run him down. Knowing all this, do you still want me to be your guest at the rancho?"

"More than before, señor," Diego declared. "I'll watch your pursuit of Zorro with keen interest. My father and I will leave for the rancho this evening as soon as the full moon is up. It will be cool then. You may meet us here at the tavern and ride beside our carriage."

"Thanks, Don Diego. I shall be here, ready and waiting when your carriage comes by in the street."

"In the meantime, Bernardo will take good care of your bay pony and see that nobody molests him. And you may be assured that nobody will be thoughtless enough to molest you personally. You are under the protection of the Vegas."

They talked a little longer, and then Diego excused himself, saying he must hurry home. He was chuckling softly as he left the tavern.

So this Señor Barney Burke was going to catch Zorro and claim the Governor's reward! Little did Barney Burke suspect that the man to whom he had been revealing his ambition was Zorro.

Burke might indeed prove to be a formidable foe, Diego thought. The man seemed to be shrewd, and certainly it would be a bad mistake to underestimate his ability. So what better plan than to have Burke at his side as a guest? He could watch the Americano's movements and make sure that Zorro never ran afoul of him. And he could watch and listen for indications that Burke was associated with the stock thieves.

Out of the tavern, Diego walked slowly to where Bernardo was caring for Burke's slashed pony.

"Bernardo, you will not ride to the rancho with us this evening," Diego explained. "Wait until the middle of the night, and then get Zorro's black horse, clothes and weapons."

Bernardo's eyes began gleaming.

"Use your riding mule and lead the horse," Diego continued. "Lash the clothes and weapons in the saddle. Go over the hills, and make sure you are not seen, and at the rancho hide everything in the usual place. Do you understand?"

Bernardo bobbed his head and made the usual guttural sounds to indicate he understood. He was showing some excitement. If Don Diego wanted Zorro's

mount and trappings out at the rancho, it meant there would be plenty of excitement before the great slaughter and *fiesta* were at an end ....

AT SUNSET, the *vaqueros* gathered in the plaza, shouting like madmen.
They got into their saddles, discharged their pistols, rode wildly around the
plaza a few times, then followed an appointed leader out of the pueblo at breakneck speed, leaving a lifting cloud of fine dust in their wake. They turned into
the trail that led to San Gabriel.

Sergeant Manuel Garcia and six of his troopers left the barracks a short
time afterward, Garcia bellowing commands as if he were leading a regiment.
Two of the troopers would be stationed at the San Gabriel mission, and Garcia
and the four others would have quarters at the Vega rancho.

Barney Burke devoured another enormous repast at the tavern, paid his bill,
and went out to make sure that his pony had been fed and watered and was
ready for the trail. He offered Bernardo a coin, which was smilingly refused,
and Bernardo hurried away.

As Burke was tethering his pony to one of the horse blocks near the corner
of the tavern, he heard boots crunch gravel and turned quickly. Don Marcos
Vargas was striding toward him.

There was nothing menacing in the manner of Vargas' approach, but Burke
nevertheless remained alert and on guard, ready for instant violent action. His
right hand dropped to his pistol holster and moved the holster around so he
could get at the weapon immediately and without lost movement should there
be necessity for doing so.

With his thumbs hooked into his belt and his body balanced on the balls of
his feet, Burke stood beside the pony and waited. Vargas came up to him smiling
slightly, stopped, and made a stiff bow.

"Señor Burke, I am happy to find you alone, for I have a desire to speak
with you," Vargas said.

"I am listening."

"I have the feeling that I have made a mistake and owe you an apology. I
am cursed with a quick temper, and to see my pet sorrel being beaten by your
pony enraged me."

"I know how that is," Burke confessed. "I have a quick temper myself."

"Then perhaps you will understand. I have rebuked Pedro Ramirez for
striking you and your pony, and you have given him proper punishment also. I
am asking you to excuse the affront I gave you. I admit the foul, and here are

the four pieces of gold I bet on the match."

"Keep your gold," Burke told him bluntly. "Perhaps we can run the race over out at the Vega rancho."

"You are going there?" Vargas revealed some surprise at Burke's words.

"As Don Diego's personal guest," Burke replied. "I want to learn how they raise cattle in this country."

"That is an excellent idea, Señor Burke. I'll see you out at the rancho. I always go there, and to the other ranchos, for the slaughtering and fiesta. At the Vega rancho there is a special attraction for me, however." He twisted one end of his mustache and leered. "A little señorita. I am sure you understand, Señor Burke."

"I think I understand," Burke told him coldly.

"I presume you are in California to find your fortune. If so, I may be able to guide you toward something profitable. I know practically everybody of importance, and often hear of rare chances for money-making."

"I am willing to work hard, if I see a good chance to profit by it," Burke assured him.

"But fortunes are not made by working hard, Señor Burke. Let others do the hard work, and sweat. But a man with the spirit of adventure in him, such as I judge is in you — for such there are fortunes to be picked up quickly."

"I will keep my eyes open and be looking around for one," Burke replied. "I'll see you at the rancho."

"We can speak further there," Vargas said.

Vargas bowed and sauntered away arrogantly. Burke was doing some thinking as he watched Vargas depart. This approach was not like the man Burke judged Vargas to be. Burke decided there was something behind it, and that it might serve him well to watch Don Marcus Vargas even closer than he had intended to watch him.

That hint of easy money, for instance. It could be that Vargas was seeking to lead him into some trap and get him into trouble with the authorities in this strange land where an alien Americano might not get much sympathy.

BURKE returned to the front of the tavern and sat on a bench there, puffing one of his cheroots and wondering where he could get more when his present supply was gone. Soft dusk had come. Lights were winking through the windows of the buildings.

In front of the adobe huts, cooking pots were steaming over the open fires.

From the distance came strains of guitar music and the murmur of a song. A pleasant land, Burke thought, especially on the surface.

The round moon came up. Burke saw Marcos Vargas, muffled in a serape, ride across the plaza and turn into the San Gabriel trail, with Pedro Ramirez riding on Vargas' left. The wind blowing in from the distant sea had a sting in it and already had driven away the accumulated heat of the day.

Then the Vega carriage, a splendid vehicle that had been shipped from Old Spain by way of Mexico, entered the plaza and came toward the tavern. The carriage was drawn by a team of black horses, with a peon coachman handling the reins.

Burke got to his feet and stretched, tossed away the remnant of his cheroot, and stood waiting. The carriage stopped, and Diego called to him. Burke strode forward and was introduced to old Don Alejandro, a man he admired at once.

"Mount your pony, Señor Burke, and ride along with the carriage," Diego invited.

Burke got his pony, swung up into the saddle and galloped after the carriage, which had been driven on. Where the trail was wide enough, he rode beside the vehicle and talked to Diego and his father, until the latter leaned back against the soft cushions and dozed. Where the trail was narrow, Burke rode a short distance behind the carriage, just far enough back to escape the dust.

The bright moon swam the sky. The wind blowing in from the sea carried a scud of clouds that obscured the light of the moon for short intervals at times.

Don Alejandro had not urged the peon coachman to make haste. He liked to ride like this through the moonlit night, perhaps remembering the days of his youth, when he often had ridden a spirited horse at top speed over this same trail, and when it was rougher than now.

Don Alejandro finally aroused himself and spoke to Diego in low tones, despite that the coachman was a trusted man who had been with the Vegas from boyhood.

"We will have at least a score more Vaqueros than usual this season," he said. "And more cattle to slaughter, too, so Juan Cassara, our overseer, has assured me. We will send long caravans of carts up the highway to Monterey and the markets there."

"It will be a prosperous year," Diego agreed.

"Wine, olives, honey — a good season for all. Tallow and hides to round out the cargo. We have a goodly estate, my son." Don Alejandro spoke with pride. "And someday it will be yours."

"Let us hope not for years and years, Father. I prefer things as they are now."

"You did not forget to bring the money chest, Diego?" his father asked.

"I remembered it, and it is under the robes at my feet as usual."

"I like to pay the *vaqueros* well and promptly, and give them prize money also. It keeps them loyal to the rancho. We can afford to give some extra prizes this year. You may make out a list."

AS THE carriage struck a rough place in the trail and lurched, Don Alejandro managed to swing his body against that of Diego and did not sit up straight again, but remained so he could whisper into Diego's ear:

"What you have told me about the theft of the mission cattle, Diego — I have been thinking about it seriously. I agree with Fray Felipe that a large band of men is concerned, and that they must have a leader with brains."

"That is my thought also," Diego said.

"Exposing the leader and breaking up the thieving band — that is a task worthy of Zorro. The mission cannot endure such a great loss and at the same time continue its charitable work and help the neophytes."

"Zorro will do all he can."

"Do you have any suspicions, any ideas?"

"None of any importance. It may be necessary to actually catch the rogues at their work."

"This Señor Burke, the Americano, a man you seem inclined to make your friend — at first acquaintance he impressed me favorably."

Diego chuckled. "He hopes to trail and capture Señor Zorro and claim the Governor's reward. He is not a man to be underestimated. However, the fact remains that he does not know Zorro, and Zorro does know him and can be on guard."

"Having him as your guest at the rancho and keeping him within your sight is an excellent idea, Diego. Have you thought that this man, a stranger, may have a part in the mission cattle affair?"

"I am considering that also, Father. I am overlooking no possibility."

Chapter VI
Danger Trail

THE trail had narrowed to ascend a long hill, and high banks and ridges of rock on either side cut off the light of the moon. The horses were walking slowly, pulling the heavy carriage, and the coachman, half asleep on the box, was letting them have their own way.

At the bottom of the long hill, Barney Burke had dropped behind to keep out of the cloud of dust. He felt his saddle slip, and stopped his pony to dismount and tighten the girth. The carriage rolled on out of sight.

In the carriage, Don Alejandro was leaning back against the cushions again. Diego made himself comfortable also, pulling a heavy serape up over his body and almost to his chin. The wind was getting colder.

As the carriage neared the crest of the long hill, the coachman prepared to stop the horses for a short breathing spell, as he always did when driving the carriage to the rancho from the town.

A huge clump of brush made a dark splotch beside the trail. As the coachman brought his team to a stop, a rider came from the dark splotch and rode out into the bright moonlight in front of the carriage.

Two men afoot came suddenly into view also, seen plainly in the bright light of the moon. The horseman menaced those in the carriage with a pistol, and the two men afoot held knives that glistened in the moonlight.

All the men were masked.

Before the frightened coachman could do more than squawk, the two men afoot were at the horses' heads. The masked rider urged his mount nearer, bending forward in his saddle and threatening with the pistol.

"This is a highway robbery, señores," he announced, speaking in a voice obviously disguised. "I'll take your valuables, please — your rings and jewels, and the cash box stuffed with coins with which to pay your *vaqueros*. I have immediate need of the money, whereas you can get plenty more."

Diego was struggling to get free of the heavy serape which had become entangled around his legs. Don Alejandro was trying to sit up straight on the cushions.

The coachman was armed with a pistol, but was afraid to use it while the mounted highwayman's weapon menaced him. Diego was carrying no weapon. But Don Alejandro had a pistol beneath one of the cushions, and now he tried to sit erect and fumble for it.

"Base scoundrel!" Don Alejandro bellowed at the masked horseman. "I'll have you hanged for this!"

"It will be necessary to catch me first, and I am not easily caught. Toss out your money chest at once! Then I'll take your rings and any other jewels you happen to be wearing. Be quick about it!"

The frightened peon coachman was holding his hands high above his head. The horses probably would have bolted had not the masked men afoot been holding their bridle straps.

Diego began fumbling for the pistol beneath the cushions also. But it had been shoved aside by Don Alejandro when he had moved the cushions to make himself comfortable.

"The money chest, at once!" the mounted highwayman ordered again. "Must I pistol you to teach you sense? There is no help for you, señores. The troopers went along the trail long ago. Nobody is following you at a short distance. You are at our mercy, señores."

Diego was remembering that Barney Burke had been riding closely behind them a short time before, and wondered where he was now, when he could have perhaps been of service.

For an instant, a suspicion flashed into Diego's mind. Had he misjudged Burke? Was the Americano an outlaw instead of an honest man, and working in league with these rogues? Was Burke now guarding the back trail against interruption while these others accomplished the robbery?

The mounted highwayman urged his horse still nearer the carriage, and the moonlight glinted from the barrel of the weapon he brandished.

"My patience has about reached its end," he informed them. "The money chest at once!"

"I'll get the chest for you," Diego replied. "It is under the rugs at my feet. Do not shoot, señor."

Diego bent over, throwing the rugs aside, and one of his hands made a futile grope to get the pistol among the cushions. But Don Alejandro found it first.

"Now, you low scoundrel!" Don Alejandro cried in rage.

HAD he fired the weapon without speaking, the result probably would have been different. But his sudden movement, the rumble of his voice in denunciation, the moonlight revealing to the highwayman's view the menacing weapon Don Alejandro held, combined to put the masked man on the alert.

The two guns were fired as one.

Diego saw the masked man reel slightly in his saddle as if he had been hit. The pistol discharges frightened the spirited horses. They reared and charged forward, knocking aside the two men afoot who were aiding the highwayman. The peon coachman grasped the reins frantically to pull the horses up.

Another pistol cracked behind them, but the ball flew wild. Diego turned to ask his father for the pistol he had used, to reload it. He found his father stretched back on the cushions, grasping his left shoulder, and blood streaming through his fingers as he held his hand over the wound.

"Stop the horses!" Diego shouted to the coachman. "Father is wounded!"

Don Alejandro opened his eyes. "Only a shoulder wound — my son," he said. "But it must — have attention — soon."

"Give me your pistol," Diego ordered the coachman sternly, as the carriage was stopped. "You should have used it at once when we were first attacked. Here — take this weapon my father used and reload it quickly."

Diego had managed to kick aside the heavy serape and the rugs. He jumped out of the carriage and looked back down the trail. He saw a few flashes of flame, and an equal number of reports soon drifted to him on the wind. Then came the loud clatter of a horse's hoofs pounding the hard road.

Diego could see that two riders were coming toward him through the bright moonlight, both bending low in their saddles and getting the best speed they could out of their mounts. One was some distance ahead of the other. Diego could not tell whether they were friends or one the pursuer and the other the pursued.

They neared him at top speed, and as the first passed almost close enough to scrape the side of the carriage, Diego saw he was the masked highwayman, who rode now clinging to the pommel of his saddle as if about to fall out of it.

Enraged at sight of the man who had shot and wounded his father, Diego lifted the coachman's pistol to fire. But the target was disappearing through

"Now, you low scoundrel!"
Don Alejandro cried in rage.

some shadows already, and Diego thought it would be better to save the shot until he was sure of the identity of the second rider.

The second rider was upon him even then, and pulling his mount to a stop. He was Barney Burke.

"Don Diego!" Burke cried. "Is everything all right?"

"That rogue shot my father," said Diego with intensity.

"I saw everything from the bottom of the hill. It was over before I could reach you. That fiend ahead shot the two men he had with him, no doubt to close their lips. I'll ride after him!"

Burke was gone, the little bay pony spurning the ground with his hoofs.

Diego got into the carriage quickly and made his father as comfortable as he could, and told the coachman to drive on and whip up the horses. But before they had traveled a mile, Barney Burke appeared again and was riding beside the carriage.

"He got away, Don Diego!" Burke shouted. "Stop your team. Let me handle the horses and I will get some speed out of them. Let your coachman take my pony and ride ahead to the mission or rancho and tell the soldiers."

Diego gave the order. The coachman got into the bay's saddle, and Burke mounted the box and seized the reins, standing and bracing himself.

"Ride to the rancho," Diego told the coachman. "Sergeant Garcia should be there. Tell him everything and let him ride back to the scene and look at the dead men. Their identity may give a clue to the mounted highwayman. Tell Juan Cassara to have everything ready to care for my father. Have them send to the mission for a *padre* who knows how to handle pistol wounds."

The coachman was away, riding at top speed. Burke started the carriage team.

"I know about gunshot wounds, Don Diego!" he shouted as he urged the horses into a run. "I know about driving like this, too. Just tell me the way."

"Follow the trail and take the right-hand turning about a mile farther on!" Diego shouted back at him.

AS the carriage lurched and bounded along the trail, Diego bent over his father. Burke was handling the spirited blacks in a masterly fashion.

"Father — " Diego began.

"I'll be — all right — Diego," Don Alejandro told him, so weakly that Diego had to bend his head close to catch the words.

Coming to the right-hand turn, Burke steered the team into it deftly. Here the ground was softer and the laboring horses could not make such good speed.

But Burke kept at them, shouting, using the whip when he could.

"About a mile more!" Diego shouted at Burke. "Take the left turn into the tree-bordered lane. Stop in front of the house."

Burke made the turn with the carriage tilting and lurching sickeningly. Diego was holding his father in his arms and looking ahead. The coachman had made good speed on Burke's pony. Lights were bobbing around the buildings, showing that men with torches were hurrying about. The front door of the house stood open and light was streaming out.

Burke slowed down the wild team and finally brought the horses to a stop in front of the door. A couple of *vaqueros* grasped the bridle straps, and Burke sprang down off the box and hurried to Diego's side.

A tall, slender man of middle age came hurrying forward. He was Juan Cassara, the trusted overseer of the rancho. Tears were streaming down his cheeks.

"Oh, Don Diego!" he cried. "How is he?"

"Let's get him into the house, Juan," Diego said. "Señor Burke will help us."

"I sent a man to the mission for a *padre*, Don Diego. He should be here before long."

"Good man, Juan!"

Burke was helping Diego with Don Alejandro, and Cassara stepped up to help also. Don Alejandro was moaning a little as they lifted him out of the carriage and began carrying him.

"Where is Sergeant Garcia, Juan?" Diego asked.

"He took three of his men and rode across the hills, Don Diego, to get to the scene, leaving one trooper here on guard."

"That is why we missed him on the road," Diego said.

With their sombreros held in their hands and their heads bowed, the *vaqueros* were standing around the veranda watching as Don Alejandro was carried into the house. Cassara had the bedchamber ready, and servants had been heating water and getting out medicines, instruments and soft cloths.

They undressed Don Alejandro, cut away his underclothing and got at the wound.

"It is high in the left shoulder," Barney Burke reported, as he sponged away some blood. He acted as coolly as a professional surgeon, like a man to whom a scene like this was nothing new. "Give Don Alejandro something to bite on, Don Diego," he continued. "A piece of leather strap will do nicely. I must probe the wound for the bullet. The wound is nothing if we can get the lead ball out and prevent infection. He has not lost too much blood."

Don Alejandro began chewing on a piece of leather strap, groaning often as Burke worked. The perspiration stood out on his face. Then he fainted.

"Let him be like that for a moment while I work, but stand by with some water," Burke said, without looking up.

He had located the bullet. And now, with an awkward pair of forceps, he worked at the wound while Don Alejandro remained mercifully unconscious. He finally extracted the ball and put it aside.

"Water, now," he ordered. "Bring him back to consciousness, and we will dress the wound. Somebody have strong wine ready."

Chapter VII
Wounded Don

SEEING a woman's small hands working beside his own, Burke glanced up quickly. Beside him was a girl he judged at first sight to be about eighteen. She was not dressed like a woman of high station nor yet as a house servant. She went at her work in a practical manner.

"I am Nita Cassara, señor," she told Burke, as they worked side by side. "I often help when one of our men gets hurt. My father is Juan Cassara, the overseer."

"I am Barney Burke, an Americano."

"I know, señor. The coachman told us all."

Don Alejandro moaned again and opened his eyes. Burke felt his pulse.

"We got the bullet out, Don Alejandro," he reported. "You will be all right. We will dress the wound now."

"Here is the dressing, señor," Nita Cassara said, handing it to him. "And cloth for the bandage."

Burke worked swiftly, and soon was done. Diego gave his father a few sips of strong wine.

"The *padre* from the mission should be here soon," Nita whispered to Burke. "His work will not be needed, thanks to you. But he can watch beside Don Alejandro through the night."

Burke smiled down at her. "You are a fine helper in a case like this," he told her. "I suppose your father is proud of you. If he is not, he should be."

She hung her head and blushed, but looked sideward at him once as he backed away from the bed.

"I'll remain at the bedside until the *padre* comes," Nita said, softly.

Diego stepped up and touched Burke on his shoulder.

"Please come with me," he said.

They left the bedchamber and went through a long corridor to the front door, then out upon the wide veranda. The Vaqueros were there, almost a hundred of them, and some were kneeling in prayer.

"Señores!" Diego shouted at them. "Señor Burke, the man here at my side, the Americano, has removed the bullet and dressed the wound. He says that Don Alejandro will survive."

A few cheered, and sombreros were tossed into the air. Diego held up his hand again in a demand for silence.

"Señor Barney Burke is my friend," he announced. "I want all here to remember it."

They cheered a little again, then started away toward the huts to begin celebrating the fact that Don Alejandro was in no danger.

Cassara had followed Diego and Burke out to the veranda, and now he approached Burke respectfully.

"I have had good care taken of your splendid bay pony, señor," the overseer reported. "He will be ready for you whenever you want him. And I, señor, am ready to serve you at any time."

Cassara bowed and turned away, and Diego and Burke were alone.

"You got any special ideas about this affair, Don Diego?" Burke asked.

"It was the case of a highwayman with two assistants trying to steal our money box and jewelry," Diego replied.

"That masked rider shot and killed his two companions," Burke reminded him. "I was in time to see that, and heard them begging him for mercy. The horseman seemed to have a sash filled with pistols. He murdered them in cold blood."

"What a fiend!" Diego said. "I hope he is caught and made to pay the penalty."

"Why did he shoot them? So, if they were caught alive by the soldiers, they would not be able to tell the name of their leader?"

"Probably that is true," Diego said.

"And their leader? Who could he be, Don Diego, except this rascal they call Señor Zorro?"

Diego had not been expecting anything like that. He thought rapidly. Such an idea must not get abroad! If it did, everybody would be looking for Zorro, searching for him. And Zorro would be unable to ride without grave danger, or carry on the work he was supposed to do.

"I fear you are wrong about that, amigo," he told Burke. "I saw the masked man tonight rather clearly in the bright moonlight. He was a smaller man than Señor Zorro, and did not sit his saddle as Zorro does. You see, Señor Burke, I have seen Zorro."

But he did not explain that the only place he ever had seen Zorro was in a mirror ….

BARNEY BURKE slept on a soft couch in one of the guest rooms of the rancho house. Birds chattering in the shrubs in the patio, men talking in the distance, awoke him at an early hour.

He left the couch, dressed quickly, bathed his face and hands in cold water ready for him on a small table just inside the door, and went to the nearest window to look out.

He could see the entire length of the big patio and through an arch. In the near distance were rows of adobe huts, many of them with fires and cooking pots in front of them. He could see a big corral, too, and *vaqueros* in their working clothes instead of the gaudy finery they had worn the day before, were busily roping horses and saddling them. They were getting ready for the day's work.

Burke opened the door and went out into the patio. He hurried through it. His eyes were glistening as he watched the scene. The *vaqueros* were not on holiday now, but were attending strictly to business, as they would until the slaughtering had ended and it was time for the grand *fiesta*.

Burke started toward the corral, and encountered Juan Cassara.

"Señor Burke, your bay pony is not in the general corral," the overseer told him. "He is with the Vega riding stock in the smaller corral over there by the trees. I'll have him saddled for you, and he will be in front of the house with Don Diego's mount and the others."

"Thanks, Cassara," Burke said. "Have you heard how Don Alejandro is this morning?"

"The *padre* was in the kitchen a few minutes ago getting something to eat, and he said Don Alejandro spent the remainder of the night well. My daughter, Nita, replaced the dressing. She has done much of such work, señor. We are always having accidents on a big rancho like this."

"I can imagine," Burke said. "Are the men starting work today?"

"Surely, señor. Our own *vaqueros* have almost finished gathering the cattle in two large box canyons. It is almost time for the lancing to begin."

"The lancing?" Burke questioned.

"I ask your pardon, señor. I forgot that you are not acquainted with our methods. The cattle are run out of the canyons a few at a time, and the *vaqueros* scatter them and ride them down and slay them with lances."

"Queer way," Burke commented.

"But it really is swift work, señor, as you shall see. Then the skinners follow and take the hides. The dead animals are scattered as much as possible. Whoever wants meat takes it, and of course the fat is taken to be rendered in the great vats we have on the other side of the hill to your right."

"And the meat?" Burke asked.

"Large pits have been dug and filled with fuel, señor, and soon there will be beds of glowing coals. The meat, great hunks of it, is turned on spits and roasted day and night. Whoever wants meat and wine can have it at any hour. Also tortillas, frijoles, sweetmeats, fresh fruit in abundance, and other articles of food."

"I never saw a roundup like that in the States," Burke told him, laughing.

Cassara hurried on about his duties, and Burke strolled on to the big corral. Vaqueros grinned at him and waved their hands and sombreros as he approached.

"El Americano!" one shouted, and many of the others waved at him and cheered.

They were getting their mounts ready for the day's hard work. Some were gnawing chunks of meat and devouring other food, and skins of wine seemed to be everywhere. Burke declined food, for he knew he was expected to eat the morning meal in the rancho house.

He turned back toward the house now. And he met Sergeant Garcia and his four troopers where they were saddling their mounts beneath the trees.

"Ha! The Señor Burke!" the burly sergeant greeted cordially. "I have been informed, señor, that you handled yourself well last night. 'Tis a pity you did not shoot the masked rogue who pistoled Don Alejandro."

"Wish I had been able to bring him down," Burke replied. "He is a cold-blooded murderer."

"And you also played surgeon to good advantage, I have been told," the sergeant continued. "I did not relish you overmuch when I first saw you, señor, but my estimation of you has been changed to your credit."

BURKE bowed and laughed.

"What did you learn about the affair of last night?" he asked.

"We found the two men the masked rider had shot and slain. They were only two ordinary rogues. Their corpses were taken to the mission, but nobody there could identify them."

"But have you no suspicions, Sergeant? Could the masked man have been the mysterious Señor Zorro?"

"Zorro has always ridden alone," Sergeant Garcia replied. "He is an outlaw and a low scoundrel who gets soldiers criticized because they cannot catch him, but he never has shown himself to be an ordinary thief."

"Perhaps he has turned bad all the way now," Burke suggested. "Something like that often happens."

"That is a possibility, señor," Garcia admitted. "But it is my opinion that the masked rider was not Zorro. He makes a specialty of punishing those who mistreat peons and natives. And the Vegas never do that, señor. In fact, they almost make pets of the rascals. Zorro would have no reason for attacking the Vegas."

"Perhaps to get money and jewels?" Burke hinted.

"Zorro has had a chance to loot many times, and never has availed himself of the chance."

A bell chimed.

"There is your breakfast signal, Señor Burke," Garcia told him. "No doubt I'll have the privilege of seeing you again later in the day."

Chapter VIII
The Letter

EXPRESSING his thanks, Barney Burke started on toward the sprawling rancho house. He entered the patio, and found Nita Cassara there gathering roses to be put in the house. She blushed and dimpled when she saw him.

"A pleasant good morning to you, Señor Burke," she said.

"You call me Barney, and I will call you Nita," he suggested. "It saves much time."

"Bah-nee?

"Well, that is near enough, and it sounds fine the way you say it," Burke told her.

"I am told that Don Alejandro spent a good night," she said. "You did your work well, señor."

"And you were a fine little helper, Nita. I never met Don Alejandro until just before we left town last night, but I like him. You know the family well?"

She smiled at him again. "I was born here on the Vega rancho, señor, and have never known any other home. My father was the overseer when I was born. My mother — she died several years ago."

"Sorry," Burke muttered.

"It is something that comes to us all, señor. I — I hope your stay on the rancho will be pleasant."

"It will be pleasant if I see enough of you," he replied bluntly.

"Señor! It is not difficult to see that you are an Americano. None of our men would say such a thing to a girl, that is, not — nicely."

"And why not?" Burke wanted to know. "I like you very much already, Nita, so why not say so? And whatever I say to you, like that, is meant to be said — nicely. Understand?"

"I understand, señor, and thank you."

"What's my first name?"

"Bah-nee."

"You remember that," he instructed her.

They exchanged smiles, and he started on. But he did not get away from her until she had put a rose in the lapel of his worn buckskin coat.

"Has that any special meaning in this country?" he asked.

"Oh, sí, señor!" she replied. "It means my thanks because you did so much last night for Don Alejandro."

She dimpled again, then laughed aloud, and hurried away like a child who had done something she should not have done.

Burke quickened his stride, went to his room and washed his face and hands again, then passed through a hallway and found Diego Vega in the big main room of the house. Nobody else was to have the early breakfast, it appeared.

Burke was amazed at the breakfast served. These people certainly knew how to provide more than enough food, he thought. He remembered many frugal breakfasts he had eaten on ranches back in the States.

Silver and china platters here were heaped high with fresh fruits. Bowls of thick cream were on the table. Several kinds of roast meat, fowls both hot and cold, hot tortillas dripping with sour cream, goblets of good wine — food without end!

"I met Sergeant Garcia and talked to him," Burke reported to Diego. "He does not seem to know much about what happened last night. He told me that he feels sure the masked rider was not Zorro."

"I feel sure of that also," Diego replied. "He was just some ordinary highwayman with a couple of assistants to help him, trying to rob the carriage. Our money box — plenty of persons know we always bring it to the rancho before the slaughter, to pay the *vaqueros*."

"The sergeant does not seem to think that this Zorro is such a bad hombre," Burke hinted.

"Many people sympathize with the work Zorro is doing," Diego replied, bending his head to hide his smile and the gleam in his eyes. "Do you wish to watch the *vaqueros* at their work today?"

"I should like to work right along with them, if I may," Burke said.

"That can be arranged easily. I'll speak to Cassara about it, and he will tell the *jefe vaquero*."

One of the house servants came hurrying into the room to announce the arrival of Fray Felipe. Diego and Burke got to their feet as the old *padre* came into the room. He looked tired.

"I left Reina de Los Angeles early, my son, and rode as swiftly as I could," Fray Felipe explained to Diego. "I got news of what happened to Don Alejandro, and must go to him at once."

"A young *padre* from the mission of San Gabriel is with him," Diego said. "His wound is not serious."

"Let us give thanks for that!"

DIEGO introduced Burke, who knelt to receive the *padre*'s blessing. Fray Felipe looked at him searchingly, as if trying to read his real character.

"Señor Burke has endeared himself to us all," Diego said, as if he had read the *padre*'s mind. "His prompt action and skill probably saved my father's life. Regarding the shooting, Señor Burke thought the mounted highwayman may have been the mysterious Señor Zorro, but I assured him such was not the case."

"Unless he has changed his tactics, Zorro would not stoop to highway robbery like that, nor would he work with confederates," Fray Felipe said.

As Diego gestured for the *padre* to sit at the table and eat, a house servant entered again with word that Señor Cassara wished to speak to Diego on a matter of importance. There was excitement in Cassara's manner as he approached the table, hat in hand.

"I have come to you about a certain matter, Don Diego, because of your father's present indisposition," the overseer said.

"That is right, Cassara."

"I have just received a report of something unusual and disturbing. Before dawn, I sent out some of our *vaqueros* to ride the hills and drive in any of our cattle that had not been driven in before. In the canyon three miles to the south, on Vega land, they found something I cannot explain."

"And that?"

"Fifty carcasses of cattle, Don Diego. The hides had been taken, and not earlier than night before last. The heads were there, and the ears were notched with the brand of the San Gabriel Mission. Who would slay mission cattle found running with our herds, Don Diego?"

"It is a matter that calls for investigation, and I'll attend to it, Cassara," Diego replied. "Thanks for bringing me such a prompt report. Be sure, before the slaughtering commences, that all mission cattle are cut out of our herds and driven far back into the hills."

Burke had started eating again, bending over the platter of food before him. He did not notice the swift glances Diego and Fray Felipe exchanged as Cassara bowed and left the room.

Nor did he see the aged *padre* dip his forefinger in wine and quickly trace on the tablecloth the letter Z, which he in turn as swiftly obliterated with other marks. It was like reminding Diego of a promise ....

It was customary for Don Alejandro to address the gathering of *vaqueros* before the work of the great slaughter began, and for Fray Felipe to offer a prayer for their safety and for the general prosperity of the rancho. This time, Diego would have to appear in his father's place.

Diego had Burke riding beside him when they went out to where the *vaqueros* were standing beside their work ponies. Fray Felipe rode a short distance behind them on his mule. The *vaqueros* uncovered as the *padre* dismounted.

Fray Felipe's service was short. Then Diego spoke to the men.

"You all know what has happened to my father," he told them. "I am here today in his place. And I am happy to tell you that my father's wound is not considered serious, though he must keep quiet for a few days."

At that, the *vaqueros* tossed their sombreros into the air and cheered.

"There is no need for me to tell you men how to do your work," Diego continued. "I simply ask you to do it as well as usual. In my father's name, I announce that all the prizes this year will be doubled."

They cheered again at that announcement, and began getting into their saddles. The *jefe vaquero* shouted orders, and the men started riding away.

Diego motioned for Burke to ride beside him again, with Fray Felipe following. They went through an orchard beneath trees heavy with fruit, and came into a trail which led to the nearest box canyon.

The canyon was choked with bawling cattle, and a heavy pall of dust hung over it. The mouth of the canyon was narrow, and riders were keeping the cattle penned in. Diego pointed, and Burke saw the *vaqueros* lining up at either side of the canyon's mouth, and noticed that they were armed with long lances like picadors in a bullfight.

OTHER *vaqueros* rode into the canyon and to either side of the herd, cut off a small bunch of the cattle and ran them toward the entrance. Diego, Burke and Fray Felipe watched from the top of a knoll where they had stopped their mounts.

As the running, bawling cattle emerged from the canyon's mouth, each *vaquero* selected one of the animals and rode after him, chasing him at a run off to one side, lancing him deftly and leaving the carcass there, and charged back furiously to get into line again and repeat the performance.

The skinning crew began its work immediately. A third band of men gathered the green hides, bundled them, carried them to lumbering high-wheeled carts drawn by oxen, and tumbled them in to be taken away.

Still another group began butchering for meat. Other carts carried choice meat away to the cooking pits, and collected fat for the rendering vats.

Diego sent a messenger for the *jefe vaquero* and introduced him to Burke. Burke rode away with the man to get a lance and try his skill.

Burke soon found his skill lacking. Lancing running cattle was not so easy as it looked. He never had heard of this method of slaughtering. Back home, they did not slaughter except for meat, but drove the herds to shipping points and sold them on the hoof.

But he saw where there was some method in this system. The *vaqueros* worked swiftly killing the stock. The skinners and cart men and butchers kept at their heels. The flaw in the system, to Burke's mind, was in the scattered carcasses that would have to be collected and destroyed afterward.

When it was time for the mid-day meal, Diego sent for Burke and they rode back to the rancho house. Fray Felipe remained behind to talk for a time to some of the *vaqueros* as they prepared to eat cold food they had brought with them from the huts, and wash it down with wine.

"Guests will commence arriving today," Diego explained to Burke. "They will keep dropping in until the house is filled. The slaughtering will be finished in about four days' time, and then will come the *fiesta*, which will last for at least two days and nights."

"Do all the big ranchos do something like this?" Burke asked.

"Sí, amigo! We lend our *vaqueros* to one another so the work can be done swiftly and at less expense. Each rancho has its annual slaughtering and *fiesta*. Then we wait for a time and soon have the sheep shearing season upon us."

"Being a cattleman, I do not care much for sheep," Burke explained. "Cattle raisers and sheepmen are always fighting in the States. The sheep ruin grazing land for cattle."

"We do not have that difficulty here. Sheep are one of our most profitable ventures," Diego said. "Wool, sheepskins, lambskins, tallow — several crops in one. And scarcely any trouble. Our herders drive the flocks up into the hills, roam around with them, and bring the flocks back multiplied."

"I am more interested in cattle and horses, Don Diego," Burke told him.

They dismounted in front of the rancho house, and Burke hurried to the guest room he occupied. There he brushed the dust from his clothing with a willow twig hand broom and washed up for the meal.

Chapter IX
Zorro Prepares to Ride

WHEN Diego entered the main room of the house, he found Marcos Vargas waiting there for him. As host in his father's absence, Diego did not reveal by speech or manner his dislike for Vargas, but merely treated him with cold courtesy.

Vargas always made the rounds of the ranchos at slaughtering time, some whispered in an effort to augment his income by playing dice and cards.

Burke entered the room, and he and Vargas exchanged polite bows. The three sat down to eat, each attended by a house servant.

"I spent the latter part of the night and the morning at the guest house of the mission," Vargas told them. "My horse stumbled and threw me on the way to San Gabriel, and wrenched and bruised my shoulder. I had Pedro Ramirez bandage it. The shoulder is sore, but will soon mend."

"Have you heard what happened to my father on the highway?" Diego asked.

"Everybody at the mission was speaking of it, and with great indignation. I was sorry to learn of it, Diego. As I rode past the same spot last night, I thought I saw some men lurking in the shadows beside the trail. But I scarcely gave it attention, believing they were peons on their way here to get work during the slaughtering."

"If I ever learn the identity of the man who shot my father, I'll punish him," Diego promised.

"If you really learn anything, Diego, it would be better for you to notify Sergeant Garcia and let him and his soldiers attend to the affair," Vargas advised.

"Is it not my proper business?"

"It is," Vargas admitted. "But — pardon me, Diego — you have had small experience in fighting, and that masked horseman may be a dangerous rogue. You could not expect fair play from such."

When the meal was finished, Burke and Vargas retired to their rooms for the siesta. Diego went to the bedchamber to visit his father. He found Don Alejandro awake and talking to Fray Felipe, who had ridden in from the canyon. The *padre* left the room to get something to eat. Diego sat beside his father's couch.

"I will be able to get up and be around tomorrow, Diego, if I use care and do not exert myself too much," Don Alejandro said. "Juan Cassara can keep things running, and I can make decisions whenever necessary. So, if you wish to attend to the matter of the slain mission cattle, you may do so."

"I also desire to attend to another matter, Father. I want to find and punish the man who shot you."

"But the other thing is more important now, Diego. There must be a quick end to this slaughter of mission cattle. The thieves must be stopped immediately. The mission cannot afford the loss." He lowered his voice to a whisper, "Zorro must do his work."

"Bernardo reached the rancho before dawn, bringing all the things I need," Diego whispered in reply.

"This Americano, Señor Burke — do you trust him fully, Diego?" his father asked.

"I have a feeling that it is safe to trust him. The way he has acted is beyond reproach."

"Yes, I know. But a very clever man might act like that for the purpose of gaining our confidence, might break bread with us and knife us in our backs an hour later. I, too, feel that he is all right, Diego. But it would be a good thing to keep an eye on him."

"He could not have been the man who shot you," Diego pointed out.

"But the man who did shoot me may have been Señor Burke's confederate and friend," Don Alejandro suggested. "Chasing the rogue and then returning to report that he got away — he may have allowed him to get away and then returned to play his little game."

"And do you think, Father, that he could have anything to do with the slaying of the mission cattle?"

"Perhaps not, Diego. Yet he could be in league with the thieves, even close to the leader of them, or the leader himself. How clever it would be for him to work his way into our confidence, be on the inside, send word to his friends when and where mission cattle can be found, where our *vaqueros* are riding, and all that!"

"His idea of making an effort to capture Zorro?"

DON ALEJANDRO nodded. He had thought of that.

"Ha! So, if he rides abroad at night on such a search, he has given you a reason for his absence. On such rides he could contact his friends, if he is connected with the cattle thieves, and allow you to think that he is out trying to find Zorro's trail."

"You seem very suspicious, Father."

"I hate to be so, Diego. But in these dreary days of dishonesty and trickery a man dare not trust anybody too much. Keep an eye on Señor Burke until you are sure."

"I intend to do that, since he is on the trail of Zorro," Diego replied, smiling.

"May he never collect the reward offered for the capture of Zorro!" Don Alejandro said fervently. "Have you made any plans, Diego?"

"Zorro may ride tonight for a short time, a sort of scouting ride. If it becomes known that Zorro is in the neighborhood, people will wonder why. And perhaps some of the guilty will grow nervous under the strain and betray themselves."

Nita Cassara came into the bedchamber with a bowl of broth for Don Alejandro. Diego greeted her with a friendly smile and got up to leave the room and prepare to ride back to the canyon to supervise the afternoon's work ....

After the day's evening meal, Diego excused himself and retired to his own quarters, pleading fatigue after the stirring events of the day, and mentioning that he would have to be in the saddle again on the morrow.

He left Fray Felipe, Burke and Vargas still sitting at the table in conversation.

Bernardo was waiting for Diego in his room off the patio. Diego spoke to him in whispers as he got off the clothes he had been wearing all day and put on slippers and draped himself in a soft thick robe.

"Zorro rides tonight," Diego whispered. "Have the horse, costume and weapons at the usual place within a short time. Make sure that no wandering *vaquero* sees you. Tonight, you need not accompany me on your mule. I ride alone."

Bernardo bobbed his head to indicate that he understood.

"When you have everything ready for Zorro, watch the private corral, where Señor Burke's bay pony has been put. It will be bright moonlight. If anybody takes a horse out of the corral, try to identify the man."

Bernardo bobbed his head again in acknowledgment of the orders. Diego stretched on the couch to get some rest and do considerable thinking.

"You may go now," he told Bernardo. "Extinguish the tapers first, so everyone will think I have gone to sleep."

Bernardo extinguished all the tapers in the room, went out quickly and closed the door behind him. Diego relaxed and listened to the sounds in the house and outside.

In a short time, he heard both Burke and Vargas go to their rooms. Fray Felipe, he supposed, had gone to visit Don Alejandro again before retiring.

Diego was trying to plan Zorro's movements for the night. He did not know where to start. He had no real objective. As he had told his father, this would be a mere scouting ride.

For one thing, he wanted to trail and watch Burke if the Americano went for a night ride, to learn whether he really was after Zorro or was riding out to contact criminal associates. Diego was inclined to trust Burke, but wanted to be sure of the man.

After a time he heard sounds from the distance — the loud voices of excited men. He heard a summons at the front door of the house, also, but thought little of that. Some of the guests had arrived late, he supposed. The servants would care for them.

Then steps came along the hall outside, and there was a gentle tapping at the door of his own chamber.

"Knock louder," Diego heard Sergeant Garcia's raucous voice saying, as he ordered a house servant. "Rouse him up. This is a matter of importance."

"One moment," Diego called.

He left the couch and lit a couple of the tapers, wrapped his robe around his body and hurried to the door. When he pulled it open, he found Garcia there, a servant behind him.

"Pardon me for disturbing you, Don Diego, but something has occurred that calls for your attention," the sergeant said.

"Come inside," Diego invited. He nodded for the servant to retire, and motioned for Garcia to sit on a stool and help himself to wine. "What has happened?"

GARCIA took a swift gulp of wine from the goblet he had filled and blew out the ends of his mustache.

"Where the story started, Don Diego, I do not know, but it is all over this part of the country now, and the *vaqueros* are getting out of hand."

"The *vaqueros*? What has happened to disturb them?"

"The story has been spread that San Gabriel Mission cattle are being slain by hundreds for their hides. That aroused them. We soldiers know of a few hides stolen, since it was reported to us, but it seems the number is running high now."

"I have heard something of it," Diego admitted.

"This is the tale that aroused them — that a big band of men is working in the district, stock thieves, murderers and rogues. And the tale also has it that they are being led by Zorro."

"By Zorro?" Diego asked.

"The thing has grown until the *vaqueros* are determined to mount and ride throughout the country until they catch Zorro and hang him, as well as getting the reward. They accuse Zorro of organizing a band of thieves and stealing mission cattle. And they are saying that it was Zorro who shot Don Alejandro."

"I do not believe Zorro would do such a thing," Diego said.

"I didn't believe it, either. But it may be true, Don Diego. Zorro may have started out doing good deeds, found how easy it was for him to outwit the soldiery, and so turned bad for his own profit."

"But the *vaqueros*?" Don Diego reminded him.

"They are coming to the house, Don Diego. I hurried ahead to prepare you. They want drop everything else and ride over the countryside chasing Zorro. They are infuriated at the attack on Don Alejandro and the slaying of mission cattle.

"Let them gather in front of the house," Diego instructed. "I'll dress quickly and come out and talk to them. If they run wild like this, the great slaughter will be delayed."

Garcia hurried out, and Diego closed the door and began dressing. He could hear the tumult easily now. Glancing through a window, he saw bobbing torches approaching. The wild *vaqueros* plainly enough had been talking as they ate and drank around their campfires, and had appointed a committee to visit the house.

Diego was seriously concerned with more than the delay of the cattle slaughtering. If the countryside was aroused against Zorro, and riders were keeping a continual watch for him, it would be perilous for Zorro to ride abroad. So how could Diego himself search for the cattle killers?

And he was not in a position to declare that the guilty man was not Zorro, for he would be asked how he knew. The tumult by this time was attracting the attention of everyone in the house.

Diego could hear the servants moving around, and supposed Burke and Vargas would be up and dressing.

AS soon as he was ready, Diego left his room and hurried through the house to the wide front veranda. On the way he met and ordered a house servant to find Fray Felipe and have him follow. He thought that possibly the *padre* could influence the *vaqueros*.

Garcia and his troopers were in front of the veranda, mounted and prepared to maintain order. Though a dozen or more led, like a committee, almost all the *vaqueros* on the rancho were packed behind them, Diego saw.

Diego stood at the veranda railing and waited. Both Burke and Vargas came hurrying out of the house to stand beside him, and a moment later Fray Felipe appeared. Speaking swiftly, Diego told them what was happening.

"It was my first idea that Zorro shot Don Alejandro," Burke declared.

"But who is Zorro, señor?" Vargas asked. "Nobody seems to know that. Despite the large reward offered by the Governor, nobody has caught the rogue. Even the soldiers cannot find his trail."

"I cannot believe that Zorro is the kind of man to lead a band of stock thieves and slay mission cattle," Fray Felipe declared. "All he has done, really, has been to punish those who oppress and mistreat the helpless. He has never played thief."

"With the following the scoundrel has gained among the peons and natives, it wouldn't take him long to build up a band of rascals," Vargas offered. "I, for one, believe he shot Don Alejandro and is leading the cattle thieves."

Then they were silent, for the *vaqueros* had marched almost up to the veranda, and had grown silent themselves.

Chapter X
Angry Vaqueros

ONE of the *vaqueros* stepped forward to act as spokesman as their committeemen advanced a little farther.

"What is the meaning of this tumult?" Diego called. "You are disturbing everyone."

The spokesman removed his sombrero and bowed.

"Don Diego," he said, "we have learned that the man who calls himself Zorro is leader of a band of scoundrels, that these men have been slaying and taking hides from mission cattle, and that it was Zorro himself who shot the illustrious Don Alejandro, a man we all admire."

"Where got you this intelligence?" Diego asked.

"Everyone is saying it is so, Don Diego. That mission cattle has been slain is a horrible thing, for the mission needs the money to help the poor."

"I agree with you in that, señor, but where is the proof that Zorro leads the thieves?"

"Where it started, we do not know, Don Diego. But there must be truth in it. And we believe that Zorro shot Don Alejandro, too."

"And what is it you wish?"

"It is our desire to scatter and ride over the hills and along the highways in pairs. We will question every suspicious man we encounter, and if any cannot answer properly we will bring him to you, that you may question him."

"And if you happen to encounter Zorro?"

"In such case, we promise not to kill him unless it is necessary. We will capture him, unwounded if we can, and bring him to you, so his identity may be learned. The Governor already has proclaimed him outlaw."

"It seems to me to be a task for the soldiers," Diego replied.

"With all due respect, Don Diego, the soldiers have not been able to accomplish anything. Zorro plays tag with them and laughs. Here is Sergeant Garcia, who encountered him once and had a blade run through his shoulder by Zorro as a result."

"Silence, you scoundrel!" Garcia shouted.

"All of you return to your huts, keep quiet, get some sleep and prepare for tomorrow's work."

"It is Don Diego's right to tell us what to do," the spokesman reminded the sergeant. "Don Diego, we ask permission to saddle and ride as I said."

"But the slaughtering?" Diego asked. "The work has started and must be continued. Everything is ready. The crews, carts, cooking pits and rendering vats — everything. And the *fiesta* awaits."

"Don Diego, we would rather catch the man who shot your father and is stealing mission cattle than enjoy the *fiesta* and win your prizes."

Fray Felipe whispered to Diego and stepped up to the railing.

"Attend me, my sons!" he called to the *vaqueros*. "I realize how you feel. But you are seeking to make the wrong move in this affair. If Zorro is guilty, and you all ride out in an effort to capture him, he will take alarm and go into hiding, and nothing will be accomplished."

"But, *padre*, if we ride tonight, now, we may discover and take him before he learns of our purpose and has time to go into hiding," the spokesman said.

There was logic in that, as those on the veranda knew. And the *vaqueros* would think it strange that Fray Felipe did not want them to try to catch the mission cattle thieves, and that Don Diego would not want them to make every effort to capture the man who had shot his father.

Diego held up his hand. "Wait a moment, señores, until I speak to the overseer," he called.

Cassara had come to the veranda, and now Diego beckoned him forward.

"You have heard everything?" he asked.

"Everything, Don Diego."

"I think it best to let some of the *vaqueros* do as they wish, but not all."

"Such an arrangement would quiet them, Don Diego," Cassara said. "They will return tired and willing to attend to their work. Refuse them their request, and they will pout and mope and do little. They are like children at such times."

DIEGO nodded and turned to the men and held up his hand again in a demand for attention.

"Señor Cassara will choose half of you to ride tonight, if you agree to be back by dawn to continue your work. The choice will be made by lot, and be fair. As for tomorrow night — that will depend on tonight's happenings."

Some of them were quiet, but the most of them cheered the decision. Cassara stepped to the veranda railing again.

"I'll number you at the big corral immediately," he told them. "Into a cooking pot we will put both white and colored stones, half of each according to your number. The white stone means you ride, the colored one means you go to your huts and sleep. Make haste!"

Within a short time, half the *vaqueros* who had picked white stones had saddled, selected their partners, and ridden wildly away from the rancho. Diego knew how they would scatter out after getting a short distance away. Some pairs would follow the highways that ran like a network from the rancho to others, to the mission and toward Reina de Los Angeles. Others would scout over the hills, hoping to come across suspicious characters.

It grew quiet around the house again. Diego had put out the tapers after returning to his room, but had not undressed. And now he got up from his couch, put on a small sombrero and wrapped his throat and the lower part of his face in a scarf, opened the door silently, went out into the patio, and closed the door behind him.

Bernardo had been waiting for some time with Zorro's horse and outfit, because of what the *vaqueros* had done. But Diego knew the mute would be waiting patiently.

For a moment, Diego remained in the darkness just outside the door. Then he slipped the length of the patio, like a shadow, and came to the entrance arch.

Before going on, he surveyed the situation well. Low fires were still gleaming in front of some of the huts. He could hear distant low voices. At the big corral, some horse was kicking and squealing.

If he happened to be seen, he could say something about the responsibility of the rancho resting on his shoulders with his father indisposed, and that he had been restless and had gone out to see if everything was all right. But he would rather not be seen.

Keeping to the deeper shadows, and wishing the scudding light clouds would obscure the moon now and then, he reached the edge of the orchard and went on. Yet this was not a place of safety. Visiting *vaqueros* were inclined to use the orchard as a rendezvous with peon or native girls during the great slaughter.

He went through it without mishap, got down into a shallow gulch, and followed the bottom of it carefully until he was in the rear of an abandoned adobe building which years before had been the rancho's first small winery.

In the darkness beside the building, he found Bernardo waiting. Zorro's black horse was tied to a stunted tree. Zorro's costume and weapons were piled against the winery wall.

"Have you been able to watch the private corral?" Diego asked, as he put on the black Zorro costume over his own clothes.

Bernardo pressed his arm with his hand twice, to signify 'yes'.

"Did any man get his horse and ride?"

Again the affirmative signal.

"Could you identify the man?"

A third time the double pressure came on Diego's arm.

"Was he the Americano?"

The answer was not what Diego expected. It was 'no'.

"Hold my arm," Diego instructed, stopping his dressing. "I will mention several men. When I mention the one you saw at the corral, press my arm twice."

At the third name he mentioned, Bernardo pressed his arm. He had mentioned Don Marcos Vargas.

So Vargas was taking a night ride. That might mean something important. Or it might mean a hasty visit to the guest house of the mission, or a meeting with a dusky maiden, Vargas being noted for the latter.

By adroit questioning, Diego ascertained that Vargas had gone to the corral for his horse soon after the *vaqueros* had left the rancho house.

Diego finished dressing, pulled Zorro's hood and its attached black mask over his head, buckled on his blade and made sure his pistol was loaded. His long heavy whip was attached to the pommel of his saddle.

"You will remain here," he instructed the mute. "Be ready to take the horse when I return, and get him under cover quickly in the usual place."

HE got into the saddle — not Diego Vega now, but Señor Zorro. His entire manner seemed to change instantly. He had cast aside the languor and inertia of Diego Vega, and now was the quick-thinking, quick-acting caballero, ready for a wild ride or a fight in behalf of some unfortunate.

As he gathered up the reins, he heard Bernardo make a guttural sound. The mute seized the black horse's bridle strap to keep Zorro from riding. Bernardo was standing at the edge of a moonlit strip, and Zorro could see he was pointing.

He was indicating the private corral.

Zorro restrained his horse. Bending forward in the saddle, he looked toward the corral. He could see some man at the gate. A moment later, the man had led a horse out of the enclosure and was putting on bridle and saddle.

Zorro moved his horse slightly, strained his eyes to watch. The man at the corral moved his horse out into a streak of the bright moonlight. As he mounted, Zorro could make out his clothing and unusual headgear. He was Barney Burke.

So Barney Burke was taking a late night ride, too. This was something for which Zorro had hoped. He was eager to trail Burke, watch him closely, see if he contacted anybody. And he would have to be cautious as he trailed. If Burke really were sincere in his pursuit of Zorro to get the reward money and give himself a start in life, he might shoot to kill instead of trying to make a capture.

Burke rode away from the corral slowly, his pony's hoofs making scarcely any noise. And Zorro was realizing, as he started to follow, that Burke had a great advantage over him. If he met any of the *vaqueros*, the Americano could say he was out searching for Zorro, the same as they. But, at the mere sight of a masked man on a black horse, the infuriated *vaqueros* would give instant pursuit and battle.

Burke rode fearlessly through the moonlight, and Zorro was compelled to go cautiously through the shadows, and spur up at times to keep the other within sight. Fortunately, the wind was blowing toward Zorro, and Burke could not hear the hoofbeats of the big black horse.

When Burke rode along the trail toward San Gabriel Mission, Zorro paralleled it. Once, the Americano pulled up suddenly, and Zorro did the same.

The man ahead seemed to be looking toward the crest of a slope on his left. And suddenly he left the trail and started riding up this slope, which was studded with small trees and dotted with jumbles of rocks.

Zorro got across the trail and followed, riding cautiously from one dark spot to another. He saw Burke reach the crest and stop his horse in silhouette against the moonlit sky, saw him lift a hand.

"Hello, señores!" he heard Burke call. "Do not shoot! I am the Americano."

The wind carried the words to Zorro's ears. He heard an answering hail from the other side of the crest:

"Welcome, señor! Ride on in!"

Chapter XI
Riders of the Hills

IT TOOK Zorro some time to reach the crest of the slope at a spot where he would not be observed. With extreme care, he guided the black horse behind a ledge of rock and finally reached a place from where he could look down the slope.

A small fire was burning, and men were grouped around it. A mule and a small donkey were grazing. Burke was still in his saddle, but leaning forward with his forearms crossed on the pommel. Zorro could hear him speaking in that atrocious Spanish of his.

"It is like I said, hombres. The *vaqueros* are riding wild and searching for Zorro. They are also looking for the men who are slaying mission cattle for their hides. If you cannot prove you are honest men, you had better put out your fire and hide in the rocks until morning. I caught a whiff of smoke from your fire. That's how I knew you were here."

"But we are honest men, Señor Americano — most of the time," Zorro heard a man reply.

"It's all right to talk to me with a crooked tongue, amigo, but don't try it on the soldiers or *vaqueros*," Burke warned. "Where are you to work late tonight?"

"We do not understand you, señor. We were thinking of going to the Vega rancho in the morning to seek work there, and to get filled with good free food."

"Do you think I am a little innocent?" Burke demanded. "It would be better to speak the truth to me always. Has Zorro been here to see you yet and give you orders?"

"Zorro?" another of the men cried. "Give us orders, señor? We do not know

Zorro. And why should he give us orders? And about what?"

Zorro, listening, was trying to decide whether Burke was playing a game, trying to gain information, or whether he was really a rogue and trying to lead these men astray.

"If Zorro has not been here to give you orders for the night, has anyone else been here?"

"Nobody, señor," the reply came. "We only camped for the night."

"And you are going to the Vega rancho to look for work — is that it? I may see you at the rancho. And if I find you have lied to me, señores, I will use a mule whip on your backs."

"You are bewildering us, Señor Americano," one declared. "We know you by sight because we were at the plaza in Reina de Los Angeles when you raced your pony against Marcos Vargas' big sorrel."

"And what do you know of Marcos Vargas?" Burke asked.

"Only that we hate him, señor, as you must since the race. He is not kind to men like us."

"Probably not," Burke observed. "Regarding work — are you the kind of men who would slaughter mission cattle?"

The watchful Zorro could see the men around the fire crossing themselves.

"Never, señor!" their spokesman cried. "We are good men who visit the padres regularly."

Zorro felt his black horse stiffen and saw his ears go up and forward, and was instantly alert. He saw shadows coming up the hillside; two horsemen. They too had caught a whiff of smoke from the fire. Their tall, peaked sombreros told they were *vaqueros* from the rancho.

Zorro could not hope to avoid them if he turned and rode back down the slope. He would be seen in the bright moonlight, and undoubtedly recognized, and the men might open fire on him. And there was no good hiding place near at hand. Zorro did not wish to fight them, even should he be victorious, for he might hurt or kill one or both.

The sensible thing would be to ride down the smooth slope on the other side, straight at the fire for a short distance, then swerve away from it and travel swiftly over a level stretch Zorro knew well. The *vaqueros* undoubtedly would pursue, Burke might become confused for a moment, and Zorro would escape.

Zorro gathered up his reins, moved his horse forward to a safe place for a speedy descent. As he heard a wild yell behind him he touched with his spurs.

The men at the fire sprang to their feet, alarmed by the sudden commotion, and darted into the shadows thrown by a mass of rocks. Zorro was watching Burke, not fearing the others. The Americano had been startled at the sudden descent of mounted men toward him. The two *vaqueros* had come over the brow of the hill, yelling wildly, and began the pursuit of Zorro.

There was a moment of confusion as Burke watched the two *vaqueros*. They swung toward Burke and the men near the fire. At that moment, Zorro swerved his horse.

He rode wildly toward a long ledge of rock, knowing that there was smooth ground on the other side of it where speed would be fairly safe. To get behind the ledge, he was compelled to be out in the open, in the bright moonlight for an instant. Burke and the *vaqueros* saw the black horse clearly, saw the masked rider dressed in black.

"'Tis Zorro!" one of the *vaqueros* shouted. "After him, amigos!"

Burke had spurred toward the two *vaqueros*, shouting his identity to prevent them firing at him. The three began their pursuit of Zorro, following him into the semi-darkness on the opposite side of the ledge.

Because Zorro knew the footing here, he had been racing the black. When the pursuit caught sight of him again, he had gained considerably. The pursuers opened fire, but the range was too great for their pistols, and Zorro rode unscathed.

He did not discount his peril, however. The firing might be heard by other *vaqueros* scouting in the vicinity, and the pursuit might be strengthened. He wanted to make an escape without engaging in a fight of any sort, so that the only report which would get out would be that Zorro merely had been seen.

As he rode and dodged through the shadows, following dim trails he knew so well, because he had ridden over this land as a boy, his mind was working swiftly.

First, he considered Burke. The talk with the men at the fire — had it been a mere 'feeler'? Had Burke been sounding them out? Was he really the leader of, or in league with, the cattle thieves, trying to recruit new labor?

And the fact that Zorro had been seen would strengthen the report that had swept like wildfire over the countryside — that Zorro was the leader of the cattle thieves, and that he had wounded Don Alejandro.

Despite the fact that every appearance of Zorro now would be fraught with

As the vaqueros swung toward Burke and the men near the fire, Zorro swerved his horse.

peril for him, the other fact remained — that Zorro had important work to do. Fray Felipe depended on him to put an end to the theft of mission cattle. His father was expecting him to do that, too.

He rode wildly over the brow of a rolling hill, on the opposite side of which were ridges of rock and several cattle trails which converged. Before the pursuit came over the hill also, Zorro had turned aside into one of the trails that led toward the distant rancho house, and had raced along behind the ridge of rocks where the moonlight did not expose him.

The wind was blowing the dust the hoofs of his mount raised, and those pursuing were compelled to stop their horses for a moment and listen to the hoofbeats of Zorro's black before they could tell which trail he had followed. He gained a considerable distance on them there.

He was swerving toward the rancho in his mad race, using routes he knew well. He could do nothing more tonight. To get back, return the horse and Zorro's clothes and weapons to Bernardo, and get into the house without being seen, was his task now.

He was compelled to ride over another rolling hill. As he rode along the crest for a moment, he was seen by the three pursuers. They began yelling and coming on at greater speed. And their yells were answered by two *vaqueros* in front of Zorro, men who had heard the distant firing and were riding to investigate. Zorro was caught for the moment between two forces.

He sent the black for a distance down the slope toward the men who presented a new menace. Just as those behind came to the crest, Zorro swung the black to the right, raced behind some rocks in the semi-darkness, and let the two forces of his enemies come together.

"'Tis Zorro!" one of them shouted. "After him!"

ALL turned behind the rocks to continue the pursuit. And as they did, Zorro rode into the open again, safely between them all and the rancho house. He had put greater distance between himself and the pursuit.

He had no fear of capture now unless the black happened to stumble and throw him. But he would have to be careful as he approached the rancho buildings. Other *vaqueros*, tired of searching for Zorro, might be near the huts and corrals.

Changing his course again, hoping that those behind would believe he had turned toward some distant hills, he rode slower and with greater caution, keeping in the dark spots as much as possible.

He saw a couple of riders in the distance, revealed clearly in the moonlight. They heard pounding hoofs and a wild yell from one of his pursuers, and turned in his direction. Zorro rode behind a heavy growth of brush, stopped his horse, and waited.

The last two riders raced toward the spot, passed him without him being discovered, and met the others a short distance away. Zorro could hear them calling to one another.

"We passed nobody — " "He did not ride in our direction." " — must have turned toward the hills — "

They wheeled their mounts and rode off wildly at a right angle. Zorro started the black again and left the protection of the brush. He circled to the left and got around the rancho buildings. Once more, he was forced to take to hiding while riders in the distance went by, toward the huts and corral.

Finally, he reached the old winery and found the faithful Bernardo waiting for him. He dismounted and tossed Bernardo the reins.

"Get the black to his safe place, Bernardo" he ordered. "I'll stow the costume and weapons here — will return and take care of them later."

He stripped off the costume of Zorro, and was Don Diego Vega again. Costume and weapons were put in a heap in a dark spot against the winery wall. Then, as Bernardo rode the black away cautiously, Diego, just as cautiously, began the trip to the rancho house.

More *vaqueros* were riding in after their futile search of highways and hills. Their enthusiasm to run down Zorro had waned. But Diego knew it would be white-hot again as soon as they learned that Zorro had been seen and chased.

As he gained the edge of the orchard, he saw Marcos Vargas lope in and stop at the private corral. Vargas, in a leisurely manner, removed the saddle from his mount, took off the bridle, and turned him in, closing the gate of the corral carefully.

Diego started on beneath the trees, keeping in the shadows. But suddenly he stopped, for Burke and the *vaqueros* came riding in.

Burke swung aside to go to the private corral and put up his pony, and met Vargas there. Two other riders appeared from the vicinity of the huts — Sergeant Garcia and one of his troopers.

Chapter XII
Suspicions

GARCIA rode up as Burke dropped out of his saddle and confronted Vargas.

"Ah, señores!" the sergeant bellowed. "Been taking a night ride, have you."

"Not together," Burke snapped. "I just rode in with some of the *vaqueros*. We were chasing Zorro."

"Chasing Zorro?" the sergeant cried. "You are sure?"

"A masked man dressed in black and riding a black horse, at least," Burke said. "He finally dodged us, and rode in this direction. If he came to the rancho, he hasn't been here more than a few minutes."

"For some time, I and my troopers have been observing all who rode in," Sergeant Garcia said. "That is why we rode over here just now — to check on you."

"You can check on me quickly enough," Burke told him. "I was with some *vaqueros* chasing Zorro, so I could not be Zorro myself. And my horse is a little bay, not a big black. By the way, Vargas, what sort of horse have you been riding?"

"As it happens," Vargas replied, "I have been riding my black tonight. I just put him into the corral. Examine him, and you'll find he has a wet hide. What of it?"

"Perhaps you are the mysterious Zorro," Burke hinted.

"Ridiculous! Why should I ride the highways and hills like a wild man?"

"It would have been a good idea," Burke observed.

"How do you mean, señor?"

"As Zorro, you could have done a lot of good work, such as helping the helpless, until you had all the peons and natives swearing by you. Then, you could have formed a band of rogues to slay mission cattle and commit highway robbery."

"Señor!" Vargas cried. "Are you daring to intimate that I would do such a thing? Why should I?"

"To get money, Vargas. I know all about you. The *vaqueros* talk, you know. You wasted your fortune. You have no money and are in debt. You like to live high. And your general character is not so good but what you would do such a thing."

"Señor!" Vargas cried, enraged. "I'd challenge you, if you were of gentle blood. But to stain my blade with blood like yours is beneath me!"

"Silence!" Garcia ordered. "You are hot about nothing, señores. Watch your words, Señor Burke. And you, Don Marcos, please curb your just anger. Let us have no trouble. Anyhow, the thing is easily settled. Don Marcos Vargas is a caballero, and will speak the truth if he speaks at all. I ask you, Don Marcos, officially, where were you riding tonight?"

"That the record may be clear," Vargas replied, "let me say that I rode forth to keep a rendezvous with a certain lady. Surely you do not expect me to name her."

"Certainly not, caballero," Garcia said promptly.

"How do you know he speaks the truth?" Burke demanded of the sergeant.

"Señor! Don Marcos is a gentleman of blood, and he would not tell a falsehood."

"That might do for you, but not for me," Burke replied. "If he is Zorro, would he tell you the truth, knowing that there is a reward offered for his capture, and that a rope waits for him?"

"Let us have an end of this bickering," Garcia ordered. "It would be better if both of you went to your rooms to get some rest. You will both see things differently in the morning."

Burke turned aside to finish putting up his horse. The sergeant rode away to inspect a couple of other men who had just come riding in.

Diego went silently through the darkness beneath the spreading trees of the orchard. Glancing back, he saw Vargas leave the corral and start strolling toward the rancho house also.

But Diego knew the shortest way. He reached the patio unseen while Vargas was still some distance away, hurried to his room and let himself in, stripped off his clothing in the darkness and wrapped himself in his heavy robe and put on his slippers.

The night's adventure, he decided, had netted him nothing but suspicions. He did not like the manner in which Barney Burke had spoken to the men by the fire. Burke could be a recruiter for the cattle thieves.

AS FOR Marcos Vargas — Diego certainly knew that Vargas was not Zorro. And it was entirely possible that, as he had said, Vargas had ridden somewhere to keep a rendezvous, possibly with some peon or native girl. It would not be an unusual thing for him to do. Yet he could have ridden elsewhere to engage in shady work.

Diego thought suddenly of Pedro Ramirez, the slimy individual who was always Vargas' shadow. Ramirez was not welcome at Rancho Vega as a guest. And Diego wondered where the man was to be found, for surely he had remained in the vicinity to be near Vargas. Perhaps he was at the guest house of the mission in San Gabriel. That was something that could be ascertained easily enough ….

Up at an early hour, Diego visited his father and found Fray Felipe there also. In low tones, Diego told them of the events of the night.

"With the countryside aroused against Zorro, he must move with great caution," Fray Felipe said.

"Yet he has a problem to solve, and it must be solved soon," Diego replied.

"The Americano, Burke, may be a scoundrel or merely incautious," Don Alejandro said. "He is speaking a language strange to him, remember, and may give words the wrong shade of meaning at times."

"There was no wrong shade in the words he addressed to Marcos Vargas," Diego declared.

"Vargas has been losing in strength of character for several years," the *padre* judged. "I dislike to say it, yet it is so. However, I would hate to think that a man of his lineage would consort with thieves, steal and kill cattle belonging to a mission, or try armed highway robbery on others of his own class, and then come here and accept hospitality. That would be the depths of depravity."

"It has been said," Don Alejandro observed, "that when a man of gentle blood turns rogue, he outdoes in meanness the rogues themselves."

"I must meet Vargas and Burke both for the morning meal," Diego told them, getting off his stool. "We will have some tired and sleepy *vaqueros* working today, but the *jefe vaquero* will drive them to their work."

"I will leave my couch today, Diego," his father told him. "I must be up and around, even if I am compelled to move slowly. Sitting half-asleep in the patio will do me more good than being stretched out on a couch."

Burke was waiting when Diego went in for the morning meal. He explained all that had happened the night before, and Diego let him talk and showed interest, though he knew everything himself, since he had been the quarry in the Zorro chase.

"But why did you go to the fire, señor?" Diego asked, when Burke had finished his recital.

"I saw the men were peons and wanted to question them," Burke replied. "I hinted at the cattle thefts and the easy money to be made, but they seemed to shudder with horror at the idea of stealing mission cattle. Of course, they may have been playing clever. Zorro showing up when he did kept me from talking to them more."

"Do you think Zorro was on his way to talk to those men, was coming to the fire for the purpose?"

"That could be," Burke replied.

"Up to this time, what are your conclusions about Zorro?" Diego asked.

Burke bent forward and lowered his voice. "You will not agree with me, Don Diego. But I believe Zorro is the leader of the cattle thieves and was also the mounted highwayman. Everybody around here thinks that. And I have another thought the others might not have."

"And that, señor?"

Burke glanced around cautiously to see no servant was near, and whispered when he replied:

"I think that Don Marcos Vargas is Zorro."

Diego laughed a little. "Señor Burke, it is natural for you to dislike Vargas, since your trouble over the horse race. But the idea that he is Zorro is, if you'll pardon me, ridiculous."

"Whoever Zorro is, I am eager to catch him and learn the truth," Burke said.

FRAY FELIPE came in to join them for breakfast, and then Vargas appeared. He bowed coldly to them all and sat at table. He busied himself making a hearty meal. Fray Felipe led the conversation into channels that were not dangerous, talking principally about the slaughtering.

"Doubtless guests will commence arriving this morning," Diego said. "My father will be able to sit in some cozy corner and welcome them for a time. But I wish, Fray Felipe, that you would remain in the house and help him, and watch over him. If any serious accident should occur at the canyon, I'll send for you at once."

"I'll be glad to be of service, my son."

"Burke, are you too tired after your ride last night to accompany me to the canyon again?"

"Certainly not!" the Americano replied. "I want to watch the skinners and cart crews today, if it is permitted. I like to talk to the *vaqueros* and get their ideas, too."

"You, Vargas?" Diego asked.

"My bruised shoulder is still bothering me," Vargas complained. "I had Pedro Ramirez bandage it again last night at the mission guest house. With your permission, Diego, I'll remain at the house this morning."

"As you will."

"Also, I do not care to ride beside and on equal terms with an alien who has been insolent to me. No offense to you, Diego. It is only a personal rule of mine." He glanced at Burke coldly, and the Americano's lips twisted slightly in a grin.

The mounts had been brought from the corral. Diego and Burke got into their saddles and started for the box canyon. The *vaqueros* had saddled up and gone to their work already.

"Though half of them had ridden most of the night in their search for Zorro, fatigue did not show in their work. They were running cattle out of the canyon and lancing them with as much speed and skill as they had the day before.

Burke soon left the knoll where Diego had stationed himself as before, and went to follow the skinners and cart crews. Diego received reports from the *jefe vaquero*, and after a time Cassara, the overseer, appeared.

"Don Diego, or the *vaqueros* who went out last night to search for Zorro, one has failed to return," Cassara reported.

"One of our men, or a visiting *vaquero*?"

"One of our men, Don Diego. He was paired with another last night, but they became separated, and the other returned alone."

"Were they friendly with each other?" Diego asked. He was thinking of a quarrel in the moonlight, perhaps over some girl, and a quick assassination.

"They have been bosom friends for several years," Cassara answered. "The one who returned can give no reason for the other not coming back. He searched for an hour after dawn, then rode to the rancho. He found no trace of the missing man or his horse."

"Pick a couple of men you can trust, and send him back with them," Diego directed. "Have them search well. His horse may have thrown him and run away, and he may be badly hurt in some canyon."

The overseer rode away. Diego, half-asleep in his saddle, watched the work going on a short distance from the knoll. After a time, he heard hoofbeats, and turned his head to see Pedro Ramirez approaching him.

Ramirez stopped his mount a short distance away and knuckled his forehead to Diego in a gesture of respect.

"May I speak to you, Don Diego?" he asked.

"Make it as brief as possible, Ramirez," Diego told him. "I do not like men who foul in a horse race."

"Your pardon for that, Don Diego. I lost my temper when I saw the sorrel losing. I knew Don Marcos would blame me if I lost the race."

"What did you want to speak to me about?"

"I wish to see Don Marcos, and thought he would be with you watching the slaughter. But I see him nowhere."

"He remained at the rancho house this morning. Said his shoulder hurt him. What has come up of such importance that you could not tell him last night?"

"But I did not see him last night, Don Diego," Ramirez said. "I understood he had a rendezvous."

SO Vargas had lied! Diego's eyes narrowed.

"Did Don Marcos not ride to the mission and have you bandage his bruised shoulder?" he demanded. "Last night, I mean."

"There must be some mistake, Don Diego. I bandaged his shoulder the night he was hurt, sí. He probably confused you with his talk, Don Diego."

"That is possible. Must you see him personally, Ramirez, or can I deliver your message?"

"It is rather a private matter."

"Another rendezvous, I presume. Are you his go-between in such affairs?" There was scorn in Diego's voice. "I give you permission to ride to the rancho house and speak to Vargas. But do not remain. You are not a welcome guest there."

Ramirez' eyes flickered a bit, but otherwise his face was inscrutable.

"Thank you, Don Diego," he muttered, and turned to ride.

Diego thought of Vargas' lie to him. Why had it been necessary for Vargas to pretend he had ridden to the mission to have his shoulder bandaged? He had already indicated that he had been on a rendezvous. That was more than likely, but Vargas may have lied about that, too.

CHAPTER **XIII**
A Vaquero Reports

NOISILY the day wore on. Bawling cattle, clouds of dust, thundering hoofs and yelling men — the din made Diego's head ache. He longed for midday, the noon meal and the siesta.

Again he heard hoofbeats and turned his head to see who approached. His eyes widened. He saw Cassara, Sergeant Garcia and three of his *vaqueros*, one bent over in the saddle and clinging to the pommel. Diego wheeled his own mount and rode to meet them.

"What is this?" he asked Cassara.

"The missing man, Don Diego," the overseer answered. "The men I sent met him and helped him home. Sergeant Garcia came along, because this may be official business."

Diego looked at the *vaquero*. "What happened to you?" he asked.

The man spoke slowly and with some difficulty:

"I separated from my companion, I to ride up one hillside and he another, with the intention of meeting at the end of a canyon."

"And then?" Diego urged.

"I heard sounds — men's voices as they called to one another, and bawling cattle — and rode up the slope. As I neared the crest, Don Diego, somebody watching there fired a pistol and hit me."

"The wound?"

"In my right leg, Don Diego. It is not a bad wound, but I have lost much blood."

"Your saddle and horse show it."

"I turned and rode, Don Diego. There was no pursuit. I began to get weak and dizzy. It was my intention to go through the canyon and find my companion, and tell him what had happened. But because of my dizziness, I must have lost my way."

"That is understandable," Diego said.

"Finally, I felt myself losing consciousness, I suppose from loss of blood. I must have fallen from my saddle. When I was myself again, I found that I was on the ground and my horse grazing a short distance away."

"Spare yourself as much as possible in the recital," Diego told him. "Give me the necessary facts only."

"Thank you, Don Diego. I got into my saddle with difficulty and looked around. During my dizziness, my horse had circled, and I was within a short distance of where I had been shot. I started up the slope again, to see if I could learn anything. I had my pistol ready, but this time there was no attack. When I came to the crest of the slope, I looked down into a little canyon. And there —"

"Yes?" Diego urged impatiently.

"I saw where cattle had been freshly slain and their hides taken. From where I was, I counted more than two score. And in the soft earth were tracks of heavy carts leading toward the distant highway."

"Were you able in your condition to make any investigation?" Diego asked.

"I forced myself to do so, Don Diego. I found where they had had guards stationed, one of whom I suppose shot me."

"But the cattle, man?"

"The heads were there, Don Diego. I looked at the ears. All were notched with the brand of the San Gabriel Mission. The cattle thieves again, Don Diego."

"Díos!" one of the other *vaqueros* swore.

"Is that all?" Diego asked the man who had reported.

"I found something, Don Diego, near where there had been a small fire. Here it is."

He urged his horse forward until he was beside Diego, and pressed something into the young caballero's hand. Diego gave it a quick inspection and stowed it away. It was a small silver ornament such as some men had on their bridles.

"I want all of you to keep quiet about this until later," Diego ordered. "Cassara, have this man escorted to his hut, and send a rider to inform Fray Felipe, who is at the rancho house, so he may be prepared to care for the wound."

ALL rode away with the exception of Sergeant Manuel Garcia.

"Well, Garcia, it looks as if there is something to this cattle thief business now, eh?" Diego asked. "I have heard that your *commandante* says nothing at all can be done about it."

"Your pardon, Don Diego, but we have found no evidence."

"Do you doubt the crimes have been committed?"

"Somebody has been killing cattle and stealing the hides, certainly. That much we know."

"You can find no trace of the guilty ones?"

"The country is filled with rogues, Don Diego."

"What are you going to do about this, Garcia?"

"I shall write out a report and send it to the *commandante* immediately by one of my troopers."

"Writing reports does not catch stock thieves, Garcia."

"We do our best."

"Do you? Understand, these are mission cattle whose hides have been stolen."

"The missions have thousands of cattle," the sergeant pointed out.

"True. At least a third of the income from the herds is used to aid the poor and educate the native neophytes so they will grow into good citizens."

"Bah! The poor and neophytes!" the sergeant exclaimed. "The poor will always be such as long as the padres feed them for nothing. And why educate the native neophytes? They are nuisance enough as it is, running around saying they are better than the heathen natives and getting big notions. They are too much under the thumbs of the padres."

He ceased speaking suddenly, like a man who realizes he is saying the wrong thing.

"So!" Diego said. "You have your orders, I see. The missions may expect no help from the soldiery of the politicians."

"Dangerous words, Don Diego."

"The Vegas fear nothing from a grasping Governor. Am I to understand that you will do nothing about this, when you are here near at hand? The tracks of the carts — "

"Ran toward the highway, your *vaquero* said, Don Diego, and I think he spoke the truth. I can take my troopers and follow the tracks to the highway, but what then? They will be lost in hundreds of other tracks, and obliterated in the deep dust. One cart track is much like another."

"True, Garcia. But the stolen hides probably are being taken to the market at Monterey. Why can you not take your troopers and ride north, overtake the carts and question the cartmen?"

"Out of my jurisdiction, Don Diego," the sergeant replied, afterward glancing away and clearing his throat.

"A convenient situation for you," Diego said, his eyes blazing. "However, the spot where this slaughter took place is not out of your jurisdiction. Nor is this rancho and San Gabriel mission. So, you can look at the scene, follow the trail that runs in this direction, question strangers and all that. Have you any ideas at all about this?"

"It is possible, Don Diego."

"Suppose you tell me."

"If, as has been suggested, there is a band of thieves led by a man of clever skill, it is the man we must find. And where to look?"

"That is the business of you troopers."

"We are only human, Don Diego. At times, we do our best, yet fail."

"You do your best in the matter of this mysterious Señor Zorro — and fail," Diego said sarcastically. "Did you have this much evidence in the Zorro case, you and your troopers would be on the move already, and you wouldn't worry about being in jurisdiction. But there is a difference, eh? The Governor wants to catch Zorro for the same reason he will not help the missions. He wants to throttle the work of the Franciscans."

"Have a care, Don Diego. You speak treason."

"Perhaps you will write a report on that, Garcia? If you have any ideas about this, speak."

"Don Diego, I have always admired you and your illustrious father. Let us continue to be friends. Remember, please, that a soldier carries out orders. As for my own thoughts regarding this affair—"

"Let me hear them," Diego broke in.

"Perhaps we have not caught Zorro because his ways of thinking and acting are not ours, because we do not understand him."

"That is possible."

GARCIA blew out his mustache importantly.

"Which means, Don Diego," he said, "that he must be an alien. And if there is a big band of thieves well-organized, with killers and skinners and cartmen and a way of marketing, and they are ruled by a leader with brains — well, Don

Diego, it is well-known that the Americanos are shrewd and unscrupulous and know how to handle other men and scheme to make money."

"Are you trying to intimate that this Señor Barney Burke may be both Zorro and the leader of the cattle thieves?"

"Frankly, Don Diego, he has me puzzled. One moment I respect and admire him, and the next I am suspicious of him."

Diego smiled a little. He felt he was in the same situation regarding Burke.

"But consider, Sergeant," he said, "that this man, this Americano, came to the vicinity of Reina de Los Angeles only a very short time ago."

"So he says," Garcia replied. "But do Americanos, or any other men, always tell the truth?"

"I think not."

"Señor Burke says he landed at San Diego de Alcalá recently, bought a pony and rode north. Everybody but me seems to have taken the man's word for it. But I did not, Don Diego. I sent a courier to San Diego de Alcalá to learn whether Señor Burke told the truth."

"A wise move," Diego said. "Are you watching him until you get a reply?"

"As much as I can. Last night, he took a ride, and we lost him in a maze of *vaqueros* turned loose to roam the hills and search for Zorro."

"I allowed that, Garcia."

"Pardon me, Don Diego, but that was a mistake. How can I and my troopers do our work if a hundred other men are riding the hills and frightening the quarry?"

Diego had a sudden thought. "I'll make a deal with you, Garcia," he said. "If you will promise me to take your troopers out tonight and search for Zorro and the cattle thieves, I'll order my *vaqueros* to remain on the rancho so as not to interfere with your efforts."

"It is an arrangement!" the sergeant declared. "Now, Diego, amigo, we are looking at things sensibly. I will try to find all evidence possible, if you will help me."

"Help you, Garcia? How?"

"The wounded *vaquero* handed you something which I take it must be in the line of evidence. If you will give it to me, it may help me."

"For the moment, I retain it," Diego said. "There may be a personal matter connected with it."

"Will you not even tell me its nature?"

"Certainly, Garcia. It is a bridle ornament of silver. Possibly, while you are occupied with weightier things, I may find the man who lost it."

Mid-day came as a relief to Diego. He galloped back to the rancho house with Burke, after the Americano had watched the skinners and cart crews throughout the morning. Diego watched him carefully. He could not make up his mind about Burke.

Guests had arrived. Several carriages were in front of the rancho house in a small park set aside for such, and the horses had been taken to the adobe stables.

"We will have a merry mid-day meal, and then a real siesta," Diego told Burke as they dismounted and natives hurried to get their mounts. "After their journey here and a heavy meal, the guests will go to their rooms and sleep. But they will be active enough this evening."

"Perhaps I would be out of place at your table, Don Diego," Burke suggested.

"Not at all! I want you beside me as much as possible, amigo. Did I not invite you here as my guest?"

"Then I will wash up, Don Diego."

Burke hurried away.

Chapter XIV
Siesta Excitement

UNDER pretense of dropping his riding whip and stooping to pick it up, Diego got a glance at Burke's bay pony before the native groom led him away. He looked at the bridle. It was entirely without ornament of any sort.

Ten guests gathered at table for the noon meal in addition to Burke, Vargas and Fray Felipe, who asked the blessing. If this meal was an ordinary noon repast, Burke wondered what the *fiesta* would be like.

Diego noticed that Burke kept silent unless addressed and then made himself as agreeable as possible. Vargas was of a different sort. He ignored the half-sneers of the men, but gave attention to any woman who would talk with him.

When the meal was over, the guests hurried to their rooms for the siesta. Diego, Fray Felipe, Burke and Vargas remained a moment longer for a last sip of wine.

"My father?" Diego asked the old *padre*.

"Up and about for a couple of hours, then I advised him to seek his couch again," Fray Felipe replied, smiling. "He is determined to be up again, however. I'll see that he does not overdo it."

"The wounded *vaquero*?"

"Gunshot wound in the leg and loss of blood, but nothing serious. The bullet went through a fleshy part and did not remain in the wound. He will be at work in a few days."

Fray Felipe left the table to attend to Don Alejandro, and the other three remained.

"Vargas, did your friend, Ramirez, find you?" Diego asked. "He came to the canyon looking for you."

"He brought me a trivial message that could have waited," Vargas replied.

"And please, Diego, do not call him my amigo. I make of him a sort of business agent at times, a man to carry messages and do errands at other times — merely that."

"And a jockey at other times," Burke suggested.

The remark brought a surge of wrath into Vargas' face.

"I seem to be all confused," Diego said. "You told me, Vargas, that you were at the mission last night and had Ramirez bandage your bruised shoulder anew. And he told me he did not see you last night."

"The man is utterly irresponsible at times," Vargas said. "But I think I understand. Ramirez probably was trying to serve me. He probably believed he was saying the right thing."

"If you mean he lied, why should he?" Diego asked.

"Oh, undoubtedly he thought that if he admitted I was at the mission and had him bandage my shoulder, you would think I had ridden on somewhere for a rendezvous. And everyone, my dear Diego, knows how you detest affairs with women. If you will excuse me, I believe I will take my siesta."

"Suppose we all do," Diego said. "I must visit my father first."

Vargas started from the room, and Burke followed him slowly. Diego watched them go, then hurried to his father's chamber. Don Alejandro was not only awake, but sitting on the side of his couch, and Fray Felipe had been talking with him.

As swiftly as possible, Diego told them of the new find of slaughtered cattle, and of his scene with Garcia.

"This grows too serious," Diego concluded. "Zorro will ride again tonight."

"It will be dangerous, my boy, with all the *vaqueros* out," Don Alejandro told him.

"I'll order the *vaqueros* to stay in tonight, saying their riding will hinder the soldiers. At all costs, whatever I must tell them and whatever penalties I must threaten, I'll keep them at the rancho tonight. Zorro must ride without being hampered. I can dodge the troopers easily enough. This is but a subterfuge of Garcia's. Probably he and his men will take a few wineskins, ride to the nearest canyon and make themselves comfortable, empty the skins there and return at dawn to report no progress."

Fray Felipe changed the subject.

"Diego, your father insists that he wants to have his siesta in the big easy chair in the patio behind the hedge. I do not think it will harm him, so I will help him there. Get your rest, my son, for you have work to do this afternoon and tonight. I'll retire as soon as I have seen your father settled."

Diego passed through the house and went to his own room off the patio. He was tired and a bit sleepy after last night's riding and the business of the morning. He removed some of his clothing and his boots, put on dressing gown and slippers, and walked to the window to look out into the patio.

IT had grown quiet in the house already. The tired guests were sleeping, storing up rest for the frolic of the evening. The servants were preparing for rest also, except in the big kitchens, where there was a clatter of pots, pans and tongues.

Diego smiled when he saw Fray Felipe help his father out into the patio. Don Alejandro's old easy chair had been put in the shade behind the high hedge. Don Alejandro sat down and made himself comfortable, and the old *padre* tucked rugs around him.

"Get yourself some rest now, Fray Felipe," Don Alejandro ordered. "You need it. I'll doze here. You may come and get me later."

Diego inhaled slowly a few times, drinking in the aroma of roses, then turned from the window to stretch upon his couch.

But sleep would not come to him. In his mind he reviewed again all he knew concerning the slaughtering of mission cattle and the attack upon the Vega carriage by the highwayman.

For actual evidence he had only a little silver bridle ornament. He had an abundance of conflicting suspicions. And he was sensible enough to tell himself that they might be of no actual worth.

Zorro could ride tonight, but he would have to stumble upon something to give him a trail to the guilty. He considered the possibility of Burke being guilty, or even Vargas, and in the end he had nothing but conflicting suspicions, as before.

How long he remained stretched there thinking, he couldn't be sure. He had ordered Cassara and the *jefe vaquero* to continue the work at the canyon, if he did not return at the usual hour, for he had anticipated being delayed by guests. So he had not planned a short siesta.

On a small table near the door was a jug of wine and one of water. Diego felt thirsty, got up from the couch and poured himself a goblet of water. Carrying it as he sipped, he strolled across the room to the patio window again.

He glanced into the patio as he heard voices.

"You are the sweetest señorita in all Alta California," a man was saying.

"Please do not talk so, señor." That was a woman's voice, and to Diego she seemed a bit frightened.

"You never give me a proper chance to talk to you," the man continued. "What better time than now, when everyone else is asleep? Come into my room now, and we'll talk. It is but a step. Nobody will know."

"How dare you, señor?"

Diego heard the man's light, bantering laughter.

"Why be so coy, little one?" the man asked.

"But it is not right."

"It occurs to me that nothing in life that is pleasant is ever right. Come!"

"Please do not seize my hand, señor. You do not realize what you are doing."

"None realizes better than I."

"If I scream?"

The man laughed lightly again. "Scream and have everyone come running?" he asked. "Have them believe any story that I wish to tell? Have them hear me say, for instance, that you screamed when I would not give you more gold?"

"Señor!"

Diego heard the sound of a slap, a girl's sob, then the harsh low voice of an angry man.

"That was going a little too far, señorita, for a girl of your class!"

That remark got Diego's instant attention. He had thought that two of his guests had been indulging in a flirtation as a lark, believing that there was nobody to see or hear. But that remark 'a girl of your class' gave a different interpretation.

Diego put the glass down quickly on a chair and got to the far side of the window, from where he could see along the patio wall. He could see them now — Don Marcos Vargas, the man who disgraced his gentle blood, and Nita Cassara, the overseer's daughter.

It was evident to Diego that Nita had gone into the patio during the siesta hour to cut roses to be put into the rooms of the guests later. She held a mass of roses in her left arm, and the cutting shears were on the ground at her feet.

VARGAS had grasped the girl's right arm, and she was trying to pull away.

"Let me go, señor!" she begged. "You are forgetting yourself."

"Your beauty would make any man forget himself, señorita. Come into my room and talk with me."

He tried to pull her along the wall. She opened her mouth to scream, and Vargas pulled her into the circle of one arm and stifled her scream with a hand. Nita dropped the roses, which fell in confusion on the flag stones of the patio.

Diego was about to leave the window, rush to the door and pull it open, and denounce Don Marcos Vargas as he deserved to be denounced. For Nita Cassara, as all knew, was a decent, self-respecting girl, devout, serving her father as housekeeper after the death of her mother. She was not a peon or native woman.

But Diego stopped as he was about to rush from the window. Another was before him. Another door had been flung open, and Barney Burke rushed out into the patio.

Diego saw Burke grasp Vargas' shoulder and twist him so he was compelled to release the girl, who cringed against the wall. Burke hurled Vargas back against the wall also, and stood in front of him with fists doubled, body balanced on the balls of his feet, his eyes ablaze.

"You swine!" Burke cried at him.

"Americano beast!" Vargas cried in answer. "How dare you touch me?"

"It takes a beast to handle a rat like you!" Burke yelled. "Putting your hands on a decent girl!"

Vargas laughed. "There seems to be a misunderstanding, Señor Burke. Did you say 'decent'?"

Then Burke hit him.

The blow crashed through Vargas' up-thrown arms and thudded against his head with a crack that could be heard all through the patio. Nita screamed once and crouched against the wall as Burke drove Vargas away from her.

"I'll teach you not to insult a good woman!" Burke raged. "Fight, you cur! No pretty blades or barking pistols now! Man fashion, Vargas! Use your fists, if you can!"

Diego saw that much, then tore open the door of his room and rushed into the patio. He saw his father's head appear above the hedge, and Don Alejandro's face was suffused with rage. Other doors were being pulled open as the guests heard the tumult. Men stepped out into the patio, and women took one look and screamed.

Vargas retreated, then suddenly stood ground and tried to fight back. But his effort was futile. Barney Burke had had many rough-and-tumble fights in cowtowns and trail camps. He may have been lacking in fistic science, but Vargas had none at all. Burke's stiff blows began battering Vargas down.

Fray Felipe appeared from somewhere, took in the situation. He helped Nita to her feet and led her a short distance away, speaking to her soothingly and learning her version of the affair.

Though a man of peace, the *padre* did not try to stop this fight. He kept his back turned toward the fighters, and pretended to be comforting the girl.

CHAPTER XV
Lost Lineage

QUICKLY Sergeant Garcia came running into the end of the patio, followed by one of his troopers, having heard the com-motion and wondering what was happening. He stopped abruptly and made no move to interfere, since Don Alejandro and Don Diego were making none and seemed to sanction the combat.

Burke got Vargas away from the wall and out into the open and began on him again.

"If my shoulder — was not bruised!" Vargas yelled, seeking sympathy and an alibi for defeat.

Burke struck the remainder of his words from his lips. Vargas began collapsing. Diego was preparing to step forward and call upon the Americano to stop, since he had Vargas at his mercy. But there was not time. Burke drove his right, and Don Marcos Vargas crumpled to the ground.

"Throw water upon the scoundrel!" old Don Alejandro called to a couple of the house servants.

Breathing heavily, Burke stepped back and looked at his fallen adversary. The others were still as a serving woman emptied a water olla over Vargas' head. Burke stepped forward as Vargas moaned, shook his head and opened his eyes. The Americano grasped Vargas by the shoulder and pulled him to his feet.

"Release me — my shoulder!" Vargas mouthed. He tried to strike Burke.

Burke hurled him back against the wall again. The move tore open Vargas' jacket and shirt and exposed the shoulder about which he had been complaining. It was bandaged, all right, and the bandage was soiled with bright fresh blood.

"What is this?" Burke cried. "A bruised shoulder, like you have been saying you had, does not bleed like that, Vargas. There is something strange here. Stand still!"

Burke held him against the wall and tore off the bandage, then turned to the others.

"No mere bruise here," he said. "A healing gunshot wound instead. How did you get that, Vargas? By turning highwayman? Perhaps by trying to rob Don Alejandro?"

Diego started forward angrily, then remembered he was not Zorro now, and checked himself.

"Don't be a fool!" Vargas said, in quick defense. "I lied about the shoulder, but it was to protect the name of a woman. Has a man never been hurt before in a quarrel with a jealous rival?"

"I ought to finish you with my fists," Burke raged at him. "Putting your foul hands on a good girl. I have smashed you for it, anyhow. I don't like to see scum like you insult a girl. In your own words, Don Marcos Vargas, son of a hidalgo, it is a personal rule of mine."

Then old Don Alejandro took charge.

"Enough!" he roared from behind the hedge. "I saw and heard the entire affair. Nobody knew I was slumbering here. Marcos Vargas, you are a stench in the nostrils of decent men!"

"All this commotion over a man trying to kiss a wench," Vargas complained.

"Do not call Nita by such a name, or I'll allow the Americano to finish you," Don Alejandro warned. "Nita Cassara was born and reared on this rancho. She is a lovely girl, and I would have her know now that none of this affair is to be blamed on her."

As Diego and all the others stood still, Don Alejandro walked from behind the hedge and faced the man he had denounced. But his denunciation was not ended.

"Marcos Vargas, I knew your father, and he was a splendid man," Don Alejandro said. "You, señor, have been a scoundrel for several years. Your acts have lost you the privileges of your lineage."

"Don Alejandro!" Vargas cried in protest.

"I am hereby ordering you expelled from my rancho, and asking others of gentle blood to turn their backs upon you henceforth, else they are no longer friends of mine. Saddle up and go!"

Vargas' face went white and then grew purple again under the stress of his emotion.

"A man with one foot in the grave can talk to me like that with safety," Vargas said. "Let your son speak in your stead. If he is afraid to do so, I term him coward and challenge him here and now!

DIEGO started forward angrily. But suddenly he stopped. He and his father and old Fray Felipe had the same idea at the same instant. They knew he was Zorro, a wonder with a blade. But Diego Vega was supposed to be a weakling, a man who never fought, but read the poets instead.

If he engaged in a duel, he would have to fight well to save his own life, because Vargas was clever with a blade. If he did that, men would wonder how he suddenly had acquired his skill as a swordsman. Sergeant Garcia, not knowing the truth and fearing for Diego, hurried forward.

"Señores, there is a Governor's edict which prohibits a duel under threat of stern punishment," he warned.

"A convenient edict for Diego Vega," Vargas said.

Don Alejandro took charge again.

"Attention all!" he roared. "Edict or not, Diego Vega, decent son of a hidalgo, need not cross blades with Marcos Vargas even if challenged."

"And why not?" Vargas asked.

"Because I have declared you a man of lost lineage. He would descend to your level if he crossed blades with you. Get your horse, and ride! You are no longer welcome in a decent house."

"A decent house?" Vargas raged. "Sergeant Garcia! I call upon you to note what I say. A decent house, he says! And at this moment it is harboring a criminal wanted by the soldiery, perhaps with Don Alejandro's knowledge."

"Name him!" Don Alejandro challenged.

"I name him — Zorro!"

Gasps of surprise came from all who heard. Diego, his father and Fray Felipe had a moment of panic, but did not betray it in their faces.

"I have been gathering evidence slowly, Sergeant," Vargas continued. "See me within a few days, and I will have enough for you to form a basis of arrest."

"The man raves!" Don Alejandro said. "Name the man you say is Zorro!"

"I'll name him. He is the Americano known as Burke."

"A poor loser — to quote your own words again, Vargas," Burke told him.

"I'll prove it! That will be my settlement with you. As for the Vegas — I am not done with you yet. Before I am, Don Alejandro, I'll see pain gnaw at your heart!"

"Take him away from here!" Don Alejandro cried. "He stenches the air."

Cassara, who had appeared some time before with a few *vaqueros* strode forward.

"Señor, Don Alejandro has ordered you to quit the rancho," the overseer said. "Come with me and my men, or we will take you, and not gently. We will see that your horse is saddled, and two *vaqueros* will ride with you to the boundary of our land. And never dare put foot upon Vega land again. Make haste, señor. For I am the father of the girl you insulted, and I may remember that if you hesitate."

Face black with rage, Vargas turned away ....

Diego did not go to the canyon that afternoon. He knew that Cassara and the *jefe vaquero* would see the work done well. He rested during the afternoon, slept some, and gathered his strength.

Toward evening, Fray Felipe mounted his mule to ride to the San Gabriel Mission and visit for a short time with the younger padres there. After the excitement of the day, Don Alejandro retired to his room, with Nita Cassara to watch over him.

Diego dressed for the evening meal, at which his guests would make merry. Then, as the *vaqueros* came riding in to the huts from the afternoon's work, Diego strolled out and met Cassara, who called the men together.

"I am asking something of you, señores, and I desire to be obeyed," Diego told the men. "Last night, some of you were allowed to ride the hills and scout for Zorro. Tonight, I wish all of you to remain here. Eat, drink, play and sing, but do not ride abroad."

He heard mutterings of protest, especially from those who had not ridden out the night before.

"I know you are disappointed, but this is necessary," Diego continued. "There is a plan afoot to learn the identity of Zorro, and if you ride tonight the plan may be ruined. If this plan succeeds, you may ride tomorrow night, all of you. Obey me in this, señores."

HE turned away with Cassara, and went to where Garcia and his troopers, who had eaten already, were saddling up.

"I have done my part, Sergeant Garcia," Diego said. "Now, you do yours."

Then Diego returned to the house to sit at the head of the table and be host to his guests. All were there, excepting Marcos Vargas. Burke, without a scratch on him, acted modestly, though the women would have made a hero of him.

After the meal came music and dancing in the patio, and some merriment. This was but a foretaste of the *fiesta* that would follow the slaughtering. But finally the guests retired, and Diego prepared to go to his room. He already had instructed Bernardo to have Zorro's horse and trappings ready. In the hallway, Diego met Burke.

"This is the first chance I have had, Señor Burke, to thank you properly for what you did today in the patio," Diego said.

"It was a pleasure," Burke replied. "I have wanted to do something like that ever since the horse race."

"The way in which you went to the rescue of a lady — we of this country appreciate a thing like that."

"She is a great little lady, Don Diego. I liked her from the first moment I saw her, when she was helping me dress your father's wound."

Diego's eyes twinkled. "Can this be the commencement of a romance, señor?"

"Stranger things have happened," Burke replied, grinning. "But I am not forgetting that I am an alien in a strange land. I would have to be a settled man, one of some substance, to ask a girl like that to marry me. And perhaps she does not even like me — though I think she does."

"If you caught Zorro and got the reward, you would be a man of substance," suggested Diego.

"I have not given up that idea," Burke assured him. "And I still think Zorro heads the cattle thieves and that he shot your father. If I have your permission, I might take to my saddle and prowl around some tonight again."

"You have my permission, Señor Burke, and also my advice if you care for it."

"I'm listening."

"Do not ride too early. Wait until the *vaqueros* take to their huts. Zorro may have a spy among them, to ride out and warn him when you start riding."

"I was thinking of taking a little rest first."

"A wise decision," Diego observed.

They separated and went to their own rooms. Diego waited for a short time, then extinguished the tapers and stretched on the couch to rest without undressing.

Tonight he would make another blind ride, hoping that he would run across something that would give him a clue. He needed something better, he thought, than a small ornament that may have dropped from almost any rider's bridle. The fact that it had been found near the place of last night's slaughter might mean nothing, he knew. It could have been dropped from the bridle of a passing rider long before.

A little earlier than the night before, he slipped noiselessly from the house. Unseen, he got to the old winery and found Bernardo waiting for him there. Zorro's horse, costume and weapons were ready. And tonight Bernardo had his riding mule, for he was to ride with Zorro.

"Has any man yet taken his horse from the private corral?" he asked the mute.

Bernardo signaled 'no'.

The Zorro costume was donned, the blade buckled on and the pistol put into his sash after Zorro had examined it.

"We must use great care tonight," he told Bernardo. "You will ride a short distance behind me, unless I signal for you to advance. Do not mount yet. I am waiting for the Americano to get his horse.

Chapter XVI
Riders of the Night

FLEECY clouds were in the sky tonight, and they blotted out the light of the moon at times. But the moon was shining brightly when Diego and Bernardo saw a man go to the private corral and saddle a horse. Barney Burke was preparing for his night ride.

Zorro signaled to Bernardo as Burke rode away from the corral. They mounted and started following, careful not to be seen. Burke took to the trail which ran toward the mission, but left it after he had gone no more than a mile, and rode up over a hill. Zorro and Bernardo followed.

Zorro was wondering whether Burke was searching for another night camp where men would be sprawled around a small fire. There still remained the possibility that Burke, despite his act of rushing to a woman's aid, was connected with the cattle thieves.

For a moment, as they reached the top of the hill, Zorro and Bernardo were in silhouette against the light sky. But they got to shadows quickly and rode on. Burke was following an old trail made by cattle, and was traveling at an ordinary rate of speed.

No sounds except the usual night noises and the patter of hoofs from Burke's bay pony reached them. The wind was moderate, and blowing toward them. Burke could not hear the hoofbeats of Zorro's horse and Bernardo's mule, Diego felt sure.

They were about halfway to the Mission of San Gabriel when clouds blotted out the moon. They rode on cautiously, listening for the hoofbeats of Burke's pony. They did not want to run into the Americano if he had stopped on the trail.

The moon appeared again to bathe the land in silvery light. No moving shadow revealed where Burke was riding. There were no sounds from his pony's hoofs.

"We have lost him, Bernardo," Zorro whispered. "Perhaps I can pick him up again somewhere. We will stop here at the end of the canyon. You will go into hiding and await me as usual, and I shall ride on."

Bernardo's guttural sound indicated he understood. The mute rode into a patch of darkness beside a ledge of rock and dismounted. Zorro rode on, leaving him there as a sort of relay station in case of necessity. It was a game they had played before.

With sudden determination, Zorro began riding toward the distant mission. He supposed that Vargas had gone there for refuge after his expulsion from the rancho, perhaps to wait for the next day when he would return to Reina de Los Angeles.

Nearing the mission, Zorro redoubled caution. Only a few torches burned around the buildings. The gates of the compound were closed. No riders or vehicles were on the trail leaving or approaching the place.

Another short season of darkness gave Zorro a chance to get near the mission wall. When the moon came out again, he was where the wall cast a deep shadow. He rode slowly along the wall. He knew the mission well, had from his boyhood days. And now he stopped near an open barred window through which light streamed, coming from a small room where the padres often met to eat their broth and discuss their affairs before seeking their pallets.

He heard Fray Felipe talking to another Franciscan.

"It is a lamentable affair," Fray Felipe was saying. "That a man of his blood could stoop so low, forget his lineage and even common decency. It is deplorable."

"There is much sin in the world," the other *padre* said.

"And many sinners. I hope the affair of the cattle thieves is soon cleared away. The mission cannot afford much more loss."

"We here at the mission are somewhat disturbed, Fray Felipe, because of the presence of these two men in the guest house. I desire to ask your advice concerning them. I mean Señor Vargas and the man with him, Señor Ramirez."

"They are in the guest house, you say?"

"Not at present. They rode away some time ago, saying they were going on a short journey and would return before dawn, and warning us to have the gate guard let them in."

"They did not say where they were going?"

"No, Fray Felipe. What shall we do about them?"

"It is against our rules to deny the guest house to any person, within reason," Fray Felipe replied. "Be he saint or sinner, he is entitled to shelter. Let us wait and see what occurs. Perhaps Marcos Vargas and his friend will return to Reina de Los Angeles tomorrow."

"Let us hope so."

"As I must now be returning to Rancho Vega," Fray Felipe continued. "I must be there early in the morning."

OUTSIDE the window, Zorro backed his horse for a distance, waited until the moon went behind another cloud, then rode away from the wall. He started back toward the spot where he had left Bernardo.

So Vargas and Ramirez were riding abroad tonight. That might mean a deal or nothing. It may mean only another of Vargas' meetings with some woman. Or it could mean that Vargas was up to some devilment by way of revenge against Burke or the Vegas or both.

Diego had made an error when he had decided that Sergeant Garcia and his men would spend the night in some cozy canyon emptying wineskins.

Though not concerned particularly about the theft and slaying of cattle belonging to the mission, Garcia had not forgotten that Zorro had been riding the night before and might be riding again tonight. And the Governor's reward was still unclaimed.

So Sergeant Garcia took his four troopers on regular patrol, and rode the trails and over the hills, watching for suspicious shadows in the moonlight.

Zorro, riding back toward the spot where he had left Bernardo, also watched the shadows, and kept off the skyline, where he could have been seen easily from a distance under the bright moon.

No scent of smoke was in the air. The wind carried to his ears no voices to arouse his suspicion. No cattle bawled in the distance, as cattle will at the smell of blood, to indicate that some were being slaughtered.

Tonight's ride would be fruitless also, Zorro decided. He would ride on and contact Bernardo, and they would make their way home cautiously.

To get to Bernardo's hiding place, still some distance away, Zorro was compelled to cross the brow of a hill, and for a short time was exposed as a dark shadow riding against the moonlit sky. He thought he heard a shout in the distance, but it was not repeated, and he finally decided he had heard nothing out

of the ordinary.

But, as he rode on, he heard a hoof strike rock, and glanced back quickly. Five men were coming over the hill he had just crossed. They were only a short distance behind. The moonlight glinted from sabres, and he knew Garcia and his men were after him.

Zorro gave his horse the spurs and raced over level ground where the going was comparatively safe. He heard Garcia yell a command, and knew the pursuit was on.

Zorro had run away from the troopers several times before in his career, and he knew his big black horse was more than a match for any animal a trooper bestrode. He made haste to put as much distance as possible between himself and the pursuit. Then he would lose the troopers and rejoin Bernardo and make his way home while Garcia and his men engaged in a futile search for him.

He rode behind a long ledge of rock, emerged on another level space, and raced across it. Stopping his mount, he listened. The pursuit was far behind and had swerved toward the south. He was losing Garcia again, as he had planned.

Zorro rode on at a more leisurely rate of speed. But he heard a sudden clatter of hoofbeats behind him, and saw a lone rider racing toward him. He had evaded the troopers, but here came Señor Barney Burke, the man ambitious to capture or kill Zorro and earn the Governor's rich reward.

Burke had been prowling the hills alone after Zorro and Bernardo had lost him earlier in the night. He had heard the sounds of pursuit when the troopers had been in chase, and had watched while Zorro shook them off. And now he was coming on alone after the phantomlike Zorro, willing to risk a fight in an effort to make a capture.

Zorro gave his black the spurs again. He remembered that Burke was a man who knew how to track and trail, and he would not be easy to dodge.

Down into a canyon he knew, where the floor was sandy and free of treacherous rocks, Zorro rode swiftly. His horse's hoofs made but little sound in the soft earth. But they did kick up the fine dust, and Burke saw it drifting away on the wind through the bright moonlight, and so knew where Zorro rode. Racing along the side of the canyon, Burke placed himself opposite his quarry.

AGAIN, Zorro heard the clatter of a horse's hoofs on hard ground above, and realized what Burke had done. He stopped his horse abruptly, allowed Burke to ride on ahead, then urged the black up the side of the canyon and to the higher ground behind the man who was seeking him.

But this was Zorro's unlucky night. His horse stumbled, and limped when Zorro started him on. And Burke glanced back and saw Zorro in the moonlight before he could get to the nearest patch of darkness!

"Stop, Zorro, or I'll shoot!" Burke yelled.

Zorro risked laming the black forever by using his spurs. Except as a last resort, he did not want to exchange shots with the Americano and possibly kill him or wound him seriously. Getting into the darkness, Zorro raced on.

When he had an opportunity to look back, he saw that Burke had lost ground by passing on the wrong side of a ledge. Zorro found his horse limping badly.

But he was not far from where Bernardo waited.

He knew that his horse was in no condition for a race with Burke's swift bay pony, even here over rough ground which Zorro knew better than the man who followed. Besides, he did not want to lame the black beyond repair.

Nor did he want to go to the extreme of shooting the Americano out of his saddle in order to escape. And he did not wish to be captured or slain himself.

If he could get to Bernardo in time, they could use the old decoy trick they had used against the soldiers several times. That was for Zorro to swing aside on his jaded horse and let Bernardo dash away on his fresh riding mule. So the pursuit would follow Bernardo, who would get away, and Zorro would be safe.

As Zorro rode on, making what speed he could and maintaining the distance between Burke and himself, he had another idea. He would change the usual procedure slightly. He could not hope to hide the black where Bernardo waited, and Burke might not be decoyed away.

He would lead Burke and the soldiers into a new way of thinking. Bernardo would ride. Zorro would abandon the horse, and leave Zorro's overall costume and mask and his weapons beside it. Burke would think Zorro had left his lame horse and trappings there and had ridden away on a fresh mount, to appear elsewhere as himself, whoever he might be.

He gave a peculiar shrill call as he rode on, which was his signal to Bernardo to be ready. Burke was pounding along behind him. A pistol barked, but the ball did not pass anywhere near Zorro.

But the shot was heard. Garcia and his troopers had swung back toward their old course and were not far away. The soldiers rode toward the sound of the shot.

On toward the jumble of rocks Zorro raced. He glanced back to see Burke riding through the moonlight, and knew he had gained a little time, enough for his purpose. He brought the lame black to a stop beside Bernardo.

"Ride!" he ordered the mute. "Lose the Americano, and go home."

Bernardo kicked at the flanks of his riding mule, and was gone, bending low over the mule's neck. He rode purposely into the moonlight to attract the attention of the pursuer.

CHAPTER XVII
The Capture

ZORRO dismounted quickly and dropped the reins over the head of his heaving horse. Working swiftly, he got off the Zorro costume and tossed it on the ground with the black hood and mask. His blade was left there also. He retained only his pistol.

He could hear Burke coming on toward the rocks. Zorro got up among them in a good hiding place. He would remain there until Burke had gone on, then get back to the rancho. If Burke stopped and found the horse and Zorro's costume, he would race on after the mule, thinking Zorro had gone on a fresh horse.

But more ill luck came to Zorro then. As Burke came thundering toward the rocks, the black horse took a few steps and revealed himself in the moonlight. Burke made a quick stop.

"Come out, Zorro!" he shouted. "I see your horse and know you are there."

In hiding, Zorro wondered what the Americano thought of the mule's hoofbeats. Perhaps he would believe Zorro did not ride alone, but had a confederate, or had simply abandoned the horse and costume to ride on as a simple citizen.

Burke rode into the shadows and dismounted. He was only a shadow himself as he moved among the rocks toward the black. And Zorro heard his exclamation of surprise as he stumbled over the costume and struck the sword with his foot and made it clatter among the rocks.

He could almost guess what Burke was thinking — that Zorro had ridden on and now was too far in the lead to be overtaken. From his hiding place, Zorro watched Burke as he examined the black. Then he picked up the costume and inspected it, and looked at the sword also. And so he was standing, holding the

"Come out, Zorro!" he shouted. "I see your horse and know you are there."

Zorro costume in his hands, when there was another sudden clatter of hoofs against rocks and Sergeant Manuel Garcia and his men, pistols held ready, rode into the scene.

"Now we have you, Zorro!" Garcia cried. "One move, and you are a dead man! Put up your arms and hold your hands high! In the Governor's name!"

"I am not Zorro, you fool!" Burke barked at him.

"Ha!" Garcia said. " 'Tis the Americano! A pretty chase you have given us, señor, but this is the end. Marcos Vargas was not so wrong as I thought him to be when he told me you were Zorro."

Two of the troopers had dismounted. They rushed forward suddenly and seized Burke. There was a short struggle, then the Americano was on the ground, and his wrists were being lashed behind his back.

"You fool!" Burke raged at Garcia. "I was chasing Zorro. He left his horse and clothes here and rode away on a fresh horse."

"I heard no man riding away."

"I tell you I am not Zorro!"

"We find you here," Garcia said, "beside your black horse, with Zorro's clothes in your hands and his sword on the ground at your feet. That is evidence enough. I take you to Rancho Vega, Americano, and let everybody know you are Zorro and that I have caught you. That is to establish my right to the reward. If the *vaqueros* take you from me afterward and hang you, what can I do?"

"You fool!"

"Hard words will avail you nothing now, señor. It may please you to know that I have not been blind. I suspected you from the first moment I saw you in Reina de Los Angeles. I did not believe the yarn you told, and sent a messenger to San Diego de Alcalá to inquire into your activities."

"Idiot!" Burke screeched. "There is my pony!"

"Oh yes, señor, I perceive the trick you would have used. You ride here on the black, leave the black and your things and ride on, using your pony. And no doubt a confederate will appear later to take care of the horse and other things."

As Zorro watched from the rocks, they got Burke into the pony's saddle and lashed him there. They bundled up Zorro's clothes and blade and tied them in the saddle of the black.

"One of you lead the black horse," Garcia commanded his troopers. "And one of you remain here in the rocks until dawn, to see if a confederate comes. If so, seize or shoot him. We go now, Señor Zorro, to the Rancho Vega. This is your last ride on a moonlight night, so try to enjoy it."

From the rocks, Zorro watched. Garcia and three of his men took the luckless Burke away, and the black horse also. And one trooper remained to await the appearance of a possible confederate.

For some time, Zorro made no move. He wanted the trooper below to feel secure and cease listening to every sound. It was his object now to overpower the trooper in some manner, take his horse and hurry to the rancho. There, he would get into the house and reappear as Diego Vega.

And it occurred to him that he was Diego Vega at this moment. His Zorro costume with its mask had gone on with Garcia and his men. He was in his own clothing. Even if he covered his face with a handkerchief, the trooper might remember the clothing afterward. It was one time when he would have to use violence.

Cautiously he wormed his way silently down among the rocks, continually watching the trooper. The man was strolling around as if to rid his limbs of saddle fatigue. His horse was standing not far away with the reins trailing.

Finally, the trooper did what Diego had been wishing he would do. He went to his horse and off the saddle-horn took a wineskin with some wine remaining in it. He tilted the skin and swallowed, then returned to the edge of the pile of rocks and sat down on a flat one in the darkness. He was directly beneath Diego.

Though Diego had retained his pistol, he did not intend to shoot the trooper, who probably was some dull fellow only doing his duty, and with no personal animosity against Zorro. But the pistol would make a good weapon, nevertheless, being heavy. A blow from the metal barrel in the right spot would render the trooper helpless. And Diego had to make haste. Barney Burke's life might depend on that haste.

The wind had increased and was whistling among the rocks. What slight sounds Diego made in his descent were drowned by the singing wind. The trooper below was giving serious attention to the wineskin, and during lulls in the wind, Diego could hear him muttering to himself.

Diego crawled nearer and finally was a pace behind the unsuspecting trooper. The fellow dropped the wineskin, and bent forward, grunting, to pick it up. Diego struck once with the barrel of the heavy pistol. The trooper groaned and sprawled forward.

Springing over the prostrate body, Diego raced to the trooper's horse and got into saddle. He touched with his spurs and rode.

He knew that Garcia and his men, burdened with a prisoner and an extra horse, would not travel swiftly. Moreover, Garcia would lose time getting over to the main trail instead of cutting across country. Diego took the latter route.

He rode cautiously, for he was himself now, not Zorro. A mere sight of him, and recognition of his identity, might arouse suspicion and call for an explanation he could not give. He kept in dark depressions as much as possible, reached the rancho and circled the buildings to come to the old winery. From the darkness, Bernardo answered Diego's cautious signal.

Diego rode in and dismounted. Speaking swiftly, he told Bernardo all that had happened.

"Remain here until I come again," he ordered. "I may be quite some time. Keep this horse here, in hiding."

Then he was away afoot, streaking through the dark spots to get to the house.

The fires in front of the huts were almost dead, and only a few men were strolling around. Diego reached the house unseen. None of the guests were in the patio enjoying the moonlight.

He got into his room, got out of his clothes and took from a closet a darker suit of apparel, which he put to one side on a stool. Then, with dressing gown wrapped around him, he waited.

There was not long for him to wait. He heard hoofs beating in front of the rancho house, then a loud summons from the throat of Sergeant Garcia.

Diego heard servants scampering through the house, and knew that tapers were being lit. Loud voices shattered the night, for Garcia was advertising his success well. Presently, Diego heard Cassara's voice as he gave some of the men directions. Then came a summons at his own door.

Diego rumpled his hair, grumbled something, and pretended he had been awakened. He opened the door to find Cassara there holding a taper. The overseer was excited.

"Don Diego!" Cassara said. "Zorro has been captured by the troopers!"

"Zorro caught? I must dress and come at once."

"And Zorro is — the Americano!"

"Ridiculous!" Diego exclaimed.

"I fear it is so, Don Diego. They found him with the black horse and Zorro's clothing and sword."

"I cannot believe it. Awaken Fray Felipe and my father and tell them the news. Ask them to meet me immediately on the veranda. And tell Sergeant Garcia to await us there. This is a serious business."

CASSARA hurried on the errand. Diego lit a taper and dressed swiftly in the dark clothes. Then, yawning and pretending he disliked having been disturbed, he went down the hallway and through the main room of the house. Some of the men guests had heard the commotion and were gathered there already. They followed Diego out to the veranda.

Servants had fired the torches in front of the house, and there was abundant light. Garcia was strutting around boasting of his success. Burke was still tied in the saddle of his bay pony. One of Garcia's troopers was missing. He had gone to inform the *vaqueros* of Zorro's capture.

"What is this, Sergeant Garcia?" Diego demanded.

"Ah, Don Diego, amigo! Here he is at last, the famous Zorro captured! They cannot avoid Manuel Garcia forever."

"The man you have is Señor Burke, the Americano, and my guest."

"He is also Zorro. I was suspicious of him when first I set eyes on him. A pretty game he played, but we have him now! He will soon stretch rope. Don Marcos Vargas was right when he said you were harboring a criminal here."

Fray Felipe and Don Alejandro, Diego's father in a robe, had come out upon the veranda in time to hear.

"We harbor no criminals, señor!" Don Alejandro thundered at the sergeant.

"Ah, I do not mean knowingly, Don Alejandro, but nevertheless here he is, the man who imposed upon your hospitality. We found him beside his black horse, with Zorro's clothes and blade in his hands. We seized him before he could offer fight, after a long pursuit."

Diego held up his hand for silence.

"Señor Burke, what have you to say?" he asked.

"This sergeant is a fool!" Burke raged. "He found me as he says, but I am not Zorro. I was chasing Zorro and almost had him. He left this black horse and his clothes behind and got away on another mount. I was inspecting the clothes when this imbecile of a sergeant grabbed me."

A chorus of mutterings approached through the night, and around a corner of the house came a crowd of *vaqueros*, some of them half-dressed. At sight of the prisoner on his horse, they began shouting.

"Silence!" Don Alejandro roared at them.

They grew quiet to listen to him.

"I ask you not to judge quickly, and perhaps rashly, señores," the master of Rancho Vega said. "There are circumstances yet to be investigated."

Some of the *vaqueros* began shouting:

"Hang the rogue! Let him stretch rope!"

"Silence!" Diego shouted in support of his father. "Would you hang an innocent man? And this man may be innocent. Moreover, he is entitled to a fair trial before the *magistrado* in Reina de Los Angeles. Sergeant Garcia!"

"Don Diego?"

"Do not let your wish to claim the reward blind you to justice," Diego said. "If a mistake is made here, you will be driven from the soldiery in disgrace and perhaps punished yourself. It is your duty to guard this prisoner until he is before the court, if he is not proved innocent before that can be done."

"How can he be innocent, Don Diego? And I know my duty, without the son of a hidalgo even, trying to tell me of it."

"Are you daring to be insolent to my son?" Don Alejandro shouted. "Why, you miserable worm of a bloated sergeant! I'll have you and your men run off the rancho by my *vaqueros*. They have little love for the soldiery."

"Treason!" Garcia cried.

"You, Sergeant Garcia, are an ass!" Don Alejandro declared. "Do as I say! We will put the horse in the private corral, and put the clothes and sword in a store hut. We will put the prisoner in an empty hut and make him comfortable, for his guilt is in doubt. Then we will make a proper investigation, calmly, and coolly when passions are not aroused."

"String him up!" a *vaquero* in the back of the crowd yelled.

"Why should you *vaqueros* wish to hang him?" Diego called. "I doubt he is Zorro. Even if he is, has Zorro ever harmed any of you? Will you share in the reward for his capture? No! Sergeant Garcia will get it all."

The *vaqueros* began muttering again. One stepped forward.

"Don Diego, Zorro is accused of having shot Don Alejandro, your illustrious father, of slaying two men, and of leading a band of rogues who have been stealing and slaying mission cattle. That is why we wish to hang him!"

CHAPTER XVIII
Zorro Reappears

LIGHTLY Fray Felipe touched Diego on the arm, and Diego stepped aside. Then the emaciated, white-haired old *padre* lifted his arms so that the loose sleeves of his robe fell down below the elbows.

"My sons," he called, "there are several things to be considered here. Do not take human life rashly. The man is entitled to a fair trial. Let us wait for another day, at least, before a move is made. Here is one reason, my sons. Zorro, if leader of the cattle thieves, must have accomplices. It is our desire to capture all, is it not? Hang this man now, and his tongue is silent forever. Let him live, and perhaps a little questioning may bring forth information we wish to have."

They could understand that. And the *padre*'s quiet voice soothed them. They began shuffling around, and one could almost see their angry passions die.

Diego had walked along the veranda a short distance, and now looked down and straight into the eyes of Burke. Diego winked at him and inclined his head a little.

"Retire to your huts, my sons, and rest for tomorrow's work," Fray Felipe told the *vaqueros*. "Trust me in this affair, as you have trusted me in many things. And Sergeant Garcia will do as he has been told regarding the prisoner. Tomorrow, heads will be clearer and we can all think better."

The *vaqueros* began slipping away around the corner of the house like men ashamed. Garcia's face was the picture of rage.

"Who is in command of the soldiery here?" he bellowed. "Who should tell me what to do?"

"I, for one, tell you!" Frey Felipe replied sternly. "I desire justice, and nothing more. Would it be a bright spot on your record if men took a prisoner away from you and hanged him? And think. Señor Sergeant! Perhaps it would be said afterward that there was not sufficient proof the man is Zorro, and the big reward be denied you. Let us get all information we can."

"There is something in what you say," Garcia agreed. "It shall be as Don Alejandro and Don Diego asked."

Diego went with them. Garcia put Burke into an empty adobe hut near the private corral, and placed one of his troopers on guard. The hut had one door and one barred window, and the walls and floor were almost as hard as granite.

The black horse's saddle and bridle were removed, and the mount was turned into the private corral. Saddle and bridle were placed beside the gate with others.

Zorro's costume and sword remained tied to the saddle.

"Garcia, I forgive your harsh remarks at the veranda," Diego said. "You are being sensible now."

"I ask your pardon, Don Diego. But I was so elated and excited. I see now how wise you and your father and the *padre* were. Had the rogue been hanged forthwith, there may have been a question afterward about his identity and the reward denied me. And what now, Don Diego?"

"Let us all get some sleep. I need it, and I am sure you and your men do. The *vaqueros* will not bother the prisoner. In the morning, we will question him and get the truth out of him.

"And the rogue's attire and sword?"

"Leave them fastened to the saddle and be kept as evidence," Diego replied.

Garcia and the others went away, Garcia to the hut assigned to him for use during the great slaughter, after Diego had whispered he would send a servant with a skin of the rancho's best wine. He sent some to the other troopers, too, including the hut guard.

The rancho settled down to sleep the remaining hours until dawn. Diego returned to his room, but not to sleep. His father and Fray Felipe were awaiting him.

"What a tangle!" Diego told them. "Since we all know that the Americano is not Zorro, he must be rescued. Zorro will have to do that."

"Then everyone will think Burke is an associate of Zorro's, and it will be almost as bad for him as before," said Don Alejandro.

"I have certain plans," Diego admitted.

"We are no nearer solving the affair of the mission cattle than before," the *padre* observed.

"I shall continue to work on that, *padre*," Diego assured him. "Do both of you get to bed now, and leave me to my own devices."

LATER, Diego slipped out of the house by his usual route. Through the shadows he hurried to the winery, where he told Bernardo what else had occurred.

"We will go to the private corral," he instructed. "My black horse and Señor Burke's bay pony are both there. You will get them out quietly and saddle them, while I attend to the guard. I will come to the corral later."

Together, they hurried through the night. Bernardo had handled the black for Zorro continually. And he had made friends with Burke's bay the day of the race in town, and knew he could get him out of the corral without noise or trouble.

So Bernardo went to the corral when they separated, and Diego in the direction of the hut in which the prisoner was confined. The heady wine had done its work. The trooper on guard was snoring, stretched in front of the door.

Diego hurried to the corral, where Bernardo had the black ready and was saddling the bay. Working swiftly, Diego got into Zorro's costume and buckled on the blade. He adjusted the hood mask.

"Tie the bay to the corner post," he instructed Bernardo. "Then return to the winery. Put up the reins of the troopers horse and let him wander. Wait for me there as usual."

Zorro mounted and rode through the shadows to a spot near the hut, where he dismounted and trailed the reins. Afoot and on tiptoe, he went on to the hut.

"Señor Burke!" he called softly through the window, in the voice of Zorro.

Burkes reply was prompt. "Who's there?"

"I am Zorro. I am here to rescue you, but you must do as I say. You will lose your life tomorrow if you do not. The guard of the hut is drunk and asleep. Be ready to come out."

Zorro went to the front of the hut, stepped over the body of the snoring guard, and unfastened the heavy latch and bar on the door. Burke was standing there ready to emerge.

"One thing I ask of you — do not try to learn my identity," Zorro said. "I am saving your life because you were taken for me. I have your pony ready, and will conduct you to a safe place. No time is to be lost. Help me put the drunken guard into the hut."

"I swore to hunt you down and claim the reward, Zorro," Burke said. "Did you know that? I have changed my mind now."

"Work more and talk less," Zorro whispered. "Men may be up and around the huts."

They put the guard into the hut, and Zorro closed and barred the door.

"Hurry to the corral and get your pony, Señor Burke, "Zorro ordered. "I'll join you there in a moment. Be careful you are not seen."

Burke went quietly through the shadows. Zorro got into his own saddle, joined Burke at the corral, and they rode through the orchard. Then they got speed out of their mounts.

"I am taking you to a cave a few miles away," Zorro said. "Remain in hiding with your pony until I come for you again. Your recapture would mean your immediate execution. Remember that. I'll get food to you as soon as I can. Here is my pistol for your protection. It is unloaded, but I will leave supplies for the loading."

"I would not cover you and take you prisoner after this," Burke declared, "but I don't blame a man in your place for being careful."

"Swear to me one thing. Have you any connection with the mission cattle thieves?"

"I swear I have not!" Burke said, with sincerity.

"I believe you. Have you any suspicions regarding them? For instance, do you think I am their leader?"

"I thought so once, but now I have my doubts."

""Truth for truth. I swear to you I have nothing to do with them."

An hour later, he put Burke into a large cave in a canyon, where the pony also could be kept out of sight. A spring of sweet water was in the cave, but no food.

"Do not show yourself," Zorro warned. "A little hunger for both you and your pony is better than hanging for you."

He waved aside Burke's thanks and spurred away.

Diego was up at an early hour, even after the fatigue of the night's adventures, though his face revealed the strain under which he had been laboring. He greeted his guests at the morning meal and bade them amuse themselves during the day, saying that he had work to do. They laughed at the idea of Don Diego Vega engaging in exertion of any sort.

The *vaqueros* were working like madmen at the canyon, slaughtering cattle, taking hides, doing the things that were necessary. The peon crews were laboring more than usual. Cassara explained the reason to Diego.

"The *vaqueros* are crazy to ride the hills tonight in search of Zorro," the overseer reported. "His mysterious escape from the hut cannot be explained. The *vaqueros*, and Garcia and his men, believe somebody helped him."

"It appears so," Diego declared.

"Garcia put the hut guard under military arrest. And he swears that he will never rest until he recaptures Zorro — that is to say, Señor Burke — and that when he does he will see him hanged immediately."

"Garcia is a bloodthirsty man," Diego observed, "especially when he has lost a reward."

"Never have I been so fooled in a man," Cassara said. "And my Nita — "

"What of her?" Diego asked, as the overseer stopped speaking.

"She is beside herself with grief. It seems she was attracted to the Americano, I presume because he beat Vargas when she was insulted. She scarcely can do her work for weeping."

"We will have to dry her tears, Cassara. Nita is a splendid girl, and deserves happiness."

"I thank you, Don Diego. I have tried to make a worthy daughter of her — Ah, here comes Sergeant Garcia now!"

Garcia came riding up as Cassara went away to attend to his duties. The burly sergeant revealed in his countenance that he had taken too much wine the night before. That same countenance also revealed that he was in a towering rage.

"Don Diego, I am a determined man," he said. "I dedicate my life to retaking this confounded Zorro. Also the men who helped him get away. A dozen of them, the hut guard declares, but I know he lies. Perhaps no more than half a dozen."

"Perhaps," Diego agreed.

"I do not wish to reproach a highborn like you, Don Diego, but let me suggest that hereafter you allow soldiers to attend to their own affairs. Instead of listening to you last night, I should have had the rogue whipped into a confession and then had him hanged straightway. Then he would not have escaped. I must retake him now, or suffer reprimand from my *commandante*. And my record is black enough already. I may be reduced in rank."

"I am sure everything will terminate satisfactorily," Diego told him.

"I and my men will rest today and ride abroad again tonight. I have sent word for my two troopers at the mission to stop eating and swilling wine there and join me."

"All this talk of chasing and bandits is fatiguing," Diego complained. "And I must manage this slaughter when my father is unable to do so."

"Be wise, amigo," Garcia said. "Let Juan Cassara and the *jefe vaquero* run things, and return to the house and get some rest."

"That is an excellent idea, and I thank you for it," Diego replied. "I shall act upon it at once."

Chapter XIX
One of the Guilty

JUST exactly what Diego wanted was a chance to rest and prepare for the work of the night. But he had wanted somebody else to suggest it. He turned over everything to Cassara and rode back to the rancho house.

During the remainder of the day he slept most of the time, and had food brought to him, sending out word to the guests that he was running a fever. He avoided the evening meal also, but sent out word that he hoped to dispense hospitality tomorrow.

His father and Fray Felipe visited him after the evening meal.

"I must ride tonight," Diego told them. "This thing must be cleared up if possible, and I am well rested. Most of the *vaqueros* will be riding the hills, and the soldiers also, but I must chance it."

"Have you any clues, Diego?" his father asked.

"None of any real consequence. Good fortune must attend me and put me on the right trail."

"You must use great caution tonight, Diego," his father warned. "In Zorro's clothing, you will be a target for all."

"One thing pleases me greatly," Diego told them. "My black was almost over his lameness when I used him last night to set the Americano free. Bernardo found the cause of the trouble, a pebble in the frog of one hoof. You may be sure that Bernardo has doctored him today, and tonight the horse will be capable of swift hard work."

Soon after nightfall, he could hear the *vaqueros* shouting as they ate and prepared for the night's patrol. Later, he heard them riding away. He knew where most of them would be riding, for, during the afternoon, he had written out a system of patrols and had given it to Cassara. So pairs of the riders could be assigned to certain districts. But Garcia and the troopers — Diego did not know where they might be riding.

At a late hour, he slipped out of the house, carrying a bundle of cold food which Fray Felipe had got from the kitchen, hinting without actually lying that he wanted it for a poor peon's family. And he had a skin of wine.

He found Bernardo at the winery. Diego got into the Zorro costume, looked to his weapons, and mounted the black.

"Remain here," he told Bernardo, "and be ready to care for the horse. I have no idea when I may return."

Though he rode slowly and with caution, it did not take him long to reach the cave. Burke appeared at his signal, and gave thanks for the food and wine.

"Stay hidden yet a while, amigo," Zorro instructed, "and all may be well. Listen for my signal, for I may ride this way again tonight. Nita Cassara is weeping, I understand, because she thinks you are a criminal and pursued, if that gives you a feeling of comfort."

Zorro spurred away. He rode in the direction of the distant mission, with no particular destination in mind. He decided to go into hiding whenever one or more riders approached him. He was hoping that he might run across a few peons around a fire, or something like that, and have a chance to question men who might accidentally give him some clue.

Twice he rode behind brush to let searching *vaqueros* pass near him, then emerged and went on. He caught no odor of fire smoke, heard no suspicious sounds.

Then, after quite a time of riding, good fortune came to him. He saw a lone rider come over the brow of a low hill against the moon and ride down the slope straight toward him.

Zorro swung the black behind some rocks and watched. He had no fear of a lone rider. The man came on, letting his horse walk down the slope, and stopped at the bottom in the bright moonlight within a short distance of Zorro.

Zorro drew in his breath sharply as he recognized the man. Here was Pedro Ramirez, Vargas' slimy companion, riding through the night alone.

Zorro got his pistol out of his sash and jumped the black out from behind the rocks and in front the other.

"Hands in the air, señor, and quickly!" Zorro barked.

Pedro Ramirez gave a frightened squawk, saw the weapon that menaced him, and put up his hands.

"Señor Ramirez, I believe," Zorro said. "Be steady while I get the pistol you are carrying. A wrong move, señor, and the devil will welcome a newcomer to his hot habitation."

RAMIREZ seemed too frightened to speak. He made no hostile move as Zorro rode up and got the pistol and backed his horse away again.

"You — you are — ?" Ramirez finally managed to ask.

"Zorro!"

"And you wish to rob me?"

"I rob nobody," Zorro snapped at him. "Is this not a strange place for you to be riding at this time of the night?"

"I was returning to the mission and lost my way."

"Returning from where?" Zorro demanded.

"From a peon sheepherder's hut, señor. He has a pretty daughter."

"Perhaps you were riding abroad like so many others, trying to catch me and earn the reward, eh?" Zorro asked.

"I would not dare try a thing like that, señor, believe me."

"I believe you," Zorro said. He rode closer again, bent in his saddle while still holding the pistol ready, and gave a sudden exclamation. "Señor Ramirez! What a careless fellow you are! I see where you have lost one of the silver ornaments off your bridle."

"I had not noticed it," Ramirez said. "It is nothing."

"It is most important, señor. The fact of its loss compels me to ask you some questions. Where did you lose it?"

"I have no idea, Señor Zorro."

"Does it interest you to know that I have the lost ornament in my pocket, señor? It was found beside a dead fire at a place where stolen mission cattle were slaughtered for their hides. It is now time for you to speak, Señor Ramirez!"

Even in the bright moonlight, Zorro could see the expression of fright that came into Ramirez' face.

"I — I scarcely know what to say," Ramirez gulped.

"Try speaking the truth for once, señor. You are concerned in the theft and slaying of mission cattle, are you not? Do not dare insult me with a falsehood, or will pistol you as I would a mad coyote."

"I — I know nothing, señor."

"Understand me, Señor Ramirez. I have been accused of being leader of the band of men committing this atrocity against a Franciscan mission. I clear my name of this only when I expose those guilty. Perhaps your own guilt is not so great as that of another. It is possible your own punishment can be lessened if you put me on the proper trail. Is my speech clear to you, Señor Ramirez?"

"I — I think I understand, Señor Zorro."

"Then speak, fully and truthfully, or I'll shoot you here and now. I know you, though you do not know Zorro. I know your caliber, señor, and it is that of a jackal, not of a lion. You are working for another, I can guess. His name!"

"It would mean my death to speak it."

"It will mean your instant death if you do not," Zorro warned. "His name — and where can I get the proof? Speak!"

Ramirez could see the pistol raised and leveled in the moonlight. Terror claimed him for a moment and rendered him speechless, then that same terror loosened his tongue.

"Do not fire, Señor Zorro!" Ramirez begged. "I'll tell everything, even if I die for it. But I ask some mercy for myself if I speak."

"Speak!" Zorro lifted the pistol an inch higher.

"There is an organized band of thieves of mission cattle, sí! They slaughter, take the hides, and have them carted to Monterey, where they are sold to swindling traders."

"And the leader?"

"Don Marcos Vargas."

"Ha!" Zorro said. "I thought as much. That is how he gets funds upon which to live, eh?"

"That is so, Señor Zorro."

"And his other enterprises?"

"He is desperate for money, being heavily in debt. The mission cattle are not all. He even tried to play highwayman, but got shot in the shoulder."

"And wounded Don Alejandro Vega?"

"That is true."

"And then went to Rancho Vega and accepted hospitality of the man he wounded? What a low scoundrel! And you, his associate — "

"He attached me to himself several years ago, señor. By serving him, I had money in my pockets always, and I had been poor."

"And to get this money, you did anything he wished?"

"That is true, señor."

"Where is Vargas now? Speak the truth!"

"His men are killing more mission cattle tonight. I have just come from them, to carry a message about the carts. They are in the deep canyon a mile south of here."

"I know the place," Zorro told him. "How many men are there, and who are they?"

About a score of men, señor. And they are nobodies — only peons and natives frightened half the time of their own shadows."

ZORRO was about to reply, but his ears caught the sounds of hoofbeats. With victory so near, he did not intend to give up his prisoner and make a run for it now.

"Ride with me behind those rocks," he ordered Ramirez. "Whatever happens, I'll pistol you if you try to escape. Riders are coming."

Ramirez was too frightened to try treachery. He rode where Zorro ordered, behind rocks within a short distance of the trail, and stopped at Zorro's left.

Two riders were loping along the trail. When they got nearer, Zorro could tell they were troopers.

"Señor Ramirez, those troopers would rather take you than me, if they knew the truth," Zorro said. "Keep quiet and let me handle this."

The troopers came on, and put their horses at a resting walk as they neared the spot where Zorro and his prisoner were hiding. Zorro gasped at sight of them when they were opposite. One was Sergeant Garcia. He warned Ramirez in a whisper again.

"Sergeant Garcia!" he called sharply then.

Garcia and his man stopped their horses at once and looked around at the shadows.

"Who calls?" Garcia bellowed.

"Ride this way, toward the end of the ledge. Here is something to interest you, Sergeant. Hasten, before he gets away!"

The urge to haste wafted aside Garcia's suspicions. This seemed to be a plea for help. He spurred his horse up the sharp slope from the trail, the trooper behind him, and swung toward the end of the ledge.

Then he heard the voice behind him:

"Stop there, both of you! Put up your hands! Do not reach for a weapon, or you both die! Take out your pistols when I say the word, and drop them upon the ground! Now!"

Garcia hesitated. But the thought of an armed man behind him, with the muzzle of a pistol pointed perhaps at the small of his back made Garcia's flesh creep. After all, he was made up more of bluff than of heroic stuff. His hand went to his sash, he drew out his pistol, and dropped it. The trooper did likewise.

"I thank you, señores, and commend you for being sensible," Zorro said. "Turn and face me•."

They turned their mounts.

"Zorro!" Garcia cried.

"The real Zorro, Sergeant, and not the man you took into custody last night. 'Twas I who released him from the hut, because he was mistaken for me."

"And how do I know you are not the same man? A voice can be changed easily."

"I'll prove that later, Sergeant. Attend me! This man on the other horse is Pedro Ramirez, as you probably know. He has just made a confession to me, and I will have him repeat it to you. Here is your chance, Sergeant Garcia, to make a name for yourself, wipe out your errors of last night and possibly win promotion."

"What is this?" the sergeant demanded.

"Señor Ramirez is connected with the mission cattle thieves. He will tell you what he told me. You can report the matter and make a clean sweep of the thieving band, and take the leader in for trial. More men will praise you for that than would praise you for capturing Zorro. In return, I will ask something of you. Speak Ramirez!"

Chapter XX
Renegades End

PEDRO Ramirez told his story again, as Sergeant Garcia listened intently.

"Marcos Vargas!" the sergeant roared, at its conclusion. "I always thought he was a low scoundrel. I thank you, Señor Zorro, for bringing this information to my attention. And I make a deal with you, señor. Tonight, I do as you say. And I make no effort to learn your identity or to capture you — tonight. But after this is over, the old chase is on between us. I catch you if I can, and earn the reward and watch you swing. But tonight, Zorro, the highwayman, and Manuel Garcia, the soldier, ride side by side. And what are your orders, Señor Zorro?"

"Bind Ramirez in his saddle and send him to the rancho guarded by your man. Then, Sergeant, you come with me. If Ramirez should see fit to repudiate his confession, I could not appear to prove him a liar. But you and your trooper have heard him, Sergeant, and that is evidence enough."

Ramirez, pleading for mercy, was trussed up in his saddle, and the trooper took charge of him. They rode away.

"Now, Sergeant, come with me," Zorro said. "Let us ride quickly and make sure none of the searching *vaqueros* get hold of us. There is a thing to be set straight."

They rode swiftly and safely, back to the cave. Zorro gave the signal, and Burke came forth. His eyes bulged when he saw the sergeant.

"What trick is this, Zorro?" Burke demanded. "Are you surrendering me to the soldiers? For what? For being Zorro? Can't the sergeant see now that I am not Zorro, and that you are?"

"That was the object of bringing him here," Zorro said. "I wanted him to see both of us at once, so he would know the truth and you would be released from all blame."

"I am befogged," Garcia complained.

"Now, Sergeant, a favor," Zorro said. "Take Señor Burke to the rancho house and explain and clear his name. There is a little lady there who will be vastly pleased."

"And you?" Garcia questioned.

"I go to capture the arch rogue, the leader of the mission cattle thieves, the man who held up and shot Don Alejandro Vega. I'll bring him to the rancho and confront him with Ramirez."

And on the way possibly have *vaqueros* take after you," Garcia pointed out. "Then, to save yourself you would have to release Vargas. You would not be safe from the *vaqueros*, who have not heard the truth and do not understand. They think Zorro leads the cattle thieves and robs the mission. They do not know he has unmasked the real leader."

"Have you something to suggest?" Zorro asked.

"I'll take Señor Burke to the rancho, pick up my men and get the *vaqueros* there. I'll lead them to the canyon where Vargas and the thieves are working, and we'll pick up more *vaqueros* on the way and tell everybody the truth."

"What else?"

"We'll raid the men in the canyon and capture or kill them all, and have them strung up."

"And possibly kill Vargas — and he is a man I want to handle myself," Zorro said. "Follow your plan, Garcia, but I'll follow you. And I'll show up at the canyon in time to do my part. Speak for me to the *vaqueros* that, for my share in this, they keep hands off me tonight."

" 'Tis done," Garcia said. "Pick us up somewhere along the way."

Zorro trailed them safely through the night. He saw Garcia and a small band of men leave the rancho, and started his trailing. He watched as they picked up more men along the way, as *vaqueros* on patrol joined the ranks. Only twice did Zorro have to go into temporary hiding on the way to avoid capture or fight.

Garcia had almost two score of men under his command when the canyon was reached. Zorro could hear the bawling of cattle, and the wind rushing out of the canyon carried the voices of men.

He never forgot the wild charge Garcia led through the mouth of the canyon. The *vaqueros* screeched as they charged. The slaughtering was being done in an open space bathed in the bright moonlight, and the frightened workers were seized before they could realize what was happening and get away.

Zorro charged in after the others. He was hoping that Garcia had explained to the others plainly, and that no ambitious *vaquero* would try to slay or capture him. And he knew that, the moment his work was done, he would have them all as enemies again.

THE thieves were shrieking as *vaqueros* and troopers rode them down or shot them. For no mercy was given these men who had been stealing cattle from a mission that sold hides to get money to aid the poor and ignorant. The *vaqueros* were devout men, though they had plenty of faults for which to answer.

Zorro was looking for Vargas as he rode, keeping to the shadows as much as possible. Finally he saw the master rogue, standing to one side of a small fire with his arms folded across his breast, offering no fight at all, as if he knew such a thing would be futile. Probably he was trying to think up some story to tell.

Zorro saw troopers surround the man, saw Garcia ride forward, and the *vaqueros* crowding behind the others, those who were not still pursuing the thieves and running them down.

"Señor Vargas, you are under arrest," Garcia thundered at him.

"For what?" Vargas asked.

"Is it necessary to ask? For being the leader of the mission cattle thieves. These other poor scum would not have the brains to engineer such a scheme."

"You are making a mistake, Sergeant," Vargas said calmly. "Order your men to unhand me."

"Why should I?"

"I was riding to a certain place, and was seized by some of these men. They brought me here and told me what work they were doing. I was to be held as hostage, if their leader was caught. I have been their prisoner."

"One side!" Zorro cried suddenly, as he spurred his horse forward.

The *vaqueros* scattered and let him through, and none said a word about his being there or sought to seize him. Zorro stopped his horse within a few feet of Vargas.

"I am the real Zorro," he said, "and not the man you named as Zorro because he gave you a beating. You have been lying, Marcos Vargas."

Sergeant Garcia, seize that man!" Vargas shouted. "Do you not realize he is Zorro? Is there not a big reward?"

"That may come later," Sergeant Garcia told him. "At the moment — What have you to say to this man, Señor Zorro?"

"Vargas, your lies will avail you nothing. Pedro Ramirez has talked and given testimony against you."

"The reprobate!" Vargas said.

"It is known that you are the leader of these thieves, that you turned highwayman and shot Don Alejandro Vega in an attempt at robbery, that you are a common cheat and swindler!"

"Señor!" Vargas cried in interruption. "Whoever you are, whichever face you hide behind that mask, if you were on the ground now I would challenge and slay you, and let these others learn your low identity."

"My blood is better than yours, Vargas, on my word, and never have I disgraced it as have you!" Zorro cried at him.

"I term you coward!"

Zorro tossed the reins over the black's head with one hand, and the next instant was on the ground drawing his blade. He was remembering that this was the man who had almost killed his aged father.

The blades met and rang. The *vaqueros* cheered and got back to give them room. There by the firelight and in the moonlight they fought, around and around, neither having the advantage at first.

Then Zorro began pressing the fighting, having felt out his man and knowing he had nothing to fear from him. Beads of perspiration stood out on Vargas' forehead as Zorro drove him backward while the *vaqueros* gave them more room, and then turned him back toward the fire again.

Their hilts locked once, and their faces were close together.

"Zorro, make an end of it," Vargas whispered. "If you are indeed a caballero, you do not want to see one of noble blood hang, though he has soiled that blood."

They separated, and engaged again. Zorro's blade darted beneath Vargas' guard and was withdrawn crimson, and Marcos Vargas sighed and sank to the ground.

Sergeant Garcia bent over the wounded man, listened to the whisper from his lips, then beckoned Zorro and two of his troopers.

"Be witnesses to this," Garcia said solemnly.

"It is — all true," Vargas whispered. "The shooting of Don Alejandro — the mission cattle thefts — everything." Then he died.

ZORRO backed away from the fire, sheathing his blade, and stopped beside his horse.

"Prepare, some of you, to take this body to the mission," Garcia ordered. "You others round up the prisoners, if any live, and march them there also. Check over the slain. And stand away from Señor Zorro, all of you. He has done people of decency a service tonight. He goes free for the present. But after dawn he is fair game again."

Zorro already was in saddle. He lifted a hand in salute, and the hoofs of his big black horse thundered as he rode ....

Shortly after dawn, there was a tumult at the Rancho Vega. Vaqueros had come riding in, cheering and shouting. Servants ran about the house chattering. Everybody was instantly awake.

The guests gathered in the big room. Don Alejandro appeared in his dressing gown and Fray Felipe in his tattered robe. The news was told. Fray Felipe crossed himself and muttered.

And into the scene walked Diego Vega, his hair rumpled and his eyes seemingly heavy with sleep. He yawned.

"What is all this tumult?" he asked in a weak voice. "Can a man never get sleep in this house? The noise has wrecked a splendid dream."

"Zorro tracked down Vargas, and killed him, my son," Don Alejandro said, as if Diego knew nothing about it. "Vargas confessed he was chief of the cattle thieves, and that Pedro Ramirez was his first assistant. Vargas also was the man who shot me. This Zorro has cleared up the entire situation, it seems."

"What a turbulent fellow he must be," Diego observed. "At least, let us be glad it is over. Now perhaps we can go ahead with the slaughtering and have the *fiesta*, and after that have lives of peace again." He yawned once more. "Pardon me," he added, "but even talking of such exertion as riding and fighting exhausts me."

Some smiled and pitied Don Alejandro as Diego turned away. But he caught sight of one couple that seemed oblivious of all that was being said and done.

Barney Burke and Nita Cassara were standing against the wall in a corner, searching each other's eyes. Diego sensed that the Americanos and Californios were soon to be drawn together, by one couple at least. As he shuffled past them on his way back to bed, he heard Nita whisper.

"Bah-nee," she said.

The *West*

Short Stories

Part 3

Zorro in West Magazine

Zorro became a regular feature in *West* magazine (Better Publications, Inc.), beginning with "Zorro Draws His Blade" (July 1944). Johnson McCulley wrote 52 original Zorro stories for the magazine, with the final installment appearing in 1952.

A Task For Zorro was published in the June 1947 issue. Certain passages in "Zorro's Masked Menace" (July 1947) read almost like a sequel to "A Task For Zorro." Ordinarily, however, the Zorro installments were self-contained, with continuity relegated to background characters.

The short stories in this volume were originally published between 1947 and 1948.

Zorro Saves His Honor

Quick and unerring is the stern justice of the fighting hidalgo when Jose Salvidar commits deeds of lawlessness!

HALF asleep in the patio of his father's house in Reina de los Angeles, Don Diego Vega heard a summons at the door. A moment later he heard his father, gray-haired Don Alejandro, greeting someone. Diego had no interest in the matter, and began perusing his book of poetry again.

But, a few minutes later, he straightened on the bench and put his book aside. He had recognized the voice of the visitor — Pedro Patino, the *superintendente* of the vast Vega rancho near San Gabriel. Patino seemed unusually excited, his voice high and shrill. Something wrong must have happened at the rancho. Generally Patino was soft spoken. Diego got up from the bench and entered the big main room of the house.

Don Alejandro was sitting at one end of the long table, and Patino was standing near him, twisting his sombrero with nervous hands. The *superintendente* ceased speaking and bowed to Diego. Diego sank into a chair beside his father. Don Alejandro explained.

"Diego, my son, thieves have been slaughtering cattle on the rancho and taking the hides," he said. "They have been working in the canyons a distance from the house. A flock of buzzards attracted the attention of one of our vaqueros, who found the carcasses and reported to Patino. He rode here in all haste."

"But thieves have done so before," Diego protested, stifling a yawn. "There are always some rogues slaying a few head of stock for the hides. What is there

in this to cause so much excitement? Have they been slaughtering wholesale?"

Don Alejandro gestured for Patino to take up the tale.

"Don Diego, young master, cattle have been slaughtered in three separate
places," Patino said. "About fifty in all. I could have my vaqueros ride at night
and try to catch the guilty ones. But there is something strange about this affair.
In all three places there has been found, scratched on rocks or marked in the
dirt with a stick, the letter Z."

"This confounded Zorro!" Diego's father exploded. "The masked highwayman who rides the hills and trails and says he is aiding the mistreated and
oppressed."

Diego sat up straight, and his eyes met those of his father squarely, and a
message flashed between them. For Don Diego, adjudged by all to be an indolent dreamer, was also Señor Zorro. His father knew that Zorro had not been
riding for quite some time.

BEFORE Diego could say anything, there came another summons at the
door, and into the room strode Capitán Alarm Sanchez, *commandante* at the
presidio of Reina de los Angeles. Don Alejandro greeted him, and the *capitán*
sat at the table. Patino remained standing.

"I see your rancho overseer has brought you the news," Sanchez said. "I
can add something to it. You, Don Alejandro, are not the only sufferer. Within
the past hour, I have requests for aid from two other rancho owners in the district."

"What do you make of it?" Don Alejandro asked.

"It is plain to me. This Señor Zorro, riding like an outlaw, has glued to him
the peons and natives. He is directing this cattle slaying, you may be sure. No
doubt he has a manner of getting the hides to a safe hiding place and to market.
His poor dupes are working to enrich him. If the thing spreads — " Capitán
Sanchez gestured to indicate that the result might very well be disastrous.

"These turbulent times!" Diego ejaculated. "Capitán Sanchez, why do you
not catch and hang the rogue, so we may have peace?"

Sanchez glared a little. Only that morning, a courier from Monterey had
brought him a sarcastic letter from the governor regarding his failure to capture
Zorro.

"Catching the rascal is no easy matter," Sanchez replied. "Peons aid him
to escape and hide. They lodge and feed him. But we shall get him one of these

days, and strip the mask off his face."

"You have no suspicion as to his identity?" Don Alejandro asked, easily.

"We have suspected almost everybody but it has availed us nothing," Sanchez confessed. "It is my firm belief that this Zorro has come here from some other part of Alta California to play his game."

"And what is your next move, señor?" Don Alejandro asked.

"I am sending Sergeant Garcia and some of my troopers out to the San Gabriel district this evening," Sanchez informed him. "They will watch for strangers, and try to gather information."

"It is in my mind to travel to the rancho myself in the cool of the evening," Don Alejandro declared. "Diego, my son, will you accompany me?"

Diego met his father's eye again. "It will fatigue me, but I'll go with you, father," he replied. "I love the rancho."

Capitán Sanchez took his leave. Don Alejandro gestured at Patino.

"Go to the kitchen and have food and drink," he ordered. "I'll have our carriage made ready."

The overseer bobbed his head and hurried to the kitchen, where he was a prime favorite with the fat cook.

Diego's father looked at him squarely.

"Well, my son?" he asked.

"It has the odor of a trap," Diego said. "Leaving the letter Z about is an attempt to arouse the rancho owners against Zorro, so they will turn their vaqueros loose in a manhunt, eager to capture the rogue."

"The rogue?" Don Alejandro's eyes twinkled.

Diego smiled slightly. "When I speak as Diego Vega, Zorro is a rogue."

"What is to be done, my son?"

"There's only one thing to be done. Tonight, Zorro will roam the range. If peons and natives are in this work, we may be sure that they have a leader. He is the one to catch, unmask and punish."

Don Alejandro clapped his hands and told a servant to have the carriage ready in an hour's time. Diego stood in an archway until Bernardo, his mute peon body-servant, came hurrying to him from an adobe hut. Bernardo's eyes were glistening as he knuckled his forehead in respectful salute.

"Bernardo, I am going to the rancho with my father," Diego said, in low tones. "When darkness comes go to the hiding place and get Zorro's black horse, clothes and weapons. By the back trails, get to the rancho and take the horse to the usual place. I'll join you as soon as possible after you arrive. Be cautious.

You must not be seen."

BERNARDO made a guttural sound to indicate he understood, bobbed his head and went away. Diego reentered the house and went to his chamber to change clothing for the journey.

It was late in the afternoon when the Vega carriage rolled away from the house and took the trail to San Gabriel. Pedro Patino, at Don Alejandro's order, left to make fast time back to the ranch.

Diego and his father noticed that, in front of the presidio, burly Sergeant Manuel Garcia and four troopers were putting food into their saddlebags and looking to their weapons. Capitán Sanchez was sending them to the San Gabriel area.

The carriage stopped in front of a tradesman's establishment while Don Alejandro went inside. From a tavern came an individual who Diego had seen strutting around the plaza before at intervals. He was short and squat, overdressed, and his fingers were heavy with rings. An uncouth, vulgar man, Diego judged him. He approached the carriage and bowed.

"Don Diego Vega, is it not?" he asked.

Diego turned his head, his face an expressionless mask. He nodded.

"I am José Saldivar, a prosperous trader not unknown up and down El Camino Real. It is in my mind that I could do some heavy business with the Vega rancho. I am buying now for a caravan I wish to send to Monterey — oil of olives, wine, honey, tallow."

"Such business as you mentioned is always conducted by Pedro Patino, the *superintendente* of our rancho," Diego informed him.

José Saldivar's eyes gleamed. A hidalgo did not bargain and argue over trade; the rancho overseer was the man who did that. Saldivar moved on toward a warehouse. Diego brushed his nostrils with the perfumed handkerchief, and Saldivar turned his head in time to see the act. Rage flamed in his face.

Don Alejandro emerged from the store and the carriage rolled out of the town. It was dusk when it reached the Vega ranch house.

Patino welcomed them at the open door, and father and son went to their rooms to cleanse themselves after the dusty journey. Patino went about his duties.

"Zorro might be inconvenienced tonight, my father, if the vaqueros were prowling around the countryside," Diego hinted, when they were in the main room again waiting for the evening meal to be served.

"I'll have Patino order them to keep to their quarters tonight and give them a couple of skins of wine. That will keep them out of Zorro's way. What are your plans, my son?"

"I have none, really. As usual, I'll pretend to retire after the evening meal, and slip out of the house at the proper time."

A full moon rode high when Diego crawled through a window on the dark side of the house and followed the wall to a corner. Keeping to the shadows, he dodged away from the buildings and got to the orchard. On the other side of the orchard, where there was an abandoned adobe storehouse. In the shadows there, Bernardo awaited him.

Bernardo had Zorro's black horse, clothes and weapons. Swiftly, Diego pulled on the black Zorro costume over his regular attire. He buckled on his blade, examined his pistol and thrust it into his sash, and made sure his long whip was fastened to the pommel of his saddle. Then he put on the black hood and mask that enveloped his head, and his eyes gleamed through the slits in the mask.

"Remain here, Bernardo," he said. "Be sure nobody sees you. Await my return."

He got into the saddle, gathered up the reins, and lifted his hand to Bernardo in parting. Don Diego Vega, the lazy dreamer, had disappeared; it was Zorro who rode the big black. He was roaming the range without destination. If cattle slaughterers were at work on the Vega rancho tonight, he did not know exactly where to look for them.

Zorro headed north, being careful not to show himself against the moonlit sky.

HE STOPPED his horse frequently to listen. Sounds came to him on the wind, but they were the usual sounds of the night. He swerved his horse toward the west. Now, some distance from the sprawling ranch house, he turned into a coulée that ran toward the east. The wind carried sounds that caused Zorro to bend forward in an attitude of listening.

He heard cattle bellowing. Hoofbeats reached him as from a far distance, and a man's voice.

Zorro went on along the coulée, where the dirt was deep and his horse made scarcely any sound. The coulée grew deeper, and Zorro followed it, stopping at intervals to listen. The voices, two of them, were stronger now. He went on cautiously. Behind a ledge of rock, he stopped his horse. He knew just which spot on the rancho he had reached.

He heard the voices again.

"We approached too openly," one said. "They heard us and got away not having time to take the hide. They must have gone toward the west. Three of you travel in that direction. Arrest anybody you find roaming the range with blood on his clothes or a skinning knife in his possession."

Zorro moved his horse forward. Against the moonlit sky he saw Sergeant Manuel Garcia and four troopers, the detachment from Reina de los Angeles. As he watched three of the troopers galloped away, and the big sergeant and one man remained. They continued their talk:

"We are to remain on this post, Sergeant Garcia?"

"Until I say to move elsewhere," Zorro heard Garcia growl. "Are you afraid of the night, infant?"

"I am not afraid. Do you really think *Señor* Zorro is behind this slaughtering of cattle and hide stealing?"

"What other man would be behind it, infant? Does he not leave his cursed letter Z at the scene of his crime? If ever I meet him face to face — "

"But you did that once, I have heard, and he got the better of you and marked you with his blade."

Garcia's voice grew bitter. "You are displeasing me, little one. I met him once — si! He took me unawares. But give me another chance to meet him face to face and the rich reward offered by the Governor will be mine"

"I hear a call," the trooper said.

From the far distance came a hail.

" 'Tis our troop call!" Sergeant Garcia said. "Ride in that direction, infant, and learn the trouble. I must remain here on post Let me know what is happening."

Zorro heard the trooper ride away. From the bottom of the coulée, Zorro could see the sergeant and his horse silhouetted against the light sky. The sergeant dismounted and began striding back and forth to rid himself of saddle fatigue and get the blood coursing properly through his veins.

Zorro got the rope off his saddle, ran a noose and began swinging it above his head.

Garcia stopped abruptly and stood with his back toward the coulée. Zorro swung the noose a few times more, and then tossed it upward. His cast was perfect. Zorro jerked it taut. He saw Garcia reel and heard the growl of surprise and fear he gave. Zorro kicked the black, and the horse sprang forward. Sergeant

Garcia came tumbling down from the lip of the coulée to the ground below, and the horse pulled him over the rough ground.

Zorro stopped the horse and sprang out of his saddle, drawing some lengths of rope from his sash. He was upon the semi-conscious Garcia instantly, lashing his wrists behind his back. He lashed his ankles together, too, and turned him over.

GARCIA groaned, writhed, and was conscious again.

"Wh-what — ?" he gulped.

"Silence — I am Zorro!" was what he heard.

"You — "

"Silence, and listen to me, Sergeant Garcia. I have no wish to harm you, but I must fight to preserve my own honor."

"Honor? You — an outlaw and highwayman?"

"This cattle slaughtering and hide stealing — it is none of my work," Zorro told him firmly. "I have not been in this district for some time until tonight. The letter Z where cattle were slaughtered was not left by me. It is but a trick to cast blame upon me."

"If you did not do it, who did?"

"I hope to learn that tonight, and turn him over to you. Now, I will help you to your feet — after gagging you with your own neck-cloth. I'll get you across my saddle and leave you where you will be fairly comfortable. Later, I'll return."

He gagged the sergeant effectually and helped him to his feet. Zorro got his horse, grabbed Garcia's legs and got him across the saddle. Then he led the horse along the coulée.

When he had gone about a hundred yards, he stopped at a place where there were masses of rocks filled with deep shadows. In a cleft in these rocks, he braced Garcia with his back against a boulder. The sergeant was gurgling behind his gag, trying to say something.

"Rest easy," Zorro whispered to him, "The troopers will return and find your horse and you gone. They may search for you. But there will be no tracks in the coulée, for this high wind is shifting the sandy earth. I'll return."

He swung up into the saddle and rode on for a distance, and where one side of the coulée sloped, he rode up out of it and stopped in the shadow of a ledge to watch and listen. Far to the west, he could hear a man shouting, and supposed it was one of the troopers calling to another. Soon, they would be coming back to where they had left Garcia.

Another sound reached Zorro's ears — from the east. It came to him on a wild rush of the wind, from quite a distance. He heard cattle bellowing, heard a distant shout. Keeping to the shadows, he rode in that direction over the rough land. Repeatedly he heard the sounds, always nearer. He doubled caution and approached warily. A wide ravine ran across the country here, and no doubt cattle had been driven into it to be slaughtered. Zorro's approach was slow, for he detoured frequently to avoid streaks of bright moonlight He came to a spot where he could hear voices plainly, and listened. Down in the ravine a man was speaking.

"Let us make haste with the skinning, Carlos. Señor José Saldivar will be riding it, us soon, and these two hides must be ready for his inspection. Then we will carry them over the hill to where the cart is waiting beside the creek, and get our money for the work."

" 'Tis easy money to earn," another man said.

"And a quick way to have your neck stretched with a rope if we are caught. You did not use your lance on the last quick enough. He bellowed like a bull."

"Some rider is coming," the second said.

"Dart into the shadows and wait until we learn his identity. Have your skinning knife ready. We are not to be caught alive!"

Zorro could hear the soft hoofbeats of horse coming along the bottom of the ravine. He left his saddle, ground-hitching his horse, and crept to the edge of the ravine and looked down into it.

Moonlight struck the wide place in the ravine. Zorro could see the carcasses of two steers, the hide off one and half off the second. A rider emerged from the shadow and came to a stop beside the slain animals. In the moonlight, Zorro recognized him — José Saldivar, who posed as a successful trader.

SALDIVAR called a signal softly, and the two peons crept from the darkness and hurried up to him.

"Snails!" Saldivar raged. "You should have been finished. Hurry now, and then go to the next ravine. Kill and skin two more there, and carry the hides to the cart as quickly as you can. Do you want daylight to catch you in this part of the district, with blood on your clothes and skinning knives in your hands?"

"We will make haste, Señor Saldivar," one of the men said. "We delayed

*"The truth or I'll cut you to
ribbons!" Zorro snapped to
the cringing trader.*

starting our work, because there were soldiers in the neighborhood."

"A sergeant and four men from Reina de los Angeles — I saw them ride past the mission. They have gone on toward the Vega rancho house. Hurry! I ride back as I came. I'll meet you at the cart and give you your pay and orders for tomorrow night."

"It shall be as you say, Señor Saldivar."

"Do not mention my name, dolt! The strong wind carries sounds, and somebody may hear. Do not forget to scratch a Z on one of those rocks beside the slain cattle. 'Tis a good joke on this mysterious Señor Zorro, eh? People are blaming him for this."

Zorro saw Saldivar wheel his horse and start riding back down the ravine slowly and cautiously. He got into his own saddle quickly and headed in the same direction. He had ridden over this part of the rancho often as a boy, and he knew just where Saldivar would emerge from the ravine,

Zorro got to the spot first and backed his horse into a patch of darkness. He got his pistol out of his sash and loosened the whip fastened to the pommel of his saddle. He heard José Saldivar's horse snort as he came up out of the ravine. Saldivar rode out into the moonlight and stopped his mount and bent forward in an attitude of a man listening. Zorro pressed with his knees, and his big black horse walked out into the moonlight behind Saldivar's mount.

"Look this way, Saldivar," Zorro said, in a tense voice. "And put up your hands as you look, and do not try to reach for a pistol. Mine is covering you."

He heard a gasp from the man in front of him. Saldivar half wheeled his horse and turned, and saw the black horse and the black masked figure in the saddle.

"What — what is this?" he gulped.

"I am Zorro. I have been interested, José Saldivar, in this affair of slaughtered cattle and stolen hides, especially since an effort has been made to convince people I am concerned. I must punish you, señor, and also clear my name."

Zorro urged his horse nearer, and Saldivar could see the menacing pistol plainly, and also the whip.

"Wait!" Saldivar begged. "I — I did not know you were in the vicinity. Marking with the letter Z — I thought it would keep people from suspecting me."

"Little wonder you are a prosperous trader, Saldivar, if you get your merchandise in such a manner," Zorro said. "You are caught now. You would have been caught eventually by the troopers, if not by me. Do you not know the hills are swarming with them tonight?"

"A sergeant and four men," Saldivar said. "Listen to me, Zorro. We can make a little business deal. Half of my profits I will give you — "

Zorro's whip lashed through the air and struck Saldivar across his back. One screech of pain escaped him. And then Zorro had pressed his horse closer, and was talking in low tones.

"Quiet, or you'll have the troopers upon us both! Take your pistol from your belt and drop it upon the ground — quickly!"

In the bright moonlight, Zorro could see Saldivar's eyes bulging, see the expression of fear in his face. The fellow was a thief, boaster and coward, Zorro decided. Saldivar removed his pistol from his sash and let it drop to the ground.

"Do not again offer me a share of your loot," Zorro warned. "I help those who need help. It is my purpose now to turn you over to the troopers and have you punished for your crimes. Take off your neckcloth and hand it to me."

RELUCTANTLY Saldivar's fumbling fingers obeyed the command. Zorro ordered the other to bend from his saddle. He stuck his pistol into his sash and hooked the whip to his pommel, threw one arm around Saldivar's neck and was gagging him almost before the other knew what he intended.

"Ride at my side, handling your own reins," Zorro ordered him. "I'll pistol you at the first wrong move. Come!"

Saldivar was gurgling behind his gag, but could not mouth words Zorro could understand. Zorro rode knee to knee with him, holding his pistol in his right hand and handling the reins with his left. He kept in streaks of darkness as much as possible and started back to where he had left Sergeant Manuel Garcia a prisoner bound and gagged.

The journey was a slow one, because of the roughness — of the ground, the need for silence and following the streaks of darkness, and the fact that Zorro stopped and listened at times. But finally he came to the coulée where he had left Garcia, and descended into it with José Saldivar riding beside him and still gurgling behind his gag.

In the distance, Zorro could hear men shouting:

"Garcia! … Sergeant Garcia! … Call out and let us know where you are!"

The troopers had returned and were searching for their sergeant, having found his horse ground-hitched at the spot where Garcia had told them his post would be.

Zorro stopped the horses beside the rocks where he had left Garcia. He dismounted and ordered Saldivar to do the same. Zorro held his pistol in his left hand now and the whip in his right. He forced Saldivar up into the mass of rocks until they came to where Garcia was propped up against the boulder.

"Attend me, Garcia!" Zorro said. "I have caught the man who is behind the slaughter of the cattle for hides. He is José Saldivar. Listen intently. He will confess it all to you. And if you will gather your men, when I release you, and hasten to the big rock slide down by the creek, you will find a cart waiting to carry away hides, and perhaps capture some of the men who have been working for this Saldivar. Tell him, Saldivar — are you not the head of this affair? And did you and your men not mark the Z when cattle were slaughtered?"

He jerked the gag from Saldivar's mouth, and waited.

"It is a lie — a trick!" Saldivar said. "Sergent, I was but riding along the highway when this masked man — "

Zorro's whip sang through the night air, and a screech came from Saldivar's throat.

"The truth, or I cut you to ribbons!" Zorro snapped at him. "And keep your voice down!"

The whip struck again, and Saldivar cringed against a rock and whimpered.

"It is the truth — *si,* " he told Garcia. "I — I engaged some peons to do the killing and skinning. I — I marked the Z wherever we worked, or had the men do it."

"The cart is by the rock slide — *si?* " Zorro asked.

"It is there."

"Get there, Garcia, and catch some of the rogues," Zorro suggested. "Get the truth out of them. They may lead you to the spot where this rogue has hidden the stolen hides."

Zorro stepped forward swiftly, took the whip in his left hand along with the pistol, drew a knife from his sash and cut the rope which bound the sergeant's ankles.

"On your feet, and back to me after I mount my horse," Zorro ordered, back away. "I am taking your pistol, Garcia, for I have no wish to be shot out of my saddle as I ride away."

He swung up into his saddle and, Garcia muttering imprecations, backed toward him. Zorro reached down and cut the rope that bound the sergeant's wrists behind his back. Garcia was a free man. His first act was to grasp José Saldivar and hurl him back against a rock, saying he was under arrest. Picking up the rope Zorro had severed, the sergeant lashed Saldivar's wrists with it.

"I thank you for, this service, Señor Zorro," the sergeant said. "But that will not prevent me from taking you whenever I have the chance."

ZORRO laughed and turned to ride down the coulée, and pulled up his horse suddenly. José Saldivar's wild screech when the whip had struck him had been heard. The troopers were coming. Zorro had some quick thinking to do then. They were coming at him along the coulée from both directions. He was in a trap. And Garcia began bellowing.

"Troopers, to me! Zorro is here!"

Zorro spurred the big black and dashed along the coulée. Two troopers appeared before him in the moonlight. Zorro fired Garcia's pistol and tossed it aside. The troopers swerved to right and left, startled at the attack. Zorro rode between them madly, turned and fired his own pistol, shooting over their heads as he had done before.

Then, before they recovered from their consternation, before Garcia could bellow the truth at them, Zorro was around a bend in the coulée and was gone. He forced his horse up out of the coulée and rode like the wind to an old cattle trail he knew. Along this the big black raced, going toward the rancho buildings by a circuitous route. On the shoulder of a hill, Zorro paused to listen for sounds of pursuit. He heard them, but they were far away and the pursuit was traveling in the wrong direction. Zorro rode on, came to where Bernardo was waiting, and dropped out of his saddle.

He stripped off his Zorro costume and weapons and dropped them in a heap.

"Hide them as usual, and take the horse to the far pasture and turn him loose," he ordered Bernardo.

Zorro was gone for the time being, and in his place was Don Diego Vega again. He made his way to the house and entered the patio. He heard his father's voice:

"Is that you, Diego, my son?"

"Si, father."

"Are you all right?"

"Everything is all right, my father. In the morning. I shall have a tale to tell. But now, my father, I wish to sit here for a time and enjoy the moonlight and meditate. *Buenas noches.*"

Don Alejandra chuckled. *"Buenas noches* my son. Ah, if I could be young again, and play at desperate games!"

"Do not suggest such a thing, my father," Diego begged, doing some chuckling himself. "The thought of it fatigues me."

Zorro and the Pirate

Out of the North come Carlos Salazar and his five ruthless killers, determined to slay Zorro, and the masked avenger meets the challenge wth flashing blade!

ON THIS particular afternoon, as he strolled slowly from his father's house on the outskirts of Reina de Los Angeles to the little plaza in the center of the pueblo, Don Diego Vega decided to take advantage of a short cut to the chapel, where he wished to talk to old Fray Felipe, his father confessor.

The short cut ran past a cluster of poor adobe huts and a scene of miserable squalor. Half-naked peons and native children, dogs, pigs, chickens, litter and assorted trash affronted the eye and offended the nose. Diego brushed his nostrils quiekly with a scented handkerchief and quickened his stride.

But suddenly Diego's eyes widened in astonishment and he came to an abrupt stop. Ahead was an adobe hut with an old bench against the front.

On the bench sat a huge, graying man with a red face and a patch over one eye. As Diego watched the man upended a half-emptied wineskin and let wine gurgle down his throat.

"Bardoso!" Diego muttered. "So he finally has returned home."

Up and down El Camino Real, the King's highway, where Bardoso was known as a reformed pirate, many were skeptical about his reformation.

Bardoso was truly a merry rogue, and one addicted to wine and dice and scandal. But behind his rascally demeanor was a keen mind.

Perhaps because opposites are attracted to each qther, the former pirate and Diego had formed a strange friendship. Bardoso, the utterly uncouth, and Diego Vega, the ultra-fastidious! Yet they seemed to enjoy each other's society.

Hearing Diego's boots crunch gravel, Bardoso turned his head and saw him. Bardoso's one good eye gleamed.

"Don Diego Vega!" the former pirate bellowed. He got upon his feet with seine difficulty. "It does one good to see you! Now I am happy again!"

"And I am glad to greet you again, amigo," Diego replied, smiling. " 'Tis indeed a long time since your departure from the pueblo. I was surprised to find you sitting before your hut, emptying a wineskin, as usual."

BARDOSO roared his laughter. "I'd offer you a swig out of the wineskin, Don Diego, except that I know you have plenty of rare good wine to drink whenever you wish. This stuff would gag you. Take my bench, and allow me to stand in your presence."

Diego sat on the bench and looked up at Bardoso.

"Where did you go, amigo?"

"As far north as San Francisco de Asis," Bardoso related, "making a slow trip. In San Francisco de Asis, which is a place of thick fog and thicker fish smells, I fell in with bad companions."

"Is that a disaster for a former pirate?" Diego asked, his eye twinkling.

"But now reformed, Don Diego, please remember," Bardoso begged. "To make the story short, these men had arranged a certain enterprise and offered me a share in it."

"Some respectable business venture?" Diego said, with sarcasm.

"A foul plot!" Bardoso threw up his hands in horror. "I refused to join with them. But they had told me too much of their plans for them to let me get away."

'What occurred?" Diego asked.

"They tried to slay me and seal my lips forever. But I managed to escape, after a ferocious battle on the waterfront, and return home where I can sit in peace and drink wine."

"Perhaps you need funds?" Diego hinted.

Bardoso's good eye narrowed to a mere slit.

"I have ample for my present needs amigo," he replied. "Because I did not join those rogues does not mean that I did not have a few little private enterprises of my own. A man must live."

Diego laughed and got up from the bench to continue his stroll. But Bardoso stepped nearer, his florid countenance serious.

Perhaps you can give me advice, Don Diego," he suggested. "As undoubtedly you know, there is a man of mystery who calls himself Zorro, who rides around masked, to punish those who oppress the poor and helpless."

"I have heard of the man and his work," Diego admitted, contriving to hide his smile. "A most turbulent fellow."

"A man after my own kidney!" Bardoso declared. "He rides alone, fights alone, and helps those who need help most."

Bardoso stopped and looked at Diego.

"But perhaps, amigo, you are not in sympathy with my speech," he continued. "You are the son of a hidalgo. Yet I always have heard that your father, Don Alejandro, treats the peons and natives who work for him well."

"We always try to treat them justly," Diego replied. "But to what is all this leading?"

"We were speaking of Senor Zorro, who rides to the defense of the poor," Bardoso said. "I, for one, admire the man. I hope that this will not shatter our friendship."

"No reason why it should, Bardoso. I — well, I rather admire this Zorro fellow also."

"Then I may speak without fear," Bardoso cried, "regarding this plot of which I told you — at the head of it is Carlos Salazar, with a band of men under his leadership — murderers and thieves. Up to now, officials never could gather evidence against any of them. But recently a slip occurred, and one of Salazar's most valued rogues was caught red-handed in the act of murder."

"And so?" Diego asked.

"Salazar was approached by an agent of the Governor, with an offer. His man would be allowed to escape jail and get to sea on some ship providing Salazar and his men accomplish a certain piece of work."

"What piece of work?"

A GLOOMY frown overspread the ex-pirate's face.

"To catch or kill this Senor Zorro, unmask him and reveal his identity to the world. Carlos Salazar can use any method. He canted me to join him because I know this territory well."

"Why didn't you join him, Bardoso?"

"Well, I don't admire Salazar's plans," Bardoso answered. "He will make no attempt to capture Zorro, but will kill him on sight. Salazar has five rogues to help him. They are armed to the teeth and have swift horses. They also have plenty of money to use in bribery. They will do everything they can to save their companion from stretching rope."

"When are they going to do all this?" Diego asked.

"Immediately. Salazar and his men are in Reina de Los Angeles already, quartered in the tavern on the plaza."

Diego stiffened slightly, like a man who feels peril in his vicinity.

"Zorro may ride into a trap," Bardoso continued. "To lure Zorro within their clutches, they are going to commence a reign of terror among the peons. They will kick, beat, torture them, knowing Zorro will ride to their rescue. Then they will slay hint. That was why 1 refused to join them."

"What about the soldiers?" Diego asked. Bardoso made a gesture of disgust. "I mentioned that to Salazar. He explained that the commandante here has been called to Monterey, and Sergeant Manuel Garcia, second in command, has orders to let Salazar and his men have their way"

"The commandante left for Monterey yesterday," Diego informed him.

"I know." Bardoso nodded. "No doubt Salazar and his men will start their mistreatment of the peons and natives immediately. I wish this Senor Zorro could be warned of the plot, so he will not ride into a trap."

Diego sighed. "Ah, well, Bardoso, we live in troublesome times," he declared. "And how will it fare with you, with this Carlos Salazar and his men here? They sought your death in the north."

"I have seen Salazar and made a deal with him," Bardoso said.

"What? After all your fine speech to me?" Bardoso laughed. "It is understood that I am only to give them information and take no active part in the work. And can a man not make a mistake and give wrong information?"

Diego chuckled a little. "Have a care, amigo, that your perfidy is not discovered. Now I must hurry on to the chapel."

Diego reached the corner of the plaza. To get to the chapel, he was compelled to pass the tavern. Outside of it, he observed strange mounts, and scrutinized them carefully. Diego knew good horseflesh when he saw it, and his eyes sparkled as he looked at these horses, six of them, steeds that gave every indication of both speed and stamina.

They belonged to Carlos Salazar and his five men, Diego supposed. Day and night they would be kept ready for instant use if Zorro appeared.

Diego slackened his steps. The door and windows of the tavern were open, and from the interior came sounds of loud talk and laughter. Then came a screech of pain, and through the doorway sailed the body of a peon, landing almost at Diego's feet.

The doorway was darkened an instant later by a stranger who was wiping his hands together.

"Stay out of here, beggar scum!" this man shouted at the peon. "If I see you in here again, I'll take the hide off your back in strips!"

Diego, handkerchief at nostrils, looked at the man on the ground. The peon's face was bleeding, a whip had ripped his left shoulder and blood was soaking through his ragged shirt.

'Get up and begone!" the man in the doorway shouted.

Diego glanced at the insured man, whom he knew by sight.

"Get up and go away," Diego advised him.

THE other man came striding from the tavern doorway, his whip gripped firmly. Diego's quick glance revealed several grinning spectators watching from the doorway and windows. Carlos Salazar's men he decided.

The peon got up. Diego quickly strode between him and the man with the whip.

"One side, senior, until I punish this rascal!" the stranger shouted.

Diego looked him over from head to feet. The peon started to scurry away. The stranger made as if to follow, and Diego again stepped into his path.

"One side, I ordered!" the stranger barked, angrily.

"Pardon me, senior, but in this pueblo or elsewhere nobody orders Diego Vega to stand aside. And we frown on the beating of peons."

"For a clipped coin, I'd put my lash across your bath!" the stranger roared.

"That would be an easy path to a swift death, senor," Diego told him.

"Ho! Perhaps you would challenge me? Be careful, popinjay. I am Caros Salazar, and you have the appearance of a weakling."

Diego drew himself up slightly. His eyes were sending out flecks of flame. He wanted to settle with this arrogant rascal, but just in time he remembered his character of Don Diego. Don Diego, the supposed fop, could not act like Zorro in public and cause talk.

From the tavern came running Sergeant Manuel Garcia of the local presidio.

"Have a care, Senor Salazar," Sergeant Garcia cried, getting between Salazar and Diego. "This is Don Diego Vega, son of Don Alejandro. Affront him, senor, and your presence in the vicinity will become impossible."

"'Since he is untouchable, I'll retire." Salazar scowled at Diego. "We'll meet again, senor."

Salazar swaggered back into the tavern, his face purple with wrath. Diego brushed his nostrils with the scented handkerchief.

"Who is the fellow?' he asked the sergeant.

"Some official from the north," Sergeant Garcia replied. "He stepped closer and spoke in low tones.

"Don Diego, the lot of a soldier is not always pleasant, when he stands between his orders and his inclinations. More, I cannot say. But I'll see to it that Senor Salazar makes suitable apology."

"I have no wish to listen to the fellow's apology," Diego replied.

He bowed and walked on toward the chapel, where old Fray Felipe was waiting. After their greeting, they sat in a cool corner, where Diego rapidly told what Bardoso had disclosed.

"Let us give thanks, my son, that the former pirate put you on guard," Fray Felipe said. "Now, Zorro will not ride blindly into a trap."

"The situation may be perilous, padre, but Zorro must ride," Diego told him. "Carlos Salazar and his men must not be permitted to abuse the peons. Except for the soldiers, there is nothing to stop this cruel work."

Hands thrust into the sleeves of his robe, Fray Felipe leaned back on the bench and pondered. Being Diego's confessor he knew, of course, that Diego was Zerro, the masked terror who rode the highway. Diego's father, Old Don Alejandro, knew this also, as did a third man — Bernardo, Diego's mute peon body servant

'You have plans, my son?" Fray Felipe asked.

"They are forming in my mind, padre."

"From what you have told me, you will be in grave danger. You will be riding in a gpod cause, but you must remember that Zorro always rides to defend the helpless, and never to destroy his personal enemies,"

"I understand, padre."

"Use wisdom. My blessings, my son."

Diego emerged from the chapel and walked on around the plaza. It was the hour for promenade following the siesta. He bowed to men of his own class, and swept off his hat when fat senoras and dainty senoritas passed. Away from the plaza, he walked faster until he came to his father's house.

IN HIS own rooms, Bernardo was waiting to serve him.

"A tepid bath, and fresh clothing," Diego ordered. In a lower tone, he added,

"Zorro rides tonight. Have everything prepared two hours after darkness falls."

Before dinner Diego told his father what had happened.

"When the chief executive of our country deals with murderers and thieves, we are in a sorry state," Don Alejandro declared. "I hope you realize your peril, Diego?"

"I do, my father. It is also a time for swift action."

"True. Remember, these men will try to shoot you or ride you down. You have made plans?"

"They have been made," Diego replied.

"One of the house servants just returned from an errand. He reports that the men from the north are riding around, roping unfortunates and dragging them over the rough ground at the end of the rope. One peon had his leg broken."

"They must be stopped," Diego said grimly. "Sergeant Garcia is not a bad sort. What he told me in the plaza showed that."

Darkness came, and Diego went to his own rooms. At the proper hour, he slipped out of the house and went like a shadow past the huts of the servants.

Some distance away was an old abandoned adobe storehouse, shrouded by thick shrubbery. Bernardo was waiting there, with Zorro's horse, clothing and weapons.

"Get your big riding mule," Diego directed, as he pulled on the baggy Zorro clothes over his own costume. Ride to the base of the first hill on the San Gabriel trail and go into hiding. Be certain nobody sees you."

Bernardo emitted a gurgling sound that meant be understood.

"If I come riding furiously toward you and give the signal, take my place and ride on swiftly while I turn aside. Lose those who follow and return here. Then put away your mule and wait for me."

Again, Bernardo signaled that he understood. Diego buckled on Zorro's sword and thrust two pistols into his sash. Into the sash he also tucked a bit of parchment upon which a message had been scrawled. He put on his black mask, his hat, and mounted. With this, Don Diego Vega ceased to exist, and Senor Zorro took his place.

He circled the pueblo and approached the rear of the barracks warily, where he could hear a tumult in the direction of the plaza. There were shrieks and lamentations, and wild raucous laughter. Evidently Salazar and his men were mistreating peons and natives to attract Zorro's wrath.

The moon was not yet up. When it did show itself, it would be a full moon to make it almost as light as day. Zorro had things to do before the moon came up.

He went on until he could see the front of the barracks. One guard was there. Zorro took the parchment from his sash and gave his black the spurs.

The black's hoofs pounded the hard ground in front of the barracks. As the guard turned around, the big black swept past, and the parchment fell at the guard's feet.

Seeing it addressed to Sergeant Garcia, the guard called his corporal and had the message carried to the sergeant.

Garcia put aside a wine mug, wiped his enormous mustache with the back of a gnarled hand, and read:

> Sergeant Garcia — I know everything, If your orders do not allow you
> to side with the fox, be honest enough not to side with the hounds.
>
> > Zorro

Garcia sprang to his feet and bellowed for the man who had brought him the message.

"Whence came this thing?"

"The guard says a masked man on a black horse rode past like the wind and tossed it at his feet."

"Zorro!" Garcia roared. "Well, he seems to understand the situation. I hope the rascal escapes the trap. Much as I would like to capture him, I'd hate to see a rogue like Salazar bring him to earth."

GARCIA refilled the wine mig and again made himself comfortable.

"If anybody asks for me," he told the trooper, "I am busy making out my day's report for the comrntandante, and cannot be disturbed. After the report is finished, I seek my couch remember!"

After riding past the barracks, Zorro had swung away from the town. He could see a bonfire blazing in the center of the plaza, and could hear laughter and shrieks of pain and fright. Shadows darted around the fire indicating where men were pursuing others. He could see a rider, too.

Through the darkness, Zorro made a circuit of the pueblo, careful to avoid meeting anybody. He approached the plaza again from behind the sprawling tavern building.

The fire in the center of the plaza had been fed afresh with fuel, and flames were leaping high and throwing an amber glow over a wide area. Through the front windows of the tavern light streamed also. Everything that happened in the plaza was easily visible to anybody back in the darkness.

Zorro rode behind a hedge, raised himself in the saddle and peered over. What he saw sickened him. Two natives had been tied to stakes near the fire, and one of Salazar's men was burning them with the point of a red-hot stick, trying to make them cry out or beg for mercy.

Another of the rogues had roped a peon and was making him run at the end of the rope which was fastened to his saddle. The peon had his arms lashed behind him. He ran like a man about ready to drop as Salazar's man spurred his horse. The peon knew that, if he dropped, he would be pulled over the rough ground until insensibility came.

Zorro urged his horse a short distance along the hedge so he would have a better view of the front of the tavern. Carlos Salazar was standing in front of the open door, his fists braced against his hips, laughing.

"Make 'em howl," he was shouting at his men.

Zorro rode on to the end of the hedge and gathered his reins well in his left hand. With his right, he took his long heavy whip from the pommel of his saddle, and slipped the wrist thong into place. Anticipating what was coming, the big black horse quivered beneath his rider.

Zorro gave a quick glance at the plaza. Salazar's men were scattered, and none near him. Only one of them was mounted. Salazar was still in front of the open tavern door

Zorro spurred the black. He sprang forward and struck the ground running. A few strides took him into top speed. Bending low over his mount's neck, Zorro rode like a madman across the front of the tavern building, through the streaks of light.

Carlos Salazar heard the thunder of hoofbeats and turned just in time to see the black horse and masked rider, to see the heavy whip swinging down toward him. This was a thing Zorro often had practiced and at which he was adept. The lash struck Salazar squarely in the face as Zorro flashed past, with a snap that could be heard by all near.

"Zorro!" some man shouted.

Then Zorro was out of the lighted space and riding in the darkness. He swerved to the right before he came to the barracks. He could tell from the sounds that only one rider was pursuing him, probably the man who had been compelling the peon to run in the plaza.

Zorro let him pass, and when he had gone a short distance started after him, as if he were another of Salazar's rascals. He overhauled the Salazar man rapidly. The rider ahead pulled up, thinking one of his comrades was approaching.

"I can't hear his hoof beats," he called back. "He may be in hiding, waiting for us."

Zorro had stopped riding and was sitting his saddle behind a ledge of rock. The full moon was coming up. One could see streaks of light and shadow now.

"Come on!" the Salazar man called. "Here, in the middle of the trail!"

ZORRO bent low in his saddle again and rode forward at a trot. He was holding the whip ready. And suddenly he jumped his horse at the rider in the middle of the trail, swerved the black at the right instant, and lashed with the heavy whip.

The Salazar man screeched as the lash bit into his back. He tried to get at the pistol he carried. But Zorro pressed the black against his mount, and continued lashing, the whip cutting into the victim and bringing blood.

The Salazar man tumbled out of his saddle to escape the punishment. He managed to get out his pistol. But the whip wrapped itself around his forearm and jerked him off his feet, and the pistol flew away into the brush.

"You deal with Zorro, rogue! Tell Carlos Salazar that I know all his plans," Zorro said. "So he will shoot me at sight, will he, that one of his murderers can go free? Starting tomorrow night, I will shoot you at sight also, any of you, even from the darkness. Tell that to Carlos Salazar."

He lashed the man once more, then wheeled the black and rode on along the trail.

But, a short distance away, he turned off the trail and followed a winding path he knew, and headed back toward the pueblo again, going slowly and allowing his horse a breathing spell.

The moon was starting to drench the country with light now. Zorro watched the shadows carefully, fearful of an ambush. Again he circled the pueblo and came near the plaza in the same place behind the hedge at the side of the tavern.

The fire still burned fiercely. Carlos Salazar was in front of the tavern, shouting at his remaining four men. And to him from the barracks came Sergeant Garcia and six troopers.

"What delayed you?" Salazar screeched at the sergeant. "I ordered you to come to my aid at once."

"Ordered, senor?" Garcia bellowed angrily. "Do I take orders from you?"

"You do!" Salazar told him. "You swill wine in the barracks while this fiend of a Zorro rides across the plaza and lashes my fare with a whip. Take your men, now, and ride in pursuit out the north trail! Only one of my men was in saddle, and he went after this highwayman. Go to his aid!"

"I'll do my best to catch this Senor Zorro," Sergeant Garcia replied. "But it is only fair to tell you, senor, that we have pursued Zorro many times and gained nothing but fatigue for ourselves and lathered coats for our horses."

Garcia growled an order, and led his troopers toward the mouth of the north trail.

Salazar called to him his four men, now all mounted.

"Two of you ride after the troopers, join them, keep them earnestly in the chase," he ordered. "You two others — one of you station yourself at the south side of the plaza, keeping in the darkness, and the other at the north side. Ride!"

His four men spurred away. Salazar shouted for the landlord, who came with a goblet of wine. He gulped the wine and dashed the goblet to the ground.

"Those two scoundrels bound to the stakes near the fire — I'll attend to them personally" Salazar declared, rage ringing in his voice. "Some of these scum must know the identity and whereabouts of Zorro, their friend. I'll have the knowledge out of them! I'll run this Zorro down and shoot him like a dog!"

He picked up a whip somebody had dropped at the door of the tavern, made sure his pistol was in his belt, and strode angrily out into the plaza, going toward the fire and the men lashed to stakes near it.

From his place behind the hedge, Zorro watched this rascal from the north. The natives, already tortured by hot sticks, were writhing against the posts but making no outcry. Salazar stopped in front of the nearer man.

"You know this Zorro and all about him, son of the devil!" Salazar cried, "Who is he? Where does he lodge?"

The native lifted his head. "I know nothing about him, senor," he replied.

"Stubborn, are you? Protect the highwayman, would you?" Salazar screeched.

The lash began singing and striking, and Zorro could see the native's body flinch as the whip stung. Light from the fire showed blood streaming from the cuts on the man's torso.

SALALZAR whirled away from him and went to the second victim.

"You saw what happened to him!" he shouted at the man, already half conscious "Will you talk?"

"I — I cannot tell you, senor. I never have seen his face. Nobody knows who Zorro is."

The whip commenced singing again. Once the man tied to the stake cried out, then his head dropped forward and he was still.

But Zorro had spurred the big black into action again, running grave risk. Hearing the hoofheats, Salazar whirled, dropped the whip, jerked his pistol out of his belt and fired. The ball fanned Zorro's cheek.

Salazar was shouting, and his men came riding from both the north and south sides of the plaza. Zorro crowded his horse forward, so the men could not fire without fear of hitting Salazar. Salazar whipped a throwing knife out of his belt. Light from the fire flashed from the blade. The point of the knife was buried in Zorro's saddle an inch from his leg.

Salazar's two men were bearing down upon him. Zorro whipped one of his pistols out of his sash and fired at Salazar, and saw him reel aside. Then he spurred the black and bent low in his saddle and rode like, a madman through the streaks of moonlight.

Pistols exploded behind him and bullets searched him out, but none struck. He heard the sounds of pursuit as the two started after him. Zorro rode at top speed now, but the mounts of the men behind were, as he had judged, speedy, and he could not gain on them to any great extent.

Out the San Gabriel trail he went, wondering where Sergeant Garcia had led his men, and whether he would crash into them or run into an ambush. Behind him came Salazar's two men.

Now he used the spurs again and the big black gave his best and gained. Zorro was nearing the place where Bernardo should be in hiding on his riding mule.

He slackened speed a little and gave a peculiar call. Ahead of him a short distance, he saw Bernardo ride out into the moonlit trail. Zorro's black stopped beside the mule.

"Did soldiers come this way?" Zorro asked. Bernardo gave a guttural grunt and pointed off to the left, toward the San Fernando.

"Ride on!" Zorro ordered.

He swung his black back into the darkness. On his half-wild mule, Bernardo rode on toward San Gabriel. From his hiding place, Zorro watched the two

Salazar men dash past, following the mule.

Zorro turned back toward the pueblo, riding slowly. Salazar was there, wounded. Two of his men were riding with the soldiers and two were chasing after Bernardo on the mule. The fifth had been handled by Zorro earlier, and where he was Zorro did not know.

He came to the plaza again and once more got behind the hedge.

Salazar was striding back and forth in front of the tavern, shouting like a wild man. His coat had been removed, and a white bandage was wrapped around his left shoulder. The wound was a mere scratch to a man like Salazar.

Looking into the plaza, Zorro saw Fray Felipe in charge of two padres and two peons who were lifting the tortured natives from the stakes. They began carrying them toward the chapel, where Fray Felipe would doctor them.

Zorro watched and listened for a moment. Several men were peering through

Zorro spurred the big black forward and lifted his weapon. Salazar dropped the whip, yanked out a pistol and fired.

the tavern windows, but most of them were men of the pueblo and Zorro did not fear them.

Sitting his black behind the hedge, Zorro reloaded the pistol he had fired at Salazar earlier and returned it to his sash. He had two pistols ready for use, and his whip, and the blade he had not drawn tonight.

And so he waited for the right moment, then spurred toward the tavern door, and was upon Salazar and covering him with a pistol before the rogue from the north could prepare to defend himself.

"Scum!" Zorro raged at him. "Torturer of better men than you will ever be!

I give you once chance, Salazar. Leave Reina de Los Angeles with your men, and never return. If you do, I'll hear of it and finish you."

" 'Tis your life against that of a friend of mine," Salazar said.

"I know the story. Your friend is a foul murderer and deserves to be hanged. So do you and the rogues you brought here with you. Answer me. Will you ride?"

ZORRO would have said more, but a clatter of hoofs stopped him. The two men of Salazar's who had gone in futile pursuit of Bernardo on his mule had returned at this crucial moment.

They took in the scene and spurred forward. Zorro wheeled his mount aside, and Salazar's hand dived to his belt and came up with his recharged pistol. He fired point blank at Zorro, and the pistol ball grazed Zorro's leg. Zorro go out one of his pistols and fired in reply. Carlos Salazar swayed and sprawled on the ground, the life suddenly gone out of him.

Zorro jumped his horse aside as Salazar's two men closed in on him. His second pistol was out now, and he exchanged shots with the nearest man. Salazar's man missed, but Zorro's pistol ball struck him in the shoulder and hurled him from his saddle, wounded but not seriously so.

He spurred the black and raced directly toward the second man as a pistol ball sang over his head. Zorro had whipped out his blade. The two mounts clashed together. The blade flashed in the light from the fire and suddenly was turned to crimson. The man toppled out of his saddle, and his mount ran away a short distance to stop bewildered near the door of the tavern.

Zorro wheeled his mount again, to see something that startled him.

Bardoso, the former pirate, had emerged from the tavern and had managed to get into the saddle of the Salazar man who had toppled from it. Bardoso was brandishing a cutlass.

"Come at me, rogue!" Bardoso roared. "I'll show you how we fought in bygone days with a slippery deck beneath our feet! At me, you pretty highwayman!"

Bardoso urged his mount forward and made a slashing attack. Zorro wheeled for an instant to avoid it. He had no wish to slay or wound his friend, Bardoso. But it was necessary that he protect his life.

Their mounts circled and wheeled, and Bardoso's cutlass made a wide sweep and was turned in the nick of time by Zorro's blade. Their mounts came side by side again, and their blades locked.

"Pretend to unseat me, then ride!" Bardoso said, so nobody else could hear. "You have done well tonight. I am with you! Ride, for the soldiers return with Sergeant Garcia and the other two Salazar men."

He made a furious onslaught as he finished speaking, and steel rang as Zorro parried the blows. Then Bardoso pretended to lose his balance, and slipped half out of his saddle, wheeling his horse. Zorro wheeled his own and spurred away from the plaza as Garcia and the others came galloping down the trail and into the town.

An hour later, Zorro rode to the abandoned storehouse where Bernardo was waiting. He stripped off the costume, gave Bernarda the clothes and his weapons — and was Don Diego Vega again.

Getting into the house unseen was an easy matter. Bernardo appeared in time and helped him salve his minor hurts. Then Diego went to his couch to sleep.

It was a late hour when he descended for breakfast. His father greeted him warmly.

"It seems, from all reports, that Zorro was riding last night," Don Alejandro said. "He slew that fiend of a Carlos Salazar and hurt some of his men. Then are leaving the pueblo today and riding north. Some peons and natives were beaten and tortured, but all will live."

"These turbulent times," Diego said, yawning. "All this violence is so upsetting, my father."

Zorro Beats a Drum

Brutal animal trainer Carlos Favela incurs the wrath
of the masked avenger — who fights to rescue the innocent!

EMERGING from the squatty tavern building on the plaza at Reina de Los Angeles, Sergeant Manuel Garcia came to an abrupt stop. He blinked to get the sun glare out of his eyes, took a swift glance at the nearest corner of the plaza, and blinked again. Having baffled his way through more than forty years of tempestuous life, soldiering in Spain, Mexico and now in Alta California, meanwhile becoming inured to unusual sights and scenes, it took something far beyond the ordinary to make Sergeant Garcia blink.

He saw a large lumbering cart with high wooden wheels entering the plaza from the highway which came down out of the north. The cart was heaped high with a strange miscellaneous cargo.

On top of the cargo sat a swarthy man of middle age, who was dressed in scarlet and yellow striped clothing. He wore huge brass rings in his ears, and a smaller one dangled from his nostrils. He was beating on a big drum, missing a couple of beats now and then as he stopped to guzzle from a wine skin.

But the strangest part of the unusual spectacle was that the cart was not being drawn by the usual oxen. In a harness on the right was a huge barefooted peon who looked as stolid as any ox. On the left was a big brown bear. Running ahead was a mongrel yellow dog which baited continually as if urging the peon and the bear to harder work.

Sergeant Garcia decided that here was an opportunity for him to make a show of authority. He drew up his shoulders adjusted his sword belt and sash,

*As
Favol lifted
the lash to punish
the cringing peon,
Zorro stepped
forward.*

blew out the ends of his enormous mustache and stalked toward the vehicle.

The cart had stopped almost in the center of the plaza. The man in scarlet and yellow clothes ceased beating the drum and stood up. The big peon got out of his harness and took the other harness off the bear. The dog stopped barking. Men of the town began gathering around the cart.

Sergeant Garcia strode forward, elbowing other men out of his path. He stopped within a few feet of the cart and stood with arms akimbo, and he put on his official glare.

"What is the reason for all this unseemly tumult?" he demanded of the man in the cart, "What queer spectacle is this? Explain yourself to me instantly!"

THE man on the cart straightened, laughing a little in a manner the sergeant did not like, and drew forth a folded document, bowed to the sergeant and handed the paper down to him. As the sergeant read. the man in the cart began declaiming to the others.

"Senores, you see before you Carlos Faveja, master showman. My professional title is Carlos Favela and His Three Beasts," he announced. "There they are Big Juan. the peon: Faroz, the brown bear; and Perro Amarillo, the yellow dog. As soon as our beautiful striped pavilion is erected, there will be a performance that will amaze you."

"What do they do?" a man shouted.

"Big Juan is so strong that he can bend a rod of iron with his bare hands, and also can lift great weights. Feroz, the bear, dances with a pole in his arms. The dog has been trained by me to do tricks almost unbelievable. As a grand conclusion of the entertainment, Juan and the bear engage in a wrestling bout."

"Wrestle?" another man in the crowd called. "No doubt they hug each other a little."

"So that is your belief?" Favela asked, angrily. "I'll have the peon remove his shirt, senores. Across his massive shoulders you will see great welts made by the bear's claws. Ferox wears a muzzle, but his paws are not muzzled. Juan!"

The big, powerful peon whimpered like a child in sudden fear at the mere sound of the voice, and looked up.

"Remove your shirt and let the senores see your back," Favela ordered.

The peon stripped off the tagged garment and turned around slowly. Some of the watchers gave exclamations of pity. Festering wounds were across the huge man's shoulders.

"Why does he wrestle the bear if he is hurt so?" one of the spectators asked.

"Because I command it," Favela replied, arrogantly. "I am a trainer of beasts, and Juan is one. He is my slave, in bond to me because I caught him once stealing meat from my cooking pot, in Mexico."

Sergeant Garcia bad been reading the document Favela had handed him. But he lifted his head quickly when somebody in the crowd shouted:

"Sergeant Garcia! I understand that you are in command here while your capitan is absent on an official journey. Will you allow a thing such as this?"

Garcia made a gesture of helplessness. "Senores this man has just exhibited to me a permit signed by the secretary of His Excellency, the Governor, and dated at Monterey," he replied. "This permit says plainly enough that this Carlos Favela may give his exhibition up and down the highway and in any and all places. He has proper official authority to do so. Do not blame me for this. senores."

Favela was grinning as the sergeant handed the document back to him, and Garcia did not like the grin.

"Senor Favela," the burly sergeant said, his voice very official in tone, "I have read your permit with official care, and it is it order. You are at liberty to give your performance of the three beasts if the people of this community desire to witness the abasement of a man."

"Abase a dog of a peon?" Favela cried, laughing loudly afterward.

"You have told us that he is in bond to you because he stole some meat from your cooking pot. Perhaps he was starving at the time, for he has a great body to feed. And for that small offense you have permission to make a beast of him and even force him to wrestle with a bear."

"Do you question the legality of my permit, Senor Sergeant?" Favela asked.

"I have said that the permit is in order. But one thing has been omitted from it no doubt through the carelessness of some hasty clerk."

"And what is that?" Favela asked, like a man a little worried.

"The permit does not state that you may beat a drum. So, Senor Favela, master of three beasts and one of them a man, do not pound your drum again in this pueblo. If you do, senor, I shall order my troopers to seize you on a charge of peace disturbance, and I am quite sure that our *magistrado*, being a humane man, will punish you severely."

FAVELA made a quick protest.

"But I always beat the drum to draw a crowd," he said.

"I am warning you not to beat it again in Reina de Los Angeles unless you are prepared to suffer the consequences for so doing."

Favela bent forward a little, and his eyes were gleaming as the corners of his lips twisted in a smile. "Ah, sergeant, I understand," he said. "Perhaps I have been too abrupt in my dealing with you. But the journey today has been hot, dusty and also fatiguing."

"For you, senor or for the man and bear you compel to pull your heavy cart?" Garcia asked.

"I think we can come to some sort of arrangement, sergeant I am not averse to buying good wine for a fine sergeant of the soldiery. And perhaps you may find a piece of gold in the bottom of your wine mug. *Quien sabe?*"

"So now you would try to bribe me?" Garcia bellowed. "Openly and in the presence of a number of our citizens! I warn you, do not beat your drum! People will think that I took your bribe."

"I only meant that I desire to be friendly with you," Favela said.

"Pitch your pavilion beside that tree and nowhere else!" the exasperated sergeant continued. "Keep the place clean. Do not let your dog bark loudly at night and disturb sleepers. And if your bear indicates violence toward any citizen. I'll order him destroyed. Is it understood?"

"Why should your manner toward me he so harsh, sergeant?" Favela whined. "I never met you until now, and I never did you a wrong."

"Beasts we have with us always, and some of them are to be admired for their qualities," Garcia pronounced. "But a brute is something else."

"You are trying to turn my audience against me. Monterey shall learn of this!"

"So now you are trying to threaten me?" Garcia asked, "You perhaps would have me punished and kicked out of the soldiery because I am enforcing the laws? Now you are worse than a brute, Senor Favela — you are a plain fool! Permits have been revoked before now. What if I complain to Monterey that you are taking an unfair advantage of that paper you carry, flouting the laws and the soldiery? Ha!"

Sergeant Garcia suddenly heard a soft drawling voice over his shoulder: "That was well spoken, sergeant."

The sergeant turned quickly and found Don Diego Vega standing behind him.

Diego yawned and brushed his nostrils with a silk handkerchief heavily perfumed. As usual, he was dressed resplendently. Regarded as lifeless, indolent, foppish, he was believed to be a thorn in the flesh of his proud hidalgo father, Don Alejandro Vega.

Only three men knew that this attitude of Diego's was only a pose, and that Diego Vega was also Senor Zorro, the wild-masked rider of the hills and highways who righted wrongs for the oppressed,

"Sergeant Garcia, here we have a splendid study in psychology," Diego said now. "The peon or bear could tear this Senor Favela to pieces if either realized his own strength. Even the dog might be able to get in a bite or two. But they are held under mental subjection."

"What manner of talk is this?" Favela shouted from the cart. "Who is this popinjay who rants at me?"

Sergeant Garcia's voice became a roar of thunder. "Senor!" he answered. This gentleman is Don Diego Vega, and scum like you will do well to keep his name off your tongues!"

"Ah — I have heard of the Vegas, and I humbly apologize," Favela said, bowing. "But your words irked me, Don Diego. I hold brute force in check because I am an experienced trainer of beasts."

"But let something happen to reveal to them that they are your superiors in strength, that even you, their master, can be handled and beaten down, and they would turn upon you," Diego told him. "If, for instance, this mysterious Senor Zorro should pay you a visit, disliking your inhumanity to man and beast—"

"Ha! I have heard of that masked fiend," Favela broke in. "Sergeant, I demand that you furnish me full protection. The permit I showed you — "

WITH an impatient exclamation, Garcia interrupted the showman.

"Made no reference about me protecting you from any man," he snapped. "At the moment I have only one concern regarding you, senor — do not beat your drum and annoy the townsmen. And keep your dog quiet after nightfall."

"How can I prevent a dog baying at the moon or answering the barks of other dogs?" Favela asked.

"That is your personal problem, senor. You have boasted that you are a trainer of beasts. Exhibit your skill." Sergeant Garcia smiled grimly.

"Keep my dog quiet after nightfall!" Favela repeated. "How can a man do that?"

He glanced down at the ground and let out a roar of rage. The dog had seized a chunk of meat the peon had tossed to the bear, and had carried it under the cart beyond the hungry bear's reach. Favela seized a heavy whip and dropped out of the car to the ground, his face a picture of fury.

"Perro Amarillo!" he shouted at the dog. "Here to me!"

Whimpering, the dog dropped the meat and crawled from beneath the car, cringing. When he was within reach. Favela struck with the whip. But no second blow fell. Diego Vega seized the showman's arm and prevented it.

"Do not strike the dog again, senor," Diego warned.

"What is this'?" Favela said. "I cannot correct my own beasts? This is too much!"

"The hungry dog has done no wrong. Feed him properly, and he will not steal food."

Diego had taken the whip from the hand of the startled showman, and now cast it aside. Uttering imprecations, Favela walked over to reclaim it.

The yellow dog rushed to Diego and began licking his hand, as if he understood that Diego had saved him from a beating. He sniffed at Diego's boots as if to get the scent of his friend, then retired quickly beneath the cart as Favela returned with the whip.

"I protest all this!" Favela told Sergeant Garcia. "I hold the Governor's permit — "

"But do not beat your drum again!" the sergeant broke in sternly. "And do not mistreat your beasts. I believe, Senor Favela, that you are not going to be popular in Reina de Los Angeles."

Garcia gestured, and the townsmen who had gathered began walking away. Diego turned toward the tavern, his manner as languid as usual but his eyes glittering, and Garcia paced along beside him.

"The low scoundrel." the sergeant muttered. "But what can I do. Don Diego? The fellow has an official permit, no douht obtained by bribery. 'Twould take a Senor Zorro to attend to this situation properly."

"That turbulent fellow!" Diego said. "Always stirring things up! But if he should hear of this affair and do something about it. What then?"

"I would have to take after the scamp with my troopers, of course, because we have orders to capture him, and also there is a big reward offered for the capture." Garcia replied, "But my heart would not be in the work. There are times when I admire the rascal."

"Have you no suspicion regarding the identity of this Senor Zorro," Diego asked, yawning.

"None. A score of men have been suspected and watched. It is my personal belief that Zorro lives at a distance, perhaps in the hills along the Coast to the north. No doubt the peons and natives aid him, hide and feed him, and act as his spies."

"That is possible," Diego admitted.

"And the padres of the missions — I do not put it beyond them to help him in his work. confess, Don Diego, that I have a measure of admiration for him — unofficially, of course. But he has been declared an outlaw, and his liberty and life are forfeit if he is caught. Since I am a sworn officer of the soldiery, I will do my duty and catch him if can."

Behind them in the plaza, with the big peon doing most of the heavy work while favela shouted orders, the colored pavilion was pitched, also a small tent behind it. The cooking pot was put out and a fire built under it, and Favela tossed meat and vegetables into the water in the pot and started a meal cooking. Then he gave Juan, the big peon, strict orders about watching the camp, chained the bear to a heavy post set in the ground, and waved the dog aside when he would have followed.

CROSSING the plaza to the tavern, Favela entered and bought cheap wine for a few loafers, boasting continually, and announcing that he would give his first performance immediately after the siesta hour. Then he returned to the pavilion to get some rest.

After the siesta hour many of the curious drifted toward the pavilion. Favela stood in front of it. Unable to beat his drum because of the orders of Sergeant Garcia, he used his heavy baritone voice and announced the nature of his entertainment. Men began paying the admission fee and passing into the big tent, where there was a small roped arena in the center, with seats and standing room in a three-quarter circle around it. No more customers being forthcoming, Favela closed the entrance of the pavilion and became the showman.

Sergeant Garcia and two of his troopers had entered the pavilion without paying the fee. And Don Diego Vega also honored the show with his presence. Diego sat a little apart from the others, his manner that of a bored man.

First, Favela put the yellow dog through his tricks, some of which were clever, always holding his whip ready. The dog acted thoroughly cowed, and eyed the whip continually as he worked. Then, Favela played a guitar and the big brown bear danced around and around, his eyes venomous at times, snarling through his muzzle, but always obeying. He caught the pole Favela tossed at him, held it as he danced and whirled, and tossed it back when Favela commanded.

So far, the show was nothing new except for some of the dog's tricks. And now Big Juan, the peon, came forward, dressed only in a loin cloth, his big body glistening with sweat, A human beast he appeared, for the expression in his face was that of a man with little reasoning.

Favela cracked his whip and began giving orders. Juan bent iron bars with his bare hands; he lifted two weights that no other man in the pavilion could have budged. Then, he moved to another and heavier weight.

The peon grasped it, tugged and strained without success. The perspiration streamed from him. He glanced at Favela and at the whip and began whimpering like a young puppy afraid.

"Lift the weight, lazy one?" Favela shout. "The senores have paid their money to watch you do it!"

He cracked the whip and Juan tried again, continuing his whimpering. Favela darted forward. The whip swished through the air, and the lash cut into the peon's sore back. Big Juan gave a cry of pain, tried again, and lifted the weight off the floor. Some of the spectators cheered. The peon staggered backward, licking at his lips as he watched the ever-ready whip.

"Rest a moment, and then we will have the wrestling match," Favela told him. He turned to the spectators. "The peon wrestling the ferocious bear will conclude the entertainment. Senores. If you have relished the show, please tell your friends. I cannot summon another crowd, because I am forbidden to beat my drum." He glanced toward Sergeant Garcia.

"That is right." Garcia called to him. "Do not beat it!"

Diego Vega had a seat off to one side.

"Senor Favela," he called out. "You hurt the peon with your whip, and his back is a thing of sores already. I am quite sure none among the spectators will object if you do not make him wrestle the bear at this time."

"I must do so, Don Diego," Favela replied. "If there is a variation of the usual program, I may lose control of my beasts. They may think I am growing weak and soft. They have been trained with a whip, and by a whip they must live."

The wrestling match began. There was nothing bogus about it, for it was no mere dancing and tumbling match. The peon screamed once with pain as the bear's claws ripped his sore back. Favela dashed in and used the whip on man and bear alike.

"Wrestle well," he yelled. "The senores have paid."

That was when Don Diego Vega slipped quietly out of the pavilion. He was breathing heavily, his eyes were aflame, and his hands had turned into fists at the ends of the arms he held rigidly at his sides.

He went quickly to his father's house and to his own rooms therein, Bernardo, his mute servant, one of the three who knew he was Zorro, was waiting to serve him. Diego beckoned to him, bent his head and whispered:

"Zorro rides tonight. Have everything ready."

BERNARDO nodded vigorously, and smiled. The only order needed had been spoken. Bernardo, after nightfall, would bring Zorro's black horse from his hiding place and make him ready. He would have Zorro's costume and weapons prepared.

It was almost a perfect night for Zorro's exploit. A swirling fog had drifted in from the distant sea. It obscured sight and distorted sounds. There was a damp chill in the air, and few townsmen were abroad, most of them keeping to their houses and huts. In the tavern, there was roistering, and lights gleamed in the barracks as they did every night.

Dressed in black costume, with a black mask enveloping his head, with blade and pistol and long black punishing whip ready, Zorro emerged from his safe hiding place and rode forth into the miserable night.

Bent on the deserved punishment of a cruel man, nevertheless his mind was dwelling at the moment on the great Vega rancho out near San Gabriel, on its vast herds and flocks, its wild vequero riders.

But he brought his mind back to present things as he neared the buildings. From a safe dark hiding spot he surveyed the plaza. Embers were red beneath the cooking pot in front of the showman's pavilion. A lighted torch burned within, and a smaller one in the tent behind it. No sounds came from the camp of Favela.

Zorro rode closer and listened for a short time, and could hear only heavy snoring. The big bear was fastened to his post but gave the rider on the black horse no attention, though the horse snorted and backed away at scent of the bear. The dog was on the ground before the pavilion, and got up with his ruff bristling, but only growled as Zorro turned his horse and rode away.

He went now to the vicinity of the tavern, dismounted a short distance from the building and continued forward afoot through the swirling mist, a shadow lost among other shadows. He came finally to a place from which he could peer through a dirty window and into the big main room of the tavern.

Senor Favela was there, drinking and playing at dice, boasting loudly about his accomplishments, and buying cheap wine for those who listened to his boasts. Zorro retreated and got into his saddle again, and rode off through the misty night. He went now to the vicinity of the barracks. Torches were burning in front of the building, and lights gleamed in the quarters of the commanding officer, where Sergeant Garcia was now installed during the absence of his capitan.

In front of the barracks under a protecting shed stood three saddled mounts, and one of them Zorro recognized as the big sorrel Sergeant Garcia usually rode. He rode safely away from the barracks to circle the pueblo and approach the plaza again, cautious not to be observed, ready to swerve aside into the darkness quickly if he heard the hoofbeats of another rider's mount.

It was Carlos Favela he wanted to punish. And he sensed that a man like

Favela would remain at the tavern until dawn, drinking wine, gambling, boasting. And Zorro wanted to have his work done and be gone long before the dawn. He dismounted a short distance from the pavilion, trailed the reins of his trained horse, and went forward carefully afoot. The dog arose and growled again.

"Quiet, fellow" Zorro said, But he spoke not in the voice of Zorro, but in that of Don Diego Vega, which the dog had heard that day. The dog whimpered and ran to him, backed away at the apparition of the masked man in black, and then came forward again cautiously to get the scent. A moment later he was jumping at Zorro in joy at recognizing the friend who had saved him from a beating.

"Quiet, boy," Zorro urged again.

The dog did not bark. Zorro went to the wall of the pavilion, keeping out of the light as much as possible. He lifted a corner of the tenting and peered inside. The big peon Juan, was stretched on his stomach and face on the floor of dirt, snoring, moaning, and by the flickering light of the torch Zorro could see that the man's cheeks were tear-stained.

It was Favela, the author of all this misery, that Zorro was eager to reach. He had to draw Favela from the tavern. He backed away from the tent wall, trying to think of a plan. Then, he saw the big drum.

IT RESTED against the wall of the smaller tent, which was Favela's own living quarters. The dog retreated when Zorro motioned. Zorro went to the big drum and took the stick from its fastening. Suddenly, he began pounding the drum. The beats shivered through the fog-ridden air and gathered volume as such sounds will in a fog. The sounds reverberated and seemed to fill the plaza, the entire town.

Zorro motioned for the dog to remain behind, hurried of into the darkness and got into saddle again. He heard loud voices as the door of the tavern was thrown open, light streamed forth and the door spewed men into the night.

He heard another sound also. At the barracks Sergeant Garcia was bellowing his wrath, and bits and sabers were jangling as Garcia and a couple of his troopers mounted and began racing toward the plaza.

Zorro, mounted, backed back into the darkness and swirling fog to watch and listen. He saw the peon, aroused by the beating of the drum, lurch out into the light cast by the torch. Garcia and his two troopers came with pounding hoofs beneath them, to reach the showman's camp and tumble from their saddles. They saw the peon and bear, and the dog snarling as he backed away from them.

Then, Carlos Favela came running and panting across the plaza to stop almost breathless near the others.

"So you did it!" Sergeant Garcia thundered. "You beat the confounded drum."

"Pardon. Senor Sergeant! I was gambling in the tavern when somebody beat the drum. I came here running. Those who were in the room there will swear to it."

"That is right, Garcia," some man called.

"Who beat the drum, then?" Garcia demanded. "It aroused the entire town." He saw the peon, and turned to Favela again. "Ah, trainer of beasts — so! You would play a trick on Manuel Garcia. eh? You train your peon slave to beat the drum while you are absent, perhaps at a given signal."

"I am innocent of any trick!" Favela cried, plainly frightened now.

"Who beat the drum, then? Juan, come to me."

The frightened peon, his eyes heavy with sleep, shuffled forward. "Did you pound that drum?" Garcia demanded.

The peon spoke in the dull monotone of a man with scarcely any wits. "No, senor," he said. "I — I was asleep."

"Asleep, were you?" Favela shouted. "I told you to guard the camp. I'll whip you for this! Had you been awake, you would have seen who beat the drum. Senor Sergeant! Some trickster, knowing I was at the tavern, did this to cause me trouble."

"That may be possible." Garcia admitted. "Remain here at your camp. Favela, and see that nothing like this happens again. And do not punish the peon. After playing ox all day and helping pull your heavy cart, after bending bars and lifting weights and wrestling with a bear, I do not doubt he was tired enough to go to sleep. You have been warned!"

Zorro watched as Garcia and his men swung up into their saddles and started back to the barracks. Favela was almost like a madman frothing at the mouth as he paced around in front of his pavilion.

The sounds of the troopers' retreating hoof-beats dwindled and died. One of the torches flared and was extinguished. Carlos Favela continued to stride around like a wild man. The bear snarled when he came near the post. The dog whimpered and kept close to the wall of the tent. The big peon stood there like a patient ox, shivering with fear, awaiting punishment. When he was sure nobody remained. Favela picked up his whip.

"Come here, Juan!" he ordered.

The peon began moaning, but he bent his head and advanced slowly.

"You pounded that drum," Favela accused. "Now, I am going to whip you until your back is raw. You are always causing me trouble."

By the light of the remaining torch, Zorro saw the peon cringe, heard him moan again, and he stepped nearer. Favela was crouched before him, whip held ready, a murderous look in his face.

"I'll half kill you this time, slave!" the crazed Favela cried. "You brought the sergeant down upon me, You have ruined business for me here."

ZORRO stepped forward through the darkness.

"Turn your back to me and take it," Favela ordered the peon.

Carlos Favela heard a cold voice behind him. It was the voice of Senor Zorro, not of Diego Vega.

"Do not touch the man, rogue!" the voice said.

Giving a cry of surprise, Favela whirled. He saw before his the masked man dressed in black. In his right hand he held a whip, and his left hand was clutching the butt of a pistol in his belt.

"Wh-what is this? What manner of man are you?" Favela asked.

"I am Zorro. I have come to punish you for your cruelty to man and beast. After I whip you, senor, get gone from this place quickly, at the morning's dawn, or I'll visit you again and give you worse punishment."

Favela dropped the whip as though frightened, and retired a step. His right hand had gone to his head, and then to the back of his neck. Zorro knew that trick — the knife concealed at the back of the neck beneath the heavy shirt.

As Favela drew the heavy throwing knife and lifted his hand to hurl it, Zorro's whip lashed out. It wrapped around the showman's forearm and jerked him forward. He dropped the knife before it could be hurled. The whip released him. Then, Carlos Favela felt the lash biting into his body as his own lash so often had bitten into the body of his peon slave. He tried to shield his head from the blows. He tried to turn and run, and the lash always wrapped around him and jerked him back.

"Help — " he began shouting.

The whip wrapped around his throat and choked the cry that had rung out on the foggy night.

Zorro drove him backward, and Favela bumped against the big drum. He seized the stick and began pounding the drum.

"Help!" he shouted again. "Zorro is here," the first beating of the drum was answered by the sounds of hoofbeats. and Zorro knew that Sergeant Garcia, exasperated now beyond endurance, was returning at top speed. He lashed Favela again.

The bear was straining at the chain that held him to the post, snarling his rage at Favela. The big peon lumbered forward.

"Juan!" Zorro howled at him. "Do not touch this man. Do not use your great strength. I, Zorro, will see that you are set free and given work where you will be paid. If you beat this man now, you will be punished."

Zorro turned and ran off into the night where his black horse was waiting. And Perro Amarillo, the dog, followed at his heels, yelping and dancing around him. Zorro motioned for him to go hack, ordered him to do so, but the dog would not.

Garcia and his two troopers came rushing into the camp.

"Help!" Favela cried at them. "Zorro was here a moment ago. He lashed me."

"Serves you right," Garcia said. "Scum that you are!"

"He is an outlaw. There is a reward."

"Which way did he go?" Garcia demanded. "I hear no hoofbeats."

"He dashed away afoot. The dog — the dog followed him."

"Running him down — trailing him?" Garcia asked.

"No. Following him as if the man were a friend. And that dog — we never have been here before. The only man at whom he has not snarled is — Don Diego Vega. The dog licked his hand today when Don Diego made me stop beating him."

Watching and listening from the darkness, Zorro had seen and heard all this. Now he spurred the black horse and hoofbeats thundered through the night. The dog yelped and followed the horse. Zorro knew he would have to lose the dog when the pursuit began, which it did immediately. And there was another danger. The fact that the dog had been friendly, the hint that Don Diego Vega was the only man in the vicinity who had made a friend of the dog — the eager Sergeant Garcia, a man holding to his duty as a soldier, might make an immediate investigation.

LIGHTLY Zorro used his spurs as the pursuit thundered behind him. The joyous yelps of the pursuing dog grew fainter as the horse left him far behind. The sergeant and his troopers were left a distance behind also. Zorro turned off the trail abruptly stopped his horse for an instant, and let the pursuit rush by. Then he used the spurs again, made a circuit, and came to the spot where Bernardo, his mute body servant awaited him.

"Be quick!" he ordered, as he stripped off the Zorro costume he wore over his other clothing and tossed aside Zorro's weapons. "Get the horse and these things away, to the usual place. I am pursued."

Zorro was gone, and it was Diego Vega who got quickly into his father's house without being seen. Silently, he gained his room stripped off his clothes and got into night attire. And there came a pounding on the front door.

He wiped the perspiration from his face, mussed up his hair, left the room and went to the end of the hallway. His father, called by a servant, had opened the door to Sergeant Garcia.

"What means this night summons?" Don Alejandro Vega asked, sternly. He knew what Diego had planned for the night, and had heard him enter the house and get to his room, and knew the troopers had pursued.

"Zorro has been at work again," Garcia said. "And it was believed that Zorro is Don Diego, because of a certain circumstance. To decide this matter — where is your son, Don Diego. now?"

Diego, yawning brushing a scented handkerchief across his nostrils, entered the room. "What is all this tumult?" he asked, yawning again and certainly presenting a perfect picture of a man just aroused from sleep.

Garcia looked at him. "Don Diego, I ask your pardon and that of your illustrious father," Garcia said. "Zorro beat the showman for cruelty, and the showman's dog followed him away in a friendly spirit. And because you stopped him beating the dog today and the dog licked your hand — "

"Oh, spare me details." Diego begged. He knew the dog had caught his scent despite the Zorro costume. "Perhaps the hound was only chasing this Zorro and trying to earn the Governor's reward. Kindly allow me to return to bed."

"I ask your pardon again, Don Diego."

"Granted," Diego replied. "But I wish these scenes of turbulence would come to an end. Why do you not catch this mysterious Senor Zorro and end them?"

But his fingers were crossed behind his back when he said it.

Zorro's Strange Duel

A brutal taskmaster meets is punishment when a masked avenger comes a-riding to deal out a taste of the whip!

DOWN the broad gradual slope that led toward the big shearing pens, bleating their plaintive protests as they traveled, came thousands of sheep heavy with their coats of wool. Herders were shouting stridently, the sheep dogs were barking at their charges, and clouds of line dust were lilting behind the flocks.

The eyes of Diego Vega were glowing as he watched the scene. He loved the Rancho Vega, which had been in his family since the vast unimproved acreage had been granted to an ancestor by the King of Spain. Re loved its great flocks and herds, its broad acres with rolling hills and shady canyons.

He liked to look over the fruitful orchards and vineyards, and inspect the scattered adobe buildings — the store-houses, workers' huts, the stables. And most of all he liked to stroll leisurely through the sprawling rancho house which nestled in a grove of gigantic pepper trees whose crimson berries stained the ground in season — the place where he had been born.

Now, sheep-shearing time had come again in California. In an hour or so, the first of the sheep would be in the shearing pens.

The regular workers on the rancho, and the extra help — peons and natives engaged especially for the shearing — were standing by, ready to commence their work. They had removed their hats and bowed their heads while aged Fray Felipe, the padre from the chapel in Reina de Los Angeles, had given them his blessing.

The extra workers would receive a red metal marker as each sheep was shorn properly and the fleece put aside, to be cashed In at the end of the shearing season. This had been a bountiful year, for the lambing had been greater than usual, and the shearing would take some time and payment would be greater than in other years.

The herders had driven their flocks in from the high bills and fertile valleys where grazing was good to report to Cassara, the rancho overseer, and have their flocks tallied to show the increase. The herders soon would receive their reward for the season's work. And when the shearing was over there would be the usual fiesta, with an abundance of food and wine, music and dancing for all.

TWO adjoining ranchos also were starting their sheep shearing today. One was the property of a proud old hidalgo, a friend of the Vega family. The other property had been purchased a year or so before from a dissolute heir by a man named Pedro Melendez. He was a person of no special standing, and was reported to be unscrupulous and cruel, and to have made his money by crooked gambling.

Because, there generally were fights between the rancho vaqueros and imported workmen, Sergeant Manuel Garcia, from the barracks at Reina de Los Angeles, was present with three of his best troopers to keep the peace. The fights were usually inspired by jealousy over some native wench, or because the vaqueros, being handlers of cattle, assumed themselves superior to the handlers of sheep.

Diego Vega was sitting his saddle on a spirited horse in a dispirited manner beside his mounted father, Don Alejandro. Diego sagged forward in his saddle and yawned at intervals as if the whole affair bored him and he considered it only a necessary nuisance.

The lips of his stern father twisted slightly at the corners as he watched his son. Only Don Alejandro and two others knew that Diego, who posed as an indolent fop, was also the mysterious Senor Zorro, the fox, who rode the highways and punished those who showed cruelty and inhumanity to men in lesser circumstances.

A short distance away, an assistant overseer with a stentorian voice was announcing the arrival of the various flocks and the names of their chief herders. The gates of the shearing pens were opened, the first sheep were admitted, and the work of shearing began.

Fray Felipe dismounted from the back of his riding mule and went among the workers like a kind father among his children, cheering them on in their work. Don Alejandro dismounted and handed his reins to a peon waiting to take them, and Diego did also. Father and son always walked through the shearing pens each year as the work began.

As father and son walked past them, the workers stopped long enough to knuckle their foreheads in salute and respect. Diego held a scented handkerchief to his nostrils as if the stench of sheep, fleece and sweat nauseated him.

As they emerged from the last of the shearing pens, their inspection concluded, Cassara, the rancho overseer, approached and saluted them.

"Is everything going well, Cassara?" Don Alejandro asked.

'The fleece is heavy this season, Don Alejandro, the number of animals to be sheared is greater than usual, and we have good workers," Cassara replied. "But there is one thing I dislike."

"And what is that?" Don Alejandro asked. "JoséAmaro, the labor contractor from Reina de Los Angeles, has furnished the rancho with twenty men, fifteen of them being natives. I am sure he is mistreating and swindling them."

"How is this?"

"He stands over them continually with a whip, urging them to work faster and harder. He uses the whip frequently across their backs. And when the red markers are given to the men he takes them to hold for cashing, saying the men are in debt to him already for food and clothing furnished by him. He is making slaves of the poor wretches, Don Alejandro."

"A thing like that cannot be allowed on Rancho Vega," Don Alejandro replied sternly. "Here, we always treat men as men. Show me where this José Amaro has his men at '~.rork."

Cassara led Don Alejandro and Diego through one of the shearing pens almost to the rear end, and stopped there and pointed.

José Amaro was a short, heavy-set man with bulging biceps. There was a deep scar across his chin, and one of his eyes drooped from an injury. He gave evidenee of having led a violent life.

Amaro's jacket was off and his sleeves were rolled up above his elbows. He held a long heavy whip with a braided lash. His men were working in a line across the end of the shearing shed. There was a narrow raised walk behind them, and José Amaro strode back and forth on this walk, shouting to the men for greater activity and threatening to use the whip.

The natives in the group of workers were laboring feverishly, like men fearing the lash. Don Alejandro and Cassara both knew that the threat held over them constantly, impaired their work instead of bettering it.

STANDING off to one side and watching, Don Alejandro and the others in the group were not observed by Amaro, who was busy scanning his men and driving them their work.

Sergeant Garcia and one of his three troopers came from outside the pen and approached to announce their presence to Don Alejandro and to be assigned to quarters by Cassara, having waited until the ceremonies were over and the actual shearing had commenced.

Diego was looking at José Amaro, estimating him. He watched him brandish his whip and listened as Amaro called the men lazy dogs and promised dire punishment if their work tally was not satisfactory at the end of the day.

"There is a base fellow," Diego whispered to his father, "and he irks me."

"To what extent, Diego?" Don Alejandro asked, his eyes gleaming as he looked at his son.

"Before I reply to that; my father, let us ascertain whether this fellow is really cruel or only blustery."

"And if he is cruel?"

"If he is, Senor Zorro may have some riding to do."

As they were speaking, aged Fray Felipe came through the long shearing shed and toward them, blessing the workers as he passed. The padre and the sergeant reached the Vegas and Cassara at the same time.

As they arrived, there was an uproar at the end of the shed. A whip cracked and a man screeched with mingled rage and pain. José Amaro's rough voice could be heard.

"Work, scum! Earn your food! Earn red markers for me! I'll shred the skin of your back with the whip!"

Cassara was the first to start forward, for he did not want this affair to get the other workers stirred up and cause them to become unsettled and fail to do their work properly. At a nod from Don Alejandro, Sergeant Garcia hurried after the overseer. Don Alejandro and Diego, with Fray Felipe between them, went forward also.

Before even Cassara reached the spot, there was a wild screech from a man's throat and a scramble as one of the native workers sprang toward José Arnaro and tried to stab him with his sharp wool shears. Amaro warded off the blow with his left forearm, then his right first crashed into the face of the native who had attacked him, smashing his nose and hurling him off the elevated walk to fall senseless on the floor of the shed.

"Any more of you scum want to try it?" Amaro howled, his eyes ablaze as he grasped the whip firmly.

Then Sergeant Garcia, who had rushed on at Don Alejandro's signal, was upon the infuriated man with his trooper at his heels. Everybody in the shed had stopped work to watch what happened. Garcia and the trooper seized Amaro, tore the whip from his grasp, and held him firmly.

"Let your blood cool," Garcia advised, as the labor contractor ceased struggling.

"That fiend — he attacked me," Amaro cried. "I'll have his hide off his back in strips! Release me!"

"We saw the whole affair," the sergeant told him. "You struck him across the back with your whip."

"These natives are working out debts to me," Amaro said. "They are lazy, slow, being so purposely."

"How do you expect them to work well when you stand over them with a whip?" Don Alejandro asked.

"I contracted with the rancho' to supply twenty men, arid here they are," the contractor replied. "I know how to get work out of them, either natives or peons. That man was not working well and I whipped him to bring him back to life."

"And now you have made him senseless with a blow, and probably will get no more work at all out of him for some days," Garcia pointed out.

"He attacked me with the shears — you say you saw it. Sergeant Garcia, I demand that you arrest the fellow and take him to your barracks and throw him into the prison room. I want the magistrado to sentence him to the whipping post!"

"One moment!" Garcia thundered. "Do you perhaps think that you are His Excellency the Governor? You demand I do this and that, do you? And you would give our magistrado his orders also?"

"I know my rights!"

"Every man has rights," Fray Felipe put in, softly.

"But this native scum — "

"Is a human being," the padre interrupted.

José Amaro laughed aloud. "A human being, and he has rights — a bronze, ignorant, lazy native! This is what comes of letting the padres convert them and tell them that they are better than they really are."

"Silence!" Sergeant Garcia roared. "You are speaking to a padre."

DIEGO VEGA felt his blood commence boiling. The brutal treatment of the native, Amaro's arrogance, this insult to the aged padre and his kind — Diego wished he dare take this affair into his own hands right now.

But he had his pose to maintain, as protection for himself and his father. He could not be Zorro at the moment. He was the fashionably dressed weakling now. He held in his rage and kept in the background.

Both his father and Fray Felipe knew what he was thinking. Besides his father, the padre was another of the three men who knew the truth about Zorro, and the padre was his confessor and could not reveal the truth — and would not have done so. The third who knew was Bernardo, Diego's peon body servant, who was a mute and could not speak.

Don Alejandro stepped forward.

"Things like this cannot be allowed on Rancho Vega," he said. "We treat everybody kindly here."

"It is a mistake, Don Alejandro, to coddle such vermin," Amaro declared. "It sets a bad example for other rancho owners."

Don Alejandro's eyes burned and his chin was thrust out as he took a step forward.

"Are you, senor, presuming to tell me how to run a rancho?" he demanded. "You are insolent!"

"If a native dolt is a man like me, as the padre has said, then I am as good as a don," the contractor said.

Diego had to fight himself well to hold himself in check then. To hear his aged, adored father addressed so by a brutal, swindling handler of unfortunate men — it was too much! But he could not rush in and handle the man with all the others in the shed watching the scene and others hurrying from the other sheds to learn of the commotion.

Don Alejandro handled the matter himself.

"Get off the rancho with your men!" he ordered Amaro.

"I have a contract — "

"Cassara!" Don Alejandro ordered the overseer. "Pay this man for one day for himself and his workers. Care for the man he has hurt. Sergeant Garcia, kindly call your other two troopers and see that this man loads his cart" and clears out immediately."

"At once, Don Alejandro," the sergeant agreed.

Don Alejandro faced the other men the contractor had brought.

"If any of you wish to remain here and work for the rancho and be paid for it, you may do so," he said. "I'll see that you are not bothered by this fellow Amaro."

"Most of them are bound to me for debt!" the contractor screeched. "It is illegal!"

"How many are so bound?"

"The fifteen natives."

"Then the other five peons may remain here and work in peace," Don Alejandro decided. "The hurt man will be cared for until he is well again. Take the others, Amaro, clean out your huts, load your cart and go. And do not let me learn later that you have mistreated any of these poor men."

"Once off your land, I'll do as I please," Amaro replied. "Even the proud and powerful Don Alejandro Vega doesn't run the entire country!"

Don Alejandro's face purpled with rage. But Sergeant Garcia's other two troopers had reached the scene, and the sergeant and his men prepared to take Amaro and his workers out of the shearing shed.

"See that they leave Rancho Vega land," Don Alejandro told the sergeant. "We do not use slave labor here."

"This is not the only rancho in the district," Amaro said. "I can hire my men to Pedro Melendez easily enough. And I'll make them work."

"I'll look in on you, to see that you do not go too far with your whip and fists," Sergeant Garcia promised. "Come along!"

As the men were taken from the shed, Don Alejandro whispered to Cassara: "Have some good man follow and watch, and bring back a report"

Cassara nodded and turned aside to see that the others had commenced shearing again. Fray Felipe had gone to comfort the workers with his presence. Don Alejandro and Diego left the shed and strolled toward where their horses were waiting.

"My father," Diego said.

"Yes, my son?"

"If the report comes back that Amaro has shown more cruelty, Zorro will ride tonight."

"He never rode in a worthier cause," Don Alejandro declared.

T HE troopers took Amaro and his workmen to the huts which had been assigned to then, and instructed them to gather their belongings, cooking pots and supplies and load them in Amaro's cart, a huge affair drawn by mules.

When the cart was loaded, Amaro got upon it to drive the mules, making his men walk beside the vehicle where he could keep his eyes on them. Garcia and his troopers escorted the cart down the road and to the highway, outside Vega land.

"Go your way!" the sergeant ordered. "I am none too soft where some of the natives are concerned, but too much brutality is too much. And you were insolent to a good padre, and to Don Alejandro Vega, known for his many acts of kindness. Get you gone!" José Amaro bowed mockingly and started the mules. The workmen trudged along beside the cart.

At a distance, Cassara's spy followed them unseen.

It was only a short distance from the Rancho Vega to that of Pedro Melendez.

There, José Amaro was greeted warmly, for Melendez, because of his reputation, had

been unable to get enough shearers.

Amaro explained what had happened at Rancho Vega.

"Here, amigo, you are your own man," Melendez told him. "How you handle your peons and natives is no affair of mine, as long as you get work done."

"I'll see to that," Amaro promised.

"Take those huts over there for your men," Melendez instructed. "There is ample fuel for your cooking pots, and you can draw food from my overseer, also a skin of wine for yourself. I'll come over this evening and drink with you, and perhaps we can have some fun making your natives dance."

"I'll make them dance!" Amaro promised. "Like they never have danced before! After what happened, they must be convinced that it is a bad thing to lift hands against their betters."

"It grows late in the afternoon," Melendez said. "Fix your camp, and put your group at work in the morning."

A couple of hours after dusk, Cassara went to the rancho house and asked to see Don Alejandro and Don Diego. His report was soon made.

"The man I sent to watch has returned," the overseer said. "Amaro hired his men to Pedro Melendez, and they made camp at some of the old huts. Later,

*As Melendez grasped his
weapon, Zorro's pistol
belched flame and lead.*

Melendez and his overseer visited Amaro's camp. Amaro had been drinking heavily of wine. He and Melendez were still drinking when our man left, after seeing much."

"What did he see?" Diego asked.

"Amaro has been punishing the men one by one, drawing out what he calls fun, and Melendez watches and laughs with him. Amaro makes a man dance until he drops from exhaustion, using the whip on him meanwhile. Melendez carries a pistol, and he threatened to use it on any man who moved against Amaro, and say afterward that the man attacked him."

"Has this story spread?" Diego asked.

"Sergeant Garcia knows what is happening, but I told our man to say nothing about it to anybody else."

Cassara bowed and left. Sitting at the table with Diego and his father was Fray Filipe. Diego looked first at one of them and then at the other, got up and paced the floor a short time, then stopped beside them.

"It is settled," he said quietly. "Zorro rides tonight"

"Punish, but do not kill save to protect your own life," the padre admonished.

Diego nodded and wandered from the room, through the patio, and to the rear kitchens. There he found the dumb Bernardo devouring food and beckoned him.

"Zorro rides," Diego said. "Get the horse and everything ready, and meet me in the usual place at the abandoned warehouse. None of the sheep shearers are quartered there. And not the middle of the night this time, Bernardo — but now."

Bernardo went back to finish his meal and then slip away unobserved. Diego strolled back into the house and found his father and the padre still there.

"This must be done at once," he explained in whispers. "My absence from the house must be covered if any ask for me."

"No doubt you will be prowling around the men's fires listening to them sing, or looking at the moon and thinking of poetry," Don Alejandro replied. "Use great care, Diego."

GOING to his own room, Diego remained there for a short time, reading, with the draperies drawn aside so anybody passing could glance through and see him. Presently he drew the draperies, waited for a short time as if preparing to retire, then extinguished the tapers in the room,

By a way he knew well, he got out of the house, avoided the huts where vaqueros and workmen were-playing music and dancing as they ate and drank, and went through the orchard and to the old adobe warehouse, where Bernardo was waiting.

Bernardo held Zorro's black horse, and Zorro's costume and weapons. Diego worked swiftly to draw on the Zorro black costume over his other clothing, buckle on blade, thrust pistol into belt, and make sure his long whip was fastened to his saddle.

He had made these preparations many times to punish some beast who mistreated the weak and helpless. But never had he prepared with greater enthusiasm than tonight.

Don Diego Vega, the indolent popinjay, disappeared. In his stead was Zorro, a man with every sense alert, every nerve on edge, who had changed in bodily carriage, manner and voice.

He instructed Bernardo to remain there and wait for his return, then rode through the night, keeping off the road and avoiding the main highway. There was a moon, but scudding clouds obscured it more than half the time. Zorro soon covered the short distance to the buildings of the Pedro Melendez rancho.

Without trouble, he located the bunch of old adobe huts where José Amaro and his men were quartered. They were at a safe distance, he judged, from the regular rancho men andt he other extra sheep shearers.

A fire burned before Amaro's hut. Zorro could hear loud, raucous laughter, the crack of a whip, a man's yelp of pain. He watched and listened carefully for a short time, then urged his powerful black horse forward.

Keeping to the shadows, and advancing once for a distance when the moon was behind the scudding clouds, he neared the spot be wanted to reach.

He could view the scene clearly now. Both Pedro Melendez and José Amaro were in a state of drunken cruelty. Of Amaro's men, several were stretched on the ground groaning. Two others had been tied to stakes with their wrists bound behind their backs.

Amaro was striding back and forth cracking his whip, and one of the natives was kneeling before him with the ragged shirt torn from his back.

"Make him dance again, Amaro," Melendez was calling. "He's your man, in bond to you for debt. I'll watch these other scum of yours. If one makes a move, I'll pistol him. That one who said he'd complain to the troopers — save that rogue for the last. He needs a dose of bitter medicine."

"He'll get it," Amaro said. "Ha! How I wish I had that proud Don Alejandro Vega and his weak son here before me! I'd make them dance."

Zorro took advantage of another cloud in front of the moon and edged the black closer, finally stopping him in the darkness at the side of the hut nearest the fire. His every sense was alert, for this was a position of danger. If a tumult began, many of Pedro Melendez' men would come running at his call. The element of surprise, quick punishment, and quick retreat were needed here.

"On your feet, dog!" Amaro barked at the kneeling native. "There's no padre here to help you now. Dance!"

"Senor, I cannot," the native whimpered. "I am so tired I cannot stand."

"I'll make you jump," Amaro declared.

The whip cracked and the lash bit into the man's back. He gave a cry of pain and helplessness and sprawled on his face in the gravely dirt. Amaro lifted the whip again.

"Up, and dance!" he ordered.

Pedro Melendez took another swig from the wineskin he was holding, and laughed. Zorro dug with his spurs and jumped his black horse around the corner of the hut, to skid him to a stop a short distance from the fire.

"Do not strike again, Amaro!" Zorro's deep voice warned.

With an ejaculation of surprise, Melendez struggled to get to his feet. Amaro dropped his arm to his side, and his eyes bulged and his lower jaw sagged.

B EFORE them, they saw the black horse, the masked rider dressed in black, and plainest of all the menacing pistol he held.

"Back up to me! And you, Peddro Melendez stand still! I will hold my pistol in my left hand as I whip, and will use it if you make a move."

Amaro was on Zorro's right as a transferred the pistol to his left hand and got his heavy whip off the pommel of his saddle. Melendez was ahead of the black horse and slightly to the left.

Zorro had no time to rearrange their positions. It was still early in the night, and the sheep shearers were roistering around their fires a short distance away. And the moon was playing hide and seek with the clouds, shining brightly one moment and obscured the next. The light from the fire exposed the scene, too, to anybody who might happen to look that way.

"Mercy, Senor Zorro!" Amaro moaned.

"A cowardly brute is always a craven," Zorro told him. "So you whine, eh? Men have asked you for mercy, and they got no more than I am going to give you now."

As Amaro started to turn and back up toward the black horse, Pedro Melendez made a bold move. He knew what it would mean for him if he could capture or kill the famous Zorro. Officials would bless him for it, and he would receive a rich reward.

He stepped aside quickly, and his right hand made a dive toward his sash to grasp the pistol there. But Zorro saw the move from the corner of his eye. His own pistol flamed and barked and belched smoke and lead. Melendez dropped his weapon without firing, staggered and sprawled as a breast wound began bleeding.

The firing had been heard in the distance, and there was a sudden commotion of singing around the fires. And, as Zorro turned his head to deal with Amaro, he heard the swish of a lash, a whip missed his head and curled over this shoulder, and the end of the lash bit into his back.

Taking advantage of the instant in which Zorro had compelled to attend to

Melendez, Amaro had whirled and began lashing with his whip, a weapon with which he was adept through long cruel practice.

Amarao continued lashing as Zorro swerved his horse, and the labor contractor shouted as he fought:

"Help! Help! Senor Melendez is being attacked!"

Zorro was using his own whip now. And this was the strangest duel he ever had fought. He felt a measure oi fear, too. Amaro's lash could mark him if it landed squarely. It would cut through his clothing, even through his cloth mask and mark his face — and possibly point the way to Zorro.

His pistol had been discharged, and he could not use that. It would be difficult to draw blade without being cut by Amaro's whip, and he did not care to stain his caballero's blade with the blood of such a wretch. Nor did he wish to kill now — only to give a cruel rogue degrading punishment and drive him out of the country.

THE whips met, wrapped around each other. Zorro Jerked Amaro toward him violently, and the whips held. Another jerk, Amaro let go his grasp, and his whip became untangled from Zorro's and sailed through the air.

"Help! Help!" Amaro was screeching.

Men had left the other fires and were running toward the spot. Zorro jumped his horse toward Amaro, and now his whip sang through the air and the lash cut into Amaro's body, until he was prone on the ground, a whining thing. "Get out of the country, or we meet again," Zorro warned.

Shouting men were rushing toward him, brandishing all sorts of weapons, as he hooked his whip to his saddle and gathered up the reins to ride. Then he heard hoof-beats.

"Well done, Senor Zorro!" the voice of Sergeant Garcia roared. "We have been watching. But now, senor — outlaw and highwayman — you belong to me. Surrender to the Law!"

Gracia and one of his troopers, having heard of Amaro's cruelty from Cassara's spy, had ridden over to learn the truth of the affair. But here was bigger game for Garcia — Senor Zorro, who bore on his head the Governor's reward for capture or death.

This was no time for hesitation. Zorro wheeled his horse, bent low in the saddle, and rode. Pistols exploded behind him and bullets whistled past him, but none struck home. The moon went behind the scudding clouds again for a short time, and Zorro, knowing this land well, rode with greater speed than the more cautious troopers.

He circled away from the rancho buildings, slowed down his horse, and made a big circle to get back to Rancho Vega. Bernardo was waiting at the abandoned warehouse.

"Hide everything — be quick!" Zorro said.

He stripped off his costume, mask, weapons then began running beneath the trees of the orchard to get hack to the house. He could feel blood soaking his clothes from the whip cut on his back. Fray Falipe could attend to the wound, he knew.

Without being observed, he got into the patio. A serape had been left on a bench there, and Diego Vega threw it over his shoulder carelessly so it would cover his blood-soaked clothing from the eyes of servants.

His father and Fray Felipe were sitting in the main room of the house talking when he entered, and got to their feet in alarm.

"Diego, your face is white!" his father began.

"A whip cut on my back is all. Fray Felipe, come and attend me. But all is well. We are shearing sheep on the rancho now, but tonight I have sheared a wolf."

Zorro's Masked Menace

Don Diego Vega pits his fighting skill against an evil disguised foe who oppresses innocent peons and natives!

LIKE a raging maniac, the masked man on the big black horse used his long whip on human backs. Into the long lash, bits of metal had been fastened, the better to lacerate skin and flesh.

His six victims were screeching and groaning, some of them stretched writhing on the ground with blood from their torn bodies oozing through their ragged garments.

Suddenly, the strength of the masked man seemed to have been expended with his insane rage. The lashing was brought to an end. The man who had used the whip laughed raucously for a moment, then became stern in manner.

"Remember this affair always, human scum!" he shouted at his victims. "Always remember that you are nothing more than worms crawling around the earth. Keep your proper places hereafter, or I'll visit you again."

He laughed once more in a tone of derision, looped the whip around the pommel of his saddle, and suddenly used his spurs cruelly and sped away through the moonlight, leaving wails of anguish behind him.

Only a few minutes before, it had been a happy scene.

In front of the little adobe hut of the sheepherder, which had been built a short distance back from the well-traveled highway, a fire was sending its red and amber flames leaping toward the sky.

Near the first was a smaller fire, and over it a cooking pot was steaming and sending off savory odors of mutton stew with vegetables. Small earthen bowls were ready for the serving. In each bowl a large wooden spoon.

Over the doorway of the humble hut had been stretched a garland of green branches intertwined with flowers. A couple of tapers were burning inside the hut, where a couch covered with skins had another garland resting upon it This was to be the sheepherder's nuptial bed.

Accompanied by four of their friends, the sheepherder and his bride had reached the hut at nightfall after walking from the mission at San Gabriel, where they had been married according to the ritual by a padre in the chapel.

The sheepherder was an honest, hardworking half breed of middle age, and his bride a pretty native girl of seventeen. She was radiantly happy in the realization that she had been married properly by a padre at the mission in the orthodox manner.

NOW nobody could point the finger of scorn at her or laugh whenever she passed. And she had acquired for husband a sheepherder who soon would be in the stock-raising business for his own account. A full moon was riding high in the sky — and making the scene below almost as light as in daytime. The six persons in the wedding party were laughing and shouting as they danced around the fire.

"Tonight, I am the happiest man in all Alta California!" the bridegroom shouted. "I would not exchange places with any hidalgo in the land. I have the prettiest bride along El Camino Real, from San Alcalá to San Francisco de Asis. And Don Alejandro Vega, for whom I have herded sheep for so long, has given me a ram and six young ewes for a wedding present. How my flock and fortune will grow!"

Approaching hoofbeats sounded from the nearby highway, but the merry group around the fire gave that no attention. Travelers were always passing along the highway during the cool hours of the summer nights.

But when the little bride suddenly stopped dancing and stifled a scream, and the others saw that her eyes were bulging, they stopped dancing and laughing also and looked where she pointed, and their own eyes bulged.

A horseman had left the highway only to come to a stop only a few feet from the fire. He was dressed entirely in black gannents, and his face was hidden by a black mask.

The six persons around the fire stood and suddenly turned into statues, scarcely breathing. Menace seemed to radiate from the somber masked rider.

Those at the fire could see the butt of a pistol protruding from his sash, a gleaming blade at his side, and a long whip coiled and looped over the pommel of his saddle. He did not speak to them. The light from the fire revealed his eyes glittering through holes in his mask like blazing fires of malevolence.

The bridegroom was the first to break the spell of silence. He gave a joyous shout and turned toward his bride and their friends, tossing his arms wide in a gesture meaning there was nothing to fear from the masked rider.

"Do you not understand, amigos?" he shouted at the others. "Observe our visitor well. The black horse and black clothes and mask! Here is Señor Zorro, our friend and protector! He has done us the honor of coming to our wedding feast. Perhaps he is pleased because we were married properly by a padre in the mission chapel."

Fright fled from the faces of the others immediately, and they relaxed and gave sighs of relief. If this masked rider before them was Señor Zorro, they had nothing to fear from him. His presence was a great honor. Perhaps he would even donate a wedding gift.

The masked man remained silent in the saddle. He bent forward slightly, his crossed forearms resting upon the pommel. The bridegroom knuckled his forehead in salute and respect — for it had been rumored that the mysterious Señor Zorro was in reality a caballero and stepped nearer the horse.

"Señor Zone, you are more than thrice welcome!" the bridegroom declared with enthusiasm. "Kindly do us the honor to dismount and eat with us, if it is only a bite, and bring honor and distinction to my poor house on my wedding night. We will all turn aside and not look as you raise your mask to eat. We have a splendid stew of mutton and vegetables seasoned with pepper both green and dried."

The masked horseman spoke to them now for the first time, his voice low and deep and obviously disguised.

"The odor that comes from the cooking pot good," he admitted.

The bridegroom beamed and his eyes dashed. "My young bride has prepared the stew, señor. It is the traditional first meal in her new home. Nobody as yet has eaten a morsel of it. Do us the honor to take the first bite."

The masked rider lifted his head and spoke again in a voice almost sepulchral.

"No doubt it would enhance the flavor of the stew to a certain extent if you tossed into the pot a few shreds of human skin cut with whip from the backs of such scum as you."

SUDDENLY afraid again, the bridegroom recoiled. The others around the fire sucked in breath quickly in terror. Señor Zorro, their protector and friend, would never use such words, they knew. The masked rider touched with his spurs and jumped his horse nearer the fire, almost riding down the bridegroom. And suddenly his whip was in his hand, and the lash was singing through the air, the bright moonlight and light from the fire glinting from bits of metal fastened in it.

"Tell me at once everything you know concerning this mysterious Señor Zorro!" the masked rider ordered, his voice a ringing menace. "What is his real identity? Where does he hide? Answer me!"

His speech was directed principally at the luckless bridegroom who had been so radiantly happy only a moment before, and who now was gulping and gasping in terror as he made an effort to speak.

"I really know nothing about him, senior," except that he rides a black horse and wears — black clothes and a mask," the bridegroom finally managed to reply.

"Do not speak to me with a crooked tongue!" the masked rider warned, sternly. "If it is necessary, I'll beat the truth out of you. So you believed I was this rogue of a Zorro, did you? I am exactly his opposite, and you will do well to understand that I have set out to undo the mischief le has caused."

"I do not understand, señor."

"A dolt such as you could not be expected to understand much about anything. Attend me closely! Because this unscrupulous rascal, Zorro, pretends to help the peons and natives, you scum are commencing to get out of hand. You believe that this Zorro will pop up from behind a rock and rush to your aid at any moment."

"But, señor — " the bridegroom started to protest.

"Hereafter, persons such as you who do not keep their proper places will find themselves visited by me. I can outdo this Zorro at any of his own tricks. I am a caballero, riding to punish all human rats who forget that they are rats and aspire to be eagles." The lash swished through the air suddenly and unexpectedly and cut across the bridegroom's breast. The victim gave a cry of pain and reeled backward, and the little bride ran to him, whimpering, and clutched his arm.

A pistol appeared in the left hand of the masked rider while he still held the whip in his right.

"You others line up here with your backs toward me," he ordered those by the fire. "I'll pistol the first who is laggard in moving, and run my blade through the others. Pronto!"

Of the four wedding guests, three were men friends of the groom and the fourth the middle-aged aunt of the bride. Trembling with fear, they lined up as the masked rider had ordered.

No thought of resistance entered their minds. They knew that an attack on the masked man would bring instant terrible reprisal from pistol, blade, and the lash that could cut to the bone. And they were all unarmed, because the Law said persons of their station could not carry weapons.

"Now," the masked horseman told them, after they were standing in a line with their backs toward him, and the bride and groom were clinging to each other a few feet away, "tell me immediately what you know of this Señor Zorro. I want the truth, and swiftly. It is my intention to run him to earth and capture or slay him."

No reply came from the trembling, whimpering, cringing persons in front of him. The lash sang again and cut into a human back. A man cried out in pain and sagged forward, and the others began groaning and twisting their bodies as if in anticipation of painful punishment.

"Speak!" the masked rider shouted.

"But we really know nothing, señor," one of the men was bold enough to reply. "We have heard of Señor Zorro, it is true, but none of us ever has seen him."

The lash immediately sang and cut again. The infuriated rider whipped the four in front of him like a man gone mad. Shrieks of pain answered the blows of the lash. He beat the men to the earth, and struck down the middle-aged woman and left her weeping on the ground.

THEN he rode on for a few feet and stopped in front of the sheepherder and his weeping, frightened bride.

"So you two would ape your betters and be married by a padre in the mission chapel?" he cried. "Perhaps you will be calling yourself 'Don' next. It is time for such as you to learn that it is your lot to walk with your heads hanging and your bare feet in the dust."

The whip sang through the air again. The lash struck the groom, and then wrapped itself like a serpent around the body of the little native bride and cut her back so that blood oozed through the cheap wedding gown she had thought so fine. She cried out in agony and fell to the ground, trying to protect her head with her arms.

The bridegroom's eyes suddenly became like twin flashing flames in the light of the fire, He screeched his rage and charged forward, tossing up his arms to ward of the stinging lash. But the lash did not strike at him. The masked rider's pistol cracked and flamed instead, and the bridegroom reeled aside from the force of a slug through the right shoulder.

But even that was not enough punishment to satisfy the infuriated masked man.

"So you would dare make an attack on me, rat?" he shouted at the wounded bridegroom. "I'll teach you not to lift your hands against your betters. I'll give you a lesson you'll never forget!"

The lash sang its diabolical song and struck and bit. It continued biting until the bridegroom was stretched unconscious on the ground. The masked man glanced around at his moaning victims, and laughed.

"Remember this occasion well," he warned. "Hereafter, keep to your proper places in life. Let no rascal of a Zorro give you ideas of equality and place you under his protection. Before long, the rogue will be unable to protect even himself."

He laughed again, used his spurs cruelly and rode wildly through the moonlit night to disappear down the highway in the of Reina de Los Angeles …

Shortly after dawn, there was a commotion at the great rancho of Don Alejandro Vega. Staggering, reeling and groaning, trying to help one another, the women and four men from the shepherd's hut had managed to reach the rancho buildings and tell their story.

An hour afterward, as they were eating the morning meal, Don Alejandro and his son Diego, heard the story from Cassara, the rancho overseer. Nor was that all, Cassara explained. A masked man, apparently the same one, had whipped two peons when he had caught them stealing a ride on empty cart instead of walking, and had beaten a young native because he had bought for his intended bride a strip of good cloth for a dress, afterward ruining the goods with his sword.

"What man could it be?" Diego asked his father, when the overseer had left the room and no house servant was within earshot "What fiend would beat a bridegroom and bride and their friends, and attack those others? Plainly, the fellow is putting himself at direct opposition to Zorro." And he attacked one of my people," Don Alejandro added. "The sheepherder is an honest fellow, and I have planned to do well by him. Yes, from his talk, this masked man is setting himself up in opposition to Zorro."

"And what will Zorro do about it?" He looked straight at his son.

"Zorro will accept the challenge," Diego replied, quietly.

Only three persons — Diego's father, Frey Felipe his aged padre confessor, and Bernardo, Diego's faithful mute peon servant knew that Diego Vega, who posed as a lifeless fop, was in reality the Señor Zorro unjust officials and cruel men had learned to fear.

"But, where and how can Zorro strike?" Alejandro asked. "He doesn't know the identity of this fiend. The masked rider who dresses like Zorro may be almost any man. He may be some haughty caballero with a twisted sense of men's rights, or some worthless rascal somebody else has engaged to do the work."

"It may be difficult to locate him, but he must be located," Diego declared. "The peons and natives must never get the idea that Zorro can be conquered, that he can no longer protect them and right their wrongs."

DON ALEJANDRO nodded. "That is true, Diego. The poor people will be bewildered. If they encounter a masked man on a horse, they will not know whether he is Zorro, their friend, or this fiend who treats human beings as beasts."

"And, not being sure of Zorro's identity, they will not help him as before," Diego intimated. "Not knowing whether the masked rider they meet is their friend Zorro, or this oppressor, they will not volunteer information, as they have so often."

"Let us go out and see the sheepherder and us bride and friends. Cassara will have treated their hurts by now. I'll order the sheepherder and bride to be cared for in a hut here, and give the man work after his body heals, until this problem is solved and it is safe for him to return to his own hut."

They left the house and walked toward the huts in the rear.

"After we talk to these abused people, we'll order out the carriage and drive to the San Gabriel mission. Everybody there will be talking about this affair, and we may learn something," Don Alejandro suggested. Have you any plans, my son?"

"Zorro must decoy this fiend into a meeting with him," Diego said. "Traps have been set for Zorro before," his father reminded him. "This masked fiend may be some officer of the soldiery sent here by the Governor to track down Zorro. He may be some famous swordsman."

"I'll chance that," Diego replied, grimly. They reached the cluster of huts, and Cassara met them and conducted them to where the victims were waiting in front of one of the Small adobe buildings.

Diego let the blaze of indignation die out of his eyes and resumed his pose of a yawning, lifeless fop in front of the victims and rancho workers who were in the vicinity. As he listened to the sheepherder and the others talk, Diego tried to find a clue in their speech, and though his face did not show it, his indignation and determination mounted.

Bernardo, his mute peon servant, approached and knuckled his forehead and awaited instructions. Bernardo had heard the story, and was wondering whether Zorro would play a part in this game. But Diego merely yawned.

"Get the carriage ready," he ordered in a drawl. "You are to drive my father and me to the mission. Pronto?"

Bernardo nodded and hurried away toward the stables.

When the carriage entered the compound at the mission, Diego and his father found a scene of unusual excitement.

Peons and natives were standing around watching and listening instead of attending to their work. Padres and neophytes were in groups talking. A detachment of troopers from Reina de Los Angeles had dismounted, and Diego saw Sergeant Manuel Garcia and heard him shouting orders. And, as he got out of the carriage with his father, he saw Don Marcos Ruiz.

"So Don Marcos has returned from his annual round of dissipation at Monterey," Don Alejandro whispered to Diego. "His actions are enough to make his father turn over in his grave. He is a dissolute wretch and a disgrace to his blood. And he is running through the family fortune rapidly."

Diego nodded in agreement. Don Marcos saw the Vegas and hurried toward them, hand outstretched and his white teeth flashing in a smile. He was a handsome man of thirty, attractive to women, a daredevil in every respect.

He bowed to Don Alejandro, who shook his hand but kept his face stern. Then he shook hands with Diego and slapped him on the back, and Diego pretended to indulge in a fit of coughing from the shock of the blow.

"Your pardon, Don Diego!" Ruiz roared. I forgot your weak constitution. A friendly slap on the back is almost enough to down you."

"You are so violent," Diego complained.

"From what I have heard here this morning, somebody was violent during the night," Ruiz continued, "it is about time men of blood began resenting these knaves of peons and natives who ape their betters."

"You approve of such treatment?" Diego asked.

RUIZ shrugged. "Why not? Let the rogues get out of hand, and we may have serious trouble to face some day. 'Tis all the fault of this mysterious Zorro, I say. He has given them the false idea that they are as good as any man."

"But to whip them like that!" Diego protested. "After all, they are human beings."

"Sometimes I doubt it," Ruiz replied laughing. "But I know how you Vegas feel about such things. Pardon me, Don Alejandro, but some of us feel you are too lenient with the workers on your rancho. You give them too many liberties and show them too much kindness — "

"Pardon me, Marcos Ruiz, but I feel thoroughly capable of running my own affairs," Don Alejandro broke in, frigidly.

Pardon me," Ruiz intoned, with a tinge of sarcasm in his voice. "But your sentiments — well, they might lead me to the belief that Diego here was Señor Zorro — if I did not know that to be impossible."

"Why impossible?" Diego asked.

Marcos Hula laughed again. "Diego? Bah! Zorro's a riding, fighting fiend. He has crossed blades with good men and bested them. He has outridden the soldiers. He is a man of blood and fire, of courage and speed, whoever he is. It is a mystery to me why he is not caught. However, anybody who knows you, Diego, would never accuse you of being Zorro. Pardon me, amigo, but you are the lazy type. Your blood is never hot. You like to read poetry, and yawn."

"You are almost insulting, señor," Diego said.

"Now, no offense. You know well yourself that you are not the dashing caballero type."

Don Alejandro entered the conversation again: "Regarding the violent type, Ruiz, is there any clue as to the identity of the man who aped Zorro last night in costume and used his whip so freely? After all, the sheepherder was a man of mine."

"Ha! You can get a hundred sheepherders m a day. What is one sore back more or less?"

Don Marcos Ruiz bowed to them again and turned away, shouting at another acquaintance. Diego and his father started to walk across the compound toward the chapel. A sudden bellow came from Sergeant Garcia, calling the troopers to attention. Diego and his father glanced toward the soldiers to see an officer, a stranger too them emerging from one of the buildings.

"The new capitan, no doubt," Diego whispered. "I heard one was being sent from Monterey to rule this district. His name is Luis Campos, a brutal fellow."

"Possibly sent to capture or kill Zorro where others have failed," his faather suggested.

"That may be. I wonder if he is starting his campaign against Zorro by — it is just a thought."

"What thought, my son?"

"Possibly the new capitan was the masked man riding last night, throwing fear into peons and natives, making them doubt Zorro's ability to protect them, making them suspicious.

Don Alejandro s eyes met those of his son squarely: "That thought is valuable enough to be considered well," he whispered.

"Capitdn Luis Campos is coming toward us, escorted by Sergeant Garcia," Diego whispered. "It appears that we are to be honored by his acquaintance."

Father and son walked on slowly. They passed a group of peons, and Diego spoke in a drawl, but loud enough for the men to hear: "I understand, father, that some of the peons and natives are to meet tonight in the Canyon of the Flowers, and that it is rumored Señor Zorro is to appear to them there and explain what is to be done in this situation."

As they walked on, Don Alejandro spoke in a whisper.

"What was the meaning of that strange statement, Diego?" he asked.

"Those men who heard me will spread the report. It may reach the ears of the masked fiend who rode last night, for he possibly has spies about. He may ride to the Canyon the Flowers to use his brutality again."

"And Zorro?"

"Zorro will contrive to meet him there Diego whispered. "This affair cannot be settled until we meet."

Then they found Capitan Luis Campos and the Sergeant before them, stopped and bowed, and Garcia managed the introductions and then retired out of earshot.

"I am happy to have met you so soon, Don Ajejandro, and your son also," Campos said.

"Naturaily, I have heard much of you. I hope my stay here will be pleasant, and that I do the work I came to do."

"The work?" Don Alejandro questioned.

'Lawlessness must cease. This Zorro fellow, for instance, who is stirring up the natives and peons — he must be caught and hanged. Every effort must be made to undo the unscrupulous work he has done."

"What of the masked man who rode last night, Capitan Campos, and mistreated men and women?" Don Alejandro asked. "One of his victims was a good sheepherder of mine. Are you and your troopers on the trail of the fiend?"

Capitan Campos laughed a little. "Scarcely, Don Alejandro. Such scum as were whipped last night are only too plentiful, and no doubt the masked man was only some young caballero having fun. I am here with my men on a more serious mission."

"Indeed?"

"Three ragamuffins stole a sheep last night, and butchered, cooked and ate the animal. Things like that cannot be endured. They must be taught to respect the property rights at the rancho owners and traders."

'Perhaps they were hungry," Diego put in.

"Hungry?" The Capitan raised his eyebrows as if the remark had astounded him. Such are alway hungry, it seems, and what of it? The thing is — they stole a sheep, killed and ate it. It is a whipping matter, and I intend to make examples of the rogues to deter others of their kind."

"And you will make no effort to run down the masked fiend who — " Don Alejandro began.

"I do not waste my troopers' energies on trivial matters," Campos replied. "They have much work to do. And it would be well, Don Alejandro, and I am sure would be very pleasing to the Governor, if some of you hidalgos in this vicinity would be more rigorous in your treatment of your workers. I'll need assistance at any time in pursuing this Zorro. I expect you to send me your armed vaqueros to aid in the pursuit?'

"In such event, your request would probably come at a time when we were short — handed at the rancho, and no men could be spared," Don Alejandro replied.

"What is it?" Capitan Campos' face flamed suddenly. "You mean you would refuse to honor my request for men?

"I would deny your authority and right to make the request," Don Alejandro told him. "My vaqueros are engaged to attend to the herds, not to chase a man the soldiers seem unable to catch."

Don Alejandro Vega bowed stiffly, then lifted his head proudly and strode on, turning his back upon Capitan Luis Campos. Diego, his shoulders hunched and his feet dragging a little as if from fatigue, walked beside his father.

"The new officer is a beast," Don Alejandro whispered. "If he is the masked fiend, I hope Zorro meets him soon."

At a later hour that night, Señor Zorro was sitting his big black horse on the hillside not far from the narrow mouth of the Canyon of the flowers. He was dressed in his usual black garments, was masked, and had his weapons.

Returning to the rancho from the mission that day, he had warned Bernardo to have Zorro's horse and trappings ready, and the faithful Bernardo had obeyed. Zorro had ridden carefully between the hills to the mouth of the canyon.

He had been there for more than an hour now. The moon was hidden by scudding clouds at times, yet he had seen a dozen men or so slip into the canyon, all walking and none riding, and he knew they were peons and natives, and that the words he had seemed to drop carelessly at the mission had been heard and spread.

What he had hoped would happen had occurred. Only a few courageous men had dared go cautiously to the Canyon of the Flowers. Others were fearful that not Zorro, but the new masked fiend, would be encountered.

The men who entered the canyon secreted themselves carefully in the brush. Zorro worked his black horse down to within a short distance of the smooth canyon floor while the moon was behind a cloud, and screened himself behind a natural hedge. He listened for distant hoofbeats, but heard none.

HE WAS wondering whether the masked fiend had heard the rumor about the Canyon of the Flowers and would come to investigate. If he was really eager to meet Zorro, he would. And Zorro had a natural curiosity, too, concerning the masked rider's identity.

The moon emerged from behind the cloud, and Zorro glanced swiftly to the spot where the narrow entrance to the canyon, almost a bottleneck, was between two lofty masses of rocks. And he saw the horseman for whom he had been waiting. He had ridden slowly through the bottleneck and had stopped his horse in a cleared spot where he could be seen plainly in the moonlight. There he waited, while Zorro waited also behind the screen of brush, and the dozen men who had entered the canyon remained hidden among the rocks.

"Señor Zorro!" came a cautious hail.

"Come to me here," the masked rider called in return.

Zorro saw dark spots moving among the rocks. Men emerged into the moonlight and went toward the masked horseman slowly, acting like men ready to turn and flee if they saw or heard anything suspicious.

"Make haste!" the rider called. They hurried toward him, then, and stood in front of him, and one spoke.

"We heard the rumor, Señor Zorro, that you would meet some of us here, so we came. Have you any message for us to carry to others like us? What happened last night — "

Zorro saw the rider hold up one hand in a demand for silence.

"Who told you I'd be here tonight?" he demanded.

"Who told us? Quien sabe? It was a rumor flying everywhere among men like us. Only a few came, because we feared it might be a trap."

"So you go running whenever Zorro calls, do you?" The masked rider's voice suddenly was raised in angry tones. "Stand as you are, or I'll pistol one of you! Tell me what you know of Zorro! You know what I did last night?"

"You — you are the man who whipped — " one of the peons began.

"I am! Stand steady, or I shoot! I am not your precious Zorro, and you can see he is not here to protect you now."

"But I am here, señor!" a loud voice cried, Zorro had ridden down cautiously to the canyon floor, and now spurred his horse out into the moonlight. And the cringing peons and natives saw two black-dressed and masked men riding black horses, and in the moonlight there was no difference to be seen between them.

The first rider had turned his head at sound of Zorro's voice. His own strong voice rang out again: "If you are Zorro, this meeting is a pleasure."

"I am Zorro, and the meeting is a pleasure for me also, cowardly beater of men and women!"

The masked unknown wheeled his horse suddenly and made him rear, and gathered reins to ride to meet him, his going swiftly to the tilt of his blade. The masked unknown did not wait to cross blades. He got his pistol out of aimed and fired. The unexpected move of his horse ruined his aim.

"So you cannot fight fairly?" Zorro shouted. "I could pistol you now, since your weapon is empty. But I prefer to soft blade with your blood, tear off your mask and learn the name of a cowardly fiend. Perhaps you are the type of man the Governor sends here."

The other had his blade out now, and suddenly charged. But Zorro kneed his black so that the other dashed past beyond sword's length. Zorro got his black under perfect control and wheeled him as the other turned and came back.

This time, the blades met, slithered, rang. The two black horses bumped and their riders fought. Zorro knew in the first instant that he had encountered a good swordsman.

The moon went behind a fleecy cloud as the horses separated. But, by the time riders could bring them together again, the moon was shining brightly again.

"The great Zorro!" the second masked rider taunted. "You must have met poor swordsmen before, to be alive now. You'll never see the face behind my mask, Zorro, but I'll see the face behind yours!"

"Perhaps I know your face without ripping off your mask," Zorro said, as they separated again for an instant "Your manner of handling a blade tells me you were trained as a soldier."

"Ha! I was trained by a soldier, at any rate."

ONCE more their horses bumped, they engaged again. Zorro began pressing the fighting now. It seemed to him that his black horse, trained to this sort of thing, was easier to handle than the other black steed, for his opponent was having trouble controlling his mount with left hand on the reins and knees against shoulder.

Zorro retreated to a place of better footing for his horse, and his antagonist came rushing after him. And Zorro happened to glance past him as he advanced, and saw horsemen riding through the bottleneck of the canyon, saw moonlight glinting from weapons, and knew troopers were upon them.

"There they are!" said a voice: "Both of them! They are at it! Capture them both — take them!"

Zorro knew that was the voice of Sergeant Manuel Garcia, who often had pursued him and had made futile attempts at capture.

His opponent engaged Zorro's complete attention at that moment. Zorro had no time to waste now. He must be victor in an instant, or turn from the duel and ride to safety down the canyon, or remain and be seized by the soldiers.

He pressed his powerful horse against the mount of the other man, and their blades clashed and rang again. The other masked rider was trying to press the · fighting and make a quick end of it also. But Zorro could feel he was tiring.

"Torturer of men and women!" Zorro shouted at him.

His blade slipped beneath the other's guard and went home to the target. Zorro jerked it away, wheeled his horse, bent low in his saddle, and rode swiftly along the canyon floor. Bullets flew past him as the troopers fired, but he rode unharmed.

"Capture him!" he heard Sergeant Garcia ordering. "There will be a reward!"

Capitan Luis Campos had not led the detachment to the canyon. So, Zorro

*Zorro began
pressing the
fighting now ...*

thought, Campos had been the unknown masked -rider. Yet, though his wrist had the feel of one trained for soldiery, there had been something weak and uncertain about it.

He rode into the darkness where an overhanging cliff shut off the light of the moon, and swerved his horse aside into the brush and stopped. His mount's hoofs had stirred up the fine sandy dust, and into this blinding cloud the pursuing troopers rode, all five of them. They rode past the hiding Zorro. The hooves of their own mounts ringing on the rocks made it impossible for them to know whether a mount ahead was sending back hoof beats.

Into the thick brush they crashed pursuing fleshing, found themselves on a narrow cattle trail, and started following it up out of the Canyon and to the floor of the mesa above, Zorro knew they would continue the chase until the mesa was reached before they realized they were chasing a shadow.

He turned his horse back, kept to the shadows, rode with great caution toward the cleared spot where Sergeant Garcia and another five troopers had dismounted and were standing around a figure prostrate on the ground. The dozen peons and natives were not to be seen. They, too, had fled at the coming of the troopers, not wishing to be jailed and tortured and questioned about Zorro.

Zorro got near enough to hear Garcia's voice.

"We have one of them, and we'll have the other. Is this one Zorro or the masked rider of last night? 'Which one got away? *Quien sabe?* "

"I wager this one is Zorro," one of the troopers said.

"I think not," Sergeant Garcia replied. "This man is Don Marcos Ruiz, a man who deserved killing if ever a man did. For all his gentle blood, he was nothing but a common cheat, and an arrogant brutal fellow. I cannot imagine such a man doing the things Zorro has done — helping the oppressed and punishing cruel men."

Zorro drew in his breath sharply. So the man he had fought, the fiend of the night before, had not been Capitan Campos, but Don Marcos Ruiz. Knowing much of Ruiz' history, he had no compunction about the slaying.

The way was practically clear for him to ride through the bottleneck and out of the canyon. The sergeant and troopers were a little off to one side, and the ground between Zorro and the bottleneck was level and safe. He gathered up his reins.

And suddenly he used his spurs, and the big black bounded forward, racing with the speed of wind toward the narrow opening of the canyon.

Sergeant and troopers whirled around as they heard the hoofbeats, but as they whirled Zorro flashed past them, bent low in the saddle again, and back on the wind to them went his ringing words:

"The dead man is not Zorro! Zorro is here, and still rides!"

He hoped the peons and natives hiding up in the rocks heard it and would spread the word.

And ride he did, at top speed, out of the canyon to lose himself in the hills and get home safely. For he knew he would be beyond capture by the time Garcia and his troopers could mount and start pursuit.

Zorro Aids an Invalid

When a mysterious placard appeal for the help of Zorro,
Don Diego Vega wears a black cloak to fight for justice!

YAWNING and half asleep, Pedro Ortez, the corpulent keeper of the tavern on the plaza in Reina de Los Angeles, waddled across the main room of his place an hour after dawn, unbolted and unbarred the heavy front door and pulled it open. He had enjoyed only three hours' sleep, due to the wild spending of a wealthy trader, Carlos Torres, who had been in the pueblo for a couple of days throwing gold around.

The cool morning air brushed against Ortez' face, and he inhaled it thankfully. It would be an excellent idea, he thought, to prop the door open and let the fresh air sweep through the main room and rid it of stale tobacco smoke and the fumes of stale wine sloppings.

As he turned to prop the door open, he sucked in his breath sharply and his eyes bulged. In less than the blink of an eye-lid he was thoroughly awake.

Somebody, during the early hours of the morning, had fastened a placard to the tavern's front door. It was an amateurish affair, but could be read easily:

TO SENOR ZORRO:
I am desperately in need of help, and know of none but you who can aid me. Whoever you are, I beg you to come to my assistance. You will be richly rewarded. Please be kind enough to respond, for my cause is just. Make haste, for I am dying.
Juan Cardoza.

The tavern keeper read the placard again, and turned with speed when he heard somebody behind him. It was a peon servant whose duties included the task of cleaning the room early in the morning.

"Make haste, son of a snail!" Ortez shouted at him. "Go with your utmost speed to the barracks and tell Sergeant Garcia to hurry here immediately. It is most important. If you hasten your reward will be a full fresh meal this evening instead of leavings from the tables; if you do not, you will get a lash across your back!"

THE servant's bare feet raised a cloud of dust as he sped across the plaza. Shivering, Ortez backed away from the door as if to touch it would mean contamination.

That such a placard should be fastened to his door! Suppose Sergeant Garcia believed he had a part in this? Such a thing might mean his ruin. A placard addressed to Senor Zorro, the masked rider who rode and fought to aid the poor and oppressed, for whose capture a reward had been offered, left here as if perhaps Senor Zorro lived at the tavern!

And signed by Don Juan Cardoza, at that! Everyone knew that the aged hidalgo, who was past ninety, was on his death bed. Why should he appeal to a masked fugitive to help him? Was the world finally coming to an end?

Ortez need not have been so much perturbed. His servant found Sergeant Garcia at the barracks, only half dressed, listening to a man who talked excitedly, and holding a duplicate of the placard in one hand. As the servant stammered the tavern keeper's message, a third man came running up, holding another placard.

"Found fastened to the door of the residence of His Excellency, Alfonso Heynoso, the alcalde," the panting messenger reported.

Sergeant Garcia blew out the ends of his enormous mustache. "It is too much!" he roared. "One on the chapel, one on the tavern, another on the alcalde's front door, a fourth on the warehouse — the things are all over the pueblo! Somebody will sweat blood for this!"

"The alcalde requests your immediate presence, Sergeant Garcia," the messenger reported.

"I'll be there as soon as I can dress," the sergeant promised. "This may be but a jest, yet it calls for investigation."

The sergeant went into his quarters and began dressing in his best uniform. His commanding officer was absent on a mission to Monterey, and Garcia at present was in command of the district. His responsibilities weighed upon him heavily.

The alcalde had a bachelor residence only a short distance away, and was served by a couple of peons, except when he held court and had a dozen standing around. Garcia knew well that Alfonso Reynoso, appointed alcalde temporarily, was feathering his nest while he had a chance, but that was none of his business. An alcalde was an alcalde, whether saint or sinner, and a sergeant had to take orders,

Garcia mounted his horse, which a trooper had saddled for him, rode the short distance to the alcalde's house, dismounted and rearranged his uniform sash, and strode toward the front door with a show of importance.

A servant opened the door before Garcia could use the knocker. Led inside, the sergeant found the alcalde pacing around the room with his hands behind his back and frowning like a man in deep thought.

"I report, Senor Reynoso," Garcia said, bowing slightly.

"These placards — "

"It may all be a sorry jest, but I assure you I'll make an immediate investigation."

"Ascertain whether Don Juan Cardoza's name is affixed to them with his knowledge and consent. He is a dying man, and may be having queer fancies. Whatever you learn, have his house watched every moment of night and day. If Zorro answers this plea, believing it authentic, you and your men must capture him. Remember the reward! I'll add something to it personally, also."

"If Zorro answers the plea, senor, he will walk into a trap," Sergeant Garcia declared, drawing up his shoulders. "If I can get my hands on the rogue — ha!"

"The reward — and I'll recommend your promotion," the alcalde said. "If Don Juan really authorized that placard, it shows his mind is wandering. But we can thank the sick old man if the affair draws Zorro into our net."

"If Zorro tries to enter the Cardoza house, we'll have him!" Garcia promised again. "I'll have some of my troopers remove their uniforms and work as barefooted peons in ragged clothing. But they'll be armed. They will watch everyone who approaches the house — and I'll be near at hand. If Zorro makes the attempt to visit Don Juan Cardoza it probably will be tonight, however."

"That is my thought also. The masked rogue scarcely would ride into the pueblo on his black horse in daytime and reveal himself to everybody. Guard the place well after nightfall," the alcalde ordered.

But Senor Zorro was visiting Don Juan Cardoza, sitting beside his bed and listening to him talk, long before nightfall ....

AS HE strolled across the plaza that day after the siesta hour, Diego Vega was never more resplendent in dress. Except for his regrettable languid air, his manner was that of a handsome young caballero, scion of a proud and wealthy family.

But all who knew the affairs of the Vega family, or even thought they did, sighed for Don Alejandro, Diego's father, because the spirited old hidalgo had such a spiritless son.

Diego knew the opinion held of him, but it did not bother him in the slightest degree. People declared he was a spineless, indolent fop who read poetry, instead of a proper young caballero always risking his life by wild riding, fighting, or playing a guitar and singing a soft love song beneath the wrong window.

They did not know that Diego was the mysterious Senor Zorro, who rode and fought to aid the poor and oppressed, and laughed at the attempts of the soldiers to capture and hang him and earn the reward the Governor had offered.

Only three persons knew the truth — Diego's father, Fray Felipe, the aged Franciscan padre, and Bernardo, Diego's mute peon servant tested and true in his loyalty.

That the public and even his friends believed him to be a weakling suited his purpose perfectly. If they believed that, never would they suspect him of being Zorro.

Now, Diego went to the little chapel on the plaza, for Fray Felipe had sent for him. The padre welcomed and blessed him and led him to a private room.

"Diego, my son," the padre reported, "Don Juan Cardoza is stretched upon a bed from which he never will arise. Death is hovering over him."

"He is a very old man," Diego suggested.

"A year past ninety and the last of the family. He has clung to life for ten years after the death of his last remaining relative. I have been attending him both spiritually and physically. He has been bedridden for the last year — and this is the end. A few days at most."

"An end that must come to us all."

"That is true, my son. But a proper man wants to pass from earth with his house in order. Don Juan Cardoza has been noted for honesty, decency, piety, and generous aid to others at time of misfortune."

"A splendid man," Diego agreed.

"Is it proper that such a splendid man should die with villains at his threat? Since he has no family, should he not have the right to dispose of his estate as he sees fit?"

"Somebody is trying to prevent that?"

"That is so, my son. The problem is beyond an old padre like me who has no weapon except a gentle attempt at verbal persuasion. It calls for a man of courage, determination and swift action — a man like Senor Zorro."

"Ah! I commence to see why you sent for me."

"Don Juan pleaded with me this morning. 'Do not let these scoundrels have their way,' he begged. 'The man called Zorro — ah, if only you could learn his identity and prevail upon him to serve me in this, I would enrich him.' He does not suspect that Zorro is a caballero and son of a wealthy father."

"But those placards about which I have heard — "

"No doubt Don Juan had one of his loyal servants make them and post them during the night. Perhaps he thought I would fail in finding Zorro, and took that measure because he knows his time is short."

"And the soldiers have been put on guard, and Zorro would find himself in serious trouble if he visited Don Juan."

"Not if he visited him in his real identity as Diego Vega."

"How can that be done?"

"Your father has been a friend of Don Juan's for almost half a century. He is absent, at the rancho. What more natural than that his son, you, would visit Don Juan in your father's absence to pay your last respects?"

DIEGO frowned. "But 'tis Zorro he desires to see, is it not? He knows me only as Diego Vega."

"I'll tell him the truth, my son, after having him take a pledge of secrecy. He is near death. Your secret would never be revealed by him. If soldiers are watching the house, they will suspect nothing if you go there with me. Members of other high families are making their pre-death calls."

"Wait, padre! Why should I go there at all? You give me the details, and then, as Zorro, I'll do what I can."

"The point is, Diego, that Don Juan has not confided wholly in me. He wants to explain his problem to Zorro. But I know a few facts. The men who are trying to undo him in his last moments are Alfonso Reynoso, our present alcalde, and Carlos Torres, a trader now living at the tavern."

"A pair of rogues! Reynoso is no better than a common thief," Diego declared. And from what I have heard of the trader he is a vulgar boaster and no doubt unscrupulous."

"It seems there is a young girl involved, one in whom Don Juan has some strange interest. That is all I can tell you."

Diego arose from the bench upon which he had been sitting. "Let us visit Don Juan now," he said.

Garcia's troopers saw them enter the Cardoza house. But they saw nothing strange in a visit there by Fray Feilpe, the dying man's confessor, and Diego Vega, the spineless fop. They were watching for Zorro.

Don Juan's head servant whispered to them that Sergeant Garcia had called about the placards. Don Juan had been in a coma at the time, and the servant pretended ignorance, so Garcia had learned nothing.

But now Don Juan was conscious and his mind was clear. His voice was weak, but he spoke his thoughts plainly enough. He had shown astonishment, and then had smiled faintly when Fray Felipe had exposed Diego as Senor Zorro.

"A true caballero," Don Juan whispered. "I knew no son of my old friend, Don Alejandro, could be spiritless. May your work be blessed! Serve me in this if you can, Diego, for it will be something just and will confound scoundrels."

The story came slowly, but simply. For ten years, Don Juan had been alone in the world. Until a few years before, he had traveled much. On one journey to San Juan Capistrano, he had met with an accident, and a passing stranger had gone to his rescue and in all probability had saved his life.

The stranger was Carlos Torres, a small trader. He had visited Don Juan frequently, and the latter had taken a fancy to him. Having plenty of money, he had established Carlos Torres in business on a large scale.

It had been a happy association at first. Torres knew how to make money, and religiously he repaid Don Juan a little at a time, and also sent a share of the profits. Tones conducted his enterprises up and down the land, and Don Juan knew little about them.

Don Juan made a will, leaving funds to the church and giving the usual ten percent to the Spanish Crown and five percent to the Viceroy in Mexico. The remainder he left to Carlos Torres, in repayment for his kindness and his honesty in returning the original investment and profits. Fray Felipe penned the will, and, according to law, the man then alcalde affixed the seal and recorded the document.

FRAY FELIPE gestured for Don Juan to keep silent for a time, then, for he feared the dying man might draw his last breath before completing his story.

"And then?" Fray Felipe urged, finally. "You tell Diego — about Carlos Torres." The padre faced Diego again. "A short time ago," he explained, "Don Juan began learning the truth about this Carlos Tortes. The man had been cheating Don Juan from the first. He sent money, but only a small percentage of the enormous profits he had made. Don Juan may have overlooked that, but he was given proof of how Tortes gained wealth.

"He swindled on every side. He formed a band of evil men about him, kidnaped natives and peons and drove them to Mexico to sell there as slaves. He seduced officials and had his way. He was in all ways the sort of man Don Juan, a decent and honest man himself, could not endure. Don Juan decided to change his will and leave Torres nothing. But he delayed because — there was something about a girl."

The dying man lifted his hand feebly in interruption. "I will explain that," he said. "Fray Felipe knows the girl, but not why I have had an interest in her. I — I had a brother young enough to be my son, who was wild and irresponsible. At an early age, he married a splendid young woman of good family. But he ran through the fortune our father had left him, and became an adventurer.

"He took his wife and child to Mexico, where his conduct was a disgrace to his blood. I kept trace of him, and learned later he had two daughters, and that his wife had died, undoubtedly had grieved herself to death.

"Then I heard of his death, and lost entire trace of my two nieces. I spent considerable money trying to trace them. I learned where they had been in a convent, but had left it as they decided not to take the veil. I learned of the death of one from the fever. The other seemed lost forever.

"Recently, I obtained a clue to her whereabouts. If I could locate my niece, and she proved to be a proper sort of girl, I had someone to whom I could leave my fortune, which would be considerable after I had cared for the usual officials and the Church.

"The girl, I learned, was a singer and dancer in a cantina in San Dieso de Alcala. I had Fray Felipe learn what he could about her, without revealing to him our relationship."

Fray Felipe nodded his head. "I understand now, Don Juan," he said.

"Tell — him the rest."

The padre faced Diego again. "At Don Juan's request, I communicated with others of our order," he said. "I learned that the girl did work in a cantina, but was not the usual sort of cantina girl. She lived with a decent widow in the pueblo, and went home immediately after her work. She was a good girl, going to mass and confession regularly at our mission in San Diego de Alcala.

"Some unpleasantness coming up, she left San Diego de Alcala and went to work in San Luis Hey, and then moved again to San Juan Capistrano. The picture I got from my communications with other padres was that the girl, a beauty, moved on to escape the advances of evil men.

"Finally, she left San Juan Capistrano — and I lost sight of her."

THE old man lifted his hand again. "But I did not. Through a man working for me, I learned where she had gone. She is here now, here in Reina de Los Angeles, She is known as Magdalena — "

Diego straightened. "The singing and dancing girl at Pedro Ortez' tavern on the plaza!"

Don Juan nodded in agreement.

"I made a new will, leaving the bulk of my estate to my niece, under her rightful name," Don Juan said. "I prepared proofs of her identity and gave them into the keeping of Fray Felipe. I sent the new will. only a few days ago, to the alcalde, Alfonso Reynoso.

"It happens, however, that he is one of the officials Carlos Torres corrupted. Torres was warned, and hurried here. Guessing I had learned of his evil deeds, he did not even come to see me. But my servants say he has visited much with the alcalde.

"Each day I have sent a servant to the alcalde with a request that he execute the will and return it so I can give it into the Fray's keeping for use after my death. Be always finds some excuse. Do you understand?"

The padre gestured again for Don Juan to rest.

"I can explain it to you, Diego," he said.

"If the new will is not signed by the alcalde and the proper seal affixed before Don Juan's death, the old will stands as the last and will be enforced. Torres, the scoundrel, will get the bulk of the big estate — and probably will give the alcalde half of it. Don Juan's niece will get nothing, the last of the family will be left destitute, compelled to work for her living, to fight off the advances of evil men — "

Diego got to his feet and paced twice around the room, then stopped at the bedside again.

"Zorro's task," he said, "is to compel the alcalde to execute the will, to deliver the will to Fray Felipe for safe keeping, and to punish Torres and Reynoso as he sees fit."

Don Juan nodded slowly.

"The scoundrels are already circulating the report that Don Juan is not in his right mind," Fray Felipe said. But when the new will was made it was in the presence of three men of the highest repute. We have nothing to fear there. But the will must be properly executed, the seal affixed, and brought to me. I'll give you a copy of the document to carry, so you'll have it handy if the alcalde pretends he has mislaid the one sent him."

"What have been his excuses for delaying?" Diego asked.

"Oh, he was ill with a cold and fever, then he saw no reason for haste — again, he had misplaced his official seal, once more he had to go on a journey of several days to San Gabriel — anything to delay executing the will."

"Let me have the copy of the will," Diego said. "And now it is best we leave Don Juan, for this scene has tired him."

Fray Felipe handed Diego a document, which he put into a pocket of his jacket.

"I'll remain and comfort Don Juan," the padre said.

Don Juan extended his hand, and Diego clasped it.

"One last request," the dying man muttered. "The padres have said my niece is good. But they are not men of the world. Visit the girl yourself, Diego, judge her without letting her know the entire truth."

"I'll do that, Don Juan."

"After your task is done, come to see me again — not as Zorro, but as Diego Vega, son of my old friend."

WITH nightfall, thick fog rolled in from the distant sea, and there was a drizzle of rain. Dressed in his black attire, wearing his black mask and riding his powerful black horse, Zorro rode slowly through the night. He was armed as usual with pistol and blade, and to the pommel of his saddle was attached his long black whip.

Bernardo, his mute servant, had brought the horse from the distant hiding place as usual, and had Zorro's attire and weapons ready. But Bernardo did not accompany his master tonight on his riding mule. He remained in waiting to be of assistance when Zorro returned after his adventure.

Zorro circled the pueblo so as to ride through the swirling fog to a position in the rear of the tavern. The night was so disagreeable that scarcely anyone was outdoors. But sounds of song and loud talk and laughter came from the tavern where men were roistering.

Leaving his horse ground-hitched in a depression, Zorro went cautiously through the darkness until he reached the tavern's side wall. By peering through a window, he had a good view of the interior of the big main room and what was occurring there.

The room was crowded. Sitting at one end of a long table, dressed in what he fondly thought was the height of fashion, was Carlos Torres, the trader. Town loafers were drinking wine at his expense and would continue to do so as long as they responded with laughter and flattery at what Torres thought was humor.

Pedro Ortez, the corpulent landlord, was waddling around, watching his native servants and rubbing his hands in delight at the prospect of heavy profits.

"Let us have music!" Torres shouted. "Music and dancing! Ortez, where is your dancing girl? We want Magdalena!"

The others shouted approval. Watching outside the window, Zorro saw Ortez notion to a guitar player to get ready. Then the landlord waddled through a door, and soon returned leading the girl by the hand. Those in the room applauded her appearance, Torres loudest of all.

To the music of the guitar, Magdalena sang as she walked slowly around the room from table to table, deftly, avoiding men who tried to put their hands on her.

Zorro marveled at the girl's manner. He never had seen her perform before. The men who listened to her now did not realize, perhaps, that she was an unusual cantina girl. There was poise in her movements, dignity in her manner, and she had a voice that had been trained.

She was not beautiful, but she was attractive. She had the manner of one of gentle blood. And in her features Zorro thought he detected a resemblance to Don Juan Cardoza, her uncle.

Her song ceased, and she began dancing. There was nothing vulgar in her dance. She was graceful, as musical in movement as the tones of the guitar were in sound. The dance ended, the men cheered, and Magdalena bowed to them and rushed to the door and out into the patio. Carlos Torres, his eyes agleam,

"Release the senorita instantly!"
Zorro's stern voice barked!

got up from his bench and reeled after the girl.

Zorro hurried along the wail and to the rear of the building, and got through a gate and into the patio, where he stood beneath the arched walkway in the shadows where light from the burning torches did not reveal him.

Magdalena had stopped beneath a shelter at the side of the patio well, and was drinking water from a gourd. Zorro watched carefully. In her face was depicted disgust with this manner of life. He was about to approach her when what he had expected happened.

CARLOS TORRES reeled into the patio and up to her. "So here you are, my pretty pigeon, drinking water when I would buy for you the best wine," he said.

"Pardon me, senor, but I do not want your wine," the girl replied, her voice rich and deep.

"Let us get better acquainted, delight to my eye. Why should you rebuff me? I am a wealthy man. I can give you whatever you desire."

"Make me a gift, then, of your absence, senor."

"Ho! A spitfire we have here! I like a girl with spirit, senorita." He stepped up to her side as she put down the drinking gourd. "A little kiss?" His arm went around her, and he tried to cup her chin in his hand.

"Let me go, senor," she begged.

She began struggling to get from his grasp, but he laughed and held her and started to bend his head for the kiss he wanted. Zorro could see that the girl's strength was not enough to cope with that of Torres.

Leaving his spot of seclusion, Zorro darted over the flagstones. His whip was uncoiled and gripped in a strong hand. Through the holes in his mask, his eyes blazed.

"Release the senorita instantly!" Zorro's stern voice barked.

Carlos Tones released the girl and whirled around in astonishment. His eyes bulged when he saw the masked, black-dressed man before him. Magdalena, on the verge of a faint, reeled against the well curb.

"What is this? Who are you?" Torres mouthed.

"I am called Zorro. I punish men like you."

"Your pardon, Senor Zorro. Excuse me. I did not know I was walking on forbidden ground, that the girl belonged to you — "

His sentence broke off and he recoiled with a strangled cry of fright and pain as Zorro's lash bit into his body.

"So you are an insulter of women, also?" Zorro asked, his voice tense. "I know you, Torres, though you do not know me. I know your life of swindling, of kidnapping and selling slaves, of your ill-gotten riches, of how you defrauded the man who befriended you and are waiting now for him to die — "

"Wait! We can make an arrangement — "

The lash bit again. Torres stepped backward with a stilled scream and made the mistake of jerking a knife from his sash. He lifted an arm to throw the weapon. But the whip curled around that arm, made him drop the knife, and jerked him forward to his knees.

"Turn your head, senorita, but do not run away," Zorro told her. "And make no sound."

But Carlos Torres made sounds. As that whip lashed him, cut into his body and brought blood to ruin his fine clothes, he began screeching. Only the roar of the wind and the noise made in the tavern kept the sounds from being heard by those in the main room.

"Get you out of the pueblo tomorrow!" Zorro ordered as he lashed. "If you do not, I'll visit you again and let your foul life out of your body."

In a lull of the wind, Torres yelled: "Help! Help! Zorro is here!"

FROM the corner of his eye, Zorro saw a native servant emerge from the tavern to get water at the well, just in time to hear. He saw the servant drop the pail he was carrying and dash back inside, and knew he had scant time left if he would escape. He lashed twice again, as hard as he could, and Torres sprawled on the flagstones more than half unconscious from pain and fear.

Zorro darted to the girl's side. "Listen, senorita! I know more about you than you do yourself. You are a decent girl of gentle blood — "

"Thanks for what you have done, Senor Zorro. But now I must move on to yet another place, Something like this always happens. I only seek to make my living but it is hard to do."

"Do not leave the pueblo. Promise me!" he urged. "An old man who is dying requests it, but do not mention that to anybody. Fear not for the future. I am a caballero, and give you my word of honor to watch over you. Now, I must go."

Men came running into the patio in time to see him in the light of the torch burning over the well. Zorro darted to the darkness beneath the arches. A pistol exploded behind him, but the ball went wild.

Then he was outside, and running through the fog and rain to where he had left his horse. They could not find him because they could not see him and did not know in which direction he had gone. And the noise of the wind and their own shouts drowned the sounds of his boots pounding the ground.

Alfonso Reynoso, the infamous alcalde, lived in an old house he had purchased some years before from its previous owner. Diego Vega had played around that house as a boy, and as Zorro it gave him no difficulty now to gain entrance without being observed. He left his horse in a secluded place not far away.

Reynoso had only two servants, both men, and they did not spend the nights at the house. That was because the alcalde had visitors to make shady dealings, who alway came at night and did not desire to be observed, nor did Reynoso wish them to be.

Zorro had not tarried in the vicinity of the tavern, so did not know that a messenger had been sent in haste for Sergeant Garcia, and that Garcia had gone to the tavern with some of his men, had heard Torres story and had listened intently.

Magdalena said only that a masked man had been there and had whipped Senor Torres and accused him of being a swindler. But Tones got Garcia aside and began whispering.

"Sergeant, there is something behind all this, and I think it has to do with the alcalde," Torres said. "Senor Reynoso is handling some business for me, and I believe this man who calls himself Zorro desires to stop the deal, perhaps for reasons of profit to himself."

Garcia rubbed his chin. "That does not fit in, senor, with what is known of Senor Zorro — unless your business is of an unjust nature," he said.

"Let me bathe my wounds and get into fresh clothes, and guard me to the alcalde's house," Torres begged.

"That is a reasonable request. I must make a report of this occurrence to the alcalde anyhow. Make haste!"

THOUGH Zorro did not know of this scene, he guessed that his appearance in the tavern patio would be reported to the soldiers immediately. So he made haste once he was inside the alcalde's house. He went silently through a hall and came to a half-opened door and peered into the living room.

Tapers were burning in a candelabrum on a table littered with documents. Alfanso Reynoso was pacing around the room as if waiting impatiently for a visitor. Zorro took his pistol from his sash and stepped into the room. As the alcalde turned to retrace his steps, Zone went forward into the streak of light from the table, and Reynoso saw him.

The alcalde betrayed instant fright and stepped toward the table.

"Stand!" Zorro ordered. "Make no attempt, senor, to reach a weapon, or my pistol will rid the country of an unjust, thieving official."

"This is an act of robbery, I presume."

"An act of justice!' Zorro corrected. "I know about your dealings with Carlos Torres, a scoundrel as great as yourself. I know why you delay signing a certain document — the last will of Don Juan Cardoza, who is dying. Sign it now and affix the official seal. Don Juan called upon me for help, and I have responded."

"So that is it! You are Zorro, then?"

"I am."

"Perhaps we can come to some arrangement which will profit you much."

"Senor Reynoso, the scoundrel Torres made me the same suggestion a short time ago at the tavern, and I used my whip on him. No doubt he still bleeds. Sit at your table and sign the will and put on the seal and hand me the document."

"Unfortunately, Senor Zorro, though you slay me for it, I must tell you the truth — I do not have the will. A careless servant, thinking it something worthless, used it to help start a fire — "

"Fortunately, senor, I have a copy, a duplicate even to the signatures of the witnesses. here it is." Zorro tossed it upon the table. "Sit down and execute the document."

The alcalde's eyes bulged. "Don Juan was insane when the will was made."

"Reputable witnesses will testify otherwise."

"If I say you made me execute the paper under duress — "

"The same good witnesses will testify that this is the will Don Juan wanted, and why you delayed executing it. You have no valid excuse, senor. Execute the will — or be executed yourself, and instantly."

Reynoso sighed and sat at the table. He unfolded the will and started reading.

"Do not fight for time, senor, for no help is coming," Zorro told him. "The will is in order. Sign it!"

Reynoso brushed a heap of documents aside with a sweep of his right arm, and his right hand darted to a pistol they had concealed. Zorro's pistol roared and smoked and flamed at the move, and the slug from it bit deeply into Reynoso's left shoulder. The alcalde dropped his own weapon and sank weakly against the table.

Zorro's blade was out, and the point of it touched the alcalde's back.

"Quickly, senor! Execute that document, or this blade will pierce your heart from behind!" Zorro ordered. "I am in no mood to be trifled with."

Reynoso was a picture of terror now. He signed the will with fingers that scarcely could hold the quill, sanded his signature, and affixed the official seal with great care.

WITHOUT moving the blade, Zorro picked up the document with his left hand and thrust it into a pocket of his costume. He picked up the alcalde's pistol and stepped back.

"Resign your official position, senor, and immediately!" Zorro commanded.

"The pueblo deserves an honest alcalde. If you do not, my next visit will leave you lifeless."

Zorro retired to the shadows near the door, watching the man before him, whose shoulder was commencing to pain. And there came a sudden pounding on the front door, and Zorro heard the hoarse voice of Sergeant Garcia.

"Senor Reynoso! Alcalde! This is Garcia! Are you all right?"

Zorro darted into the hallway, and was gone. Out of the house he got, to run through the swirling fog again and mount his horse. The chase was wild and never endangered him. And within a short time he turned Zorro's horse, clothes and weapons over to the faithful Bernardo at the rendezvous — and was Diego Vega again as he entered his father's house without being seen and got to his own rooms.

It was the next afternoon When Diego Vega and Fray Felipe walked with bowed heads toward the house of Don Juan Cardoza. Diego had given the will to the padre earlier, and the latter had informed Don Juan of what had happened.

"Torres, the trader, has left town," the padre whispered, as they walked. "He is afraid Zorro may visit him again. Our alcalde spent several hours, after his wound was dressed, in rebuking Garcia for being an inefficient officer. He is sick of the job of alcalde, he has told certain persons, and intends to quit it and move to Monterey, where there is more chance of advancement."

Diego smiled slightly, then went with the padre into the house to receive a dying man's blessing.

Zorro Saves an American

**Bill Walsh, Americano, runs into trouble when he faces
Carlos Ramirez, crooked magistrado, but a masked avenger steps in!**

A S DON DIEGO VEGA, taking a leisurely stroll after the heat of the day,
neared the door of the tavern on the plaza in Reina de Los Angeles, the
door was jerked open suddenly and slammed back against the wall with a
bang.

Startled, Diego glanced up quickly, in time to see a human body shoot
through the doorway and strike against the ground as if it had been hurled from
a catapult.

Then Diego realized that he bad been hearing loud voices as of men quar-
reling, but had given it little attention because of mental preoccupation regarding another matter. He stopped his stride abruptly and looked at the man who
had been tossed out of the tavern.

Diego recognized him instantly as a certain Carlos Ramirez, a trader with
a reputation for being unscrupulous in his dealings, who overdressed his station
in life, boasted of his own accomplishments and in general made himself
obnoxious to people of the right sort.

As recognition of the victim came to Diego and he was thinking that at last
Ramirez had received his just deserts from somebody he had swindled, he found
himself a witness of the continuation of the affair.

Through the doorway of the tavern charged another man, a stranger to
Diego. He was tall, heavy-shouldered, red-faced, and dressed in the buckskin
clothing and coonskin cap favored by the Americans. Diego felt a sudden inter-

est. He had liked the few Americans he had met so far.

He listened and watched while this man spoke a jargon of mixed Spanish and English that could have been understood readily by users of either tongue.

"So you'd try to use crooked dice while playing with Bill Walsh, would you?" the American demanded, angrily. "Get on your feet, scum, and put up your fists! I'll batter in your face and knock your teeth down your throat!"

Carlos Ramirez remained prone on the dusty earth, and groaned like a man in agony. Diego guessed that he had not been injured badly, but feared he might be if he got upon his feet. After a second and longer look at Bill Walsh, the American, Diego did not blame Ramirez for remaining prone.

BUT Ramirez found that the trick did not serve him to any extent. Bill Walsh bent forward quickly and grasped Ramirez by the shoulders and jerked him to his feet. He swung a wicked blow with a fist, which Ramirez managed to dodge more through luck than fistic skill.

"Fight, you cheap swindler!" the American roared, as men came pouring from the tavern and running toward the scene from across the plaza. "I've met up with your kind before. Marked cards and crooked dice! Give back the money you stole from me — pronto!"

Another man pressed through the small crowd that had gathered already, and Diego saw he was Sergeant Manuel Garcia, attached to the local barracks. The sergeant got between the belligerents quickly.

"What is this?" Garcia howled. "A brawl in front of the tavern during the hour of promenade? Do you not realize that you are frightening the ladies?"

"Let's get behind the tavern and out of their sight, then," the American suggested. "I'm going to teach this fellow a thing or two. Thought I'd be easy prey for him because I'm an American, did he? It's time he was taught a lesson."

"Silence from you!" Garcia roared at him commandingly. "Ramirez, explain this matter."

"We were dicing, Sergeant, and the fellow lost," Ramirez whined. "And suddenly he became like a mad man, and attacked me and threw the out of the tavern. Sergeant Garcia, I demand that you arrest him. Let the *magistrado* decide the affair."

Sergeant Garcia tugged at one end of his enormous mustache and closed one eye significantly. "Ha! The *magistrado* is your cousin, I believe," he hinted.

"That is true. And this man who attacked me without reason is an Americano, an alien, one of the detestable crew of vagrants and petty thieves — "

He was interrupted by a wild bellow of rage that came from Bill Walsh. The American toppled the big sergeant aside and sprang forward, grasped Ramirez by the throat and commenced shaking him as a terrier shakes a rat.

"Vagrants? Thieves?" Walsh roared, "I'll teach you not to misname your betters!"

Ramirez squawked with fear, tugged helplessly at the strong hands on his throat, and began turning purple in the face. Sergeant Garcia shouted an order, and two burly troopers rushed to his aid. They tore Walsh away from Ramirez and held him. Panting, angry, Garcia confronted him.

"Are you perhaps seeking serious trouble?" the sergeant demanded. "Did I not say you would frighten the ladies?"

"Oh, since you'd side with him, you're the same kind," Bill Walsh complained.

Birds out of the same nest. What hope can an American have for justice here? But one day soon, perhaps, the boot will be on the other foot. You may be glad to be friendly with Americans then."

"Silence!" Garcia snapped at him. "I do my duty regardless of a man's nationality. By speaking as you have to me, you have insulted one of His Excellency's officers, and that is a serious offense."

"Let me at that swindler and cheat!"

"Back! We will give you an opportunity to cool off your hot blood." he gestured to the troopers behind him. "Take him to the barracks and lock him in the prison room. I'll attend to his case later."

Bill Walsh started to fight, but one of the troopers cracked him on the head with a club, and half stunned the American allowed them to lead him away.

"Sergeant Garcia, you have acted in an appropriate manner," Ramirez declared. "I shall be glad to report as much to my cousin, the *magistrado*."

"Hand me the money you swindled out of that man, so it may be returned to him," the sergeant ordered.

"You dare accuse me of swindling?"

"Ha! 'Twould not be the first time you have used crooked dice and marked cards," Sergeant Garcia informed him. "I have watched you play often, senor. No man of the pueblo would play with you. But this Americano, this stranger is not acquainted with your reputation."

FOR a moment Ramirez stared at Garcia, amazed at his insolence.

"You are daring to speak so to me?" Ramirez raged. "Your superiors shall lean of this! I'll have you demoted and removed to another post."

"Ha! If I am ordered to some new post because of you, be sure you do not show yourself in the vicinity," Garcia warned. "But I do not fear your animosity: I feel positive, senor, that neither you nor your cousin, the *magistrado*, has influence enough to have me punished for attending to my duty."

"You slurred me."

"One cannot blacken the wing of a raven, senor," Garcia broke in.

Ramirez choked, and his eyes glittered. 'Perhaps you are displeased and angry, Sergeant Garcia, because I met this strange Americano first," Ramirez suggested. "You are adept yourself at handling dice and cards."

"What is this?" Garcia raged. "You are now accusing me of being a cheat like yourself? Now you are the one who insults an officer of His Excellency's soldiery. I try to deal fairly with all, so to the barracks you go!"

"You would dare?"

Garcia beckoned two more troopers. "Take this rascal away and shove him into a prison room," he ordered his men. "But do not put him in with the Americano. That Americano probably would beat him to death, and then we would be put to the nuisance of burying him."

Carlos Ramirez protested vociferously, but his wild protests availed him nothing. Garcia gestured again, anti the troopers led Ramirez away.

"That was very well done. Your action was commendable," a voice behind Garcia said.

The sergeant tuned quickly and saw Diego Vega standing a few feet away, bent forward like a man fatigued, and brushing his nostrils with a scented silken handkerchief as if even the very air he was compelled to breathe offended his sense of smell.

"I am glad that you approve, Don Diego," the sergeant told him, bowing slightly. "It is time someone handled Ramirez for his cheating. I would not have jailed the Americano had he not used the words he did. The *magistrado* undoubtedly will order me to punish the Americano and release Ramirez, his cousin. And he will be furious with me for putting his cousin in jail."

"Does the *magistrado* rank you in authority?" Diego asked.

"Unhappily, he does. My superior is absent, so I am in command at the barracks. Our *alcalde* is also absent, so the *magistrado* acts in his stead. I had strict orders from the *capitan* to bow to the orders of the *alcalde* always. And since Jose Reyes, the *magistrado*, is now in the *alcalde's* place, I must now bow to him. 'Tis a sorry mess … "

Diego went to the chapel for a chat with aged Fray Felipe, his confessor, and some time later started to stroll homeward.

He saw men of the pueblo converging on the barracks, and asked a passerby the reason for it. And he learned that Jose Reyes, the *magistrado*, had ordered an immediate trial of the two men Garcia had taken into custody. So Diego turned aside and went to the barracks and into the courtroom there.

Jose Reyes sat on the dais like a king upon his throne, his manner excessively arrogant. The sergeant sat on one side of him and a clerk on the other, Diego observed as he was ushered to a place on the front bench. The room was crowded, for a trial of any sort, with the expectation of punishment out in the plaza, always attracted the curious.

Sergeant Garcia gave his testimony, and was followed by a couple of bystanders who obviously had been coached by Jose Reyes before the trial began. Then Ramirez was called to the stand.

"We were dicing in the tavern, and this Americano wormed his way into the game," Ramirez declared, trying to act like an injured man. "Suddenly the Americano went wild and accused me of cheating, because he had lost a small sum. Then he made a vicious attack on me and hurled me out of the tavern, and followed and started beating me. The troopers pulled him away."

"You're a swindler and cheat!" Bill Walsh shouted at the witness. "And you're a liar as well!"

"Silence!" Jose Reyes roared. "You are affronting this honorable court."

"Call more witnesses," Walsh suggested. "Ask those who saw us dicing."

RAMIREZ slammed his hand down upon the table.

"This court has all the testimony and evidence necessary for a verdict, senor," the *magistrado* replied. "The pueblo cannot endure to have aliens enter it, become drunken and brawl and attack reputable citizens. You also defamed an officer of the soldiery."

"For that last, I apologize," Walsh said. "But this fellow Ramirez is a swindler and cheat."

"Silence!" Reyes interrupted. "The court has decided the case. It is my judgment that the defendant Carlos Ramirez is the injured party in this affair. He will apologize to Sergeant Garcia for what he said, and his case is dismissed."

"Spanish justice!" Walsh growled.

"As for you, Senor Walsh, it is quite another matter," Reyes continued. "You are an alien and refuse to abide by our laws. You make infamous charges against reputable citizens, defame our soldiers, and render yourself generally obnoxious to this court. It is our judgment that you receive ten lashes across your naked back in the plaza at sunrise tomorrow."

"It'll take more than one strong man to give them to me!" Walsh howled.

"But there is another and more serious matter," Reyes went on to say, his eyes glittering again. "Since your arrest, we have been gathering evidence along a certain line concerning you. Your remarks against authority and officials made us suspicious. Our investigation has convinced us of your guilt."

"Guilt of what?" Walsh asked. "What trick is this? What trap have you built for me in a short space of time?"

"Senor Walsh, you rode into this pueblo on a fine black horse, did you not?"

"I did, and I own him legally. I bought him some time ago from a man in Santa Barbara, and have the bill of sale here to show for it."

"Your ownership of the horse is not questioned, senor. It only helps to prove your guilt. That is not all. There has been found a bundle containing black clothes which would fit you well. In the bundle also was a black mask, a pistol, a sword, and a long whip. These articles were found hidden beneath some rocks near where you picketed your horse. Moreover, as you were scuffling with the troopers in the plaza, you scratched in the dust with the toe of your boot, no doubt as a notice to your unknown friends to help, the letter Z."

Those in the courtroom stirred, gasped, and their eyes bulged as they looked at the prisoner. "This court is satisfied," Reyes continued, "that you are the notorious Senor Zorro, the highwayman, for whose capture dead or alive the Governor has posted a large reward. I adjudge you guilty of being this notorious Zorro."

"You must be mad," Walsh said.

"You will receive the ten lashes in the morning on the first charge, and immediately thereafter will be hanged by the neck until dead. You see now, Senor Americano, to what dire straits your unjust defamation of a reputable citizen and our soldiery has brought you. Senor Carlos Ramirez should be acclaimed because his trouble with you has brought you to our official attention and revealed your true identity."

"It's a bunch of lies!" Walsh cried. "I was never in this district until a few days ago. I rode down from the north on my way to San Juan Capistrano."

"But what of the evidence we have unearthed, senor?"

"It's bogus evidence you had arranged yourself," Walsh accused. "You want revenge on me because I handled this rogue of a Ramirez, and want to make a hero out of him, because the cheat and swindler is your blood kin."

"The court has finished," Reyes announced. "Sergeant Garcia, take charge of the prisoner and see that the sentence of the court is carried out as ordered. Let the room be cleared."

Diego arose from the bench to follow the others out of the room. Outwardly, he was calm, but inwardly he was seething at the injustice. Bill Walsh, the American, had been adjudged guilty of being Zorro and would be hanged to appease the anger of the *magistrado*.

Diego knew that the evidence must have been prepared purposely by Reyes and some of his hirelings. Walsh would be hanged. And if the truth came out afterward Reyes would say that it was to be regretted, but that it really amounted to nothing, since Bill Walsh was an alien and of no consequence.

DIEGO knew Bill Walsh was innocent of the charge, that he was not Senor Zorro, for Diego Vega, who always pretended to be a languid fop, was in reality Senor Zorro himself.

Fray Felipe was one of three persons who knew Diego was Zorro, and Diego went to the chapel again now and told the *padre* what had occurred.

"This Americano must be saved," Diego said. "Only the real Zorro can save him. Nor is that all."

"What else, my son?"

"Jose Reyes, the false *magistrado*, must be exposed and punished and his cousin, Carlos Ramirez, also dealt with. Those tasks, too, belong to Zorro."

"That is true," Fray Felipe acknowledged, after a slight hesitation. "Let us hope Zorro does not encounter peril tonight, and that he may accomplish his object without the necessity of taking human life."

"Such official action is a stain on Alta California," Diego went on to say. "Senor Walsh should know that not all of us are the same as Jose Reyes. And, if I may say so, the condemned man should be comforted."

The *padre's* eyes twinkled. "Why not speak out directly, my son, and suggest that I go to the prison room and comfort him? I shall do so immediately, for it is my duty whether the man is of our faith or not."

Diego hurried home after that, and had speech with another of the only three who knew his secret, his august father, Don Alejandro Vega. He told his father the story, and Don Alejandro paced around the room thoughtfully, thinking of the problem.

"It is understood that Zorro must save the American," he said, after a time. "You have plans, my son?"

"One is forming in my mind, Father."

"You desire me to do something?"

"Invite two or three reputable men here for the evening meal. So late an invitation will tell them there is a necessity. Get them to go with you to Jose Reyes at a certain time, to protest against the hanging of the Americano."

"And this Senor Zorro may appear while we are there?" Don Alejandro asked.

"That is it, Father. Witnesses of standing."

"It shall be done, Diego. What is the rest of your plan?"

"I am still thinking of it."

Then, Diego went to the third person who knew his secret. He was Bernardo, the huge peon, dumb from birth, who acted as Diego's body servant — who could not speak and tell the secret had he wished to do so, and who would have died rather than reveal it had he been able.

"Zorro rides tonight," Diego told him, when he found Bernardo by the servants' huts in the rear of the house. "Have everything ready soon after nightfall."

Bernardo gave a gurgle which meant he was both excited and delighted, and Diego returned to the house to conclude his plans.

Two men of birth and importance replied to Don Alejandro's invitation to supper, house servants having been sent to invite them. Yawning and languid, Diego appeared at the table. After the repast, Don Alejandro spoke of the arrest of the Americano.

"Without doubt, senores, this fellow Reyes is only avenging his rascal of a cousin," Don Alejandro told his guests. "He hopes to have the Americano executed immediately, before the return of the capitan from Monterey. He may say afterward that a sad mistake was made, but a dead man cannot be brought back to life."

"That is true," one of the guests said, nodding in agreement.

"I suggest that the three of us pay a visit to Jose Reyes and ask him to rescind his order of execution and await the return of the *capitan*, who will conduct a proper investigation into the affair. He would not dare refuse us. He has no valid reason for not issuing a stay of execution."

Diego arose from his chair and bowed to his father and the two guests.

"I have had a busy day and am fatigued," Diego told them, stifling a yawn with his silk handkerchief. "With your permission I'll seek my couch and get some sleep. *Buenas noches!"*

"'Noches!" the others chorused.

Diego lounged across the room and disappeared, and Don Alejandro and his guests prepared to take a last sip of wine and start for the house of Jose Reyes, the *magistrado.*

BEFORE they passed through the front door, Diego was out the back without being seen by a servant. He skirted the huts in the rear of the house and hurried through the darkness to a depression behind a mass of rocks some distance away.

Bernardo was waiting for him there. He had Zorro's black horse, clothes and weapons. Swiftly, Diego put on the black Zorro costume over his usual attire, donned the black mask and hat, buckled on the blade and thrust a pistol into his sash. Then he mounted the big black horse and gathered up the reins.

His entire manner had changed. Now he was keenly alert as his eyes glistened through the holes in the mask. He adjusted his scabbard, made sure his pistol was in its proper position. Don Diego Vega had disappeared, and in his place was Senor Zorro, defender of the helpless and oppressed.

Clouds had scudded in from the distant sea, and a slight mist was falling. Through the darkness Zorro rode to a spot near a corner of the plaza, and surveyed the scene.

A bonfire had been built in the plaza, and by its light men were sawing and hammering, building a gallows for use at sunrise. Many of the town's loafers and curious were watching the builders. One of Garcia's troopers strolled around to keep order and see that the builders were not disturbed.

The door of the tavern was open, and through the doorway Zorro could see men eating, drinking and playing at dice and cards — the usual evening scene there.

He watched for a moment more, then gathered up his reins, settled himself in the saddle and touched with the spurs. The big black sprang into a running stride. Hoofs thundered against the hard packed ground, and those around the fire and gallows tuned and looked quickly.

As Zorro emerged from the darkness and entered the circle of light cast by the fire, they recognized the masked rider. Some yelled in surprise and others

*The troopers
found themselves
looking into
the muzzle of
Zorro's pistol!*

stood as if suddenly turned to marble. The trooper started to draw his saber, but
Zorro stopped the horse a short distance away, and the trooper found himself
looking into the muzzle of a pistol.

"Attention, senores!" Zorro shouted. "You can see plainly that the man held
at the barracks for execution in the morning is not Zorro, for Zorro is here before
you. Your *magistrado*, José Reyes, condemned a man to death through revenge
for what he thought was an affront to his worthless cousin, Carlos Ramirez. See
to it that this murder by hanging does not occur."

He backed his horse a few feet, and his eyes glittered at the trooper. "Take
out your pistol and toss it away!" Zorro ordered. "Pronto!"

The trooper obeyed, knowing it would be futile to try a shot while the muzzle
of Zorro's pistol was covering him. Zorro laughed a little, and used his spurs
again.

He dashed out of the lighted space and disappeared in the, darkness. Behind him, the men around the fire began shouting, and the trooper retrieved his pistol and fired it into the air as an alarm for Sergeant Garcia and the other men at the barracks.

Zorro thundered past the barracks as some of the troopers emerged, and out of the pueblo. At a distance, he stopped his horse and turned away from the trail, to circle through the black night and approach from the rear the old house occupied by José Reyes.

Zorro knew the house well. He had played around it as a boy, before the owner had died and the property had come into Reyes' possession. He knew Reyes had only one servant, an elderly peon.

Dismounting a short distance behind the house, Zorro tied his horse in a clump of stunted trees and shrubs and went forward afoot with no more noise than a shadow would have made. The wind was coming up and it carried to Zorro's ears sounds of tumult in the plaza and the pounding of horses' hoofs as some of Garcia's troopers started in pursuit.

Zorro slipped into the house through a rear door. The old servant was washing pots and pans in the kitchen. From the front of the house came a hum of voices.

PASSING swiftly and almost silently through the rear hallway, Zorro came to a half opened door and could peer through into the spacious main room of the old house. José Reyes sat behind a long table heaped with books and documents, lighted by a huge candelabrum at each end. In chairs on the other side of the table sat Don Alejandro and his two friends.

The *magistrado* was speaking, his manner somewhat pompous and what he considered to be official:

"It would pleasure me to oblige you, senores, but I am an official and must act in an official capacity."

"We are asking you only to delay execution of sentence until the *capitan* returns and can make a thorough investigation," Don Alejandro pointed out.

"To my mind, the evidence against the Americano is conclusive," Reyes declared.

"He was given no chance to make a defense."

"Pardon me, Don Alejandro, but I am the *magistrado,*" Reyes said, softly. "Why should you gentlemen concern yourselves so much regarding an Americano?"

"Whatever he is, he is entitled to justice," Don Alejandro replied. "Injustice even to an alien would be a sorry reflection on Alta California. The Governor —"

"I'll answer for my actions to the Governor," Reyes interrupted.

There came a pounding on the front door. Reyes got up and opened it, and Sergeant Garcia strode into the room. He bowed to the three hildagos and faced the *magistrado*.

"They are working on the scaffold?" Reyes snapped at him.

"The scaffold is almost finished, senor, but it will not be used in the morning," the sergeant replied.

"What is your meaning?"

"You have ordered me to hang the Americano because he is the notorious Senor Zorro, have you not?"

"That was my order."

"Then it may interest you to know, Senor Magistrado, that the real Zorro rode across the plaza only a short time ago, and that some of my troopers are now pursuing him."

Watching through the doorway, Zorro saw his father suddenly put up a hand to stifle a smile.

"That cannot be!" Reyes raged. "The Americano is Zorro. I have evidence to confirm it. This is a trick!"

"How can it be a trick, Senor Reyes?" Garcia asked.

"Are you blind? Do you not see? One of Zorro's friends has dressed like him and ridden through the plaza in an effort to save the real Zorro, now a prisoner in your barracks."

Garcia drew himself up and blew out the ends of his large mustache. "Senor Reyes, I cannot and will not hang the Americano in the morning," he declared. "I will keep him prisoner until the return of my *capitan*, and let him decide this affair."

"Do you not have orders to obey me during your *capitan's* absence?"

"I had orders to obey the *alcalde*, but he was called away and left you in his stead. Under the circumstances, I refuse to take such an order from you."

Reyes' face turned almost purple with wrath. "Do you not realize that such conduct on your part is insubordination?"

"I'll risk the consequences, Senor Reyes. Fray Felipe has visited the prisoner to offer the usual offices to a condemned man. I talked with the padre. He understands men, and he tells me that he knows the Americano is innocent."

"Are you taking orders from your superiors, or from some old fray who has been softened by age?" Reyes demanded.

"In this case, senor, I listen to the *padre.*"

"I order you again to carry out the execution at sunrise! If you do not, I'll prefer charges against you. That is all, Sergeant. Go about your duties. If you think the man in your prison room is not Zorro, catch me the real Zorro, and I'll have the Americano released at once." Reyes smiled.

Garcia's face grew purple in turn. "It is true that the soldiery has failed so far to catch Zorro," he replied. "The rascal is a clever rogue. But we'll catch him one of these days — or nights." He saluted the three guests again, tuned on his heel and strode out of the house.

REYES closed the door behind him and walked back to the long table, fighting himself to regain his composure.

"I trust, senores," he told the three guests, as he seated himself, "that you understand the situation. Undoubtedly, one of Zorro's friends has aped him to put a doubt in the sergeant's mind. Garcia is a stubborn fellow. I'd hate to have him punished, perhaps demoted, incarcerated and afterwards dishonorably discharged and ordered out of the country. But I'll be compelled to do so if he does not obey me. It would be a kindness to him if you gentlemen would urge upon him that he conduct the execution in the morning as I ordered."

Don Alejandro Vega opened his mouth as if to reply, but at that moment Zorro slipped into the room, and Don Alejandro shut his mouth without speaking.

"There is no doubt that the man in the prison room is Zorro and the man who impersonated Zorro in the plaza a poor counterfeit," Reyes continued.

"You call me a counterfeit, senor?" a stern voice asked from a corner of the room.

Zorro strode forward into the bright light, a menacing figure in black, holding a pistol ready for use. Jose Reyes sank low in his chair, gasping.

"You — you — " he gulped.

"I assure you that I am the real Zorro, and that the man in the prison room is not. He is guilty of nothing except punishing a cheat and swindler — your cousin, I understand. Prepare to write an order for Sergeant Garcia to release the Americano immediately with the understanding that he mounts his horse and leaves the pueblo at once. Make sure he can go where he wishes without being hindered."

"I'll give an alarm."

"Order Garcia to reimburse the Americano for his losses through your cousin's crooked gambling, and promise you will reimburse Garcia or have your cousin do so."

"You dare to make such a suggestion?"

"Silence!" Zorro barked at him. "Include in the order that Carlos Ramirez is to serve five days at hard labor for cheating, and that a part of his labor will be to tear down the gallows in the plaza. During this labor, he is to wear chains."

"Are you mad to think I'd write such an order?" Reyes thundered.

"If you do not, senor, there will be another *magistrado* named as soon as word can be sent to Monterey that you are dead and buried," Zorro warned. "Nor is that all. You will also write out your resignation of the post you hold unworthily, and give the resignation to Sergeant Garcia with orders to forward it to Monterey by courier. Commence writing, senor!"

Reyes' eyes had been bulging, and they bulged almost out of his head as Zorro advanced toward the table with determined stride. Zorro's pistol had been raised until its muzzle covered Reyes' heart.

"Make no mistake about it, Senor Reyes — I am the real Zorro! You know the work I have done against unworthy officials and in behalf of the downtrodden. I have been watching your acts for some time, and this affair of the Americano is but the culmination. Write as I have said, and immediately, or you are a dead man!"

Reyes gulped and tried to talk, but there was no courage left in him. With a hand that trembled, he began writing. Zorro stood back a few feet and watched, pistol still held ready.

"Senores," he said to the three who had called on the *magistrado*, "there must be no misfire in this matter. Though you do not know me, I know all of you as honorable men. Don Alejandro Vega!"

"Well, senor?" his father asked.

"You will read what Senor Reyes has written when he has finished. You will take charge of the documents and see that they get into the hand of Sergeant Garcia, and you and your two friends will see that the orders are carried out."

"Though you are a rascal and a rogue," Don Alejandro said, his eyes twinkling, "in this case I believe you represent Justice, and I'll do as you ask. Confronted by a pistol in the hand of a man I fear, what else can I do?"

Zorro bowed. "That was a pretty speech, Don Alejandro, but the knowledge

I have of you tells me you do not fear the devil himself," he replied, his own eyes twinkling through the holes in his mask.

BY THIS time Reyes had finished writing and sank back into his chair as Don Alejandro began reading.

"This is not the end, senor," Reyes told Zorro. "I'll never rest until you are run down and hanged."

"They will have to catch me first, senor."

There came a pounding again on the front door, and those in the room heard Garcia's voice:

"Open, Senor Reyes! Are you all right? A man has said he saw a masked man on a black horse riding this way."

Zorro threatened Reyes with the pistol again, and the *magistrado* remained silent.

"The papers are in order," Don Alejandro said, softly.

"See that the sergeant gets them, and that Reyes does not countermand them," Zorro warned. *"Senores, a Dios!"*

He backed a few steps, whirled, darted through the doorway and was gone. In the hall, he crashed into the old servant and caused him to drop pots and pans and make a general clatter. The old servant and Reyes both began shouting, and Garcia pounded on the door again.

Zorro did not escape from the house. He feared troopers might be around it. He hid in a closet off the hall, and listened. Reyes was shouting at the sergeant, who put his head through the door and howled for troopers to comb the hillside and watch the highway. And then Zorro heard Don Alejandro explaining the circumstances and giving Garcia the papers Reyes had written. The sergeant's gruff voice came to Zorro's ears:

"I knew the Americano was not Zorro, and that it was the real Zorro who rode across the plaza tonight. A dozen men who have seen Zorro have told me he is a much smaller man than the Americano. I'll catch the real Zorro when I can, and hang the rogue and claim the Governor's reward."

"Attend me, Sergeant!" Reyes barked. "I was compelled to write those papers with a pistol under my nose. I repudiate them now. Give them here, and I'll destroy them."

"I have them, senor, and am handing them to the sergeant now," Don Alejandro said. "And you are utterly without authority here. I say so, and these two friends of mine say so, and if you care to take up arms against the three foremost men of this pueblo say the word now. And you forget, do you not, that you have resigned? Take the papers, Sergeant Garcia, and see that the orders are carried out."

Zorro got out of the house to find that a heavy rain had started falling. One trooper was groping around, but Zorro dodged him and found his horse. He swung up into the saddle. Despite the rain, he did not return home, but circled the pueblo again and returned to the highway a distance from the town. Under a spreading tree, he waited.

He was drenched before the shower ended and the moon came from behind the clouds, and Bill Walsh came riding along the highway. Zorro rode out to meet him, pistol ready.

"Do not be alarmed and try to shoot me, Senor Walsh," he said. "I am Zorro."

"Zorro! They told me what you did. My thanks, amigo! I have heard a lot about other things you've done. This country needs more men like you."

"And more men like you, senor," Zorro said. "I like Americans, though some of my people do not. Some day many more of you will come, and we will get better acquainted. May good fortune travel with you, Senor Walsh. *Buenas noches!*"

Zorro wheeled his horse and rode furiously along the highway, to leave it presently and circle to the place where Bernardo waited to take the black horse and Zorro's clothes and weapons. And before long, drenched to the skin, but happy, Don Diego Vega entered his father's house and hurried to his room, to undress and put on a robe and quaff the hot spiced wine he knew his smiling father would bring him.

Zorro Meets a Rogue

**When the blackmailer threatened to reveal the identity
of the black-clad avenger, disaster rode the highways!**

SHADOWS were starting to lengthen that afternoon as Don Diego Vega strolled across the plaza in Reina de Los Angeles on his way to the tavern. He desired to purchase a pot of crystallized honey, a delicacy the innkeeper made one of his specialties.

Diego observed the thick high fog rolling in from the distant sea. No doubt nightfall would bring a dismal mist, and the thought of it made him shudder. For he was to attend a small *fiesta* that evening at the home of Don Juan Romo, an old friend of his father's. Magdalena, Don Juan's eldest daughter, was to be betrothed to a friend of Diego's. And Diego was somewhat interested in Don Juan's youngest, Rosita.

As he neared the tavern, Diego glanced ahead to where some barefooted peons and natives were resting lazily against the front of a vacant building. And he saw, approaching them from the opposite direction, an overdressed, heavy-set stranger who had been living in the pueblo at the tavern for several days.

The man had given the name of Carlos Portillo, and he had hinted that he was a man of means traveling leisurely along the highway while recuperating from a wound he had received during a duel with blades in which he had slain his adversary.

The peons and natives scurried away like so many rabbits at sight of Portillo, which indicated that he had treated some of them cruelly and they feared he might do so again. So it happened that Diego and Carlos Portillo met where there was nobody near enough to overhear anything they said.

Portillo bowed and smirked.

"Don Diego Vega, it gives me pleasure to address you," he announced. "I am Carlos Portillo, of Monterey. I desire to have a few words with you."

"If it is a matter of important business, you should address yourself to my father," Diego informed him. "Lesser affairs are handled by the overseer at our rancho. If you wish to speak to me socially, allow me to say I do not think we would be congenial in social intercourse."

ANGER flared in Portillo's face, but he managed to gain control of himself.

"A pretty speech, Don Diego," he complimented. "This is a matter of business of which I would speak to you, and does not concern your father or his rancho overseer, but you personally."

"I cannot imagine what it could be. I never attend to business," Diego informed him. "I do not have the knack of it."

Portillo stepped closer and glanced around furtively to be sure nobody could hear him.

"My business, Don Diego, is this — I know the real identity of the man they call Senor Zorro," he whispered.

By the way of reply, Diego merely gave him a blank stare. He in no way revealed the shock the words had given him. For he, Don Diego Vega, supposed to be a spineless fop and an ache in his father's heart, was also Zorro, the wild masked avenger of the poor and oppressed. And only three persons were supposed to know this, and the man who called himself Carlos Portilo certainly was not one of them.

"You said — ?" Diego prompted.

"I said that I know the identity of Zorro."

"And why should that concern me, senor. I'd say that you are a fortunate man. I understand the governor has offered a rich reward for the rascal's capture. Why not report what you know to the soldiery so that you can share in the reward?"

"Why should I share the reward with soldiers who do not have the knowledge I possess?"

"If you do not wish to do that, capture Senor Zorro yourself and claim the entire reward," Diego suggested. He brushed a scented handkerchief lightly across his nostrils in a gesture the meaning of which could not be mistaken.

"Knowing his identity, I might do that," Portillo replied.

"I understand the rogue is handy with a blade," Diego remarked. "It is said he rides like a mad fiend, can shoot a pistol with unusual accuracy, and has a long whip which he wraps painfully around the bodies of such men as deserve punishment."

Portillo smiled slightly. "I also am handy with a blade, he boasted. In some quarters, I have quite a reputation as a swordsman. Also, Don Diego, I am an excellent shot with a pistol."

"Then you should have a fair chance at wounding the rascal and should be able to capture him."

"I am a practical man, Don Diego, and I judge Zorro to be the same. Perhaps he would give me the amount of the reward secretly to seal my lips. I would go my way, and he could continue frightening the countryside and making fools of the troopers who wear out their horses chasing him."

"And if he should refuse to make such an arrangement?"

"Then, as a last resort, I'll go to the soldiers and tell them what I know, let them make the capture and share in the reward. 'Twould be better than nothing. He would be foolish not to make the deal I suggest."

"But the reward is of large amount, and this Zorro probably is a poor man," Diego judged.

"I happen to know that he is rich in his own right, and his father is rich also. In real life,. Zorro is a young caballero, son and heir of a hidalgo of proud lineage."

"A man of my own social class?" Diego asked, his brows lifting. "Perhaps I know him."

"I am sure you do, Don Diego. And you see his face each time you look into a mirror."

"I do not understand your meaning."

"Ah, Don Diego, you are clever! This business of Zorro has puzzled me for some time, and I love to solve puzzles. So, in my spare time I gathered evidence."

"An interesting occupation, no doubt," Diego replied. "You remarked, I believe, that I see Zorro's face each time I look into a mirror. Can you possibly believe I am Zorro?"

"Absolutely!" Portillo declared.

"Ridiculous! Preposterous! I, Diego Vega, ride like a wild man and use blade and pistol defending peons and natives? You say you have evidence, senor.

I'd be interested in knowing what it is, how you have been misled."

"I have evidence, Don Diego. Be assured of that. If I had not, I'd not have approached you."

"Pardon, senor, but we have been standing here talking for quite some time, and that may attract attention. Suppose we stroll into the tavern and discover whether the good host has wine fit to drink. We may continue this interesting conversation."

THEY started walking slowly toward the tavern door, and Diego continued.

"As I understand this, senor, you say that I am Zorro, and demand that I pay you a large sum to prevent you giving this information to others."

"That is correct, Don Diego."

"If I were Zorro and did such a thing, what assurance would I have that you would not make other demands upon me, using the same threat?"

"I could only give you my word of honor."

Diego smiled. "A man who takes money to hide another's guilt from the world should not speak of honor, senor."

"I can endure your insults, Don Diego, since I know you are about to pay well for them."

"Let us talk of other things for the moment, senor. We are nearing the tavern door, and ears may be open around us. Talk to me of your travels, in a natural manner."

Portfflo talked as they walked on, but Diego heard scarcely a word he said. He was thinking intensely. This was a dangerous moment, he knew. Perhaps this rogue of a Portillo had leaned something damaging.

For an instant there flashed through Diego's mind what exposure would mean. Like many grandees, his father was at odds with a rascally governor who , sought to humble all men of better birth and character than himself. If caught and condemned, Diego might be hanged. If the governor was afraid to go so far, he at least would exile Diego and his father and confiscate the Vega estates. And his father's proud head would be bent with a weight of shame.

This rogue of a blackmailer must be undone! Not only must other men be convinced that Diego could not be Zorro, but Senor Portillo himself must be convinced that he had made a mistake, regardless of any evidence he had collected.

A plan flashed into Diego's mind even as he entered the tavern with Portillo. The fat innkeeper, bending and bowing; hurried to meet the son of the Vegas. A look of surprise flashed across his face when he saw Diego's companion, but immediately that face became a mask again.

Diego had glanced rapidly around the main room of the tavern. It was the after siesta hour when men of the town patronized the place. Sergeant Manuel Garcia, of the local barracks, was there with some of his troopers. Men of the town and travelers off the highway were scattered around the room also, eating and drinking, dicing and playing cards.

Diego waved the innkeeper aside and walked the length of the room to stand in front of the wide fireplace. Portillo followed a step behind him, and seemed surprised when Diego did not go immediately to one of the tables.

Diego faced those in the room and tossed up one arm.

"Ho, Sergeant Garcia! Senores!" he shouted.

He had spoken during a lull in the din, and his voice rang through the room. All turned to look at him, and there was instant silence.

"Ha! 'Tis my friend, Don Diego Vega!" the burly sergeant cried. "A good day to you, Don Diego!"

"I am instructing the innkeeper to serve all here with good wine at my expense," Diego continued.

They shouted at that, and the fat innkeeper clapped his hands for his native servants to begin pouring the wine. Diego Vega, he knew, would pay any bill rendered without glancing at it except to ascertain the amount.

Diego gestured to Portillo, then to a small vacant table at the side of the fireplace. Portillo, basking in this moment of glory, sat on the bench beside the table when Diego motioned for him to do so. The innkeeper himself poured the wine at that table while Diego remained standing at the fireplace, pouring Diego's in his finest goblet. Then he bowed to the scion of the Vegas and handed him the goblet.

"Senores, most of you here know me and my family well," Diego said. He spoke in a lazy sort of voice, his appearance that of a man who disliked exertion of any sort. He held the goblet in his right hand and with his left brushed from his right satin sleeve an imaginary speck of dust. Those in the room were silent out of respect, but hoping Diego's speech would be short so they could drink the good wine he had bought them.

"You all have heard of this rogue, Zorro," Diego continued.

"May the rogue be blasted!" Sergeant Garcia growled. Only that morning he had received by courier from Monterey a written rebuke and threat of reduction. in rank because he had not caught the masked rider.

"Sitting here at this table," Diego went on to tell them, "is the stranger who calls himself Carlos Portillo. A short time ago, he accosted me in the plaza. He told me that he had proof that I, Diego Vega am this rascal of a Zorro. And he demanded that I pay him considerable gold to seal his lips."

A MOMENT of stunned silence followed, then a roar of laughter. Men there could not restrain themselves. The very idea of indolent Diego Vega, who seemed to go around in a fog all the time and was known to read poetry, being Zorro, brought on a fit of merriment.

He groaned whenever he had to get into a saddle, made the journey between the pueblo and the Vega rancho in a carriage with soft cushions at his back, never gave the eye to a senorita, never revealed the caballero spirit in a quarrel, and never had been seen to handle a blade or aim a pistol. That such a man could be the fiery Zorro — the thing was ridiculous!

Diego lifted his hand for silence and got it, and continued:

"I tried to convince Senor Portillo of his error, but he refused to be convinced. Drink your wine, senores — unless you find it distasteful to drink wine bought by a rascal some people call a highwayman."

They laughed again, and drank, and Diego lifted his goblet and took a modest sip. Then, Sergeant Manuel Garcia, looking like a huge avenger, got up from his bench and stalked toward the table where Portillo was sitting. The sergeant's face was like a thundercloud.

"You, Senor Portillo!" he barked. "How dare you think such a thing? And you are a blackmailer, it seems. My good friend, Don Diego Vega, is Zorro? We who know him — well, that is to say, he is scarcely the type."

"Perhaps he has made fools of you all," Portfflo suggested. He was furious at the turn events had taken. "I have gathered some evidence — "

"Ridiculous!" the sergeant thundered. "If it comes to that, Senor Portillo, as you name yourself, what do we know about you? Nothing! What if you are this rascal of a Zorro, living here openly in our midst and laughing at us? You might be, and consider it a jest to accuse Don Diego.

"My evidence! Do you, an officer of the soldiery, refuse to consider it? Do Don Diego Vega's wealth and social standing blind you?"

"Ha! What is this? You now accuse of dereliction in duty? A little investigation of you and your affairs might not be an official error. What is your evidence? Give me good proof that you had reason to accuse Don Diego, or on his statement that you tried extortion I'll throw you into the barracks jail and have the magistrado order you out of town in the morning!"

"I'll give my evidence to you secretly, Senor Sergeant, and all here are my Witness that when I have proved my point and you have arrested Don Diego Vega for treason I claim a share of the governor's reward."

"Prove that Don Diego is Zorro and I'll give you the whole reward," Garcia declared. "Speak openly, here and now. Convince me and I'll make an arrest at once, before all this company."

Portillo gulped some of his wine. Diego remained standing at the fireplace, holding the goblet. He had taken only a sip.

"Don Diego Vega, in the first instance, has a powerful black horse he keeps hidden somewhere near the town," Portillo declared.

"Every rancho owner has black horses by the dozen," Garcia replied. "Why keep this one in secret?"

Diego lifted a hand. "Probably, sergeant," he said, "the man refers to a big black my body servant, Bernardo, is training. Bernardo has a strange way with horses, as you know."

Portiflo sprang to his feet.

"So! The way is clear for you, sergeant. Get this Bernardo and interrogate him, beat the truth out of him!"

Diego smiled slightly. "You seemingly do not know, senor, that Bernardo is a mute peon," he told Portillo. "He can hear and understand. But he cannot speak, and he does not know how to write. It would be difficult to interrogate him."

"Very clever!" Portilo admitted, his lips curling. "Perhaps, Don Diego, you will deny that while you were at school in Spain you received instruction in Swordsmanship from a master?"

"I admit it. Every young man in school received such instruction."

"You are proficient in horsemanship, are you not?"

Diego yawned. "I know how to ride," he admitted, "but do not like the exertion."

"You, who pretend to be so ladylike — are you afraid to let the sergeant feel your biceps and find they are those of a man of strength enough to wield a blade?"

"My biceps are very good, I believe," Diego replied. "I wrestle regularly with Bernardo, who is a huge strong man. My father tells me I must at least do that much to keep up manly strength necessary to health. You may ask my man

Bernardo — but I forget for a moment that he cannot speak and tell."

SOME man near snickered his amusement. Portillo's face showed his rage.

"Is it not true," he demanded, "that you and your father pet and coddle peons and natives treat them better than they deserve, and hence it would be natural for you, as Zorro, to attack men who kick and cuff them around?"

"It is true," Diego replied, "that we treat them as men in less fortunate circumstances than ourselves, who are not responsible for their lot in life, and who are to be shown kindness instead of brutality for that reason."

Sergeant Garcia bellowed again. "Enough of this nonsense! Senor Portillo, I am going to incarcerate you for the night and take you before the maqistrado in the morning."

"Wait, Garcia!" Diego protested. "I want this fellow to be convinced that I am not Zorro. Let him remain free to watch me every hour of day and night—"

"And, what of that?" Portillo shouted. "Would Zorro make a move if he knew he was being watched?"

"Not if he has good sense," Diego replied. "But if Zorro did something while I was elsewhere being watched by you, that should be convincing."

Garcia took charge again. "Senor Portillo, I let you retain your liberty for the time being. Watch Don Diego day and night if you wish."

"From the tavern, I am returning to my father's house," Diego explained. "This evening my father and I are guests of Don Juan Romo at the betrothal celebration for one of his daughters. After the fiesta, I'll return home and go to bed. My plans for tomorrow are not known yet even to myself."

"And you, Carlos Portillo," Garcia added, "will learn that Don Diego is not Zorro. After you have learned it, I'll remember you attempted extortion and see you well punished for it. Nor will you run away from the pueblo, senor, for starting this instant, you'll be watched continually by my troopers."

Portillo looked at Diego, and a sneer curled his lips. And Diego, with a quick flick of his right wrist, dashed the contents of his wine goblet into Portillo's face. The extortioner gave a scream of rage and wiped the wine out of his eyes.

"For that, I challenge you, Don Diego Vega!" he cried. "Let us get our blades and have a settlement."

Diego knew he had to avoid that. This fellow might be good with a blade, and Diego dared not expose his skill even to defend his life, with everybody believing he was a man who knew little of swordsmanship.

"Senor Portillo," Diego replied, haughtily, "first convince me that you have blood good enough to entitle you to cross blades with a Vega in an affair of honor. A caballero does not grant a fair and honorable fight to the death to a blackmailer."

Then, Diego bowed to all in the room and walked slowly down the length of it, stopped at the counter to pay the innkeeper for the round of Wine, and went on through the door and out into the plaza. He yawned and brushed his nostrils with the scented handkerchief as he started strolling slowly homeward. He had forgotten to buy the crystallized honey.

At home, he told his father, Don Alejandro, all that had occured, and they talked, and Diego made plans. Then he sauntered out of the house and located Bernardo near the servants' huts, and beckoned him.

"Zorro may or may not ride tonight, but everything must be ready," Diego explained. "It is almost sunset. As soon as it is dark enough, take one of the black carriage horses from the stable and lead him to the hidden corral where Zorro's big black is kept.

"Leave him there and bring Zorro's horse to the stable here. Let nobody observe it. At a later hour, take the horse and Zorro's clothes and weapons to the place I shall name, and have them ready. And listen carefully now, to further orders!"

Diego gave them in a whisper.

Bernardo's eyes glistened as they reflected the sunset. Strolling back into the house, Diego ate a small meal with his father — for there would be feasting a little later at Don Juan Romo's house — then retired to his own room to put on his most resplendent clothes.

WHEN he met his father again in the main room of the house, Don Alejandro was ready to set out. Don Juan lived hut a short distance away, and they would walk, with a servant carrying a burning torch ahead of them to light the way. Diego's fears had been realized — a heavy mist was falling. Where he had not desired it before he was glad of it now — Zorro could work much better on a dark, misty night.

The servant with the torch walked ahead, and Don Alejandro let his steps lag and talked to Diego in whispers.

"While you were dressing, I overheard some of the servants talking. After you left the tavern this afternoon, that scoundrel Portillo beat two natives unmercifully to work off his rage."

"Zorro will remember that."

"Be cautious, my son. That beating may have been a ruse to draw Zorro out of his shell. And, according to what you told me, Sergeant Garcia will have one of his troopers near the fellow all the time. Do not forget, in your eagerness to settle things with this Portillo, that the soldiers would be delighted to capture Zorro."

They were greeted by Don Juan at the door, and as soon as they had divested themselves of damp ponchos and serapes and taken the drink of welcome with the host, they mingled with the crowd. About a hundred guests, the foremost people of the pueblo, had been invited to Magdalena's betrothal ceremony.

Diego located Rosita Romo and paid her cautious court under the eye of her *duena.* The serious ceremony of betrothal was conducted by old Fray Felipe, and the feast began.

They were long at table, and though Diego posed as the indolent man they thought him to be, inwardly he was seething at the delay. When the feasting ended and musicians played and the dancing began, Diego danced with each of the sisters, and then with another senorita, and finally joined his father in a corner of the room.

"I contrived to slip out upon the veranda, my son, Don Alejandro whispered. "That rascal of a Portillo was loitering around, a trooper with him. I overheard their conversation."

"Was it interesting?" Diego asked.

"The trooper was grumbling because he had to be out on such a night instead of comfortable at the tavern drinking wine. Portillo agreed that you would be here for hours feasting and dancing, and suggested they return to the tavern for a time to get warm. The trooper was scoffing at the fellow for thinking you could be Zorro."

"It is time for me to become Zorro," Diego said. "My absence must be covered."

"In what manner, my son?"

"I'll dance once more, then complain of a headache. Leave that to me, my father."

He danced with another senorita, spoke to old Fray Felipe, mentioned his headache to everybody who would listen, and finally slipped unnoticed into the patio.

The merriment was at its height. His absence would not be missed unless someone deliberately looked for him. The inclement night was keeping everybody out of the big patio.

Through the darkness, Diego slipped to a couple of dark huts in the rear of the house, and behind them the faithful Bernardo was waiting with Zorro's black horse, costume and weapons.

Working switfly, Diego pulled on Zorro's attire over his own, put on belt and blade and mask and tucked his pistol into his sash. He mounted and rode away silently through the wet night. Don Diego Vega had disappeared for the time being, and in his stead was Zorro, a man of different manner and voice.

Cautiously, he rode toward the plaza and skirted it toward the tavern. He encountered nobody, nor saw anybody around the buildings. From the tavern came sounds of roistering. At the horse blocks three mounts were tethered, and Zorro identified them by the saddle blankets as the mounts of Sergeant Garcia and two of his troopers. Streaks of light coming through the tavern windows revealed the horses and illuminated the ground in front of the building.

FORTUNE was with Zorro this night. The tavern door was pulled open, and Carlos Portillo emerged, a trooper a step behind him. The trooper closed the door, and they stood in a streak of light from a window, adjusting their ponchos. The wind carried their talk to Zorro's ears as he bent forward in his saddle in the darkness not too far from the corner of the building.

"This is nonsense, Senor Portillo," the trooper was saying. "Don Diego Vega will dance until dawn, then go home to bed. And suppose you did meet Zorro? How do you expect to handle him?"

"I wear my blade and have a pistol handy," Portillo replied. "I beat those natives today to attract Zorro. If we meet, you stand back and allow me to have first chance at him alone. If he beats me, then shoot him down and claim the reward."

Muffled against the swirling mist, they bent their heads and started forward. But they heard a stern voice above the sound of sudden hoofbeats:

"Stand, senores! Trooper, toss your pistol and blade aside! You, Senor Portillo, be cautious in movement if you do not wish to die!"

The trooper squawked his surprise and did as he had been commanded. Portillo gulped. In the streak of light was a black-dressed masked rider on a black horse. He held a pistol that menaced them.

"So!" Portillo cried. "Now we will get at the truth. I'll show the world your

Portillo tried to slash the torturing whip with his sword.

identity now, Don Diego Vega."

"I am Zorro, fool. I have come to punish you, Portillo, for beating helpless men."

"Give me time to cast aside this poncho and draw blade," Portillo said. "Dismount and draw your own." Portillo unwrapped and dropped his serape and got off the poncho with a single jerk.

The trooper had stood back a few feet, wondering whether he should shout to Sergeant Garcia and his comrades in the tavern. The wind was drowning ordinary sounds, and nobody was in the vicinity to give an alarm. The trooper decided it would be safer after Zorro and Portillo began fighting.

Zorro did not dismount and draw blade.

Portillo turned to see something swishing through the air, and the next instant he gave a cry of pain as the lash of a long whip struck his side and bit through cloth to the skin.

"Do you think I would stain my blade with blood as foul as yours, scum?" Zorro said in a deep voice. "The whip honors your hide as it is."

He began lashing. Carlos Portillo whipped out his blade and tried to slash at the whip, but always missed. And the lash was torturing him, striking his arms and legs and hips, cutting into his back.

"Help! Help!" he began shouting. "Zorro is here!"

The trooper risked a pistol bullet by taking up the cry, and turned to run, bent almost double, to the door of the tavern and jerk it open, shouting for Garcia.

Zorro struck with the whip again, rode closer and called to the cringing Portillo:

"Get you out of the pueblo at dawn, and never return! It will not be the whip the next time, nor a blade, but a pistol bullet that will end your foul life instantly."

Through the door of the tavern and into the streak of light spewed men, Garcia at their head. Zorro wheeled his horse and fired his pistol into the tavern wall.

"Help!" Portillo was calling, his arms wrapped around his head as he feared another cut of the lash. "Zorro is here!"

Zorro laughed and gave the big black the spurs. Two pistols were discharged behind him, but the slugs went wild. And on the wind he heard Portillo's wild call to Garcia:

"It was Don Diego, I tell you! Sergeant, hurry to the Romo house, and you will find Diego Vega missing. Send men to the little hidden corral and see if the black horse is there. If it is not, you have your answer. If it is, you will find the horse wet, as if recently ridden hard."

GARCIA was shouting orders and his men were running for their mounts.

Zorro rode past the end of the plaza, his horse's hoofs pounding to show in what direction he went. Then he began circling toward Don Juan Romo's residence.

He was thanking his fortune that the Zorro costume had kept his fiesta clothes dry, and that it had been made so his boots would slip into larger ones fastened to the trouser legs, else he would have wet and muddy boots to explain.

Before Garcia had the chase arranged and was riding to the Romo house himself with one of his men, sending the other two to the corral, Zorro stopped the black behind the huts and sprang out of his saddle.

He stripped off the weapons and black costume and handed them up to

Bernardo who had mounted the black.

"Be careful not to encounter the soldiers," he warned the mute. "Ride slowly toward the hills, then circle back and put the black in the stable stall. Go!"

Darting into the patio, Diego Vega reduced his breathing to normal and strolled into the big main room of the house as another lively dance began. He saw a senorita who was something of a wallflower, approached, and a moment later was delighting her by being her dance partner. And the senorita was delighted also because, whereas Don Diego generally was not animated, now he was laughing. She did not know that he was laughing at how he had fooled everybody again, and not because of his happiness at having her in his arms.

As he danced, he saw Sergeant Garcia standing in the doorway with Don Juan Romo beside him and Carlos Portillo a step in his rear. Diego guided the senorita past them.

"Bueiuts nochesP' he greeted the sergeant. "From your clothing, it is damp out. And what has happened to that fellow beside you? He seems to be in a pitiable state." He smiled and danced on. But he heard Garcia's growl at Portillo:

"You see, dolt and ass? Your suspicions were groundless. In the morning, the magistrado will deal harshly with you. Come with me!"

Diego laughed happily again and danced on, and mayhap he gave the senorita a little squeeze. He was thinking that when the troopers went to the hidden corral they would find a black horse that was not laboring after a run. And they would not suspect it was one of the Vega's carriage horses.

Don Juan Romo greeted him as the dance ended. "You are enjoying yourself Diego?" he asked.

"More than I have any evening for quite some time," Diego replied.

Zorro Races with Death

***A Don Diego Vega story in which the fighting hidalgo
mounts his black and rides the judgment trail in pursuit of a vicious
peon-punisher whose stock in trade is brutal mass torture!***

SERGEANT MANUEL GARCIA, presiding over the barracks at Reina de Los Angeles in the absence of his superior, strutted along one side of the plaza and sank his bulk in a shady spot on a bench in front of the tavern.

The sergeant ran to brawn more than brains, was a jovial fellow at times and a stern disciplinarian at other times. The responsibility of attending to military matters in the district in the absence of his *capitan* weighed heavily upon him.

Recently, he had not been jovial at all, not even when in his cups. In the habit of bursting into roaring song when filled with wine, he had not flung his basso-profundo into the air of Alta California for weeks. He had become a grouch and a menace, and wise men kept out of his vicinity.

But today he seemed to have brightened somewhat. And he brightened yet more when he glanced up and saw Don Diego Vega, only son of rich old Don Alejandro, walking toward the tavern as if the exertion of locomotion fatigued him.

Between Garcia, the uncouth soldier, and Diego, the fastidious scion of a hidalgo, there was a strange friendship, perhaps the attraction of opposites. Diego bought the sergeant wine, and the sergeant regaled Diego with wild tales of his past experiences, many of them the figments of his own imagination.

What Garcia did not know was that in his cups he often told the secrets of the soldiery, in which at times Diego was vastly interested, desiring to know what movements of the troopers were contemplated.

For Diego Vega, in appearance a lifeless fop who caused many to cluck their tongues in sympathy with his proud father, was at intervals Senor Zorro, the masked rider who battled to protect and avenge the oppressed peons and natives, and Zorro certainly wished to know where the troopers were going, so he could operate in an opposite direction.

SEEING Diego approach, and knowing his company would mean free wine, Sergeant Garcia brought his huge body off the bench and straightened to something like a soldierly stance, brushed aside the ends of his enormous mustache, and got a gleam into his eyes.

"Ah, Don Diego! *Amigo!*" he greeted. "It gladdens my heart to see you again!"

Diego stopped in front of him, brushing his nostrils with a scented silk handkerchief. He was a picture of sartorial splendor in satin and fine linen and ruffles. He yawned slightly as he looked at the sergeant.

"Garcia, though it tires me to walk about, I came to the tavern to get a jar of crystallized honey," Diego said. "The tavern keeper has it for sale. We have tons of honey on our rancho, but none of it is crystallized. I do not know the process."

"I understand, Don Diego," Garcia replied.

What he did not understand was that Diego's trips to the tavern for honey were for the purpose of overhearing talk and gathering information that might be of service to him.

"I'll be glad to have you join me over a goblet of wine, Garcia," Diego said, "if it will not interfere with your duties."

"I'll struggle to keep it from doing so, Don Diego. And my duties soon will be lighter. A new *capitan* is coming."

"Indeed? Did you say a new *capitan*?"

"That is the gist of it, *amigo*. Our old officer is detained in Monterey, trying to explain to the Governor why he has not been successful in capturing that confounded masked highwayman, Senor Zorro."

"That turbulent fellow!" Diego complained. "He is always stirring things up and causing excitement."

"It is possible, Don Diego, that your nerves will have an opportunity soon to be settled for all time, as far as this Zorro is concerned."

"How is that, Garcia?"

"It is quite a long yarn, and I grow thirsty when I do a deal of talking."

"Let us go into the tavern and to some quiet table in a corner, and have wine while you tell me," Diego suggested.

The fawning tavern keeper ushered them to a table, clapped his hands for a native servant, set before Diego his best goblet, gave Garcia an earthen mug, and filled the vessels himself with his best wine from a wine skin. Then he gave the skin to the servant, with orders to stand by and refill the goblet and mug whenever necessary, but to keep a proper distance so he could not overhear conversation.

"Our new officer is Capitan Pedro Gomez," Garcia explained. "He brings twenty troopers with him to add to our detachment. He is a terrible man, this Capitan Gomez. And he has explicit orders, as I happen to know, to work his troopers as he pleases and capture this Zorro fellow and hang him."

"Why are you always mentioning that rascal and upsetting me?" Diego complained.

"But when we make an end of him, Don Diego, you will have peace of mind. No more turbulence," Garcia reminded him.

"No doubt that is true," Diego observed, without a smile.

"Capitan Gomez is a furious man. I have heard tales of him. With his troopers he has traveled from Monterey. They are all picked men. They will ride through tonight and be here at dawn tomorrow. He will find Zorro, you may be sure. He is a ruthless fiend, it is said. He will make some of the peons and natives reveal Zoro's identity and whereabouts, for he is an expert at torture."

Diego shuddered. "Your talk makes my wine turn sour," he declared. "Have another mug while I get my honey."

Diego left the sergeant, got his jar of honey from the landlord. Then he left the tavern and made his way homeward slowly and thoughtfully.

***

WEARY from long riding, Capitan Pedro Gomez and his detachment of troopers reached Reina de Los Angeles on jaded horses at dawn. The horses were cared for, and the troopers went into the barracks to get some sleep. Gomez received Sergeant Garcia's report, inspected the barracks and other buildings, ate a hearty breakfast, and then retired to the quarters of the *commandante* and sought his own couch.

But he was up again in a few hours, ate another hearty meal, then mounted, and rode with Garcia down to the plaza. He made a swift survey of the town, dismounted finally with the sergeant in front of the tavern, and entered that hostelry like a conquering hero.

Gomez was tall and slender, and gave evidence of having great physical strength. His long black hair and piercing black eyes made him look ferocious. He made natives and peons shiver with a single glance.

Officer and sergeant sat at a table and were seated by the tavern keeper. As they drank, Gomez talked of his plans. It was apparent that they were waiting for someone.

The man they were waiting for arrived soon on horseback — Esteban Silva, overseer for the rancho of Don Ricardo Rivera. The owner had been absent for almost a year, having gone to Mexico to attend to business and political interests and to mend his broken health, and it was said he would be gone another year at least. He trusted Silva to manage the rancho in his absence.

Silva was short, squat, swarthy. He was honest enough, and a good manager. But he was known to be ruthless toward his workmen, many of them enslaved for debt and under his direct rule according to the laws of peonage.

Sergeant Garcia introduced the officer and Silva and then retired so they could engage in confidential conversation. He strolled to the counter to talk to the landlord, and at that moment Diego Vega entered the tavern.

It was unusual for Diego to make his appearance until after the siesta hour, unless it was necessary for him to go to the chapel on religious matters. Garcia and the tavern keeper greeted him warmly when he stepped up to the counter, stifling a yawn with his silk scented handkerchief.

"Don Diego! *Amigo!* What brings you out so early?" Garcia asked. "Your illustrious father is well, I hope."

"Quite well, thank you," Diego replied. "I am on my way to the chapel to confer with Fray Felipe, and dropped in for a moment."

"Our new *capitan* has come," Garcia indicated. "It takes a weight off my shoulders."

Diego turned slowly and yawned as he inspected Gomez, the officer who had been sent to catch and hang Zorro.

"He has a look of meanness about him," Diego observed, quietly. "And Meanness sits beside him. I mean Esteban Silva, who mistreats his workmen so."

Capitan Gomez was speaking now to Silva in a voice loud enough to be heard by all in the room, as he intended it should be.

"I anticipate no difficulty, Senor Silva, in catching this fellow Zorro," he was saying. "I have some ideas about the matter. Some of the peons and natives know his identity and where he hides. He gets help from somewhere. If a man comes to me secretly and tells me of Zorro, he will be richly rewarded. But I'll not wait for that. I am going out into the rancho district with some of my troopers. I'll line up the peon and native workmen and make them talk. I know methods of loosening tongues."

"I feel sure you will succeed," Silva replied. "Honor me by making the Rivera rancho your headquarters."

"I accept. Today I and my men must get some rest, and our mounts also. I have a report to prepare. We will leave early in the morning with one of the local troopers to guide us on the way."

"It will be a blessing to us all when Zorro is caught," Silva declared. "His actions give the peons and natives courage. They become surly when they are punished for a fault. That is bad for discipline."

They lowered their voices, and Silva motioned for their wine cups to be refilled. The tavern keeper hurried away to do that himself.

"A brutal fellow, your new *capitan*," Diego observed to Garcia. "Always turbulence! Why do we not have more peace in the world? I am going on to the chapel, where there is no talk of violence."

He gestured languidly and strolled to the door and went out. He had inspected the new *capitan* well, and knew Zorro would have a formidable foe in him. He would have to be doubly cautious. And, if Gomez intended to inspect the workmen in the rancho district, it would be a good thing for Diego and his father to be out at the Vega rancho.

Instead of going on to the chapel, Diego went toward home to confer with his father.

As a result of the conference, the Vega carriage rolled out of the pueblo that afternoon, proud gray-haired Don Alejandro sitting with Diego in the comfortable back seat among the cushions. The spirited team was driven by Bernardo, Diego's mute peon body servant. Bernardo the mute, Don Alejandro the father, and Fray Felipe the padre, were the only three persons in the world who knew Diego was also Zorro.

FOR two days, they received reports of Gomez' activities. The new *capitan* had inspected the workmen of the Rivera rancho first, and Silva had stood aside grinning as peons and natives who worked for him were lined up and questioned, lashed with a long whip the *capitan* carried, had their arms twisted and bones broken. Gomez demanded knowledge concerning Zorro.

The second day, Gomez and his troopers visited a smaller rancho operated by an elderly man, and used the same tactics. But he learned nothing. And the pity of it was that none of the workmen on the ranchos or elsewhere could tell him anything, for they were innocent of knowledge concerning Zorro.

"It is time for the man to be handled," Diego told his father the second evening after they had eaten. "The peons and natives are growing frightened, and they will be taking to the hills, leaving the flocks and herds and vineyards and orchards to go to waste."

"In my estimation, this fellow Gomez is no fool," his father decided. "Perhaps by his cruel treatment, he hopes to bring Zorro out of hiding."

"His hope will be realized."

"And no doubt he has arranged a trap, or several of them. I know he has twelve troopers with him, having left the others in town to nose around. Do not let your just rage lead you into an incautious move."

"I'll use great care, my father. I'll make plans, and perhaps tomorrow night will be the time Zorro rides."

Diego's just rage reached the boiling point the following day. In the middle of the morning, Capitan Gomez and his twelve troopers arrived unexpectedly at the Vega rancho. Don Alejandro went out to meet him, Diego beside him. Gomez introduced himself and stated the object of the visit.

Don Alejandro, looking stern, did not invite the officer into the house or patio to receive refreshment. Drawing himself up proudly, he made his reply.

"Capitan Gomez, I understand your mission," he said. "I realize how eager you are to accomplish it. So I must tell you that you would be wasting time on my rancho. None of my workmen know anything concerning Zorro."

"Would you know if they did, Don Alejandro? Would they tell you, a rancho owner and employer of men? You would be one of the last to know. I shall investigate your household servants and the rancho hands later when they come to their huts. I call upon you in the name of the Governor to supply myself and troopers with the mid-day meal."

Don Alejandro's eyes flamed at Gomez's arrogant manner.

"Never, Capitan Gomez, has the Vega rancho refused to feed a hungry man," he replied. "But I protest against your examination of my servants."

"Have all of them been with you for some time? Do you know them well?"

"Not one but what has been me for years. Some were born on this rancho."

"Because you treat them so well — too well, I have heard — make pets of them and are soft where proper punishment is concerned, no doubt none would raise a hand against you. But they have a deep sympathy for others of their kind. They would help hide this confounded Zorro. Why, Don Alejandro, for all you know, they may give him sanctuary and protection even here on your rancho, under your very nose!"

"Senor!" Don Alejandro's eyes blazed again.

Gomez turned to wave at his troopers. "Gather them in!" he ordered.

The troopers started away, some to go to the huts in the rear of the main house, some to the kitchens, and others entered the patio boldly and passed from it into the house itself.

"I resent this intrusion on my privacy, Capitan Gomez," Don Alejandro told him, shaking with rage. "You do not have the right to send your men into my house without permission."

"You dispute my authority?"

"Certainly not, senor. But I detest the way you misuse it. I shall send a report to the Governor concerning this occurrence."

"I will send one also, Don Alejandro, telling him I received no aid from you, that on the contrary you obstructed my efforts to carry out the orders he gave me."

"I am not hindering your efforts. But I tell you my workers know nothing of Zorro's identity, and that I do not wish to see any of them mistreated."

The troopers were commencing to return with the servants. The latter were badly frightened, for they had heard what had occurred on the Rivera rancho and the other. They glanced toward Don Alejandro, a master who always had been kind to them, and at Diego, always friendly.

DIEGO snapped erect for an instant when he saw that one picked up by the troopers was his faithful and loyal Bernardo, his own huge mute body servant. Bernardo was watching these proceedings as if stunned and not understanding.

The troopers lined the unfortunates up, and Capitan Gomez paced back and forth along the line, carrying his heavy whip, glaring at them, trying to terrify them.

Gomez finally stopped at the head of the line and made his announcement:

"I want information concerning the person known as Senor Zorro! Many of you know his identity and where he hides. If one steps forward and reveals the truth to me, he will be rewarded. If you refuse to speak to me, an officer in the army of His Excellency, the Governor, I'll see you are properly punished.

We have had quite enough of you scum shielding and hiding the man. Any found so doing hereafter will be seized and hanged for giving aid to a highwayman and outlaw."

He strode back and forth along the line again, and stopped before the huge Bernardo.

"Tell me!" he ordered.

Bernardo merely shook his head and pointed to his mouth. The gesture told he was a mute and was innocent enough, but Gomez took it as an insult. He gripped the butt of the whip, and Diego took a quick step forward as Don Alejandro gave an exclamation of rage.

"Speak, dog!" Gomez roared.

He struck with the whip, and the lash fell across Bernardo's breast, cutting the skin. Bernardo, eyes aflame, reeled backward. He might have hurled himself upon Gomez and throttled him before others could prevent, which would have meant hanging. But Diego called to him to stand still, and launched himself forward.

This mute peon, faithful and loyal, and not any too quick in thinking, had been struck like a beast. Moreover, a Vega man had been struck, a man under protection of the Vegas.

Gomez turned quickly and started to lift the heavy whip again when he heard boots pounding the earth behind him. Diego seized the whip and jerked it from Gomez' hand before the *capitan* realized what he intended.

"You beast!" Diego cried at him.

"You dare call me such!" Gomez roared. "You dare tear a whip from my hand? Return it to me instantly! Be glad if I do not use it on your own back, though you are of noble blood!"

"You insulting upstart!" Diego raged. "This man you struck is my personal servant. He was born a mute. He cannot speak and answer you. If I had not jumped forward, he probably would have seized you and choked you to death or snapped your neck, for he has great strength."

"Who commands here?" Gomez roared. "You, Diego Vega! For this I'll challenge you — "

"Perhaps you have heard I am not skilled in swordsmanship and such things, that you are so ready with a challenge," Diego said in scorn. "Get decent blood in your veins before you seek to challenge a Vega!"

"I bear the commission of the Governor."

"He would not be Governor long if the hidalgos of this rancho district desired it otherwise!"

"Is this treason?"

"No," Diego told him. "I doubt whether the Governor knows your methods. Why did you not acquaint yourself with the people of this district before you began your cruelty? Everybody here knows Bernardo is a mute, a faithful servant not easily moved to anger."

The troopers had moved closer to watch the quarrel. Though Gomez was their *capitan*, none admired his methods. And they would hesitate before lifting theft hands against a hidalgo and his son. The servants began slipping away as the troopers gave their attention to the quarrel. Only Bernardo remained, his slow mind trying to get at the truth of this.

"Give me my whip!" Gomez ordered. "If you do not, and also apologize instantly, I'll place you and your father under arrest, jail you at the barracks and hold you for trial and punishment."

"There are men enough around Reina de Los Angeles to tear down your jail and release us," Diego informed him.

"I order you to give me the whip!"

DIEGO stood still, his breast heaving, his breathing labored because of his rage, his eyes blazing, and he did not reply. Diego realized that he must not go too far. Rage against the striking of Bernardo the people would understand, but too much show of strength might cause suspicion. They might wonder at this sudden change in the man they had looked upon as a spineless fop who could not endure violence or physical exertion.

Gomez made a grave mistake. He sprang forward and grasped the whip and tried to tear it from Diego's grasp, and the other allowed him to do so because he did not want to make a show of too much strength.

Bernardo gave a guttural cry and sprang forward, thinking Gomez was about to use the whip on Diego. At the same instant, Don Alejandro, thinking the same and wishing to prevent the indignity, started forward.

Bernardo seized Gomez by the shoulders and pressed down upon him, making the *capitan* kneel in the dirt. The troopers surged forward to the defense of their officer.

"Bernardo! Release him!" Diego ordered.

Bernardo bobbed his head and obeyed and stepped to one side. Then, Don Alejandro was at Gomez' side.

"Enough!" he cried. "Capitan Gomez, take your troopers and get off the

Vega rancho."

"I take that mute with me, to hang him for striking an officer."

"He did not strike you, only subdued and held you — easily. He thought you were about to strike my son with the whip. It is not against the law for a man to protect the one he serves."

"A man? A skunk of a peon."

"Enough! You may order your troopers around, and you may mistreat and abuse men elsewhere, but not on this rancho. I hold this property under a grant from the King of Spain himself, and I am not without influence with the Viceroy in Mexico. Take your troopers and go! Do not try violence. From the windows of my house and from the archway of the patio, you are covered at this moment by guns in the hands of my overseer and his assistants. They are under cover, and you are out in the open. Is it your desire to start a battle under the circumstances?"

Gomez glanced around quickly and saw that Don Alejandro spoke the truth. At the first coming of the soldiers, the head of the Vegas had warned Juan Cassara, his overseer, and Cassara had taken precautions to be ready in case of serious trouble.

"Don Alejandro," Gomez said, trying to make a show of dignity, "I retire with my men for the moment. I return to the Rivera rancho and draw up an indictment against you and your son, and will send it to Monterey by fast courier. I shall ask the Governor for permission to place you both under arrest on several charges, to confine you, and to take charge of your rancho in the name of the Governor."

"I, too, shall indite a message to the Governor," Don Alejandro told him. "I shall write the truth. And I am quite sure, Capitan Gomez, that my message reach the Governor first, for I have swift horses and good riders, and my messenger can get fresh mounts at any rancho or village between here and Monterey. I do not fear the result if the Governor has to decide between me and my friends and a common *capitan* of his hired soldiery."

"Senor!" Gomez purpled at the intentional insult.

"Mount and get gone!" Don Alejandro ordered.

Gomez hesitated an instant, then gestured for his men to mount. He was raging as he got into his own saddle. What he was pleased to call his pride and dignity had been humbled in front of his men. He lifted a hand in a signal and trotted down the lane to the road that ran toward the Rivera rancho.

***

THAT night there was no wind, but a fine mist was falling. Clouds obscured the moon and stars. The wind might come and blow the mist away, or it might turn into a torrential rain. It was a night to keep men indoors.

The moisture-laden air carried and magnified sounds, but also distorted them. So, as he followed a narrow trail made by wandering cattle, far off any regular road, Zorro went forward slowly and with extreme caution.

The faithful Bernardo had prepared his horse and brought out Zorro's costume and weapons as usual. And as Zorro mounted he had given Bernardo a pat on the shoulder and had told him, "Tonight, Zorro will avenge the blow you received."

As he neared the Rivera rancho, he stopped his big black horse frequently to listen for sounds that might indicate the near presence of human beings, especially such things as hoofs striking rocks, saddle leather creaking, sabers rattling. Despite the evil night, troopers may have been stationed around the rancho buildings at a distance to guard their officer against any attack.

News of what had happened at the Vega rancho had spread through the countryside like wildfire, spread in the mysterious manner such news always was spread, and few men knew how. Peons and natives passed the word along, signaled one another with smoke and in other ways. They needed no telephone, telegraph or radio.

Around the San Gabriel mission a short distance from the Vega rancho, men gathered in groups and whispered of the event. The padres went about in their robes shaking their heads. The cruelties already practiced by this Capitan Gomez had aroused indignation. The striking of mute Bernardo was the climax. On every side, men were whispering: "If Zorro is near, and learns of this!"

Through the swirling mist, Zorro rode carefully. He knew this country well, for he had been reared in it as a boy. He knew obscure back trails, ravines where a man could hide, hills that cut off the view, where travel was safe and where caution must be observed if a man rode with speed.

He was wondering what Don Ricardo Rivera, a splendid and humane man, would say if he knew that a man like Capitan Gomez was quartered on his rancho at his overseer's request. There was no mistreating of men there when Don Ricardo was home.

From a safe spot, Zorro looked down upon the rancho buildings. A small fire burned in an open space between the ranch house and outbuildings, but no men were around it. The mist would gradually drench and kill it.

From the quarters of the *vaqueros* came sounds of song and laughter. No doubt the troopers were drinking wine and having a merry time there with the rancho men. Lights gleamed in the ranch house itself, and Zorro visualized Capitan Gomez being entertained by Silva, the overseer no doubt trying to ingratiate himself with the officer by supplying an abundance of good food and Don Ricardo's best wine.

It was Zorro's wish to punish Gomez where men could see and spread news of the *capitan's* degradation. Unless compelled to do it, he would not use a pistol bullet on the officer or give him the honor of a sword thrust. He would use the long black whip he always carried on his saddle.

He would give Gomez what Gomez had given poor Bernardo, though in much greater measure. If he could accomplish that, Gomez' assumed dignity and pride would be a mockery and men would laugh behind his back. Such a man, losing prestige, could do nothing but get away quickly, and resign his position.

ZORRO surveyed the buildings again. Horses filled the corral, but he saw only two saddled and ready, and they were tied to horse blocks near the front of the house. Because he did not know the number of Silva's *vaqueros*, he could not tell whether all the troopers' mounts were in the corral, or whether some were carrying their riders around in the night.

He moved his black horse down a slope and to a position nearer the buildings. In his black costume, he merged with the night, even his white face obscured by a black mask. And suddenly he pulled up and swung beneath a tree. Half a dozen riders came dashing in, to dismount in front of the corral and shout at those in the quarters of the *vaqueros*.

Zorro saw them plainly in the light thrown by the bonfire. They were some of Gomez' troopers. The door of the quarters was pulled open, and a streak of light shot out.

"Out with you!" one of the riders shouted. "Our patrol is done. Saddle and mount and relieve us. Come out into this fine night and get the mist in your whiskers!"

Zorro swerved his horse and reached for his pistol.

Zorro understood. The patrol had ridden in to be relieved. So Gomez did have men riding the trails and watching.

Troopers hurried out and ran to the corral for their horses. The wind carried talk to Zorro's ears.

"Orders are to watch the road between here and the Vega rancho. Station yourselves a distance apart. The second group covers the road between here and San Gabriel Mission."

The troopers who had come off patrol unsaddled and turned their horses into the corral as the others saddled and prepared to ride. Their duty over for the night, those who had come in hurried into the building to dry and enjoy themselves.

The door of the ranch house was flung open, and Gomez and Silva appeared.

"I want one man for escort!" Gomez shouted. "Senor Silva and I ride to the tavern near the mission."

Zorro knew the place — a disreputable establishment patronized by scum off the highway, unscrupulous traders, smugglers and their ilk. He wondered why Gomez and Silva were riding there, and learned at once.

"We intend to have a little rough entertainment," Gomez explained, laughing. "And I wish to look over the scum in the tavern, and see if I can get a clue to this Zorro from their drunken talk."

Zorro got away from the scene and rode cautiously through the misty blackness of the night. He went over a hill and located a trail he knew, and sent the black along it as swiftly as he could without endangering himself. All the troopers were behind him now, as were Gomez and Silva. So he cut down another hill and got near the road, and traveled along it, prepared to pull off and go into hiding if any rider approached.

As he neared the tavern, he left the road again and approached the building with caution. It sat back a distance from the road, with trees on three sides of it. But there was a cleared space in front where a huge bonfire was burning, being constantly fed with logs by a couple of native servants.

Perhaps a score of mounts were tied to hitch-rails at the sides of the clearing while their riders enjoyed the merriment inside. Loud voices, laughter, ribald song poured from the place. It was the disgrace of the district, and a direct affront to the devout *padres* at the mission, which was not more than four hundred yards away.

Zorro rode down a slope and into a grove of trees at one side of the building.

There, he waited and watched. Men wen passing in and out, some mounting and riding away, others riding in and dismounting and tethering their horses. It seemed to be a big night at the tavern.

He saw Capitan Gomez, Silva and the trooper escort ride in. There was a sudden hush as they passed the fire. The sign of a uniform was not pleasing to most of the men in the clearing around the fire and in the tavern.

AS THE three dismounted, there was a sudden riot in the tavern, and the door spewed men. Two were fighting, and had been thrust out into the open to do their fighting there, and the others crowded out to watch. They were howling, screeching encouragement to their favorites.

They fought their way to a spot near the roaring fire and knives flashed in the light from the flames. Gomez, Silva and the trooper went forward to watch. Somebody separated the brawlers and men tore the knives from their grasps. Then a drunken man began howling:

"Soldiers! Look!"

Capitan Gomez had made another grave mistake by coming there with only one trooper. The trooper was seized first, before he had time to get his pistol from his belt. As he was hurled to the ground, others seized Gomez, tossed his pistol and sword away, and jerked him close to the fire.

"Soldiers! Spies!" the drunken mob was shouting now.

"Hang them!" another man cried. "Hang all soldiers!"

Shouting, laughing raucously, they started pulling Gomez and the trooper toward a tree at the edge of the clearing. Silva tried to prevent them. So they seized him also, took his pistol away.

"Hang Silva, too!" some man yelled. "The soldiers are his guests."

Zorro knew the proper moment had come. He jumped his horse into the clearing and dashed to the fire.

"Hold!" he shouted in a voice that carried above the din. "Leave the *capitan* to me!"

They turned to see the masked black figure on the black horse. Zorro's appearance was well known, for he certainly had been described enough.

" 'Tis Zorro! Zorro!" they shouted.

"Bring him near me!" Zorro shouted. "Hanging is too good for such a beast, a torturer of men better than himself. Let me use my whip on him. Hold Silva and the trooper so they will not interfere."

The idea appealed to the drunken mob. They pulled Gomez over the ground.

Zorro got the long whip off his saddle and swung the lash and cracked it.

"Turn him loose!" Zorro ordered. "And then stand back."

They released Gomez and darted aside. Zorro jumped the black. The whip sang through the air and the lash cut into Gomez' back. He tried to grasp it, and was only jerked to his knees for the effort. Then Zorro began riding around him, using the whip that cut every time it struck, and brought blood. Gomez wrapped his arms around his head and bent so his face might not be marred. As he whipped, Zorro shouted at him:

"How do you like the bite of the whip, beater of men? Take some of your own medicine, coward! What a fine proud *capitan* you are now! Men will laugh at you and mock you when news of this travels up and down the king's highway. Get out of this part of the country, or you will get more than the whip!"

The men in the drunken crowd were laughing and cheering. Zorro suddenly swung his black horse, and dashed to the side of the clearing, prepared to ride.

Gomez lurched to his feet and began howling.

"A hundred pieces of gold to whoever catches that masked fiend for me! The Governor's reward also!"

There was silence as they realized what he was saying. The mood of the mob changed instantly. They knew Zorro only as a masked man, not as a known friend. And gold was to be desired.

Men began rushing to get their horses. Zorro started riding toward the highway — and saw a trooper riding toward him, one of the patrol who evidently was coming to make a report to Gomez.

Zorro swerved his horse quickly and got his pistol out of his sash. Gomez was yelling at the trooper, who saw the masked man, took in the scene and realized the situation. The trooper fired quickly, and missed. Now he had nothing but his blade, for it would take him some time to reload the pistol. Zorro returned his own weapon to his sash for use later, laughed loudly, and turned to ride.

But the short delay endangered him. Already, some of those wild riders had mounted and were starting to spur toward him. He bent low in his saddle and gave the black the spurs.

Led by the trooper, they thundered after him, wild drunken riders who were thinking only of golden reward. Pistols spoke behind him, but the balls flew wild. He could not ride back toward the Rivera rancho and on to his home, for he knew men of the patrol were stationed along the road.

So he turned into the king's highway and spurred toward distant Reina de

Los Angeles. Some of the pursuers were mounted on good horses. Through the night Zorro raced with death close behind. Those who pursued knew the Governor's reward was for Zorro dead or alive.

He managed to distance them a little, and suddenly turned off the highway and up a narrow winding ravine he knew well. As the pursuit thundered by, he sent his big black slowly along the bottom of the ravine. And then he went across country, taking a circuitous route that brought him finally to the place where mute Bernardo was waiting.

"Care for the horse," he told Bernardo as he dismounted. "Hide my clothes and weapons as usual. You have been avenged, Bernardo, you and the others Capitan Gomez has mistreated. His back will be sore for many a day. And his dignity and prestige and pride are wounded beyond repair. No doubt he will leave the vicinity, for he is the kind who cannot face men's laughter."

Then, Don Diego Vega went slowly under the trees of the orchard to let himself into the house quietly and be greeted by his proud father.

Zorro Fights for Peace

A masked avenger takes time out to dabble in politics — with sword and pistol!

A S HE sagged to one side of his saddle and bent forward slightly like a man fatigued from long riding, Don Diego Vega was following the dusty trail that ran from San Gabriel to the little pueblo of Reina de Los Angeles.

It was about the middle of the afternoon on a day late in the summer, and hot. A merciless sun blazed down out of a cloudless sky, and a brisk hot wind swirled clouds of dust.

At the side of Diego rode Fray Felipe, the elderly Franciscan padre now attached to the chapel on the plaza in the pueblo, who attended and guided the members of the illustrious Vega family in religious matters. The padre was mounted on his big black riding mule, an animal known for ferocity and stamina.

Diego and the padre had been out to the vast Vega rancho in the vicinity of San Gabriel Mission, the padre to officiate at a wedding ceremony and Diego to witness it and have fun at the *fiesta* afterward.

Desiring to return to the town with the padre, and his father having need for the family carriage, Diego had taken to a saddle with much groaning complaint. It was the usual pose of Diego Vega to appear as an indolent dreamer and avoid all forms of physical exertion as much as possible.

Only three men actually knew — and no others even suspected — that Diego Vega, the apparently languid fop, was also the noted Senor Zorro, the masked rider of the trails and hills who could ride like a fiend and fight like half

Captain Zapata
dropped his sword
in the fire and reached
for his pistol.

a dozen of them in defense of the downtrodden and oppressed. He made fools of the troopers who tried to catch and hang him and claim the rich reward offered by the Governor.

THROUGH the blazing sunshine and the swirling clouds of dust, the two riders were traveling down a long hill with their mounts at a walk. The rushing wind that stirred up the fine dust and half blinded them with it also carried sounds to their ears.

They heard the shrill cries of a man in peril: "Help! … help! … I am being slain!"

There was a tone of agony in the man's voice that reached the ears of the riders on the wings of the wind, the agony of a man already suffering from a mortal wound. Diego straightened suddenly in his saddle and tightened his reins, and Fray Felipe became instantly alert.

At the foot of the hill on the right side of the highway was a tangled mass of high brush, and beyond that was a small cleared space. The cries for help had come from this clearing, but because of the high brush wall Diego and Fray

Felipe could not see what was happening.

With spurs and knees they urged their mounts into an instant burst of speed and rode down the hill madly, Diego forgetting his usual pose of being languid. At that moment, he was more Zorro than Diego Vega.

As they neared the bottom of the hill, they saw a rider dash through a gap in the hedge of brush. He tuned in his saddle and observed them, then bent low as if to hide his identity and spurred down the highway toward the town. But Diego had a good look at him, and knew he would recognize him instantly if he saw him again.

Fray Felipe skidded his big mule to a stop and turned into the gap in the brush wall, with Diego a few feet behind him. They saw a man propped up against the bole of a tree.

His sombrero was on the ground beside him. A pony stood a short distance away with trailing reins and hanging head. The man against the tree had his clothing torn almost to shreds, his sash had been ripped off, his pockets turned inside out. His breast had been bared, and now was covered with blood from a couple of stab wounds. On the ground beside the sombrero was a folded gray serape, as if the shawl had dropped there from the man's saddle.

Diego and the padre sprang off their mounts and hurried forward. The wounded man was conscious. He saw them, saw the padre's brown robe, and spoke: "Padre. Padre."

"I am here, my son," Fray Felipe replied, softly, kneeling beside him.

"Help me ... padre. My time is near ... there is so much to tell."

"What would you say to me, my son?"

The wounded man hesitated and seemed to be gathering strength. Fray Felipe turned to Diego, now kneeling beside him.

"I know this young man, Diego," the padre said. "He is a neophyte at the Santa Barbara Mission. He is also a mission messenger and courier."

Diego nodded. He saw that the wounded man, little more than a boy, was mixed native and peon in blood. And he saw also that the stabs the man had received were mortal. He indicated as much to Fray Felipe, and the padre bowed his head.

The wounded man was speaking again: "The gray serape, padre! Guard it well, and send it on. It is the message."

"A message?" the padre queried. "And where must it be sent? Talk slowly, my son, and in low tones. Save your strength as much as possible. This is Don Diego Vega with me, and he will listen also."

The wounded man lowered his voice and spoke slowly as he told the story, sometimes almost in a whisper. His first words held the attention of the listeners:

"They must have learned I carried the message ... I was seized and stabbed and my clothes torn almost off me as he searched ... the man who stabbed me. But he did not find the message ... the message is on the serape ... a message in red threads on the end ... signed by Padre Carlos ...."

"What is this?" the padre asked. "You mean Padre Carlos of Santa Barbara? He is one of the heads of our order here in Alta California. I have knowledge of certain things, but tell me more, my son. Diego Vega is to be trusted."

So they got the story, told haltingly and with pain.

IT WAS the usual story of a planned uprising by natives and peons. They would seize arms if they could, raid the big ranchos and the small villages, perhaps try to pillage the warehouses at the missions.

There had been several such uprisings through the years, usually stirred up by unscrupulous men who hoped to profit by making the peons and natives their dupes. But they always had been put down promptly by bloodshed and swift punishment from the soldiery.

But there was more behind this than a few unscrupulous leaders who hoped to loot during the trouble. Fray Felipe knew it, for there had been many consultations in the missions regarding the situation.

It was the period when Spanish politicians coveted the wealth of the missions and sought to end the influence of the padres with natives and peons. The latter, caused to believe that the padres made them work for nothing and serve them in all things, might be influenced to turn from the missions. Then the unscrupulous leaders would have them, pass a few laws, make them slaves in truth.

The wounded man, being a mission messenger, knew the situation well. His painful words told the padre and Don Diego that a high army officer had been sent from Mexico to aid in fomenting the trouble. The plot was to make the people believe the uprising had been planned by the padres themselves. Claims would be filed against the missions afterward. The men who were actually in the uprising would be slain by the soldiers and those remaining told to put the blame on the padres. But the peons and natives, though stirred up, were not easily fooled. They had even been told that the plotters had been instructed by the padres, who wanted the uprising. Instead of being duped easily this time, they had sent word to Fray Carlos of Santa Barbara, and asked for guidance in the matter.

"Send us the true word," was the appeal. "Is it to be peace or war?"

Up and down the king's highway, secret committees of peons and natives awaited the word. They would do as Fray Carlos said. But the enemy had learned of this, for they were watching the committees. They preached that if the word for peace did not come by a certain time, they must go ahead with the uprising before the soldiers became suspicious.

And soldiers would be ready when the blow fell, ready to use firearms and swords to slay, and blame the slaying on the padres, to seize men and throw them into jail and torture, and perhaps make so the weak ones confess the padres had planned it all.

The wounded man almost lost consciousness as he told this story. Fray Felipe urged him to be quiet for a moment and renew his strength. His life's blood was ebbing fast. But after a short time, he went on with the story.

Being a wise man and knowing the messenger must get through quickly, Fray Carlos did not send a message written on parchment. He gave the messenger a gray serape to carry. In case of attack, he would be searched well for a document, but the serape, since every man carried such a shawl, would not get a second glance.

The messenger had contacted three secret committees so far, and had been striving to reach the one in Reina de Los Angeles. He had been seized by a stronger man, rushed behind the hedge and stabbed immediately and searched. Hearing the approaching riders, the murderer had mounted to get away without being recognized.

He had not found the message, but he knew he had slain the messenger. He would go to the committee, members of which thought he was one of them and a friend, and urge them to immediate action, declaring Fray Carlos had sent no message and that they must strike at once or plans would be ruined.

"Who stabbed you, my son?" Padre Felipe asked. "Do you know the man's name?"

"He is the officer … sent from Mexico … Capitan Juan Zapata … the fact has just been learned."

"I saw him well, padre, as he rode away, and will know him again," Diego whispered.

"The committee … waiting … tonight … at midnight … old Gonzales corral. Carry the message, padre! I — I am going — "

DIEGO stood, removed his sombrero and bent his head as Fray Felipe attended to the dying. When it was over, the padre got to his feet.

"His body must be left here and the authorities notified," the padre said. "I am glad you were with me if this had to happen, my son. Had I been alone, word might have spread that I had done this to stop a man's mouth. Our foes will stoop to any iniquity. Wait a moment!"

Fray Felipe walked over slowly and picked up the serape. He unfolded it, bent his head and inspected the shawl closely. Suddenly, he straightened and nodded for Diego to come to him.

"Here it is," he said. "The all-important message. Red threads sewed into the border of the serape."

He handed the serape to Diego, who read:

> *The word is — peace!*
> *Carlos, Santa Barbara.*

"What is to be done, padre?" Diego asked.

"This crime must be reported to the soldiers in Reina de Los Angeles. That is the first thing."

"But this man who died said that Capitan Juan Zapata was the man who killed him."

"Then he must be unmasked and the news of his deed spread. A report at the barracks may reveal to us the reaction of those there to the news. They may not be concerned."

"I'll make the report," Diego said.

"I'll go along with you, my son."

"No. If I have to mention you saw it with me, they may question you and get nothing but the truth. But that fact may not come out. If you appear there with me now, the way things are between the missions and the politicians —"

"I understand, my son. You may do as you wish. I'll ride to the town with you and go to the chapel and pray. And the serape?"

"It must be safeguarded. Wrap it around your body under your robe, quickly, and let us ride."

"And the meeting tonight?" Fray Felipe questioned further. "The men must be warned. If that scoundrel goes to them and talks them into instant action because the message has not been received, it means soldiers will cut them down and drench the land with blood again. Yes, my son, they must be warned."

"Zorro will attend to that," Diego said, softly. "The man must be unmasked. Here is a task, padre, that Zorro will be delighted to accomplish. I'll come to the chapel after nightfall and get the serape."

They mounted and hurried on to the town. Fray Felipe turned aside to go to the chapel, and Diego Vega rode straight to the barracks and told the guard at the door he wished to speak to Sergeant Manuel Garcia.

Garcia, in charge of the post while his commanding officer was visiting Monterey, had Diego admitted at once. He was a huge man, rather uncouth, who did his duty under orders whether he liked that duty or not.

"Don Diego Vega, amigo!" the sergeant greeted. "I am proud to welcome you. How is this? You must be fresh from the trail, for you are covered with dust and streaked with perspiration. How you must be suffering — you, a man who dislikes exercise and loves to read the poets!"

Diego took the seat toward which Garcia gestured. "I have come to you to make an official report regarding a foul murder."

The sergeant bulged his eyes and blew out the ends of his enormous mustache. "A murder, you say? How terrible! Don Diego, my friend, you should not excite yourself with such matters. Leave them to the soldiers."

"It is a law that I make an official report."

So Diego made it, speaking rapidly and giving only the essential facts. Before he had finished, Garcia was drumming nervously on the tabletop with the tips of his chunky fingers.

"Ah, that affair!" the sergeant said, when Diego had concluded. "Do not trouble yourself about it, Don Diego. I understand the fellow was a mixed breed of no consequence."

"But he was foully murdered! And how do you know about it, Sergeant Garcia? Nobody else was there, and I saw nobody ride away — except the murderer."

"The murderer?" Garcia sat up straight. "You saw him?"

"And would know him if I saw him again."

"Ha! I see you must be told a certain amount, Don Diego, and warned. I admire you very much, *amigo*. You often buy me wine at the tavern. You are the son of a hidalgo, and I am a rough soldier, yet we have been friends. May I give my friend a hint of importance, believing he will retain it unto himself only for his own guidance?"

"You may speak," Don Diego replied softly.

"You are my opposite in everything, Don Diego. You run to brains instead of brawn. You live a quiet life and read the works of the poets. Do not ruin your life by dealing with violent matters. Leave such things to the soldiery. That is what we receive pay and rations for — as much as we get."

"But, this murder, Sergeant Garcia?"

"Don Diego, there are things a young gentleman like you, following a genteel life, does not understand. Let me hint to you that this was not really a murder, but a sort of execution against a fellow who resisted authority. The fellow was a spy, and he was caught by an officer of the army and slain when he resisted arrest. I already have the report of it. If you saw the slayer and remember his face, you will be wise to forget it."

"Very well, then," Diego said, getting to his feet and yawning slightly, covering his mouth with a silk handkerchief as he did so. "I am fatigued from my journey, and must return home and get some rest."

"Ah, that is sensible, Don Diego! Allow me to escort you to the door, *amigo.*"

DIEGO hurried to his father's house and turned his horse over to Bernardo, his mute peon body-servant.

"Take him to the stable," Diego directed, "and then attend me in my room."

Bernardo bobbed his head and hurried away, leading the horse. Of the three men who knew that Don Diego Vega was also Zorro, the mute Bernardo was one. Fray Felipe, being Diego's confessor, was the second. And proud old Don Alejandro, Diego's father, was the third. His secret was safe with them.

Hurrying to his rooms, Diego started stripping off his travel-stained clothing. Bernardo soon appeared, panting from his haste, and carrying a small porcelain tub for ablutions. As Diego went on undressing, Bernardo came back with warm scented water and thick towels and wash cloths, filled the tub and put cloths and towels handy. Diego spoke to him in low tones.

"Zorro rides tonight!"

The big mute's eyes gleamed, and he made a grimace.

"Have my black horse and Zorro's attire and weapons ready two hours before the middle of the night, at the usual place. You will remain there until my return, instead of riding after me. The matter is a serious, one."

Between splashes, and while toweling, Diego whispered the story. A look of rage came into Bernardo's face as he listened, and his nostrils dilated with his angry breathing. Then he helped Diego into fresh clothing taken from a huge chest in the corner of the room, and handed him a perfumed silk handkerchief.

Diego Vega was the indolent fop again — outwardly. Inwardly, he was seething with rage himself at thought of the brutal murder, of the diabolical plot. He realized the necessity for quick and decisive action. Zorro must be wary tonight. He must not fail!

When dusk came, Diego, after eating the evening meal alone, left the house and strolled to the plaza and around it toward the chapel. Fray Felipe was waiting for him.

Diego told of his talk with Sergeant Garcia, and the padre frowned slightly.

"Then we know the soldiers here are in the plot," Fray Felipe said. "They may have planned a trap. Zorro must use care tonight."

"He will be doubly cautious and alert, padre."

"The body of the poor neophyte has been brought into the town, and I will conduct a service tomorrow. I have sent a messenger to Fray Carlos at Santa Barbara, telling him what has happened."

"Be prepared to send him another message tomorrow, after this night's work," Diego whispered. "Now — the serape."

"I have a thought, Diego. I have a robe that is torn and needs mending. Your seamstress servant often mends them. I'll wrap the robe around the serape, and you can take it home. If you are questioned, you may say you are taking a robe of mine home to be mended — and be telling the truth."

A few minutes later, Diego left the chapel with the bundle under his arm. He passed the tavern where men were roistering and went on through the shadows. The moon was almost new. It and the stars gave a little light, but there was no bright full moon to reveal everything plainly. It would be a perfect night for Zorro's exploit.

At the appointed hour Diego, who had pretended to retire early because of his day's journey, slipped from the house by the patio entrance, carrying the serape, and went like a shadow past the huts of the house servants in the rear. Once away from the house, he traveled swiftly through the deeper shadows to the abandoned storehouse where Bernardo was waiting.

The mute had Zorro's black horse, clothes and weapons. Over the clothing he wore, Diego slipped the baggy Zorro costume, put on the black hood and mask, buckled on his blade and put a loaded pistol into his sash. The long black whip had been attached to his saddle by Bernardo.

"Await me here," Diego ordered the mute.

He mounted and gathered up the reins and put the serape over his saddle. His entire manner seemed to change instantly. He was not Don Diego Vega now. He was Zorro.

THROUGH the night he rode cautiously, going away from the buildings of the town, alert to dodge passersby.

The old Gonzales corral was only a small box canyon a short distance from the town, which once had a fence of stakes and brush across its narrow mouth. Years before, when the pueblo was very small, a rascal named Gonzales, a stealer of horses and cattle, had used the place in which to keep stolen stock until it could be driven away safely some dark night and sold to unscrupulous dealers.

Gonzales and his men had been caught and hanged by the soldiers, but the place was still called Gonzales' corral. And it was at this place, according to what the dying neophyte had said, that the meeting was to be held tonight.

Zorro approached the old corral cautiously, riding slowly through the shadows, stopping frequently to listen for sounds that might presage danger. He had serious work to do tonight; he did not want to be seen and chased without being able to accomplish it.

He worked his way up a slope to the rear end of the small canyon, careful to keep to the brush and not get in silhouette against the starlit sky. When he reached the crest and went a short distance down into the canyon, he stopped and looked below.

Almost up to the canyon's mouth, a campfire was burning. A few men were squatting around it, eating. And one man was striding back and forth beside the fire, making wild gestures with his arms. Zorro guessed he was haranguing the others.

Only one horse was in sight, and he stood a short distance from the fire, his reins trailing. Zorro suspected the man delivering the vehement oration was Capitan Juan Zapata, the murderer of the neophyte and arch-plotter from Mexico, and that the horse was his mount.

Working slowly and cautiously down through the brush, Zorro came to the soft, sandy floor of the canyon. He kept in the edge of the brush as he advanced, making his way toward the fire.

Soon he was close enough to see better, and to hear. The orator stopped at the edge of the fire as he gestured, and Zorro could see his face plainly in the firelight. He had guessed correctly. It was Capitan Zapata talking to the men.

Not more than ten of the latter were around the fire, and they were stolid and quiet as they listened.

"Why are you such dolts?" Zapata was demanding. "I have worked like a dog to help you plan. Everything is in readiness. The message has not come. That means simply that Fray Carlos wants you to strike, but is cautious about sending a message telling you directly to do so. Do you want something to go wrong and the good padre to be seized and possibly hanged?"

Now, one of the men at the fire spoke: "We await the message. We will wait until midnight for the messenger."

"That is not more than an hour or so away. If the message does not come, will you carry out the plans at once, and strike? Think of the revenge you will have! Think of the wealth! You can have your pick of horses and cattle and sheep. You can take good food and cloth for clothing from the warehouses on the big ranchos. You can feed and clothe your wives and children. The padres have made fools of you. Do not be their slaves longer."

The spokesman at the fire waved his hand. "We have no quarrel with the padres," he declared. "We await the message."

"It will not come," Zapata assured them. "I have given you the explanation why it will not come. Are you such ignorant fools as to fail to understand?"

Zorro worked his horse nearer, and took his pistol from his sash. Zapata started striding back and forth again, continuing his wild oration. He drew his sword and began chopping at an imaginary enemy.

"We await the message," the spokesman at the fire responded to Zapata's tirade. "We will wait until midnight. If it does not come by that time, we will go away and consider the affair with our friends, and meet you later — "

"Later!" Zapata broke in. "Always delay! If the soldiers learn of our plotting they will be down upon you before you can strike. I tell you the messenger will not come."

Zorro used his spurs and jumped his black horse close to the fire. The men around it sprang to their feet in alarm. Capitan Zapata whirled around and dropped his sword in the fire as he reached for his pistol.

But he found himself looking into the muzzle of a pistol held by the masked man on the black horse.

"Zapata, you lie! The messenger is here!" Zorro cried. "And I have the message, too."

"You — who are you?" Zapata demanded.

"I am known as Zorro."

"Zorro! Zorro! *Amigo!*" the men around the fire shouted.

"So you are the notorious Zorro?" Zapata asked. "And you claim to have brought the message?"

"I have it. Do not make a wrong move, Senor Zapata, or I'll pistol you. Spokesman for the others — come forward!"

ONE of the peons hurried up to Zorro's horse. Zorro gave him the gray serape.

"Here is the message," Zorro said. "Padre Carlos of Santa Barbara feared the soldiers knew of the plot and might capture the messenger. A written document would be found and destroyed, and you never would receive the true message. So the good padre stitched the message with red thread in the border of the serape. Take it to the fire, and read the message. And you, Senor Zapata, stand perfectly still."

Zorro glanced only once at the men at the fire as they unfolded the serape and began examining it closely, then he watched Zapata with keen, narrowed eyes, the pistol held ready.

From the men at the fire came glad shouts.

"It is here — the message from Fray Carlos!" their spokesman said. "It reads, 'The word is — peace! Carlos, Santa Barbara.'"

"A false message!" Zapata declared.

"No, Senor Zapata," the spokesman replied. "Here in the corner, stitched with red, is a sign we know, one used by the padres. This is the true message. Peace he wants, so we will not fight and raid."

"This Zorro!" Zapata cried. "He is making fools of you. His face is covered with a mask. You do not know his identity. He may be a soldier trying to trick you into not starting the insurrection. Make him remove his mask, so we may learn who he is and see whether he may be trusted."

Zorro laughed a little. "You would like that, eh?" he asked. "And perhaps I am a soldier, eh? There are many who would like to see my features — for purposes of their own. My friends, those I help, do not demand to see my face. You men at the fire — pay close attention!"

They suddenly were quiet. Zorro spoke rapidly, but never took his eyes off Zapata.

"This man here, you have trusted," he said. "He would help you right his wrongs, eh? Let me tell you the truth concerning him. He is an officer of the army, sent here from Mexico to plot for your undoing. You were to be fooled into rebellion, and shot down, and the padres blamed for starting the trouble. Then the padres would be arrested and their goods at the missions confiscated."

"What insane talk is this?" Zapata shouted.

"It is the truth, Senor, and you know it. My friends, make no move when I speak the truth, but, leave everything to me. This man, Capitan Juan Zapata, seized the neophyte messenger from Santa Barbara this afternoon, and stabbed him to death and searched for the message. But he never looked at the serape, looking only for a document he could not find. Then he came here to urge you to quick insurrection and send you to your destruction. Even now the soldiers may be ready to pounce upon you."

The men at the fire began muttering angrily, their voices rumbling like growls of beasts about to attack. Capitan Zapata stepped aside suddenly and jerked out his pistol and fired. The pistol ball sang past Zorro's head and went on into the night to strike a rock and scream away in ricochet.

ZAPATA dashed to his horse as Zorro made no effort to return the fire. As he sped through the shadows, he began screeching:

"Garcia! Troopers! Zorro is here! Ride in and capture him, and slay these other rogues!"

Zapata reached his mount and sprang into the saddle. He whipped out the blade he had fastened there. A shout came from beyond the mouth of the canyon as Sergeant Garcia, waiting there in ambush with some of his men, answered the capitan's order.

Zorro shouted to the peons, "Run quickly! Scatter and hide yourselves, or you'll be slain! I'll finish the affair here."

He heard them give shouts of alarm and start running into the brush. With blade ready, Zapata was driving down upon him. Zorro swerved his big black aside as he returned pistol to sash and whipped out his own blade.

Zapata turned and rode back furiously, and they met beside the fire. Their blades clashed and rang, they strained in their saddles. From the near distance came the sounds of pounding hoofs as Garcia and his troopers came charging.

Then there was a quick thrust, and Zorro drew back his blade with crimson on it. Zapata gave a cry and began toppling from his saddle. Swerving his horse, Zorro used his spurs and rode wildly along the floor of the little canyon, away from the fire.

He was in the shadows before the troopers got near enough to the fire to see in which direction he had gone. The pounding of hoofs of his horse made little sound in the sandy earth. Garcia, shouting orders, stopped beside the wounded Zapata with a couple of his men. The others scattered and began their search for Zorro.

But he was in the brush where the shadows were deeper, and following a narrow trail to the top of the blind end of the little box canyon. He reached the crest and went over. And within a short time he was where he could use his spurs and ride at top speed. If there was pursuit, he did not see or hear it.

He circled the town carefully and came to the spot where Bernardo was waiting.

"Everything has been done," he said, as he dropped out of his saddle. Working swiftly, he got off the costume of Zorro, put the weapons aside, and stood forth Diego Vega once more.

At his order, Bernardo gathered up costume and weapons and led the big black away toward the hiding place. Diego strode toward the rear of the house, went carefully past the huts of the servants, got into the house and went to his rooms.

A few minutes later, he was stretched on his couch ready for a night of sound sleep and even into the late morning, since the night was so far gone.

After a leisurely breakfast, Diego dressed in his usual resplendent attire and strolled toward the plaza, acknowledging the salutations of friends and acquaintances he passed. He slackened stride as he neared the tavern, for groups of men were there talking in an excited manner. Diego got snatches of their talk as he passed:

" — was really an officer of the army ... a plot against the padres ... Zorro revealed the truth ... there would have been a war of blood and fire ... Zapata, the rogue, was badly wounded and may die — "

Diego brushed his scented handkerchief across his nostrils and yawned and went on toward the chapel, to see Fray Felipe and discuss the affair.

Zorro Serenades a Siren

Don Diego Vega wears his black cloak to do battle with black-hearted oppressors!

WITHIN the space of ten days, two arrivals aroused the keen interest of the residents of the little pueblo of Reina de Los Angeles. The first was a young woman who announced that she was known to the public merely as Senorita Juanita. She arrived with a cart caravan, sitting in the end of the first ox-drawn cart and letting her feet hangout.

She had a haunting smile, and beneath long black lashes her smoky eyes surveyed the pueblo and its inhabitants in what might be called a speculative manner.

"That one," said the first man who noticed her, "is no mystery." Wherein, despite appearances, he was wrong.

The caravan was one of empty carts returning to a rancho down San Luis Rey way after delivering a cargo to Monterey.

The senorita had boarded the cart, the pueblo soon learned, at Santa Barbara, where an indignant alcalde and a frowning padre from the mission had made sure of her departure. It was whispered that the commanding officer of troops there had regretted her leaving, and that she had danced and sung for the officers the evening before.

She spoke to the driver of the cart when Reina de Los Angeles was reached, and he gestured toward a distant building. When its vicinity was neared, she sprang out of the cart, taking from it a huge bundle covered with a shawl, containing her personal belongings. She laughed at the driver of the cart and blew

"Enslaver of the poor and helpless! Your dastardly work is done forever!"

him a kiss, and went up the gentle slope carrying her bundle, her hips swinging gracefully.

The building was the barracks, where at the moment Sergeant Manuel Garcia was in command during the absence of his capitán, who had been summoned to Monterey to explain to an irate Governor why he had not caught Senor Zorro, the masked man who rode a big black horse at night and used blade, gun and whip against those who mistreated and oppressed the poor and downtrodden.

When she reached the entrance to the barracks, Senorita Juanita made eyes at the guard. The trooper eyed her in return, but with some hostility. He was a middle-aged man who had been caused considerable trouble by a woman in days gone by, and for the fair sex had no feeling except an abiding hatred.

"Be off!" he ordered.

At that instant, ponderous Sergeant Garcia happened to emerge from his office to see and listen. The girl noticed his badges of rank and appealed to him.

"It is an urgent matter, senor," she told Garcia. "I have important information for you. I have just arrived on the cart caravan—"

"Into my office, senorita!" Garcia ordered. "And you," he added to the trooper on guard at the door, "be more careful in your reception of persons who come to the barracks. One never knows."

WITHIN the half hour, Senorita Juanita appeared again with Sergeant Garcia beside her. She tilted her nose as she passed the guard, and the sergeant glared at him. The pair went down the slope toward the plaza. It was after the siesta hour, and those of the town were taking a leisurely promenade. The sergeant and his unknown charge were seen and word of her arrival spread.

They went directly to the tavern, where Garcia beckoned the fat innkeeper.

"Senor," he said, in low tones, "here is Senorita Juanita, a singing and dancing girl who has entertained at the best cantinas in Alta California. She is to work here for you."

"For me? Never have I employed a cantina girl!" the innkeeper protested.

"You are about to employ one now, senor," Garcia informed him. "She is to have the best treatment—a nice room off the patio, an abundance of good food and drink. She will arrange her own program. She is under my protection."

"But, my Sergeant! Business is poor. I am almost ah impoverished man—"

"When the senorita dances and sings your business will pick up amazingly," the sergeant promised him.

"I can see at a glance that the senorita is one of those highly paid for her talents, and I cannot afford it. Ah, how ravishing it would be to have such a one perform in the main room for my customers! But, as I remarked, I cannot afford it! I am impoverished already—"

"Attend me, and silence your tongue as you listen! The senorita will do her best for your patrons, singing and dancing both, and the only cost to you will be her living quarters and her food and drink. She is to retain any small coins your customers may bestow upon her. If you desire, you may hint that you have engaged her at an enormous salary, and thus gain prestige."

"Ah, that is different! No doubt she will be worth room and food," the innkeeper replied. "But, who pays her, Sergeant? You, with your small wage—"

"Dolt and fool and ass!" Garcia barked at him. "Must you know everything—the secrets of government, perhaps? Do as you are told, and guard your words. Escort the senorita to a good room, give her what she wants of eat and drink, and see that she is treated courteously."

"As to the last—" the innkeeper began.

"Do not despair, Senor," the senorita told him, smiling slightly. "I shall see to it personally that I am treated courteously. I carry a poniard with me always— and where I can reach it easily."

The tavernkeeper shivered slightly, glanced again at Sergeant Garcia, then bowed.

"The affair is settled," he said: "Please to come with me, Senorita, and I'll see that you are properly domiciled in this my place of business and residence."

Because Garcia saw that it was spread, the news promptly went through the town that the tavernkeeper had engaged at enormous expense the cream of all cantina girls, fresh from triumphs in Monterey and San Francisco de Asia. That same evening, Senorita Juanita was pleased to strum a guitar and sing, and then dance while someone else played.

A native servant followed around after her as she danced and picked up the coins tossed her way to hand to her later. Then the senorita disappeared, and the tavern-keeper let men hope she would return as long as they spent money, finally being obliged to explain that she was greatly fatigued from her journey and would not appear until the following evening.

ON THE third evening, Don Diego Vega, dressed in his usual resplendent raiment, appeared in the tavern to buy a jar of the crystallized honey the inn-keeper sold. Yawning behind a lace-edged handkerchief which had been deli-cately-scented, and seeming to be bored with life, he tossed a coin upon the counter and listened to the fulsome compliments of the tavern man.

"And, Don Diego, you are just in time to see and hear my new acquisition, Senorita Juanita," the innkeeper related. "Ah, what beauty and grace! What singing and dancing!"

"Do you criticize or praise?" Diego asked. "From your tone, one cannot tell."

"Wait until you see her, Don Diego! At great expense, I have had her sent me from Monterey."

He would have continued, but at that instant those in the tavern, the main room of which was crowded this evening, began clapping their hands and shout-ing, and Diego looked toward the patio door and saw the senorita.

She already had observed him through the doorway, and she knew the real thing when she saw it. Regardless of her other activities, she would not ignore the opportunity of attracting the attention of the scion of one of the richest and most powerful families in all Alta California.

Diego sat on a bench after the innkeeper had brushed the dust off it with his apron, and yawned behind his handkerchief again as the girl began playing and singing. She moved among the tables, talking with her eyes, her movements graceful. Twice she passed near Diego, who looked at the ceiling and seemed to be listening to her song.

Then she danced. lie did not look at the ceiling now. He watched her closely as she moved faster and faster, her skirts swirling and at times exposing a neat ankle to fire the imagination. She brushed her skirts against him as she passed the bench, turned and looked over her shoulder to see how he had taken it. Diego yawned.

Anger flamed in the senorita's eyes. She increased the tempo of her dance and when it reached an end she sank to the floor with head bowed and arms outstretched. Those in the room tossed coins for the native servant to pick up for her; sprang to their feet and yelled, begged her to sit at table with them and drink the best wine in the house. But Diego only yawned again.

He arose from the bench and went to the counter for his jar of honey.

"What think you of her?" the innkeeper asked him.

"Did you say you had acquired her at great expense?" Diego asked. "A sad waste of good money, my friend. However, toss her this coin for me. One should pay such persons." He gave the innkeeper a gold piece and strolled from the tavern.

Senorita Juanita had been watching and listening, and now she appeared behind the counter.

"The coin is for me," she told the innkeeper, as he was starting to pocket it. "Tell me! What is the name of that half-dead caballero who yawns when I dance and sing?"

"He? That was Don Diego Vega. only son of Don Alejandro, the best catch in the country—except that no senorita has been able to catch him."

"No doubt they did not try. He is like a lifeless fish! Where is his fire, this young caballero? He will die of yawning."

"Careful how you speak!" the innkeeper warned. "The Vegas are most powerful."

"His father should take the son in hand, then, and remake him. Yawn when I sing and dance, will he? 'Tis a wonder this bold Senor Zorro, who rides the highways in these parts with his face behind a mask, does not prick this blood-less Vega with his blade to see if he could draw a drop of blood. If he did, no doubt it would be as thin as water and as cold."

She went away angrily to rest in her room until it was time for her to dance again, innocent of the knowledge that the spineless Diego was also the Senor Zorro she had mentioned.

SOME days later, there was another arrival in Reina de Los Angeles, this time a senor who seemed to be a man of some importance. He came riding an excellent horse, and with a peon servant following with a pack mule.

The stranger announced that he was Alfredo Romo, and his talk intimated that he was a wealthy trader traveling from Monterey to San Diego de Alcalá and spending some time in each district, seeking for likely places. in which to build a branch of his business.

His arrival gladdened the heart of the tavernkeeper, for Senor Romo was a free spender, buying wine for all, ordering the most expensive dishes, making friends with everybody and paying for the privilege.

It was observed that Senor Alfredo Romo paid a visit to the barracks and exhibited his traveling papers to Sergeant Garcia. The latter showed most pro-found respect, which was nothing new for Garcia if he scented free wine.

Senor Romo asked a multitude of questions about the district, the native and peon help, the numbers of men working on nearby ranchos, and all that. But that was a natural thing in a man who spoke of opening a branch of his business. He was merely estimating the trade territory, men supposed.

On a certain afternoon, Diego strolled along the side of the plaza and toward the little chapel, for aged Fray Felipe, his confessor, had sent for him. Their ceremonial greetings over, the padre escorted Diego to his private room, where they could converse without danger of being overheard. Fray Felipe was one of three persons who knew the identity of Senor Zorro. The others were Diego's father and Bernardo, his mute peon servant.

"We have had two new arrivals in the pueblo recently," the padre men-tioned.

"I have seen them both," Diego replied. "The senorita closely and the fine new senor from a distance."

"As to the senorita—" Fray Felipe began.

"I can imagine your thoughts concerning her," Diego interrupted. "But such always have been and perhaps always will be."

"I had no intention, my son, of speaking of her possible morals or lack of them," the padre continued. "I doubt whether what you have in mind is her real reason for traveling about the country. In fact, I am sure it is something else, something far worse."

"How is this?"

"I have reports of her—and of another," Fray Felipe said. "Confidential reports that have come to me from missions to the north. She began in Monterey, after remaining there for a time after her arrival by ship from Mexico."

"Began what, padre?" Diego urged.

"Allow me, my son. From Monterey, she traveled south, always pretending to be nothing more than a cantina girl. She stopped at each pueblo and mission. And always she asked a multitude of questions, like an innocent child desiring to learn."

"Perhaps she did desire knowledge."

"Of the rancho district, of natives and peon workmen, of men living without remunerative labor? Would such a one be concerned in those things—naturally?"

"What then, padre?"

"Always, after a few days of time, she has been followed by this man who calls himself Alfredo Romo and pretends to be a wealthy trader."

"Perhaps an infatuation lures him on and on," Diego suggested. "I have heard of such things."

"Bah! Wherever she stops, the senorita goes to the authorities and speaks with them—"

"A traveler is supposed to show his or her papers, padre."

"That is true, my son; but wait until I have finished. I happen to know that in every case some man in authority has put himself to the trouble of getting her an engagement to sing and dance, as if he had orders to do so. Here in Reina de Los Angeles, Sergeant Garcia actually compelled the tavern keeper to engage her. When I rebuked him for having a cantina girl, he defended himself to me by explaining. Garcia told him he had only to give her lodging and food. Her fees are being paid from some other source."

"I grow interested, padre."

"I had thought you would. Behind her, I have said, always comes this Alfredo Romo with his multitude of questions. And in every ease, immediately thereafter, many men are seized and sent north to Monterey."

"What is this?" Diego cried.

"Alfredo Romo is a government recruiter. It is peonage. The poor creatures are rounded up unexpectedly like so many cattle, torn from their families in some cases, packed into carts, tied together, threatened and beaten, and taken to Monterey in secret. And from there they are shipped in foul vessels to Mexico, on the Gulf side, are then driven overland and scattered among the plantations and sent to work in the mines. Especially the latter — where they do not live long."

"Is that a fact?" Diego cried, getting to his feet and starting to pace the floor.

"A pretty thing, is it not? A thing we of the Franciscan other have not been able to touch. We can do nothing but warn, and that avails us little. This, my son, is a task for—Zorro."

Diego breathed deeply, and his eyes met those of the padre.

"You are right," he replied. "It is a task for Zorro. No doubt Zorro will learn of this and act accordingly."

THE following evening Senorita Juanita danced before a crowd that jammed the big main room of the tavern. The Innkeeper was jubilant. He had put more native servants to work. He had two peons carrying wineskins from the cellar. Coins poured into his purse. If this sort of thing continued long enough, he would bench.

Senorita Juanita, he observed, kept herself aloof from all with the exception of Senor Alfredo Rome. She revealed some consideration toward him, and the innkeeper believed him to be the favored one. He watched carefully, but they appeared to have no meeting outside the common room.

If he happened to be puzzled at times regarding the real status of the senorita, happened to wonder why she worked there for no more than food and lodging and what coins were tossed to her, he cast such thoughts aside. He had more sense Than to look a gift horse In the teeth to estimate his age.

Having finished her dance on this evening, the senorita retired to her private room to rest for her next appearance. It was a well-furnished room, and she was comfortable In It. She latched the door and stretched upon her cot, putting a scarf over her eyes to keep from them the light of the one taper burning.

A moment later, something came through the open barred window and thumped upon the floor. The senorita gave a squeal of alarm and sprang off the cot, reaching for her dagger. On the floor she spied a folded sheet of parchment, attached to which was a rock held by a thong. Working quickly, she unfolded the parchment and read:

Sweetest senorita! One who cannot make himself known at this moment would have private speech with you. Circumstances are such that he dare not speak to you in the common room of the Inn. His standing in the community will not admit of it. When you are tough singing and dancing tonight and all have retired except the few wine guzzlers In the common room, no doubt you will feel the necessity for a breath of such sweet fresh air as can be found only at the end of the patio on the left hand side.

There was no signature. The senorita folded the parchment and thrust it into her bodice. She was smiling slightly. One of such standing in the community that he could not speak to her in the common room, eh? That meant a hidalgo, or the son of one. Perhaps, she thought, that spineless fop of a Don Diego Vega was not so dead to emotion as she had judged. Either him, or another.

It was not the first episode of the sort in Senorita Juanita's career. Often she had received such epistles, in Mexico and also here in Alta California. There promised to be a rare profit in this. So long as it did not interfere with her official duties, she could learn whether the profit existed In fact.

She danced and sang better than before, and finally retired to her room as though to go to bed. After an interval during which it grew quieter in the common room, she extinguished the taper. She waited still a few moments, then wrapped a shawl around her shoulders and draped a mantilla over her head and the high comb adorning her thick raven hair.

Opening the door, she found the patio deserted. She went from the room like a shadow, closing the door behind her, and strolled toward the end, keeping to the shadows beneath the arches as much as possible.

In the spot the note had indicated, she waited. No one was in sight. She did not fear the appearance of Romo, for they thought it better to avoid each other in secret as much as possible. And there was a soft mist falling, so none of the few roisterers remaining in the common room would venture into the patio.

The mist was commencing to make itself uncomfortable to the senorita herself when, from dose by, she heard a whisper:

"Senorita Juanita!"

"Si?" she asked. She was holding the dagger in her hand as she spoke. Life had taught her to trust nobody.

"'Tis I who sent you the communication."

"And what is your identity?" she questioned. "I cannot even see you."

"Since I find it safe, I'll approach. Kindly do not scream at sight of me and call attention to my presence. You are in no danger from me, senorita."

She heard a movement at her left, and then, In the faint streak of light that came from the nearest flaring torch in the patio, she saw him—a man dressed in black, with a black hood over his head and a gleaming sword at his side.

SENORITA JUANITA laughed a little. It was not the first time a man of high birth had approached her masked. But usually they cast aside the mask after the first meeting.

"How are you named, senor?" she asked him. "And why have you sought this interview in such a remarkable manner?"

"Is it necessary for you to ask that last, Senorita? What man would not seek a meeting with such a rare beauty, such a sweet singer and graceful dancer? My heart pounded at my ribs as I watched you, as I listened to your song."

"Ah, senor! Your speech is most romantic."

"You would make the dullest of men turn romantic, senorita, believe me!"

"Pardon me, senor, but this meeting is to what end?"

"To many more meetings, let me hope."

"But you have not yet revealed your identity to me."

"Promise you will not be frightened when I do so."

She laughed softly again. "High names do not frighten me, senor. Many men of high birth have sought to gain my acquaintance."

"You have perhaps heard of Senor Zorro?"

"I have. The bold man who rides the highways and laughs at the foolish troopers who try to catch him? What a man he is!"

"I am he, Senorita."

"You? You are—Zorro?"

"Please keep your voice down, Senorita. Do not forget that a large and flattering reward has been offered by the Governor for my capture."

"As if I would betray you! Where did you hear and see me sing and dance, Senor? How could you have done so?"

"Men do not know me when my mask is off, Senorita. I move among others freely at times. Let us say that I happened to be here present in the pueblo, and was one of the crowd that heard and saw you."

"And you were attracted, Senor?"

"Would I be here else, Senorita?"

"But what comes of the meeting?" she asked.

"Another—and another! Unless—"

"Unless what, senor?"

"I have heard a whisper that you are interested in one man only and will never grow interested in anyone else. If that be true, my time is being wasted, and you have kept this rendezvous only through curiosity."

"Name the man."

"Alfredo Romo, the rich trader."

"Did it not attract attention, Senor, I should laugh at that statement."

"You do not know him well, then?"

"I never saw him until he came here to Reina de Los Angeles. It is true he tossed a gold coin to me, and asked me to meet him after I had done my evening's entertainment. But I am here talking to you, am I not?"

"That is true."

"Unmask, Senor Zorro, and let me see your features."

"My ugliness might cause you repugnance."

"Ah, no! A man who does and dares as you do could not be ugly."

"If we could become attracted to each other, Senorita, what a life of thrills we could lead!"

"Listen, Senor! If such came to pass, what profit we could have together! Thrills, love, riches!"

"Riches, Senorita?"

"Si! I have traveled down the coast from Monterey and have acquired knowledge. I know where rich people keep their gold and jewels. I could lead foolish young rich caballeros into an ambush for you. We could reap a harvest! And then—to Mexico, to live like king and queen!"

"You paint a beautiful picture, senorita."

"And you—you risk liberty and perhaps life to speak to me here tonight—"

"It is nothing! To do so I would risk much more. But I cannot tarry now. Shall we meet again?"

"Tomorrow evening, Senor, at this hour."

"I shall have to make it the hour safest and most opportune for me. Senorita. To announce my presence, I will serenade you tomorrow evening beneath your window. Meet me a short time after my song."

He extended his gloved hand across the palings and took her own, bent and kissed the palm of it, and then was gone Into the deeper shadows with not the slightest noise.

SHE STROLLED back to the door of her patio room—and there encountered Alfredo Romo. "I came for a short conference, and found you gone," he whispered. "You were talking to some man at the end of the patio."

"Is it not my duty to get information?" she asked.

"Not in such a manner. There may be spies about. If my object is learned, my usefulness will be ended and the Governor will dismiss me. You never have been careless before. Can it be possible you are indulging in a romance?"

"If so?" she questioned.

He grasped her arms. "Do not play with me, Juanita! If you encourage another man, he dies! In both business and love, you are mine! This should be the district of my greatest success. I'll strip the ranchos of natives and peons. What a cargo we'll have to send to Mexico! And the reward will be huge. Can you match that in any other man?"

"Perhaps," she taunted. "I may find a man who can give me a thrill an hour, some one who rides with a price on his head, who takes gold where he finds it, and quickly without secret planning and the asking of thousands of questions."

"Do not talk like a fool! With whom were you speaking at the end of the patio?"

"Some fool, perhaps, who waited to catch me there and plead his love and ask for a rendezvous. Has such not happened scores of times before? Is it not a part of the game I must play? I am tired now, and must get to bed. Buenas noches, senor!"

Romo returned to his own room to find a communication had been tossed through his window. He picked it up and read it swiftly.

Your affairs are in danger of being betrayed. A recruiter for peonage should be wary of his co-workers. Your fair assistant may meet her admirer again tomorrow night Would it not be best, and quietest, to deal with him personally? Quietly—say with a blade. A pistol might attract attention and let it become known to Sergeant Garcia that he should report to his superiors that you are not discreet.

After he had read that unsigned missive, Romo paced around his room like a man enraged. So, somebody knew! But evidently a friend, since he sent this warning.

Juanita, he supposed, had met some man and had conceived a swift infatuation. Both jealousy and rage at his affairs being threatened with disaster impelled Romo to handle this matter personally, as Zorro had thought they would.

He did not wish to lower himself by going to Garcia for help and exposing his weakness. Garcia impressed him as a man who would send in an adverse report on him. And this had been a profitable business.

Be watched Juanita the following day. She could not keep from betraying a sudden interest and agitation foreign to her. But Romo held back bitter speech and spoke to her only in the presence of others early in the evening when they met in the common room of the tavern.

After she had danced the second time and had retired, Romo bought wine for all present, pleaded fatigue and a headache, and went to his own room. He buckled on his blade. Whoever had warned him had been wise; a pistol shot might ruin everything. He wondered as to the informer. Would somebody appear afterward and try blackmail? In such case, Romo would know how to handle him.

This night, there was no mist. A bright moon sailed the sky, obscured at Intervals by scudding clouds that came in from the distant sea. Zorro rode his black horse to within a short distance of, the sprawling tavern, and left him In a spot of darkness behind a storage shed.

CARRYING an old guitar the loss of which would cause him no regret, he went through the deep shadows and got outside the window of the senorita's room. He strummed the Instrument and began singing a love song in a low voice. She spoke from the window: "That is enough for the signal, Senor. Someone may hear you, and we do not wish to be observed. I'll go at once to the end of the patio."

"A moment, Senorita," he whispered. "This meeting may lead to a decision between us. Have you considered well? In case you see my face and like it, and are pleased with me tonight, would you give up everything to ride with me?"

"Without a regret, senor."

"But your present employment is profitable, I understand. To work as you do with the peonage agent—"

"Senor! You know?"

"It is necessary for Zorro to know many things if he would preserve his own life and take a profit."

"What you have said is true, senor. I have worked with him at his order. I have infatuated men to get them to talk, so I could learn where peons and natives could be seized with ease."

"And sold into slavery?"

"At so much a head, Senor. But what do we care about such cattle? All that will be over. I'll ride with you. We'll have a thousand thrills a day. We'll grow wealthy—"

"Get to the rendezvous and await me there," Zorro broke in.

He went silently through the shadows again, leaving the old guitar behind on the ground. He was cautious now, knowing that Romo would be lurking somewhere near, realizing that the fellow might take him with a foul and unexpected thrust.

A streak of moonlight revealed the senorita to him as she took up position Inside the paled fence. Zorro's eyes searched the shadows. He had to risk a shot, but thought Romo would not fire and attract attention. He would try ambush instead.

The moonlight was bright for some distance around where the senorita was waiting. Romo could not get within sword's length without being seen. Zorro loosened his own blade in its scabbard and put hand to hilt, then stepped into the moonlight and advanced rapidly toward the waiting girl.

"Ah, here you are!" she whispered. "How I long to see your face!"

"We may be interrupted, Senorita."

"Who is to bother us? None suspects I ant here. Come closer to the fence and let me clasp your hand. Let me remove the mask—"

"Tell me again, Senorita—you will cease serving the peonage agent and ride with me?"

"To the end of the world, Senor, If we are pleasing to each other."

A bellow of rage came from a nearby dark spot, and Romo charged forward, blade in hand. Zorro side-stepped quickly and whipped out his own weapon as the girl gave a cry of fright.

"She traitor!" Romo yelled at her. "I'll attend to you after I have finished with this lout—"

"Lout? You fight with the famed Zorro, you fool!" she replied to him. "He'll laugh as you die! He is a man—"

The blades were clashing already, and for Romo there was no retreat. The tone of the girl's voice told him she spoke the truth. A great fear came upon him.

Zorro was speaking as they fought, as he tried out Romo's wrist and got the feel of his blade and learned he had nothing to fear from this antagonist: "Enslaver of the poor and helpless! Your dastardly work is done forever!"

Romo gave ground, before what he thought was a furious attack. The perspiration came out upon his brow in great globules, perspiration induced by a great fear. "Help!" he screeched at the top of his voice. "Zorro is here!"

"Too late to call now," Zorro told him. "I but play with you, Senor. Were you not such a fiend, I'd disarm you and go my way. But to send men to slavery and death as you have done—that deserves the worst punishment."

He laughed as Romo fried a rally, and beat the man back to the fence of palings. Senorita Juanita, her hands clutched at her breast, had retired a few feet into the shadows to watch from there.

"Do not slay me," Romo whined.

"Craven! I could thrust you through the heart at any moment. But I'll spare your life. Through the lung—"

Romo gave a cry as the blade entered his body, dropped his own weapon, sprawled. Zorro stepped back, sheathing his sword, knowing that Fray Felipe would be pleased that he had removed the menace to men's liberty without actually taking a human life.

The senorita rushed from the shadows to the fence. "Now," she whispered. "Show me your face. Then I must get to my room. Tomorrow night, here—"

"No tomorrow night," Zorro told her. "Think you I would have romance with a thing like you? Get you gone from the pueblo, from Alta California, else hide from the sight of all men. You are no less bad than this man on the ground. You knew the foul work you were doing. I only used you as a lure to bring this man within the reach of my blade."

He saw her dagger flash in the moonlight, and laughed as he dodged the blow. Romo's yells had been heard, and the landlord of the urn came charging out with other men at his heels. Zorro laughed wildly again, and turned to flee through the streaks of moonlight to the dark place behind the storage shed, where he had left his horse.

"Buenas noches, Senores!" he taunted.

Hoofbeats sounded as he rode off through the night, to circle the town and approach it again cautiously, dispose of his horse and costume and weapons, and enter his father's house, to report to proud old Don Alejandro what he had done.

Zorro Meets a Wizard

It was a time for feasting, dancing, and love, but a deadly evil was loose — and only Don Diego Vega could conquer it!

AT LAST the long hard work of the roundup was over. The cattle had been brought in from the hills and canyons and slain for their hides. The big tallow vats had been cooking for days. The vaqueros and the rancho workmen were tired — but not too tired for play.

Here, on the big rancho belonging to the Vega family, only a short distance from the San Gabriel mission, there was always a gay *fiesta* after the work of the roundup was done. It was a time for feasting, a time of music and dancing and making love. There were competitive athletic events, with large prizes as rewards. And there were always pony races, when the vaqueros bet heavily on their own mounts and every horse seemed to have scores of backers.

Don Alejandro Vega, the aged head of the family, and his son and heir, Diego, sat their saddles now on the side of a little knoll a short distance from the sprawling ranch house. In a long line before them were the vaqueros, dressed in holiday finery and mounted on their best ponies. The racing was about to begin.

Fray Felipe, the aged Franciscan who served now at the little chapel in Reina de Los Angeles, had asked a blessing. Don Alejandro had made his usual annual speech. Diego had read a list of the prizes and entries for the races.

As the riders scattered to get into position for the various events, Juan Cassara, the rancho overseer, rode up beside the Vegas, father and son, and touched his forehead with his knuckles in salute and respect.

"What is it, Juan?" Don Alejandro asked.

"Perhaps I should not bother you with such a trivial thing, Don Alejandro, but it has me worried."

"If it worries you, it is important enough for us to hear," Don Alejandro replied. "You are a man not easily worried, Juan."

Cassara was the serious type. He considered his position of responsibility one of the utmost importance. Had the rancho been his own, he could not have served its interests better. He never bothered Don Alejandro or Diego about things he felt he could handle himself.

"Just outside our property line, beside the road that runs to the mission,, a pavilion has been erected," he reported. He then went on to say that tacked to the front of the pavilion was a sign which read:

Alfonso, The Wizard

"This Alfonso is a fat man with an evil face," Cassara continued. "He wears outlandish clothing. He has a fair young daughter, named Inez, who walks about in front of the pavilion and smiles at men to get them to enter."

DON ALEJANDRO frowned and stared at the overseer.

"And what does this wizard do?" he asked.

"For a coin he foretells the future."

"Only God knows what the future holds," Fray Felipe rebuked him sternly.

"All good men know that, padre," Cassara replied. "But this man who calls himself a wizard pretends to tell what it holds. Some men take his nonsense seriously."

"To what extent, Juan?" Don Alejandro asked.

"Most of the peons and natives are superstitious regardless of the teachings of the good padres," the overseer replied. "This man who calls himself a wizard tells them of good fortune to come. If the fellow is young, he is promised a beautiful bride and a life of prosperity. But he does not stop there, with all that which is told by other so-called wizards."

"What else, Juan?" Don Alejandro asked, impatiently.

"He has told some of the men — and one related it to me and asked my advice — that a dark cloud is hanging over them and over this entire district of Alta California. There is a demon abroad, the wizard declares, a clever demon who pretends to aid the poor and downtrodden and oppressed. But, in reality, according to the wizard, this demon is preparing to lead them to destruction."

"And the demon?" Don Alejandro asked.

"The man known as Señor Zorro."

Don Alejandro and Fray Felipe exchanged swift glances. Diego Vega looked at them — and yawned. His father and the padre were two of the only three persons in the world besides himself who knew that Diego Vega, apparently an indolent, spineless fop, was in reality Zorro. The third man was Diego's mute peon servant, Bernardo.

"Interesting," Don Alejandro observed. "What else, Juan?"

"The wizard looks into a huge crystal ball and makes motions with his hands and says that any man who knows the identity of Zorro and will come to him and reveal it will receive some gold coins, and also will be known as a benefactor of his people. He will have prosperity the remainder of his life, and other men will look up to him."

"What nonsense!" Fray Felipe exploded.

Diego spoke: "Must we always be hearing of this confounded masked rider who travels about at night and whips, shoots and stabs people? Such turbulent times!"

"But that is not the worst," Juan Cassara continued. "Also, there is something that concerns this rancho."

"What now?" Don Alejandro asked.

"The scoundrel of a wizard has told some of the men, even some of our vaqueros, that a dark cloud is hanging over the Vega rancho. Disaster is to come, he says. The wise man who now works for the rancho will do well to leave it immediately and seek work elsewhere. If he does not, he faces ruin. Accidents will occur, the wizard says. Men will be maimed and killed."

"This grows serious," Don Alejandro admitted.

"So serious, Don Alejandro, that about a score of men have come to me already asking that they receive their pay immediately after the fiesta, since they are seeking work elsewhere."

"Why, the low scoundrel!" Don Alejandro fumed. "No rancho in the land cares for its men better than do we. They have good huts and food, and we do not drive them too much at their work. They have good pay. We give them liberties they would not receive on any other rancho. Does this wizard suggest where they may get work if they leave Rancho Vega?"

"One of the men asked him that. He suggested the rancho of Marcos Melendez."

"Ha!" Don Alejandro's face purpled with wrath and, had not the padre been at his side, no doubt he would have resorted to profanity, a thing he seldom did. "Marcos Melendez, eh? The explanation of this affair is appearing to me."

The others understood his meaning well. Marcos Melendez, a vulgar upstart who had amassed considerable money by methods adjudged unscrupulous, had come to the vicinity a year before and had purchased a rancho from the heirs of the former owner.

His method of running a rancho was as unscrupulous as some of his other enterprises had been. Men of decency would have nothing to do with him.

HE SWINDLED the small stock-raisers, mistreated the peons and natives who worked for him, fed them poorly and drove them to hard labor by whipping and kicks and cuffs. He also mistreated his horses and oxen, disregarded the laws, and held boisterous parties in his house attended by questionable characters traveling along the highway.

Don Alejandro had rebuffed him once in Reina de Los Angeles when Melendez had presumed to address him with familiarity, and Melendez had sworn to have revenge. It would be like him to scheme to make the Vega rancho hands dissatisfied and induce them to leave Don Alejandro's employ.

"So this fellow who calls himself Alfonso the Wizard is warning his dupes to betray Señor Zorro and also leave this rancho and take employment elsewhere," Don Alejandro said. "Without doubt, he acts in the employment of somebody. Of Melendez, of course, regarding our men. But who is paying him to try to get somebody to betray Zorro?"

"Possibly the soldiers," Diego suggested. "It is common knowledge that the Governor has reprimanded them for not catching this Zorro and hanging him."

"Thanks, Juan, for bringing me this information," Don Alejandro told the overseer. "I'll attend to the matter."

Cassara rode away. The vaqueros were preparing for their first race. Fray Felipe rode his mule a short distance away to hold speech with a friend. And Diego pressed his horse closely beside that on which his father was mounted. He spoke in low tones, hiding the motion of his lips by brushing his scented handkerchief across his nostrils.

"If you will be kind enough to award the prizes yourself, father, instead of having me do it, I think I shall take a little ride," Diego said.

"A ride?"

"It is in my mind to visit the pavilion of Alfonso the Wizard and possibly have the fellow foretell my future. But do not mention my plan to the good padre, or he will make me do a penance for listening to the rogue."

Don Alejandro smiled. "I'll not inform him where you have gone, nor for what. Is there anything else on your mind?"

"Only the thought that Zorro perchance may ride his black horse tonight."

Don Alejandro looked at him sharply. "If Zorro does, he will be wise to take every precaution. Behind the so-called wizard is Marcos Melendez, of course. But there may be a stronger force behind him also."

"That is my own thought, Father. Sergeant Garcia is here from Reina de Los Angeles for the fiesta, as usual. When he rode in a short time ago, I noticed that instead of the three troopers he usually brings with him this time he has brought six. The hounds expect a fox hunt."

The pavilion was back a short distance from the road, in the shade of a small grove. The cloth which formed it was striped red and green. Behind the main pavilion was a smaller tent which served the wizard and his daughter as living quarters.

Diego rode toward it at an easy lope, wiping his face with the lace-bordered handkerchief, like a man making his way leisurely to the mission at San Gabriel. As he neared the pavilion, he brought his horse down to a walk, bent forward in his saddle as though fatigued, and allowed his keen eyes to search the scene.

The girl was pacing back and forth in front of the pavilion. She eyed Diego as he approached, and in turn he eyed her. She was a handsome, robust girl with a swagger in her walk, and she increased the swagger as Diego neared her.

"Buenos dias, senor!" she called to him, boldly.

Diego nodded, and pulled his horse to a stop. "What is all this?" he asked, indicating the pavilion.

"It is what the sign says, señor. I am Inez, and my father is Alfonso the Wizard. Will you not dismount and let him look into the future for you, señor? The fee is whatever you wish to pay."

"My future may frighten me."

"I am sure that Don Diego Vega has nothing to fear."

"You know me then?" Diego pretended to be surprised.

"Ah, who does not know the handsome caballero who makes the hearts of all the senoritas hammer at their ribs? They tell me you are not yet wed, though you could have your pick. Perhaps you are difficult to please, señor?"

"That may be it," Diego admitted. "I believe I will dismount and rest a moment in the cool of the pavilion, and listen to what your father has to say."

DISMOUNTING, he led his horse toward one of the trees. Inez brushed against him as she pretended to help tether the mount, flashed her eyes at him and gave him one smile after another.

"One moment, Don Diego, until I see whether my father is engaged," she murmured, and disappeared into the pavilion.

Diego heard a murmur of voices, and knew she was informing her father of the visitor's identity. A moment later, the girl held aside the flap of the tent and indicated he was to enter.

Alfonso the Wizard was dressed for the role, with a robe decorated with strange symbols and a high peaked hat similarly adorned. He sat behind a table upon which was a huge crystal ball. The wizard waved toward a stool on the opposite side of the table.

Diego tossed a gold coin upon the table, at which the eyes of the wizard gleamed, and sat down. Alfonso bent over the huge crystal ball and brushed his palms across it.

"You are of a proud and noted family you have everything except love but that will come to you soon."

"How do you know I do not have it now?" Diego asked.

"The crystal ball tells me everything. Ha! There it is again!"

"What?" Diego demanded.

"It comes between me and every client. It intrudes itself; and is becoming a nuisance. It must be a warning."

"Do not frighten me!" Diego begged.

"Ah, señor, this thing means no harm to you. It deals with the man known as Señor Zorro. The Powers are warning people of him. They tell me he is an impostor and should be removed. They say that the man instrumental in bringing him to justice will have great honor."

"What has that to do with me and my future?"

"Seemingly nothing, señor. But the sign always comes to me. Perhaps it means that you should question the men who work on your father's rancho, Don Diego, and make them tell what they know of Zorro, so you can report it to the soldiers."

"That would be too fatiguing," Diego declared.

"Think of the honor that would come to you! The Governor himself would reward you."

"Confound this Zorro!" Diego said. "Tell me of myself."

"You will live long and prosper, the crystal ball tells me. You will wed in four years, and be the father of six children, four of them sons."

"Remarkable!" Diego exclaimed. "I must wait four years?"

"For marriage. Take love where you find it."

"If my padre could hear you talk! Tell me of other matters … our rancho, its future prosperity, all that."

Alfonso waved his palms over the crystal again and looked at it. "Ah! The Powers say for you to do everything you can to get information about Zorro, and tell the soldiers. Then the prosperity of your family will be doubled."

"That confounded Zorro again!"

"Thoughts of him are being sent me by the Powers."

"Have you no fear, Señor Wizard? From what I have heard about Zorro, he may pay you a visit if he learns you are interesting yourself in his affairs. You are quite fat, Señor Wizard. If his long whip ever cuts into your body, it will be like whipping a big cushion — except that it would draw blood."

The Wizard shivered, but immediately had his composure again. "I — I have the feeling that the Powers will protect me," he declared.

"No doubt" Diego was thinking of Sergeant Garcia and his six troopers. He got up from the stool and brushed his scented handkerchief across his nostrils. "You have been very amusing, Señor Wizard — well worth the fee. No doubt many men will visit your pavilion. We are having a fiesta at the rancho today and tomorrow, and if news of you gets abroad you may have many clients."

THE WIZARD shrugged. "I hope to prosper. A man must gather coins to pay for clothing and food. And I have a daughter to support. Say a kind word to her as you go out, Don Diego, if you will.

She gets lonesome at times, with nothing to do but help me. She seldom has a chance to stroll in the moonlight with a romantic man. A señorita enjoys such things."

"Without a *dueña?*" Diego asked, seemingly aghast.

"Ah, señor, we are simple folk. We do not pay strict attention to the conventions."

Diego smiled slightly and went through the flap of the pavilion to find Señorita Inez only a few feet away. He knew she had been listening.

"Was the fortune good, señor?" she asked.

"I can think of a better one."

"And that?"

"Come to the rancho tonight to the fiesta. All are welcome. No doubt your father will be too busy to attend. But you can come alone?"

"Possibly." She flashed him a smile.

"During the evening, I'll contrive to speak with you."

"Ah? I have the thought, señor, that I'll be present at the fiesta."

Diego got into his saddle. "I was thinking of riding to the mission, but have changed my mind," he told her. "I shall return home and rest, so I'll have strength tonight for a great amount of dancing."

She smiled again as she swaggered beside his horse, and waved at him as he rode away.

"It were better that she not be at the pavilion if Zorro pays a visit to the Wizard tonight," Diego muttered to himself as he rode. "She is the sort who might have a dagger in her garter, and no doubt would try to protect her rascal of a father. I have no desire to fight a woman."

The races were over when Diego reached the ranch, and the vaqueros, peon and native workmen had hurried to their huts to rest for a time and then get ready for the evening of feasting and dancing. Under the spreading pepper trees, long tables had been placed, and in the kitchen chattering women were preparing an abundance of food.

Diego held speech with his father and Fray Felipe and outlined his plans. Sergeant Garcia and his six troopers were going among the men, making themselves at home, attacking the various wineskins that were scattered around the place for the use of all.

Diego strolled out through the patio and encountered the burly sergeant.

"Ha, Don Diego, 'tis a pleasure to be with you again," Garcia greeted. "What a fiesta! But 'tis always so at the Vega rancho."

"You and your men are welcome," Diego replied. "Let us hope nothing occurs to mar the festivities. But you and your men will keep the affair orderly."

"You may depend on that, Don Diego. We will prevent the vaqueros from knifing one another over some *señorita*, and the peons and natives from drinking too much wine."

"I delight in such an event, but am always fatigued before the middle of the night," Diego told him. "It is, as you know, my custom to retire long before the others have ceased their merriment."

Garcia bowed to show he understood, and Diego strolled on. He came upon a group of rancho riders who were playing at dice on a serape spread on the ground beneath a tree, and stopped to watch their game. They greeted him affectionately, for it was Diego who posted each year such rich prizes for the athletic contests.

"I am grieved in a measure today," he told one man who had worked for the rancho for years. "I have been told that some of the men are leaving the rancho. I like to see old friends about instead of new faces."

"Some of them have gone mad, I think," the rider replied. "They listen to silly talk."

" 'Tis easy to understand, amigo. That wizard down the road would lead them astray. He is paid to do so — by Marcos Melendez. I pity them if they take service on the Melendez rancho. He serves poor food, assigns men to dirty huts, makes them work themselves and their horses to death."

FOR A moment there was silence. Then a the rider made a gesture of disgust.

"You say Melendez is paying the wizard?"

"To frighten the men from the Vega rancho — si! He is offering employment because he is short-handed. Many men have left his rancho because of bad treatment. The fellow — the wizard, I mean — should be driven away from the vicinity."

"But he has a license, Don Diego, to set up his pavilion. And he is under the protection of the soldiers because of that. As I rode back from the mission this morning, I saw Sergeant Garcia talking to the rogue."

Diego strolled on, and after a time returned to the house as if to rest. In his own room, Bernardo, his mute servant, was waiting.

"Tonight, I shall wear the new clothes I had made especially for this fiesta, Bernardo," Diego said.

Bernardo nodded that he understood. "And another thing ... Zorro rides tonight."

The mute's eyes gleamed. Diego stepped close to him and continued: "Have Zorro's horse, weapons and costume in the usual place an hour before the middle of the night."

Bernardo bobbed his head up and down, grinned, hissed a little to show he was pleased. Then he hurried from the room, and Diego stretched himself upon his couch to rest and mentally check over his plans for the night.

Two hours after nightfall, the fiesta was feverish with activity. Guests crowded around the tables, visited the wineskins, sang and danced, and couples strolled beneath the trees in the orchard and along the lane.

Dressed in his resplendent new clothes, Diego moved languidly among the guests and made them welcome. He had eaten the evening meal in the house with his father, Fray Felipe, and owners of nearby estates.

Now, he danced with a couple of *señoritas*, then watched the others. Inez, the wizard's daughter, had come to the affair as she had promised, and was surrounded by romantic vaqueros who were commencing to glare at one another already.

Diego kept an eye open for Sergeant Garcia and his men, too. The burly Sergeant was boisterous because of the wine he had taken, but his men were keeping fairly sober, under orders to do so, no doubt.

The great bonfires blazed as everybody roistered. Song and laughter rang through the still air. A half moon swam lazily through a sky dotted with fleecy scudding clouds. Women kept carrying great trays of food from the kitchen and putting them upon the tables.

Diego showed himself in all parts of the celebration, but finally began yawning behind his handkerchief and mentioning that he was growing fatigued and sleepy. He smiled at Inez once to give her a thrill of hope, then avoided her.

In the presence of several men, he told his father that he felt a headache coming on and would retire. Sergeant Garcia was one who heard him.

In his own room, he waited for a time and then extinguished the tapers and dressed swiftly in an old, tight-fitting suit of clothes over which his Zorro costume would slip easily. Getting out of the house unseen was easy enough, but he had to be careful as he went past the huts and skirted the orchard to get to the place where Bernardo would be waiting.

He found the faithful Bernardo in a spot of darkness with Zorro's black horse, attire and weapons. Diego slipped the costume on quickly over his other clothing, buckled on his blade, stuck a loaded pistol into his sash, and made sure that his long whip was fastened to the pommel of his saddle.

"Await me here, regardless of how long I may be absent," he instructed Bernardo.

Bernardo made a sound that said he understood. Diego had disappeared into his other self — now, he was Zorro. He rode away slowly through the shadows, jumped the black over a low rock wall, and then put on some measure of speed, circling toward the pavilion of Alfonso the Wizard.

THE WALLS of the pavilion revealed that there was a light inside. Zorro rode cautiously to the small grove of trees, his keen eyes searching the shadows and his ears attuned to every sound. Not for an instant did he forget that the Governor had offered a handsome reward for his capture, nor that his capture would mean pain for his father and possibly the seizure of the Vega estates on a trumped-up charge of treason.

The soft breeze carried to his ears a mumble of voices from the pavilion. Zorro rode up to the back of the establishment and stopped his horse in a dark spot and listened.

"I have done my work well, Señor Melendez," he heard the wizard saying. "I have frightened several of the peons and natives who labor on the Vega rancho. And I have heard through a friend of mine, who is spying around the place, that several of the Vega vaqueros have told the overseer they are leaving to work elsewhere."

"Good, Alfonso! Maintain your pavilion here tomorrow, until the end of the Vega fiesta, then move it down to the main highway at the corner of my rancho and set up there."

"It shall be done as you say, Señor Melendez."

"How I yearn to get my hands on some of the Vega native workmen! They have been going around saying ill things of me. I'll whip their backs into ribbons!"

"Why do you dislike Don Alejandro Vega so much, señor?" Zorro heard the wizard ask.

"Because he is of proud blood and will not make friends with a man like me. Because he talks of my business methods and calls all my little tricks of moneymaking dishonest. And especially because he and some of his high-born friends coddle and pet their workmen, treat them to fine food and wine, let them live in good huts, and permit them to get by with only a little work. How can a man prosper if he treats the swine in that manner? And because Don Alejandro does it, the peons and natives think all rancho owners should do the same. Why are such animals alive if not to be the slaves of their betters?"

As he listened to Melendez, Zorro drew in his breath sharply and felt the blood pounding through his veins. That was the sort of thing against which he had been waging a dangerous war. Melendez was the kind of man he had sworn to punish.

He realized that the task
before him was a delicate one,
that he would have to move and
speak with care to keep from betraying
his identity. He could not reveal too much concern
about the Vega workmen being led astray, for men might wonder at his interest
in the Vegas.

But he could punish Melendez for cruelty to his workmen, and Alfonso for
aiding him. And he could punish the wizard for trying to get his visitors to betray
Zorro — something they could not do, since none knew Zorro's identity. The
wizard would believe, no doubt, that some faithful friend of Zorro had carried
the news to him.

Zorro listened and watched a moment longer, satisfying himself that nobody
was approaching on the road from either direction. The cleared space in front
of the pavilion was moonlit now. Zorro rode to the corner of the square striped
tent and called softly:

"Melendez! Alfonso! Come here to me!" He heard startled exclamations from the two inside, and then the voice of Melendez: "Who calls?"

"Do you want me to shout and reveal things better left secret?" Zorro asked. "Hurry, or you will be caught in a trap."

That alarmed them. Sounds of movement came to Zdrro's ears from the interior of the pavilion, and the flap at the door was tossed back and Marcos Melendez emerged with the wizard a step behind him. They advanced a short distance into the cleared space. Melendez, a tall, brawny man with an evil countenance, glanced around quickly.

"Who are you?" Melendez asked. "Where are you? I can't see you."

ZORRO jumped his black horse out of the shadows and came to a stop within a few feet of them in the moon-drenched open space. They whirled at sound of his approach and beheld the masked mounted man who held a pistol in one hand and a long whip in the other.

"The time has come for your punishment, *señores*," Zorro told them, as they stood before him seemingly half paralyzed with sudden fear. "You, Marcos Melendez, mistreater of other men, must be taught a lesson. And you, Alfonso, self-named wizard, have been in his payment and aiding him, and you had best call upon those mysterious Powers of yours now, to see if they will come to your aid. Did you read, in your crystal ball, what is about to happen to you?"

The wizard was not made of stern stuff. He dropped to his knees and held up his hands in a plea. "Mercy, *señor,* mercy!" he begged. "This man paid me gold — of which I have sore need."

"You will need it to purchase salve for your sores," Zorro informed him.

Melendez tossed up his hands also. "Wait — wait!" he implored. "I'll give you gold!"

"You poor specimens of men seem to think of nothing except gold," Zorro broke in, sternly. "It will purchase many things, Marcos Melendez, but will not keep you from punishment now. You have beaten and kicked and cuffed helpless men, half starved them, driven them to excessive work, treated them like dogs."

The whip lashed out, and Melendez gave a shriek as the lash bit through his clothes and his skin. He turned to run, but Zorro jumped his horse forward, and the long whip lashed out to wrap around the rogue's body and jerk him back to his knees again when Zorro threatened him with the pistol.

Melendez was almost prone on the ground, trying to cover his head with his arms, screeching at the top of his voice for mercy and help. Zorro swung his black horse, and the whip struck Alfonso in turn. The self-styled wizard sprawled face downward and began howling.

"Pack up and get out of this part of the country!" Zorro ordered him. "If you do not, I'll visit you again and use something more deadly than a whip."

"I — I'll go, *Señor* Zorro!" Alfonso promised.

"See that you are away by dawn and do not return." Zorro tuned back to Melendez. "And you, *señor* — I'll be watching over you! Treat your workmen decently. Use polite courtesy to your neighbors."

Melendez howled again. Zorro reined back his horse. And suddenly he heard hoofbeats in the distance, and a harsh voice he knew belonged to Sergeant Garcia:

"Faster! There is trouble of some kind at the pavilion!"

Zorro backed his horse toward the dark spot at the side of the tent.

"Say nothing of my presence, or I'll pistol you!" he warned the pair on the ground.

He was back in the spot of darkness now. His whip was coiled and fastened to the pommel of his saddle, but he held the pistol ready. There had not been time to get away without riding through the moonlight, and he wanted to learn, if possible whether Garcia and the soldiers had any deal with Alfonso.

Zorro's eyes widened slightly, as the riders came into the moonlight and turned off the road toward the pavilion. Garcia had one of his troopers with him, and riding behind the trooper and clinging to him was the girl Inez.

"What have we here?" the sergeant thundered, as the riders stopped.

Melendez and Alfonso staggered to their feet, but neither gave explanation, aware of Zorro's nearness and fearful of the pistol he held.

"Speak!" Garcia roared. "Have you lost your tongues? Ha! You have been whipped. So this Zorro has been at you, eh? You, Alfonso, dolt and ass! I paid you to get me information concerning Zorro, and you let him come here and whip you. And you, Melendez! Tell me what happened! You won't speak? Ha! That means Zorro is near and you are afraid of a pistol shot."

SERGEANT GARCIA turned to his trooper. "Quick, Pedro! Dump that pretty baggage on the ground and get out your pistol! You, *Señor* Alfonso — keep this girl of yours at home. She is a menace. She had half the vaqueros at the celebration at one another's throats. She is a worthless flirt, and I brought her home to prevent carnage."

Inez was dumped to the ground, and her language was not that of a tenderly-reared *señorita* as she picked herself up and ran toward the pavilion.

More hoof beats thundered in rapid approach, and Sergeant Garcia and his trooper, forgetting Zorro for an instant, tuned to see who was approaching.

Half a score of wild vaqueros came rushing toward the pavilion with their ponies at a run. They skidded their mounts to a stop around the sergeant and trooper.

"What have you done with the *señorita*?" one demanded of Garcia. "What right had you to carry her away? We'll take her back to the fiesta!"

"Hold!" Garcia thundered at them, "She was causing sore trouble amongst you. I want no knifing over a wench. And attend me! Zorro has just been here. He has whipped these two men. After him, all of you! There is a reward."

Zorro knew this was the moment for swift retreat. He swung his black horse and touched with his spurs. Across a wide patch of bright moonlight he rode, the hoofs of the black spurning the ground. Zorro knew no trooper or Vaquero could catch him.

"Buenas noches, señores!" he shouted at them.

They yelled and began the futile pursuit. Zorro led them astray, dodged them, let them scatter in useless hunting as he returned by a circuitous route to the spot where Bernardo was waiting.

He sprang from his saddle, stripped off his Zorro costume and dropped his weapons. "Hide everything as usual, Bernardo," he ordered.

A moment later, Diego Vega was striding through the shadows. The merriment was at its height. Great platters had been emptied of food and empty wineskins were upon the ground. But the musicians were still playing and couples were dancing.

Zorro got into the house unseen and hurried to his own rooms. He stripped off the old clothes he had been wearing and adorned himself quickly in his fancy attire. Then he made his way to the big main room, where his father and Fray Felipe were sipping wine and talking to other rancho owners.

"My headache is gone," he explained, yawning behind his scented handkerchief. "I shall look at the fun for a time, and perhaps dance once with some *señorita*."

He was smiling slightly as he glanced at Fray Felipe and his father. And they understood that everything had gone well.

Zorro Fights with Fire

*Don Diego pits himself against an unscrupulous judge —
and his villainous, scheming partner!*

IN HIS usual manner, Diego Vega entered the tavern on the plaza at Reina de
Los Angeles that afternoon after the siesta hour. He seldom drank a goblet
of wine there, having much better vintage in his father's house. And on each
visit his sole errand seemed to be the purchase of a jar of crystallized honey, of
which the tavern keeper made a specialty and none of which was to be found
in the Vega warehouse.

None guessed that these visits, which threw the keeper of the tavern into a
sort of rapture, since the presence of a Vega in his establishment gave it prestige,
had another motive. For none knew that Diego Vega, scion of a proud and
wealthy family and famous for his indolence and perpetual fatigue, was at other
times the Senor Zorro who rode the highways with a mask hiding his face and
laughed at the troopers who sought to catch and hang him.

Visiting the tavern to get honey and have a bit of gossip with the fat landlord,
gave Diego a chance to attune his keen ears to the talk of men in the big main
room as they ate, drank and gambled with dice or cards. And what Diego learned,
Zorro knew also, and often turned the knowledge to his own use.

The fat tavern keeper bowed with what grace he could, considering his
obesity, and hastily got the jar of honey Diego desired. Meanwhile, Diego
glanced around the room, which was in something of an uproar.

At the end of a long table sat a corpulent man who seemed to be the center
of attraction. Diego observed that he wore too many jeweled rings, that his

*Zorro ordered Big Carlos
to use the torch*

clothing was too ornate for good taste, and that his voice was loud to the point of being obnoxious. With a languid gesture, he indicated the stranger to the tavern keeper.

"That is Pedro Ortiz, Don Diego," the tavern man whispered. "He is a wealthy buyer of wool. I understand the men are shearing at your family's rancho near San Gabriel now, and that other rancho owners are shearing also. No doubt this Pedro Ortiz will desire to purchase many a fleece for shipment by cart to the market."

"Our overseer, Juan Cassara, attends to such details," Diego mentioned. "I am thankful that neither my father nor I have to deal with that Ortiz fellow. There is something about him that is almost repulsive.

"He brings a profit to my house, yet I wish I could have the same profit from a man of another sort," the tavern man admitted. "He boasts too much, is vulgar in his speech, and orders my servants around as if they were swine."

"Indeed?" Diego's brows lifted slightly. "Ah, well, many such travel up and down the highway, and there is nothing we can do to relieve the situation.

As a padre once told me, some offshoots of Adam grow on a crooked limb."

Diego yawned, brushed a scented silk handkerchief across his nostrils, picked up the jar of honey he had purchased and turned toward the door.

FROM the plaza outside came sounds of a sudden tumult. Men were shouting, whips were cracking, there were screams of rage. And Diego could hear the brazen voice of Sergeant Manuel Garcia, head of the soldiery in Reina de Los Angeles during the absence of his superior officer:

"Drive the dogs on to the barracks and put them into cells! I'll notify Senor José Villesca, our *magistrado*!"

Diego sauntered toward the door with the fat tavern keeper at his heels. Others in the big room got up from benches and stools to go to the windows and look out, Pedro Ortiz among them.

"Ha! 'Tis but a bunch of drunken sheepshearers the good troopers are herding to jail," Ortiz announced. "The *magistrado* no doubt will fine them all, and they will have to work out their fines if they have no money. 'Tis too often so! I wait to buy wool, and those rascals drink and do not shear, and so I am delayed in my business."

Diego had passed through the door to view the scene in the plaza. Several mounted troopers were driving the prisoners, who had their wrists tied behind their backs and were also fastened together with ropes. Sergeant Garcia rode behind, shouting orders.

Diego's eyes bulged. Among the prisoners, all of whom gave evidence of having participated in a debauch, were several peons and natives who worked for the Vega rancho.

Diego could not understand that. The rancho hands drank a little thin wine at times, when it was given them, but he never had known them to become wildly intoxicated. Almost all these prisoners were raving like madmen, staggering and making grotesque gestures.

A horseman came clattering down the highway to pull up in front of the tavern, spring out of his saddle, and hurry forward. He was Juan Cassara, the dependable overseer of the Vega rancho.

"Don Diego, a word with you," Cassara begged.

Diego stepped aside with him.

"There is something wrong, Don Diego," Cassara whispered. "Some of those prisoners are our men. They never have been in trouble before. I have heard that shearers from several ranchos were missing from their huts last night for a time. They returned mad with intoxication before dawn. There were several bad fights, and the soldiers were sent for."

"Ride quickly to our house and tell my father of this," Diego instructed.

Cassara mounted and rode away. Diego looked after the troopers and their prisoners. They were almost to the barracks now. They would be herded into filthy cells, and in the morning José Villesca, the local *magistrado,* would hold, court and no doubt punish the miscreants severely. Diego was about to start for home, sauntering in his usual indolent manner, when another horseman came to the tavern and dismounted. He was José Villesca, the *maqistrado.*

"Ah, Don Diego, a happy meeting!" Villesca greeted, bowing and almost fawning.

"For you, no doubt, senor," Diego observed.

"I have just been informed of this business. After the usual custom, I would hold court in the morning. But I have planned to ride to San Juan Capistrano with some friends during the cool of the night. So I will hold court at sundown today. It will be only a short business. Peons and natives, crazed with drink — such are a menace."

Diego did not like Villesca, who had attained his position by bribery, as everybody knew. His court scarcely was one of justice. So Diego merely bowed slightly, yawned and brushed his nostrils with his handkerchief in a significant manner, and turned away to go home.

When he had gone some distance and knew he would not be observed by those in front of the tavern, he quickened his stride. At the house, he entered through the patio, and could hear Juan Cassara's voice as he went into the main room.

"I got it from one of the men, Don Alejandro," the overseer was telling Diego's father. "Word was passed around that a wealthy man who admired them and felt sorry for men who had to work so hard, would provide free drink. They were told to go to the old abandoned storehouse on the Tres Piños rancho, quietly and without being seen."

"Even so, I fail to understand," Don Alejandro said. "The men have had wine before."

"But 'tis not wine, Don Alejandro. It is some sort of queer spirit distilled from cactus juice. It makes a man mad, so mad he does not know what he is doing or saying. It is not a liquor to drink, but a poison!'

"But what can be behind it?" Don Alejandro asked, as Diego stopped at the end of the long table beside which his father was sitting.

"That is something to be learned," Cassara replied. "As it is now, several of our best workers, the sheep-shearers we need sorely, are in the jail and will be tried tomorrow."

"Tonight," Diego corrected, and told what the *magistrodo* had said to him.

Don Alejandro looked startled. "So they will be tried this evening? There is something behind this, *si*! And it is plain to me that José Villesca is involved in the affair in some manner — which you may be sure will be to his profit. Cassara, get some rest and eat, and we'll attend this trial."

CASSARA bowed and hurried toward the kitchen, and Diego sat across the table from his father.

"Do you have any idea regarding this, my son?" Don Alejandro asked.

"At the tavern, I saw a man named Pedro Ortiz, who poses as a wool buyer," Diego replied. "I did not like him."

"Wool buyers are always around at such a time and they seldom are the sort of men we would like," his father remarked. "But Cassara attends to such things for us."

"There were seventeen prisoners, Father, and six of them were our men," fleigo said. "José Villesca will punish them all with fines which they will not be able to pay."

"And what will follow then, my son? I'll tell you," Don Alejandro explained. *"If* there was public work, they would be compelled to work out their fines. But the roads have recently been repaired, and there is no public building being done. And so they will be sold into peonage for the amount of their fines, and whoever pays the fines will be entitled to take twice the amount from them in poorly paid service."

"It is in my mind to attend the trial with you and Juan Cassara," Diego said. He lowered his voice: "This may be a matter to concern Senor Zorro and enlist his activities."

Diego walked to the barracks, where court was held in a large room, between his father and Juan Cassara. At the door, they met the aged Fray Felipe, the Franciscan attached to the chapel, and one of the men who knew Diego was Zorro.

"I have talked to several of the unfortunates," the padre told them. "They have said that a huge fellow known only as Big Carlos invited them to the old warehouse and gave them the liquor. Who is behind this Big Carlos, I do not know."

Inside the courtroom, Cassara sat in the rear, but Don Alejandro, Diego and the padre were ushered to a reserved front bench. José Villesca took his position, and Sergeant Garcia and his troopers ushered in the seventeen prisoners.

Diego could tell at a glance that all had been ill. They acted as if half dazed, as if the effects of the strong cactus juice liquor had not yet left their systems.

Garcia's testimony was short and official:

"I received news of trouble and hurried out to the rancho district with some of my men. These fellows were wild with drink. They were fighting and even tried to set fire to a sheep-shearing shed. I seized them all and brought them in to the barracks."

José Villesca sighed and straightened. "An ordinary case," he judged. "Excessive drinking and rioting must be curbed, especially among the peons and natives. How did they get the liquor; Sergeant Garcia? I understand they had not yet received pay for their labor of sheep-shearing."

"Some fellow gave the liquor to them, I have heard."

"Whether it was given them or whether they bought it makes not the slightest difference," Villesca stated. "They are guilty of drunkenness, creating a disturbance, fighting and attempting to destroy private property. It is time an example was made. I fine each of these men a gold piece."

A chorus of moans came from the luckless seventeen. Few of them had more than a couple of small coins, and it would mean at least a couple of years of steady labor for them to earn a gold piece.

"If they cannot pay immediately," Viilesca continued, "I make them liable to indenture and peonage, and will indent them to any man who desires to pay their fines into the coffers of the state, the man so doing being allowed to work them at usual wages until he has received through their services twice the amount of the fines advanced by hint"

Another chorus of groans came from the men thus being sold into peonage. Many were married and had children, and they might be driven away like cattle to some far rancho or settlement.

From the rear of the courtroom, Pedro Ortiz strode forward to address the *magistrado*.

"May it please you, senor, I am owner of a plantation near Monterey," Ortiz said. *"I* will take all seventeen of these men into peonage and pay their fines, I feel sure they will be good workmen."

"I thank you, Senor Ortiz. So be it," Villesca decided. "We will transact the affair at my residence in two hours' time. Please be prompt, for I am to leave for San Juan Capistrano at an early hour tonight."

Don Alejandro Vega was quickly upon his feet. "Not so fast!" he barked, angrily. "I would say to the *magistrado* that this proceeding has odor of having been prearranged. Six of the prisoners are workers on my own rancho, and I will pay their fines myself and so gain their release."

"It irks me, Don Alejandro, that you did not speak sooner," Villesca told him in an oily voice. "Senor Ortiz made the first offer, and the men go to him. I have made the decision, and it cannot be changed."

"A man who acts as a *magistrado* should know at least something of the law," Don Alejandro replied. "You will find, if you care to look into it, that the employer of men in such circumstances as these, has one full day in which to decide whether he will pay their fines and has first claim to their services under the act of peonage."

"Much as I dislike to do so, Don Alejandro Vega, I must make the decision that this case has been disposed of. You can easily get workers to take the places of your six, no doubt."

"There are some circumstances of this affair that should be investigated," Don Alejandro said. "This is not a trial, but a farce. I shall report this affair to the Governor unless there is more justice shown here."

VILLESCA'S face paled. "That is your privilege, Don Alejandro," he replied. "However, my decision stands." He arose and held up his hand. "Court is adjourned."

Pedro Ortiz called out, "Sergeant Garcia, kindly, lodge the seventeen in your barracks at my expense until tomorrow. I'll arrange to have them sent to Monterey."

"It shall be done, Senor Ortiz."

The troopers herded the luckless ones back to the cell room, and the spectators began leaving the courtroom.

Out In the open, Juan Cassara whispered to Don Alejandro, Diego and Fray Felipe: "I know the Monterey district well, and never heard of an Ortiz rancho. That rogue will sell his clairm to some ship owner. He is recruiting for ships, no doubt. They will, be worked to death, beaten — "

"Something must he done," Don Alejandro broke in. "Ride back to the rancho, Cassara, and proceed with the sheep-shearing. I may come out tomorrow."

As Cassara hurried away, Sergeant Garcia approached Don Alejandro and saluted. "Please understand, Don Alejandro, that I only did my duty," he said. "I regret some of the men were your workmen."

"Can nothing be done about the man who gave them the liquor?"

"The fellow they call Big Carlos? There is no law against giving liquor to men. Big Carlos is working for someone, in my opinion. This smells of a plot. But 1 — my hands are tied."

"I do not hold you to blame," Don Alejandro said.

The sergeant hurried after his men. Diego walked with his father and the padre to the corner of the plaza.

"The plot is plain," Diego said, in low tones. "The men were made drunk purposely. They were arrested legally, but fined ten limes the usual amount and sold into peonage. Pedro Ortiz is behind the plot, which also concerns Villesca, of course. He must be paying Villesca a pretty price per man to make the rascal of a *magistrado* be insolent to my father. Ortiz, of course, will drive the men to Monterey and sell them into slavery to ship owners, and, they will 'be seafaring slaves until they die."

"What can be done?" Don Alejandro asked. "Two of those men of ours have been on the rancho for years. They have families. They have never been in trouble before."

Diego glanced around cautiously. "I think, my Father, and you, padre, that this is something in which Senor Zorro should concern himself," he muttered,

It was a dark, misty night, which suited Zorro's purpose. He rode his black horse around the pueblo and approached the house of José Villesca from the rear. In his black clothes and wearing the black mask, Zorro scarcely could be seen. His blade was at his side, his pistol in his sash, and the long whip he often used to punish oppressors was attached to the pommel of his saddle.

He had left his father's house about an hour before, going to the hidden place where his mute servant, Bernardo, had horse, costume and weapons ready. Soon after he had left, Fray Felipe had arrived there in haste, too late to catch him.

"I had speech with Sergeant Garcia," the padre told Don Alejandro. "I convinced him he should do something. He has no power to prohibit this Big Carlos from giving the men liquor. But he agreed to take two troopers and go to the abandoned warehouse and loiter around there, which will scare men away if more free liquor is to be given out tonight. It was in my mind that the affair would be repeated so Ortiz would get more slaves."

"But Diego has gone already. Zorro is riding!" Don Alejandro said. "No doubt he will visit the warehouse. He did not tell me his plans. If he runs into the troopers, he will be in peril."

"I am quite sure that Zorro always rides with his eyes open," the padre replied. "Let us hope for the best."

BEHIND the Villesca house, Zorro dismounted and tied his horse to a stunted tree. Through the swirling mist and blackness of the night, he went forward cautiously.

Villesca was a widower who lived alone save, for a peon and his wife, who acted as servants but did not sleep in the house. Zorro doubted that either of the servants would be in the place now if Villesca had private dealings with Pedro Ortiz.

Through a window over which the curtains had not been drawn too carefully, Zorro peered into the main room of the house. José Villesca and Pedro Ortiz were sitting at a table with goblets of wine before them. On the table was a small pile of gold coins.

Getting into the house presented no difficulty, for a rear door was unlatched. Once inside, Zorro went forward with extreme caution, pistol held ready. He could hear the voices of the men in the main room as he went silently along the hall. Standing in the dark hallway, he could glance through the partially-open door and view the scene.

"The papers are in order, Senor Villesca, so you may pocket my gold," Ortiz was saying. "'Tis a pretty plot. But what if that old fire-eater, Don Alejandro Vega, gets you into trouble with the Governor?"

"He will not," Villesca answered. "In the first place, the Governor and I understand each other in such deals as this. He gets his percentage. And in the second place the Vegas irk the Governor exceedingly, since they have the quaint idea that all public officials should be scrupulously honest."

Ortiz laughed. "There will be another haul tonight, and no doubt a larger one," he said. "I'll contrive to have Big Carlos dish out the cactus liquor he distills while you are on your journey, and the jail will be full when you return. Then you may hold a private session of court, assess the fines, and I'll take the men over, giving you so much per head as tonight."

"But, after this haul, will not the peons and natives be cautious?"

Ortlz laughed again. "Not so. You do not understand human nature, Senor Villesca. They will think the men arrested were weaklings unable to take such potent liquor, and believe that they can stand up under it."

"I will start for San Juan Capistrano inside the hour," Villesca said. "The affair will blow over with me gone."

"And there will be no ill after effects for you," Ortiz promised. "I shall rush the men to Monterey and herd them aboard ships. They will not know that the shipping company for which they slave is two-thirds owned by the Governor himself. We are both safe, Senor Villesca, except for any unpleasantness you may encounter here."

It was Villesca's time to laugh. "For the gold I am getting, I can endure the unpleasantness," he replied.

Zorro's rage had been mounting as he listened just outside the door. Suddenly he strode through it, his pistol held in a menacing manner.

"Look this way, senores!" he said.

Half getting out of their chairs, their hands flat upon the table between them, Villesca and Ortiz jerked their heads around to face him. They saw the masked man dressed entirely in black; saw his menacing weapon and his eyes glittering through the slits in his mask.

"'Tis a robber!" Ortiz said, his hand straying toward the gold coins on the table.

"'Tis Senor Zorro," Vlllesca corrected. "He has been described to me often."

"Do not move, senores, if you wish to live," Zorro told them. "After listening to your talk, it irks me to delay slaying you both. Deliberate enslavers of men!"

"Perhaps — that is — if you wish a share of the gold — " Ortiz stammered.

"So you would make me a partner in your infamous dealings?" Zorro asked.

Menacing with his pistol, he drove them back against the wall, where they stood side by side with their hands held high. With his own left hand, Zorro swept the gold coins from the table, scattering them around the room.

"Your plot is known and your words were overheard," Zorro told them. "Senor Ortiz, be gone from Reina de Los Angeles before dawn, and do not return, else your life will be forfeit.' As for you, José Villesca, sit you at that table now and write your resignation as *magistrado* and hand it to me.

"Write also an order to Sergeant Garcia, at the barracks, that you have remitted the fines of those seventeen men and that he is to release them immediately. At once, senor! If you do not, you will soon sprawl in a pool of your own blood on this expensive rug, which no doubt was purchased with stolen money."

ORTIZ, his fat body a-tremble, remained standing against the wall. Villesca went to the table when Zorro gestured again with the pistol. His hands shook as he wrote what Zorro had demanded.

"It may be in your mind, Senor Villesca, to repudiate later what you write now," Zorro hinted. "I gather as much from your lack of protest at this moment. If you do so, I shall visit you again, and that visit will be the last you will receive from any man. Be assured of that! If more sheep-shearers are arrested tonight because of the fiery liquor Big Carlos gives them, I am sure the new *magistrado* who takes your place will deal kindly with them, and justly, and not seek to make an illegal profit from their plight."

Zorro watched carefully while Villesca wrote, then motioned for him to return to the wall. Stepping forward, Zorro read the papers swiftly and stuffed them into his sash. He backed toward the door through which he had entered the room.

"It often has been said that Zorro works alone, that no man aids him," he told the pair. "Ba not too sure of that! You will remain in this room for at least half of one hour after I have departed. If you try to emerge sooner, you may meet with disaster. If you doubt it, make the trial and learn."

He darted from the room, ran the length of the hallway and let himself out of the house. A moment later, he had reached his black horse and was in the saddle again.

Through the swirling mist, he rode to the barracks, before which torches were burning in wall sockets, and where one lonely guard yawned as he marched back and forth in front of the entrance. Zorro appeared to the guard suddenly out of the night.

"Drop your musket!" he ordered.

Caught off guard, the frightened trooper obeyed.

"I mean no harm to you, senor. Here are two documents for you to put into the hands of Sergeant Garcia immediately. He tossed the documents at the guard.

"But the sergeant and a couple of men have gone away," the guard reported.

"See that Garcia gets the documents the moment he returns, then. It is an official matter," Zorro told him. "One of those documents calls for the release of the seventeen men who were found guilty at dusk. If the release is not made at once, your superiors may cause you serious trouble. Tell Garcia as much."

"And you?" the guard asked.

"I am Zorro, as you may have guessed. But you will not claim a reward for my capture tonight. Make a move toward your musket, and I'll pistol you!"

Zorro touched with his spurs, and the big black horse plunged into the swirls of mist and was gone from the small spots of flickering light cast by the torches.

Zorro left the highway a short distance from the town and followed a cattle trail over the sloping hills. He knew the old work so hard, would provide free drink. They were told to go to the old abandoned storehouse on the Tres Piños rancho well, though it had been cut into three properties in recent years and had other names. And he knew the location of the old tumbledown ware-house, no longer in legitimate use.

When he was near the warehouse, he rode off the cattle trail and proceeded slowly through a sea of short brush; it was green at this season of the year and his passage created little sound. From the crest of a low hill, he looked down upon the old building.

Zorro knew it was constructed of adobe and had heavy wooden beams and a wooden floor that had been cured and dried through the years. Now a torch burned in front of the door, and on the air was an odor that indicated a still was being run either inside the building or behind it.

But what startled Zorro most was the presence of three horses in front of the place in the light of the torch. Zorro could see their trappings and knew they were the mounts of Sergeant Garcia and two of his troopers. So this was where the burly sergeant had come!

SLOWLY, cautiously, Zorro rode down the slope and neared the old building. He could see now that a still was in use at the rear of the warehouse, and the odor of its cooking was on the damp air. Stopping behind a clump of thick brush, Zorro watched and listened. He could hear voices plainly.

"It is none of my business, Big Carlos, as you are called, if you make this foul liquor we have tasted and give it gratis to peons and natives," Zorro could hear Garcia saying. "There is no law against it at this time, though there should be. But it is my business to arrest and take in for trial any man who drinks the stuff and gets crazy and creates a disturbance!'

"None have come tonight," Big Carlos replied.

"Because they have seen me and my troopers in the neighborhood, that is why."

"Have another mug, sergeant, since it is a damp night."

"No more. The stuff is vile. I'll ride on with my men to the mission and drink a little real wine. But I'll be coming back to see if you have any drunken guests."

"Why should you care, sergeant, if the poor devils drink themselves out of an hour or two of their misery?" Big Carlos asked.

"Personally, I do not care if they drink themselves into their graves," Garcia replied. "But the old padre at Reina de Los Angeles has been after me about it. I promised him to look in upon you tonight. I have done so."

Zorro saw Garcia and his two troopers emerge from the building. Behind them walked a huge man who was undoubtedly Big Carlos.

"One thing intrigues me," Zorro heard Garcia say as he got into his saddle. "Who is behind all this affair? What man is paying you to make the stuff and give it away?"

"I have promised not to disclose his identity, sergeant. Just let us say that he is a man who feels sorry for the hardworking peons and natives."

"You may say it, but I think otherwise," Garcia replied. "However, it is none of my business unless a complaint is made by some man of standing. I shall ride on to the mission. No doubt men will come creeping out of the brush the moment my back is turned. Warn them, Big Carlos, not to create a disturbance or destroy property while in their cups. If they do, they will find themselves sold into peonage."

The sergeant and his troopers touched with their spurs and rode away through the misty night, going toward the highway to follow it to the mission. Zorro heard Big Carlos laugh as he turned back into the building.

Zorro was cautious as he neared the place. Sounds of the hoofbeats of the soldiers' mounts died away in the distance. Zorro gave them time to get to the highway, then urged his horse to another clump of brush and dismounted and tied him there.

As he went forward afoot, he held his pistol in his left hand and his long whip in his right. He took up a position at the corner of the building where light from the torch would reveal him, and called:

"Carlos! Big Carlos!"

The huge man waddled through the doorway almost immediately. "Who calls?" he demanded.

"I am over here."

Big Carlos turned, stiffened, and his eyes bulged. He saw the masked man dressed in black, and light from the torch danced in reflection from the silver mountings of the menacing pistol. Nor did Big Carlos fail to see the whip that was swinging lightly through the air and causing a sibilant sound that made the cold shivers run up and down his spine.

"Who — what — " Carlos mouthed.

"I am Zorro!"

"But what — what do you want?"

"I know all about Pedro Ortiz's dealings, you dog. I know why you make cactus liquor and give it to peons and natives. I have dealt with Ortiz and the rascal of a *magistrado*. And now I am here to deal with you."

"I only work for hire."

"There is better work for a man," Zorro told him. "You know what you have been doing. You have helped Ortiz in his scheme to make hopeless slaves of men. Approach and kneel before me, with your broad back toward me. We'll see how my whip can cut through your tough hide and into your fat body."

"The soldiers have been here — "

"I saw them."

"They may return and catch you. I have heard there is a big reward — "

"Do as I say, or you'll feel the hot impact of a pistol ball tearing into your body!"

"Throw the pistol aside, and I'll break you with my bare hands!" Carlos raged.

"No doubt you could do it," Zorro admitted. "But in the work I am doing I must hold an advantage. You do not merit consideration such as an honest man would receive — or even a half-honest rogue. You are a beast and a fiend, Big Carlos! How would you like to be sold into peonage? Yet you help send other men into that state. Come forward!"

Big Carlos lumbered forward like a huge bear, his hands hanging at his sides, his head bent forward, eyes agleam. Suddenly he rushed, his arms coming up, his fingers curved into claws that reached for Zorro's throat.

BUT ZORRO had been watching for a move like that. He darted quickly to one side, and the whip hissed as it slashed through the air. The lash struck Carlos as he passed, cutting deeply, and the big man's cry was one of mingled rage and pain.

Before Big Carlos could regain his balance and charge back, the whip coiled around his neck and jerked him off his feet. Then the lash began singing as Zorro struck repeatedly, keeping Big Carlos on the ground to take his punishment.

"Mercy, Senor Zorro!" the rogue began crying. "I was but making a living —"

"There are better ways to make one. It is not necessary to degrade your fellow men."

"Why not punish the others?"

"I have punished Ortiz where it will hurt him most, in his purse. I have punished the dishonest *magistrado* also by compelling him to resign his post. Now get upon your feet and lead the way into the warehouse."

Sobbing, Big Carlos got painfully upon his feet and lurched toward the door.

"Remember the pistol I hold," Zorro warned, as he coiled his whip. "Do not try treachery again. Inside with you!"

A torch burned inside the old building, too. Zorro saw two casks of the cactus liquor, and an old table and bench half drenched with it.

"Take the torch out of its socket," Zorro ordered. "Touch it to the casks. Quickly!"

"They will burn like — "

"So I know!" Zorro interrupted. "Act quickly!"

Big Carlos got the torch and held it against the side of one of the casks. Liquor that had seeped caught the flame, and fire spread rapidly.

"The table and bench," Zorro ordered. They caught quickly also. The first cask was starting to burn, and the second would catch soon. Flames were leaping already, reaching for the dry beams and eating at the wooden flooring.

"Outside, now, to your still!" Zorro commanded.

They went outside and to the rear of the building. Beside the still was a cask being filled slowly. At Zorro's order, Big Carlos used the torch there.

Zorro then drove him around to the side of the building. The beams had caught fire and the floor was burning. Clouds of black smoke rolled from the structure through the door and the roof and drifted through the light of the flames.

"Be glad I do not pistol you!" Zorro told Big Carlos. "And do not remain in this vicinity. If you do, I shall learn of it, and my next visit to you will be more unpleasant."

Heat from the flames was becoming unbearable, and Zorro started a slow retreat. There was an explosion inside; rocketing lances of sparks soared through the holes in the roof and flashed toward the sky. Then above the roar of the flames Zorro heard the sudden thunder of hoofbeats.

HE TURNED and ran behind the clump of brush, to the place where he had left his horse. Into the cleared space in front of the warehouse dashed Sergeant Garcia and his two troopers. Garcia was shouting as Big Carlos ran toward him, holding up his hands and yelling at the top of his voice that Zorro had been there.

As he settled in his saddle, Zorro saw Garcia spurring in his direction, the troopers behind him. Zorro rode madly out of the brush, and the light from the burning building revealed him.

Pistols exploded behind him, but no bullet came dangerously near. Zorro held his own fire. He bent low in his saddle and rode. Away from the bright light of the fire, he turned into a narrow trail he knew, and which forked after he had ridden only a short distance.

He had ridden around this country as a boy and knew trails and hiding places Garcia and his troopers had not discovered. He left the pursuit a distance behind, then turned into a cattle path where the traveling was less dangerous.

He knew now that he had dodged the peril Garcia and the troopers had lost the trail, and Zorro had been spared the necessity of fighting with them.

Now he had only to ride cautiously to the town, deliver his horse, weapons and costume to Bernardo, his loyal mute peon servant, and get into his father's house without being seen, a thing he had done often before. He felt a glow of satisfaction from work well done.

Gold for a Tyrant

**When taxation becomes extortion, the fighting hidalgo
dons his black cloak of battle!**

IT WAS A bright morning in Reina de Los Angeles, with a soft breeze blowing in from the distant sea. Diego Vega enjoyed the day as he strolled languidly toward the plaza, and the little chapel, for a talk with Fray Felipe, his confessor and friend of the Vega family.

Diego held a perfumed handkerchief to his nostrils as several vaqueros galloped up, the hoofs of their spirited mounts lifting clouds of sandy dust. He was known to be fastidious. Some whispered that he bordered on the effeminate. But those who whispered did not know that Diego Vega, heir to wealth, an apparent fop, was also Senor Zorro, the masked daredevil who rode the highways to right the wrongs of the downtrodden.

Diego went on leisurely, only to curl his lips in an expression of disgust as a long line of lumbering oxen-drawn carts appeared, creating new dust clouds. Diego was coughing when he finally was able to get out of the drifting dust. But it was the busy season in the rancho district, and it was a great rancho that poured new wealth into the coffers of the Vega family.

"Enough discomfort for one day," Diego muttered. "I'll soothe my nerves as I listen to Fray Felipe."

As he neared the tavern he heard a man bewailing his unjust fate, heard raucous laughter, the swish of a whip and a howl of pain. A short, obese man in rather expensive clothing yet in poor taste stood in front of the tavern, a whip in his hand. Kneeling before him was a barefooted peon, his arms wrapped

"Keep your distance!"
Zorro warned

around his head for protection from the whip. Off to one side four strangers to Diego held an ewe with a thong about its neck.

"Enough of this!" the man with the whip shouted to the peon. "I desire no more argument. Be on your way, or this whip will cut the skin from your back in ribbons!"

"Have mercy, senor," the peon screeched. "The ewe is all I have in the world."

"You err," the other man replied. "You do not have the ewe. It is now the property of His Excellency, the Governor. You have not paid your tax, so we

335

take your ewe. And for trying to evade payment of this just tax, I shall ask the magistrado to sell you into peonage for one month, unless you pay a fine. Since you had no money for taxes, you have none with which to pay a fine; hence you will work out double the amount in peonage."

"My wife and children will starve — "

"The sufferings of your wife and brats do not interest me."

Diego stopped beside the tavern keeper, who stood in his doorway.

"Who is the man who threatens the poor fellow?" Diego asked.

"He is Carlos Barbosa, a new tax gatherer sent by the Governor from Monterey. Those other fellows are his assistants. Never have I seen a tax gatherer work more thoroughly. He does more than take the shirt off a man's back—he takes the hide beneath it."

"The peon has worked on our rancho," Diego explained. "He is a worthy fellow."

The peon looked up. "Don Diego!" he cried. "Help me, Don Diego!"

AS DIEGO shuffled forward in his resplendent garb, the tax gatherer turned his head quickly. "What is this tumult, senor?" Diego asked Barbosa.

"The rascal owes taxes, and I am gathering them, senor. He declared he had no property, and I find he had an ewe about to yean."

"Tell him, Don Diego, that your august father gave me the ewe," the peon begged.

"That is true," Diego said.

"The start of a flock!" the tax gatherer said, laughing boisterously. "We should watch out, Don Diego, or some of these fellows will be owning our fine ranchos."

"How much is the tax?" Diego asked. "It would have been half a peso. But because he hid his property, the tax is doubled."

Diego turned to the peon. "Why did you hide the fact that you owned an ewe?" he asked.

"It is all I have, Don Diego. And I did not have a coin with which to pay."

Diego took a coin from his pocket and tossed it to Barbosa.

"Here is thrice your tax, senor. Take it, and give this man his ewe."

Barbosa pocketed the money. "As you say, Don Diego. But be soft with one of his ilk, and thousands will beg mercy, and then where will the taxes come from? The Governor is in sore need of taxes. Maintaining a position of state is expensive."

"I understand," Diego interrupted. He faced the peon. "Take your ewe, and go home," he ordered. "Your tax has been paid."

"Ah — but one moment!" Barbosa said. "What now?" Diego raised his brows slightly.

"The matter of the tax is settled, Don Dego. But there remains the criminal act of refusing to declare property. For that, the rascal must be jailed and fined. No doubt the fine will be a large one, and he will go into peonage to work out its double worth."

Diego's eyes glittered. "Can you not overlook such a little thing at this time?"

"I must enforce the laws, Don Diego."

"It would mean that the man must work for months for no pay. His family will have difficulty — "

"Bah! Such families scourge the land!"

"Why are you so bitter?"

Carlos Barbosa stepped nearer and lowered his voice. "Such men are born to be exploited by us, by men of the upper classes. Whenever I bring a fellow to justice, I get a percentage of the fine." He laughed lightly.

That sent a surge of resentment through Diego. "It is my advice to you, senor, to take this man before the magistrado immediately," he said. "I intend to pay his fine, whatever it is, and have him in peonage to me."

"I can see you are an excellent business man, Don Diego! Put him on your rancho with a good overseer who does not spare the whip, and you will get the worth of your money."

DIEGO BRUSHED the scented handkerchief across his nostrils again.

"It is my intention to remit the deed of peonage to him and let him attend to his own affairs," he replied. "Take the man to the magistrado immediately."

"I am handling this affair; Don Diego. I am an official."

"Have you ever heard of the power of the Vega family?" Diego asked him.

"I have, senor. And have you ever heard of the power of His Excellency, the Governor?"

"I have heard of many things concerning the Governor," Diego replied. "I have even heard how the hidalgos from one end of Alta California to the other have petitioned the Viceroy in Mexico for the Governor's removal — which undoubtedly will occur. It is natural for His Excellency, and His Excellency's henchmen, to grasp all they can before that comes to pass."

"You dare speak treason?"

"Were it treason," Diego declared, "the Governor would not dare assert it to be such. Let us go to the barracks and have this man tried. He will walk beside me. Have your men bring along the ewe, and hold their pistols ready. A tired, hard-working peon and an ewe about to yean — dangerous things that should be under the muzzles of pistols always."

"We go to the barracks, Don Diego, but I will make a report of the occurrence to Monterey."

"Oh, certainly, senor! Send your report by a swift courier. I would not be in your boots, senor, for half the world."

"And why not?"

"I was thinking of the fellow who calls himself Senor Zorro. He attends to affairs like this. No doubt this cruelty of yours will be reported to him."

"Ha! If the rogue shows himself in my neighborhood, I will earn the Governor's reward for his capture! Don Diego, I do not like your words and attitude."

"That pleases me exceedingly, senor. Let us get to the barracks. And be kind enough to walk on my left. There is a stench about you. I do not desire to have it offend my nostrils."

With Diego Vega sitting on the bench reserved for men of position, the man acting as magistrate in the absence of the alcalde was disposed to be lenient in the case of the luckless peon. He fined him five pesos, and bounded him in peonage to Diego, who paid the fine. Diego at once entered an order that the fine had been worked out, and the peon went on his way a free man, leading his ewe and shouting his praise of Diego Vega and all his family.

Sergeant Manuel Garcia, acting as commanding officer in the pueblo, met Diego outside the barracks.

"Don Diego, my friend, I am a rough man," the sergeant declared, "but men like this tax gatherer turn my stomach."

"He is a rascal serving another rasal higher in rank," Diego observed.

"This case is only one of many. He is frightening our peons and natives half to death. They will be taking to the hills until this tax gatherer is gone, and no work will be done.

"The affair has unnerved me," Diego complained. "I was going to converse with Fray Felipe, but now shall return home. Why cannot we have peace and quiet in the world?"

"Ha! We are like to have still less of it if Senor Zorro hears of this occurrence."

"There you go, adding to my misery by mentioning that turbulent fellow!" Diego rebuked. "How is it that you and your soldiers do not catch the rascal?"

"Don Diego, this Zorro has been too clever for us. But we shall catch him. He will make some little mistake. I shall contrive to have troopers in the vicinity of the tax gatherer continually, so if Zorro appears to punish him he will run into a trap."

"What sort of a trap could you contrive?" Diego asked. "You would shoot him on sight, perhaps?"

"Not if we can catch him alive, Don Diego. The Governor is eager to have him hanged as a lesson to the peons and natives. Ha! I am anxious to see the face behind the mask the rogue wears. It might surprise me."

"That is possible," Diego admitted.

"He brushed his scented handkerchief across his face quickly to hide his slight smile, then turned and walked slowly toward his father's house.

SENOR CAROLS BARBOSA, the tax gatherer, must be punished. The peons and natives would expect Zorro to do that. Barbosa had stripped men of their last small coins and their goods. Zorro, if possible, should see that the men were repaid. They labored hard to keep themselves and families half fed, and even a coin of smallest value meant much to them.

Diego reached home to find his aged father sitting in the patio sipping wine and eating little cakes. Diego sank upon a bench beside him and, in low tones, told Don Alejandro what had happened.

He clapped his hands to call a servant, and ordered the servant to send Bernardo to him. Bernardo, Diego's huge deaf mute body-servant, was one of only three persons in the world who knew Zorro's identity.

Bernardo appeared and stood before Diego and Don Alejandro, his head bowed.

"Have you heard of the doings of the new tax collector?" Diego asked him, in a low voice.

Bernardo made a guttural sound, and rage flamed in his face.

"Zorro rides tonight," Diego told the mute, almost in whispers. "Have verything ready an hour after darkness …. "

Clouds drifted in from the sea, a mist came with them, and the mist finally changed to a drizzle of rain. None was abroad save those compelled by business.

Dressed in his black costume with black mask, riding his powerful black horse, with his blade at his side, a pistol in his belt and his long whip fastened to the pommel of his saddle, Senor Zorro traveled cautiously through the inclement night.

A short distance from the town, a small fire burned beside the highway, and around it were three men in ragged clothing and without shoes. One was gnawing fragments of meat from a bone, and the others were hunched in misery.

Out of the night came the masked rider to stop his horse near the fire. The three men sprang up in quick alarm.

"Do not be afraid," the rider told them. "I am zorro. Have any of you been mistreated by Carlos Barbosa, the tax gatherer?"

All three had been. One exhibited a raw back where the lash of Barbosa had fallen. Another had run away when the tax gatherer would have arrested him and held him for peonage. The third had given his last small coin.

"Leave your fire," Zorro instructed. "Seek out others who gave their money to the collector. Tell them to have their tax receipts with them. If I am successful in what I shall attempt to do tonight, they will be repaid. Tell all to await me in the little hut off the highway, about a mile north of town. Keep quiet. The troopers may be out tonight."

Zorro rode on, and the men extinguished their fire and scattered.

At the edge of the pueblo, Zorro tuned aside, fearing some wayfarer would see him. He rode behind a large adobe building near the rear of the tavern.

Lights streamed through the windows of the tavern to turn the falling raindrops into Jewels. From the place came raucous talk, loud laughter and ribald song. Men were making merry, no doubt seeking to purchase friendship with the tax gatherer with gifts of wine.

Zorro's eyes searched the shadows. He saw nothing to inform him where horsemen might be lurking. Finally he dismounted and ground-hitched his horse. He went forward afoot, pistol ready, eyes alert and ears attuned to catch the slightest warning of danger.

When he was near enough to look through one of the windows, into the main room of the tavern, he could see Carlos Barbosa sitting at the end of a long table with a goblet of wine before him. It was evident he was the host.

Men were drinking with him and listening to his experiences. The tavern keeper's peon servants scowled at the tax gatherer. And at one table sat a single trooper. Sergeant Garcia would have more than one trooper stationed near Barbosa, Zorro thought, so other troopers must be in hiding in the vicinity.

ZORRO retreated from the window and made his way to the patio in the rear. One torch was burning beneath the covered arches. Nobody was at the well or beneath the arches.

A sudden streak of light shot into the patio, and Zorro withdrew quickly. The door of the main room had been pulled open. Standing In the doorway, weaving a little, was the tax gatherer.

"I am not leaving you, amigos," he called back to those in the room. "I merely go to my room to get more money for wine. I find it better to pay cash than to let the landlord keep account which can wander at times."

A burst of laughter greeted the sally. Barbosa started to reel along beneath the arches, approaching the burning torch. Somebody in the main room closed the door to keep out the storm.

Zorro wondered if this could be a trap. His eyes searched the dark spots of the patio again, but saw nobody. He saw the tax gatherer open the door of a room and light a taper, and nobody appeared.

Zorro opened the lattice gate carefully and slipped inside the patio, keeping to the darkness. He stepped cautiously toward the door of the room Barbosa had entered, flattening himself against the adobe wall.

No sound caused him alarm. He advanced to the side of the door and stood waiting, watching, listening, his pistol held ready.

He could hear the tax gatherer inside, fumbling around, and humming a drinking song. There was no sound in the patio except the rush of the wind and pattering of the rain.

The door was pulled open slowly. Zorro was inside instantly, had pushed Barbosa back, and closed the door behind him. With a squawk, the tax gatherer recoiled against the wall, his face a picture of fright in the light from the guttering taper.

"Not a sound!" Zorro ordered. "Not a move, if you care to live!"

It seemed to Zorro that Barbosa's fright disappeared swiftly, as if a reassuring thought had come to him. Zorro's dramatic entrance had startled him, no doubt, but he seemed to have remembered that there was actually little to fear.

"What — what — " he mouthed.

"I am Zorro — but perhaps you have guessed that I have come to deal with you for your mistreatment of peons and natives. You are a cheap swindler, senor, who preys upon his fellow men as a buzzard upon carrion. Hand me at once a bag of money sufficient to restore to those you have robbed the few poor coins you took from them! Then, senor, I shall deal with you."

"If you dare seize the Governor's tax money — " Barbosa began.

"The Governor may have one less jewel to buy for some light woman," Zorro broke in. "Let him anguish! At once, if you care to continue living!"

Zorro watched carefully while Barbosa went to a large piece of luggage, unlocked it and took from it a leather sack with neck tied with a thong.

"Put it upon the table and open it," Zorro ordered.

The tax gatherer did so with trembling hands, then stepped back. Zorro took a swift step forward and saw that money really was in the bag. Watching Barbosa carefully, Zorro tied the bag again and attached it to his belt with the thong.

"Senor Barbosa," he said, "a man like you does not deserve to live. But you should be punished for your actions. Today you cut the backs of a couple of poor men with a whip. When I have finished with you, senor, you will need a deal of salve for your back."

"If you dare attack an official — " Barbosa began again.

"I have attacked some higher than you," Zorro reminded him. "It occurs to me, Senor Barbosa, that you are not sufficiently frightened. Perhaps troopers are awaiting my exit, eh? Garcia and his men are guarding you, believing I would attack you for what you have done?"

Barbosa's facial expression changed swiftly, and Zorro knew his guess had been correct.

"Perhaps you think you have me in a trap," Zorro told him. "The window is too small for me to get through it. I must go through the door, it appears, to make my escape. But I will hold my pistol's muzzle at your back, senor, and use your fat body as a shield. If troopers attack me as we emerge, you die!"

"No — no!" the tax gatherer cried. "They instructed me to do this. They thought you would attack me here to get the tax money."

"And they are waiting outside, eh? Face the door, senor, and raise your hands above your head. Instantly!"

THE tax gatherer did so. Abject terror had seized him. Holding his pistol in his right hand, Zorro picked up the taper with his left. He stepped up behind

Barbosa and jabbed the muzzle of the pistol against the base of the man's spine.

"A shot would crack you in two," Zorro Informed. "Put out your hand, and when I extinguish the taper unbolt and open the door. Hesitate, and you die!"

The tax gatherer extended a shaking hand and seized the bolt.

"Now!" Zorro ordered, and smashed the burning taper against the wall, to plunge the room into darkness.

He thrust harder with the pistol muzzle. The tax gatherer pulled the door open and faint light from the patio torch revealed him.

"He has a pistol at my back!" he began screeching. "He will slay me if you make a move! Do not attack him!"

Zorro put his left arm around Barbosa's neck and choked, and the man's wild cries ended in a squawk. Zorro could see three troopers within a short distance.

"Zorro!" one called to him. "Deliver yourself!"

A rumble of laughter came from Zorro's throat. "Keep your distance, senores, or you will be responsible for the death of one of the Governor's officials," he warned.

He pulled the tax gatherer along beneath the arches, out of the streak of light from the torch and toward the gate in the patio railing. He released pressure on Barbosa's throat, and the tax gatherer began howling again:

"Do not attack! He will pistol me!"

They came to the little gate, and Zorro kicked it open. A gust of wind spattered the rain upon them. The storm was increasing in wildness, which suited Zorro's purpose. He pulled Barbosa through the gate and started him toward where the black horse was waiting.

"Do not attack!" the tax gatherer continued howling.

Zorro whispered for him to be silent. He could see nothing in the black night, and no sounds reached him from the direction of the horse. But the sound of boots squashing in the mud told him the three troopers were following carefully.

"Do not come too near!" Zorro called. "This man dies if you do! My regards to Sergeant Garcia, arid tell him to think of a better trick next time."

As he spoke, Zorro was wondering how tt happened that Garcia was not with his men. It would be a torment to the sergeant if he had been taking his ease before the roaring fire in the main room of the tavern while this happened.

He pulled Barbosa along again and reached the horse.

"Senor," Zorro told him, "you are fortunate. Were it not for the troopers, and that I have something else to do, I'd use my black whip on you with my full strength. But I shall be watching your antics, senor. And you will receive another visit from me if you mistreat any more men or work hardships upon them. Cheap swindler that you are!"

Zorro struck twice with the barrel of his pistol, knocking Barbosa to the ground and marking his face. As the tax gatherer howled with pain and fright, Zorro got into saddle and gathered up his reins.

He shouted a mocking farewell to the troopers, touched with his spurs and rode. Behind him pistols exploded, but no bullet came near him. The troopers were firing wildly in the darkness, at the sounds of his horse's hoofbeats.

There was no pursuit. Zorro decided the troopers' mounts had been tied at the side of the tavern, and that it would take them some time to get into saddles, and pursuit then through the black, rainy night would be futile.

He got away from the pueblo and started toward the distant hut where he instructed the peons to wait with their fellow sufferers at the hands of Barbosa. Zorro rode with caution, though nobody seemed to be on the highway.

As he neared the spot, he circled to the rear of the hut. As he guided his horse down the slippery slope, the wind carried voices to his ears.

"Make a sound to warn him, and I'll have you hanged!" some man was threatening.

That was the voice of Sergeant Garcia. So this was why Garcia had not been at the tavern.

"It was told me," he heard Garcia continue, "that Zorro had instructed you to be here and get back your tax money. One of my spies got the message, eh? After we capture the rogue, I'll deal severely with you. No longer can you claim you do not know Zorro."

"But we never have seen his face, Senor Sergeant!" one of the men replied.

ZORRO heard the crack of a whip and a man's howl.

"Do not lie to me!" Garcia cried. "If Zorro is not caught at the tavern, he will be caught here. We'll see the face behind his mask. And he will swing at the end of a rope! Some of you, his friends, will swing also. And the others will spend a long time in prison, or be sold in peonage into Mexico."

Garcia gave a command for silence, and there was no further talk.

Zorro moved his horse on down the slope and to the hard ground at the bottom. A streak of lightning stained the sky, and by its fleeting light, Zorro saw five horses standing together, the saddles empty. Garcia had dismounted his troopers, then, and no doubt had them stationed around the hut. And the peons were being held prisoners inside.

"Garcia!" Zorro yelled suddenly. "I ride into no trap tonight! Your own voice warned me!"

He heard exclamations of rage. Zorro fired his pistol and sent a ball in the general direction of the hut. And he touched with his spurs and sent the black thundering past.

The troopers fired wildly even as Garcia was howling for some of them to mount and pursue. As Zorro reached the highway, he pulled up behind a jumble of rocks and reloaded his pistol swiftly.

He counted them as they passed — all the men Garcia had with him except one. Zorro turned back, doubly cautious now. Since the sergeant's presence had been discovered, he was no longer silent, but raged.

"We'll take these rogues to the barracks!" he yelled at the trooper remaining with him. "Get the rope from your saddle, and we'll lash them together. I'll start a fire in the hut"

Zorro watched until a tiny flame had sprung up. The fire grew swiftly and its light revealed five peons huddled together. The trooper was uncoiling his rope. Garcia stood near the prisoners, a pistol in his hand.

"Garcia!" Zorro shouted from the darkness. "Your silly troopers are chasing shadows through the rain. I have you covered with my pistol. Drop the one you hold. You and your man get on your horses and ride to the highway. At once!"

Not for an instant did he expect Garcia to obey without protest. Garcia was a tough soldier who had been long in service.

Garcia could not be sure where Zorro was waiting, for the rushing wind and the rain distorted sounds. Garcia suddenly kicked at the fire, scattering it, almost obliterating it. He yelled at his trooper, and the man ran to mount. Zorro sent a shot toward them, then urged his horse away from where he had been standing. The horse's hoofs made little sound as Zorro rode past the hut and behind it. But Garcia and his trooper made noise enough.

"After the rogue!" Garcia was shouting. "Follow me!"

They went, as Zorro had hoped, toward the spot where he had been. And Zorro moved his horse toward the hut.

"Pedro Ortez!" he called softly. "Zorro is here. I saw you by the light of the fire. Come to me, quickly."

A man shuffled toward him through the mud.

"Over this way," Zorro guided. "Listen to me well. I have here a bag of money I took from the tax gatherer. I put it in your charge. Return to your friends the amounts the tax collector took from them. Be honest in this dealing. Then, you and the others divide the rest among you and hurry down the highway to San Diego de Alcala and remain there. If you do not, Garcia may put you into prison. Do you understand?"

"Si senor! May the saints bless you, Senor Zorro!"

Zorro tossed the bag at the man's feet, then wheeled his black horse and rode.

Less than an hour later, he had delivered the horse, his Zorro costume and his weapons to his faithful Bernardo, who was waiting to take them away to safe hiding. And, not Zorro now but Don Diego Vega, he was comfortable in his father's house, telling him of the night's adventures.

The Hide Hunter

*Don Diego Vega takes the whip-and-spur trail
of a cowardly bounty seeker!*

A S SENOR ESTEBAN SCALO sat on a bench in front of the tavern on the plaza in Reina de Los Angeles and talked in a loud voice, he knew he had a large audience, though he spoke to the fat tavern keeper alone. And only two other men, both his own employees, lurked near.

But peon and native servants were working in the tavern, and others were passing back and forth in front of the building as they went about their business. They heard Señor Scalo's words easily enough, and they formed the audience he wished to reach, though he addressed the landlord. The tavern keeper was only a sounding board for Scalo's propaganda.

"Never was I as much astonished as when this masked rogue who calls himself Zorro approached me," Scalo declaimed. "My two men were gone from the camp, and I was alone. I expected to be murdered, or robbed at least. But all the rascal wanted was something to eat and drink and somebody with whom to talk."

"And he did you no harm, señor?" the tavern keeper asked.

"He was courtesy itself except when he compelled me to turn my back so he could lift his mask and eat and drink without revealing his features. His voice was deep, and his eyes gleamed through holes in the mask."

"An interesting experience," the landlord suggested.

"The fellow seemed lonesome, as an outlaw might well be if he does not have companions in crime. After drinking wine, he unburdened himself of his thoughts. They were interesting, too. I am surprised that he told me what he did."

"Indeed?" The tone was an invitation to continue.

"It seems he is carrying out a carefully prearranged plan. He laughed as he told me how he has posed as protector of the poor and downtrodden and avenger of the oppressed. He has worked hard to gain that reputation, it appears. As for his real thoughts, he told me, 'I despise such low scum. I intend using them only for my own purposes.'"

"What purposes did he mean, senor?"

"The rogue is a spy for the authorities," Scalo declared. "The officers of the soldiery know his identity and pretend to try to capture him. That is but a little play, señor. They could take him tomorrow did they so desire."

"I fail to understand," the tavern keeper protested.

"The rogue is compiling a list of men who will be seized one day unexpectedly and pressed into the army. They will be sent down into Mexico, perhaps into the hot country, and there be compelled to work like slaves for the poor food and scant coins the troopers receive."

"I scarcely can believe it!" the landlord exclaimed. "He has done so many things to aid the oppressed."

"Certainly, señor—to gain the confidence of the peons and natives so he can betray them later. Is it not dastardly? The officials up at Monterey know his work, and laugh about how he makes dupes of the wretches who praise him and his deeds."

THE conversation was continued until the words of Señor Scalo were being repeated in whispers throughout the pueblo, and even out into the country. House servants in the town heard, and workers around the warehouses. And so, in time, the story reached the house of Don Alejandro Vega, who overheard some of his people talking of it, and told his son, Diego.

Half sprawled on a bench as he fanned himself languidly, Diego Vega listened, yawning. The yawn did not fool his proud father, but it did fool the servant who brought into the patio a tray of little cakes and a bowl of fruit for father and son to devour.

Diego Vega, scion of a proud family, heir to the entire Vega estate, was the exact opposite of what a young caballero was supposed to be. He did not ride like a demon, fight at the blink of an eyelash, drink and gamble to excess, or indulge in numerous flirtations. People believed Don Alejandro was slowly dying of shame because he had such a son.

But the public did not know this was only a pose, that Diego Vega was also the famous Señor Zorro. Only Diego's father, Fray Felipe of the chapel, and Bernardo, a mute peon servant, knew the truth.

Diego straightened on the bench as the servant disappeared, and addressed his father in low tones.

"It is a trap, of course, my father. We know that this Señor Scalo lies. He pretends to be a stock buyer, I understand. He is making a plain effort to turn the peons and natives against Zorro. But why?"

"That is the thing to be considered," Don Alejandro decided.

"How can it profit a stock buyer to do such a thing? Such men generally work only for a profit. It is in my mind to contact this Señor Scalo and get the truth out of him, though no doubt it will gag me to do it."

"If you try that, my son, use extreme care. The Governor will do anything to get Zorro into his clutches. This fellow who calls himself Scalo and says he is a stock buyer may be a clever spy."

"That is to be ascertained," Diego replied.

After the siesta hour, when people of the pueblo took a promenade around the plaza if the day was fair, Diego left his father's house and joined the procession.

He was in resplendent attire and appeared almost effeminate, but fat señoras smiled upon him, and dainty señoritas eyed him slantingly, for Diego Vega made up for what he seemed to lack in spirit with social prestige and wealth. He was the most eligible young bachelor in the country. But he did not seem attracted by the dainty señoritas, and, when compelled to dance with them at social gatherings acted like a man bored with a necessary duty.

Diego slackened his pace as he neared the tavern. Señor Esteban Scalo was no longer on the bench in front. He had retired to a bench beside a table inside, where he was drinking and boasting and in general making a fool of himself.

The tavern keeper bowed low when Diego entered, and escorted the scion of the house of Vega to a choice table, carefully dusting the bench before he allowed Diego to seat himself. He brought wine in a golden goblet and bowed again as he placed it before his guest.

"I hope you are well today, Don Diego," the tavern keeper said.

"I am more than usually fatigued," Diego replied.

"Ah? Perhaps you read too much of the works of the poets."

"'Tis not that," Diego explained. "'Tis the confounded chattering around me about things which disturb a man's tranquility. It appears that everybody, even our own house servants, speaks again of this confounded rogue of a Zorro."

"How is that, Don Diego?"

"I do not know all of it. But it seems there is a rumor that Zorro is making dupes of peons and natives. Why do the soldiers not catch the rascal and have done with it? It should not be difficult. A smart man could put his hands on this Señor Zorro in a moment."

Scalo had been listening.

"Could you do it, senor?" he called.

Diego eyed him. "I could, señor," he replied. "Any of my friends could, no doubt. But the Governor's troopers cannot, it seems."

SCALO arose and strutted to the table where Diego was sitting, though the tavern man frowned, knowing Diego disliked men of Scalo's sort.

"Allow me, señor! I am Esteban Scalo, a buyer of cattle and sheep. This talk of Zorro intrigues me. Would you allow me to sit and talk with you, señor? I shall be glad to buy our landlord's best wine, for talking is thirsty work."

The tavern keeper paled, and glared at Scalo. A man like the stranger did not take such liberties with Diego Vega. Scalo — a man overdressed, flamboyant, loud, arrogant and ignorant — were anathema to Diego Vega and his sort.

The tavern keeper expected to see Diego's patrician face reveal an expression of deep scorn, or to hear Diego's voice in blistering rebuke. He wondered if Diego would ever enter the tavern again.

But to the landlord's great surprise, Diego only brushed his scented silk handkerchief across his nostrils as if they had been afflicted with a stench and bowed slightly.

"I have a moment, Señor Scalo," Diego said. "Seat yourself at my table. As for the wine — I now have before me all I require. I seldom take wine except in the house of my father or his friends."

Scalo bowed in an exaggerated manner and seated himself on a bench on the opposite side of the table. The landlord hastened to serve him. Diego Vega, he judged, was investigating the lower classes. That must be it!"

"Your words, Don Diego, lead me to believe that you think the capture of this Zorro should be an easy task," Scalo said. "You said a smart man could put his hands on Zorro."

"That is possible, señor. I have heard the talk today of how Zorro is playing a little game with the natives and peons."

"One of them may betray him," Scalo suggested. "Even a peon does not like to be duped."

"Ah, señor, they would be afraid to go to the soldiers with information," Diego replied. "Peons and natives fear the troopers, and with good reason. Our officer here at present is Sergeant Manuel Garcia, who is ruthless in handling such men."

"Could some peon or native not go to a man other than a soldier and reveal Zorro's identity and hiding place?" Scalo asked.

"Why should he, senor?"

"Perhaps a deal could be made by the peon or native who has information. He could tell somebody not afraid of the soldiers, and that Señor Somebody could go to the authorities and earn the Governor's reward, and share it with the informer."

"That could be possible," Diego decided.

The landlord had retired from the table to attend to the wants of a customer, and Scalo bent over the table and lowered his voice so nobody could overhear.

"To a man like you, Don Diego, I am not afraid to make a little confession. I am not a buyer of cattle and sheep."

"You are not, señor?"

"I am not. The fleece of sheep and the hides of cattle do not interest me — yet I am a hide hunter."

"Pardon me, Señor Scalo, but I fail to understand you."

"I make my money — and plenty of it — by hunting human hides, Don Diego. When a rogue cannot be captured, even after a large reward has been offered, they send for Esteban Scalo. It is my specialty to capture wanted men, for the head money."

"What a noble career," Diego told him witheringly.

"I flatter myself I serve the people and the country, Don Diego. I travel with those two fellows at the table beneath the window — Pedro and Juan. They are clever with pistols, knives, fists and ropes. When we get on the trail of a wanted man, we soon have his hide — and good pay for getting it."

"But what has this to do with that rogue of a Zorro?" Diego asked.

"The story about Zorro making dupes of the peons and natives — I started it, Don Diego," Scalo said, with a touch of pride. "One of two things will happen as a result — perhaps both. Some man may come to me with information concerning Zorro, which will put me on the right trail. Or Zorro himself may try to attack me for what I have said, in which case my two men and I will take him and turn him over to the soldiers. It will be my pleasure, Don Diego, to show you how we work."

"That should be interesting," Diego told him. "But suppose, señor, there is a little slip? What if this terrible Señor Zorro should get at you and punish you for what you are doing?"

Scalo laughed a little. "I am too well-guarded, Don Diego. How I wish Zorro would try it! I'd have him then! Pedro and Juan, my rogues, would care for him. Nor is that all."

"There is more?"

Esteban Scalo spoke in whispers again.

"Your sergeant, Garcia, here in Reina de Los Angeles, knows of me and my mission. He has orders to watch over me in a degree. If Zorro attacks me, he may find not only my two men but also Garcia and his troopers upon him."

"If Zorro has spies about, no doubt he knows of you and your mission also," Diego said. "He would not be so idiotic as to attack you under such conditions. Perhaps you will have to rely on some peon or native coming to you and betraying Zorro."

"If it becomes necessary, I'll give this Zorro a chance at me," Scalo declared. "I'll make it possible for him to get at me where he thinks I am not protected. As to that, Don Diego, I would not be afraid to meet him alone."

"You would dare?" Diego's eyes bulged.

"I am expert with a pistol. A quick shot — say through a leg — and I'd capture him."

"But suppose he tries a quick shot also — say through the heart?"

Scalo shuddered slightly. "Such a risk is a part of my trade," he replied.

"I fear you will have to waste time waiting," Diego said. "Surely Zorro would be too wise to attack you when your two men are near, and perhaps soldiers also. I have a thought!"

"I shall be glad to entertain it, Don Diego."

"Why not spread abroad the rumor that you are going to be in some place where Zorro could get at you? Then you could make arrangements for your men to be in the vicinity. Thinking he would catch you alone, Zorro might make a move at you."

"Splendid!" Scalo replied. "Don Diego, I admire a quick thinker like you.

I'll start a rumor immediately. I'll grin and hint that I have a rendezvous with an attractive señorita for tonight. Naturally, I'll not take my men or the soldiers along."

"Naturally not, señor."

"But my men and the soldiers can be in the vicinity ahead of time, in ambush."

"There you have it!" Diego told him. "And now you must pardon me, señor. I must hasten home."

Scalo arose and bowed almost double. Diego bent his head slightly, strode to the counter, paid for the wine he had been served, and went outside. The tavern keeper noticed that he drank deeply of the fresh air as if clearing his lungs of an impure atmosphere.

As he walked home in a leisurely manner, Diego's mind was busy with the problem confronting him.

To punish Esteban Scalo would not be enough. Even though he did, some peons and natives might think Zorro was really making dupes of them and had punished Scalo for revealing the fact, instead of for falsehood. The hide hunter must be proved to be a lying rogue, and the peons and natives must know him to be such.

In the patio at home, Diego found Bernardo, his faithful mute peon body servant, trimming rose vines, and beckoned him.

"Zorro rides tonight," Diego said in low tones. "Have everything ready."

As dusk descended, Diego played eavesdropper, deeming it necessary, and judging it was in a good cause. He listened to the chatter of the kitchen servants, and strolled within earshot of the huts in the rear, where some of the Vega men and their wives and children were squatting around the cooking fires.

He leaned what he desired to know. Esteban Scalo had been hinting at an amorous intrigue, and had said he would pay a visit to the object of his passing affection that evening. He even had said he had rented a certain hut about a mile from the town for the scene of the rendezvous.

Also, he had made further statements regarding Zorro and the manner in which he was duping peons and natives, and they were relaying the intelligence swiftly. Some believed in Zorro's honesty and others doubted it, which was to be expected.

Diego knew the location of the hut. It was a place where men could easily be in ambush among the rocks and trees. To attack Scalo there would be to run into a trap. Diego was compelled to make plans.

"Not a sound, or you die!" Zorro warned, his pistol held menacingly.

AN HOUR after nightfall, after having s a short conference with his father, Diego slipped out of the house and walked to the spot where Bernardo awaited hint Bernardo had Zorro's black horse and his costume and weapons ready. Swiftly Diego put on the costume and changed his identity. He thrust his pistol into his belt, buckled on his blade, and mounted.

He had been giving Bernardo instructions in low tones. As soon as Zorro had mounted the mute fled through the shadows of the moonlit night to get to the servants' huts.

The evening meal was over, and men were squatting around the fires talking and laughing when Zorro rode into the circle of light cast by the largest fire. Men sprang to their feet and looked at him with awe.

"You know me," Zorro said, speaking rapidly. "A certain man has been telling falsehoods concerning me, and tonight I punish him for it. But I want to prove to you that he lied. Pass the word to your friends. Gather around the plaza and watch for me to appear. I do not think the soldiers will be in the town. They will be out along the highway trying to catch me."

He wheeled his horse and rode through the shadows, going away from the town.

For quite a distance, he paralleled the highway, then cut across country and approached it cautiously. He stopped his horse within a few feet of the road, behind a mass of rocks half covered with brush and screened by stunted trees.

There he waited. There was a bright moon, but fleecy clouds were scudding through the sky, and at times the light of the moon was blotted out. There was little travel along the highway in either direction.

He had been waiting for almost an hour before he saw what he had expected. Along the highway came Sergeant Garcia and almost his entire detachment of troopers. Seemingly the sergeant had left only a small guard behind at the barracks.

The sergeant, Zorro guessed, was determined to make a capture of Zorro this time. No doubt he had joined forces with Scalo, or the hide hunter with him, and had some arrangement about dividing the reward. For Garcia, capture of Zorro would mean promotion also.

Garcia and his men were riding slowly, passing along the road toward the rendezvous hut, which was half a mile away to the southward. They rode by within a short distance of Zorro, who remained in the shadows of the rocks, and disappeared around a curve in the highway.

Still Zorro waited. Again he was rewarded, this time with the sight of Scalo's two men, Pedro and Juan. They were riding slowly also, and Zorro could hear their talk as they approached and passed.

"Catching this fellow Zorro will be the biggest thing we have done, Pedro," one was saying.

"Catching him may not be easy, Juan," demurred the other.

"Ha! He is but a man, and rumor has it that he always rides alone. If he tries to take Señor Scalo, we will have him."

"Zorro may not have heard of Scalo's remarks about him, and may not know Scalo is coming along the road to the hut."

"As to that, we can only wait and see. We ride on to the hut and hide a short distance from it, one of us on either side. Señor Scalo follows us at a short distance. He desired to ride alone, so if Zorro happens to be watching, he will not think this is a trap."

They rode on. Zorro gathered his reins and prepared for action. A cloud hid the moon for a time, but when it passed Zorro could see a lone horseman approaching from the direction of the town.

Esteban Scalo sat his saddle like a lump of lard. The horse he bestrode was an ordinary mount, no match for Zorro's powerful black. Zorro kneed his horse and got to the side of the jumble of rocks.

Pedro and Juan had disappeared around the curve ahead, after a backward glance had assured them that Scalo was following safely. A squawk of fear came from the obese hide hunter as the masked man on the black horse spurred out from the rocks and was beside him immediately.

"Not a sound, or you die!" Zorro warned, his pistol held menacingly. "Turn your horse. We ride back along the road."

"Wh-what is this?" Scalo stammered, "You would rob me?"

"Do as I say, or I pistol you! You know who I am and what this means. I have heard of the lies you have been telling about me. So we will return to the pueblo, señor, and let everybody hear the truth."

ZORRO'S black bumped the other mount and half turned him, and the frightened Scalo turned him the remainder of the way. He found Zorro riding beside him, still threatening with the pistol.

It had not been the voice of Diego Vega the hide hunter had heard, but the deeper and more threatening voice of Zorro. And this man riding beside him certainly did not have the manner of Don Diego, but that of a man used to violent pursuits. Caught in this fashion, Esteban Scalo felt a sudden panic seize him.

He did not dare cry out to Pedro and Juan who had ridden on around the curve. There was nobody coming along the highway. Scalo, the hide hunter, was at Zorro's mercy.

"Ride!" Zorro ordered. "Use your spurs! And do not for an instant forget the pistol I carry."

Zorro urged the black forward at higher steed, compelled Scalo to ride beside him, and they rushed along the road toward the town.

Zorro slackened speed as they neared the outskirts, and forced Scalo to do the same. He guessed that the hide hunter was wondering at this return to Reina de Los Angeles. It would have been more natural had Zorro taken him to some lonesome spot out in the country.

And it dawned upon Scalo that his two men, Pedro and Juan, and also Sergeant Garcia and his troopers, were in ambush around the hut far behind him. Such thoughts did not decrease his fear.

They came near the corner of the plaza. "Señor Scalo, I have decided we shall go to the tavern," Zorro told him. "It is the center of activity in the pueblo at this hour."

"Dare you risk capture?" Scalo asked.

"Since I apparently do not fear the activities of a professional hide hunter like you, would I fear the men who may be loitering around the tavern?" Zorro countered.

"What are you going to do?" Scalo asked.

"I can have it over with almost as quickly as I could tell you," Zorro replied. "Keep your mount close beside mine. And do not forget my pistol."

There was a small bonfire in the center of the plaza, as there was almost every night, and a few peons and natives were around it. Others were strolling along the plaza walk, and one group was in front of the tavern listening to two men argue.

Zorro put on a little more speed and forced Scalo to do the same. The hoofs of their mounts beat against the hard earth and attracted instant attention. The buildings cut off some of the bight of the moon, casting shadows through which they rode, but the light from the bonfire was strong enough to reveal the black-costumed masked man on the black horse, and the squatty rider beside him.

Some man shouted, and the others turned to look.

Zorro stopped the horses in front of the tavern door.

"Dismount!" he ordered the hide hunter. "Stand with your hands held high above your head. Quickly!"

Scalo dismounted like a man glad to do so. He was thinking that it was only a short distance to the open door of the tavern, and that inside he would be comparatively safe. But he thought also of the pistol Zorro held, and of how a bullet could cut him down before he could reach the sanctuary of the tavern.

Scalo looked up when his feet were upon the ground, and saw that Zorro had transferred his pistol to his left hand and was taking from the pommel of his saddle a long heavy whip. The hide hunter had a pistol hidden in his sash, but it would take some time to get it out.

Even as Scalo wondered whether he could get the pistol out and fire, Zorro's long whip whistled through the air. It struck around Scalo's fat middle and brought a howl of pain from him. He turned as if to run, and the whip wrapped itself around him and jerked him backward and to the ground, where he knelt with his arms wrapped around his head.

The hide hunter began screeching as the blows rained upon him. Men poured from the tavern. Peons and natives came running from the fire. They kept at a respectful distance, but could see and hear.

Zorro stopped using the lash.

"You, Esteban Scalo, tell the truth!" he shouted, so all near him could hear. "The straight truth, or I shoot you! You lied, didn't you, when you said I was a spy for the Governor? You lied when you said you had met me and that I had told you I was using peons and natives as dupes. Did you not?"

"I — I lied," Scalo moaned.

"Say it louder! Shout it!"

"I — I lied—*si!* Do not strike again,"

DOUBLED over as he was, Esteban Scalo had an opportunity to get the hidden pistol from his sash without Zorro being able to see his move. And as he pretended to dodge a blow from the whip, he got suddenly to one knee, lifted the weapon, and fired hastily.

The ball sang past Zorro's head, so near that he could feel the hot breath of its passing. Zorro did not fire in return. But he jumped his horse forward, and his whip hissed and sang as the lash cut through Scalo's clothing and into his flesh.

The hide hunter screamed, then ceased screaming and began moaning like a dying man. Zorro backed his horse a few feet and glanced quickly around. All the spectators were keeping their distance.

"Have you men heard?" Zorro shouted at them. "This hide hunter has been telling lies about me. That is what he is — a hide hunter. He hunts down men for pay, and he hoped to capture Zorro. I am your honest friend, and want you to know it!"

They shouted that they believed him. Zorro coiled his whip and fastened it to his pommel as Esteban Scalo got to his feet with great difficulty and stood there reeling, blood staining his clothes. His face was white with fear.

"Señor Scalo, your work here is done," Zorro told him. "Get you gone from the pueblo. If you are not gone before the next sunset, with your two rogues, I shall visit you again — and use my pistol."

There came to Zorro's ears a sudden clatter of hoofbeats. He glanced up quickly to see the peons and natives scattering like frightened rabbits, running to cover.

Into the plaza at a gallop came Garcia and some of the troopers. Pedro and

Juan were with them.

Not until afterward did Zorro learn that Scalo's delay in reaching the hut had made the men suspicious. So they had started along the highway back toward the town and when they did not meet Scalo quickened their pace. Then at last they were near enough to hear the hide hunter's howls, and put on speed.

Zorro wheeled his black horse and used his spurs. He did not fear that any of the mounts in pursuit could catch him. But as Sergeant Garcia bent forward in his saddle and tried, Zorro emptied his pistol so that the ball flew over the sergeant's head and made the men behind him spread to right and left, delaying them a moment.

Pistols barked, and slugs sang in Zorro's direction, but none came as close to him as Esteban Scalo's shot had done. The moon went behind a cloud and Zorro spurred down the highway a distance, then left it to turn abruptly up over a hill.

From behind a hedge, Zorro watched the pursuit flow past him on the road below. He urged the black down into a narrow gully and rode slowly and cautiously where he would not be seen in sharp silhouette against the moonlit sky.

Within a short time he had reached the spot where Bernardo was waiting. He dismounted, tossed his weapons aside and stripped off the Zorro costume. He was Diego Vega again.

"The hide hunter will not bother us any more," he told the mute.

Bernardo made a sound indicating pleasure, and Diego strode through the night toward the rear of the house.

He let himself in and got to his own room without being seen. Quickly he removed his clothes and put on a heavy robe and soft slippers. He tousled his hair, left the room and shuffled to the big main room of the house, where he knew his father would be waiting to hear a report of the night's adventure.

One of the house servants saw him and hastened to the kitchen for a glass of warm milk for Don Diego.

"No doubt he cannot sleep," the servant muttered. "Never in my life have I seen a young caballero so lifeless!"

Johnston McCulley

Author, creator of Zorro

The creator of Zorro, Johnston McCulley (1883-1958) was born in Ottowa, Illinois, and raised in the neighboring town of Chilicothe. He began his writing career as a police reporter and became a prolific fiction author, filling thousands of pages of popular pulp magazines.

Southern California became a frequent backdrop for his fiction. His most notable use of the locale was in his adventures of Zorro, the masked highwayman who defended a pueblo's citizens from an oppressive government.

He contributed to popular magazines of the day like *Argosy*, *Western Story Magazine*, *Detective Story Magazine*, *Blue Book* and *Rodeo Romances*. Many of his novels were published in hardcover and paperback. Eventually he branched out into film and television screenplays.

His stable of series characters included The Crimson Clown, Thubway Tham, The Green Ghost, and The Thunderbolt. Zorro proved to be his most popular and enduring character, becoming the subject of numerous television programs, motion pictures, comic books, and cartoon programs.

After assigning all Zorro rights to agent Mitchell Gertz, Johnston McCulley retired to Los Angeles and died in 1958.

Joseph A. Farren

Illustrator

Joseph Farren (1884-1964) was born in Boston, the youngest of five sons. After high school, he drew comic strips and sports cartoons for various Boston newspapers. He was an avid golfer, and he competed in Massachusetts statewide tournaments. In 1926, he began drawing political cartoons for *The New York Times*. From his home art studio in Queens, he freelanced illustrations to pulp magazines such as *Clues Detective Stories*, *Detective Fiction Weekly*, *Popular Sports*, and *West*.

Farren balanced his art career and golf by a weekly routine of visiting midtown Manhattan to pick up and deliver illustrations, then heading to the golf course in nearby Flushing.

Watch for the Curse of Capistrano's wildest adventure!

ZORRO ®

and the
LITTLE DEVIL

A thrilling new novel
by New York Times
best-selling author
Peter David

BOLD VENTURE
www.boldventurepress.com

Made in the USA
Columbia, SC
20 August 2023

21872162R00198